Literature of Fantasy and the Supernatural

Revised Edition

Edited by Gail Finney

University of California, Davis

Poe- gothic
Unrealiable narrator- James
Uncanny
marvelous, fantastic, uncanny

cognella
San Diego, CA

First published in the United States of America in 2013 by Cognella, Inc.

Printed in the United States of America

ISBN: 978-1-62131-421-9 (pb) / 978-1-62131-422-6 (br)

cognella™

www.cognella.com 800.200.3908

Contents

The 20th Century 177

Introduction

By Gail Finney

In the largest sense, all literature can be said to represent fantasy, since literature portrays fictional or imaginative worlds rather than reporting on actual phenomena in the manner of journalism or scholarly research. Yet a subcategory of literary texts seeks overtly to depict characters and events which not only transcend the everyday, empirical realm that we perceive with our five senses, but contradict the laws of nature and rationality. Such phenomena may be labeled supernatural—literally "above or beyond the natural." The readings in this anthology portray varying manifestations of the supernatural, all belonging to the realm of fantasy, or the counterfactual.

Whereas the world around us—the room, the house or building, the natural scene, the city—is finite, the imagination is infinite, unlimited in time and space. In our imagination we can be anywhere, anytime. As the product of imagination, fantasy runs counter to natural laws, conventional ground rules, normal perceptions and perspectives. To look ahead to some of the readings in this anthology: it seems unbelievable for a human heart to continue beating after death, as occurs in Poe's "The Tell-Tale Heart," and it contradicts the laws of nature for a man to turn into a giant bug, as happens at the beginning of Kafka's *The Metamorphosis.* Works of fantasy such as these establish new conventions, based not on empirical reality but on imaginative visions.

The defining element in literature of fantasy is the supernatural. The reader's perception of the supernatural is crucial in talking about the fantastic quality of these texts. One of the most influential approaches to the fantastic is the typology generated by the Bulgarian critic Tzvetan Todorov. The supernatural is his point of departure: when a literary character inhabits a world in which an event occurs that cannot be explained by the laws of this same familiar world—a supernatural occurrence—the way the reader and/or character perceives and explains or fails to explain the supernatural event determines the mode of the work. If the event turns out to be not supernatural but scientifically motivated, so that the laws of reality remain intact, Todorov characterizes the mode of the work as "uncanny." If the supernatural events are accepted at face value, so that new laws of nature must be generated to account for these phenomena, Todorov's typology terms the mode "marvelous." When the reader or character is unable to determine whether the supernatural events are real or imagined, we have arrived at the domain of the “fantastic,” in Todorov’s terminology. Is the character dreaming or not? Is the character confronting an illusion or reality? The fantastic occurs during this period of hesitation, uncertainty, ambiguity.[1]

Todorov’s typology provides a useful framework for talking about the works in this anthology. To cite only a few examples, the fanciful phenomena in *Alice’s Adventures in Wonderland*—talking animals, magic potions, cats fading in and out of view—are revealed in the end to be part of a long dream Alice has had. Since the supernatural is explained, or shown to be a function of natural laws, this work can be characterized according to Todorov’s typology as uncanny. In Márquez’s “A Very Old Man with Enormous Wings,” the title character lands in a village where he is regarded as an angel before eventually flying away. Since the supernatural is accepted at face value and new laws must be formulated to understand the events of the story, it belongs to the mode of the marvelous. Most of the texts in this anthology belong to the fantastic mode: The line between the uncanny and the marvelous is blurred, so that the reader cannot definitively determine whether supernatural events are real or illusory within the fictional framework. In James’s quintessentially ambiguous *The Turn of the Screw*, for instance, the reader is ultimately uncertain whether the tale is meant to be a ghost story, in which supernatural beings exist as it were on their own terms, or whether the governess’s sightings of ghosts are the product of an unbalanced mind.

Although elements of fantasy and the fantastic have been found throughout literature—in fairy tales; Greek, Roman, and Nordic mythology; the Bible; and medieval and Renaissance works—the manifestations of fantasy are especially rich and varied during the 19th and 20th centuries, the period embraced by this anthology. Although the book is divided into two sections according to these larger time periods, two major themes tie the sections together:

Madness or apparent madness: The literary character’s difficulty in distinguishing between reality and illusion can produce a state of insanity or near-insanity. The interest in insanity is heightened in the late 19th century by the prominence of psychology and psychoanalysis as new branches of science, growing out of the study of the human psyche by Freud and others, which included the analysis and interpretation of dreams.

Bodies in pieces: Like the 19th-century novel, the fantastic tale attends to details of setting, clothing, physiognomy, and the general accessories of life, yet in contrast to the realist novel’s holistic depiction of unity between character and environment, fantastic literature is often pervaded by a sense of partiality and the fragmentary. This impression is reflected in the abundance of disembodied body parts—hands, hair, teeth, eyes, even heads—populating these tales.

The readings that follow offer many and varied manifestations of these and other features of the literature of fantasy and the supernatural. In studying these works, we will see that the fantastic is present not simply for its own sake but to illuminate human behavior. By portraying phenomena in a supernatural guise, writers often shed light on very real aspects of our character and our lives.

---

1 Tzvetan Todorov, *The Fantastic: A Structural Approach to a Literary Genre*, trans. Richard Howard (Cleveland: The Press of Case Western Reserve University, 1973), esp. pp. 24–57.

The 19th Century

Introduction to the 19th Century

By Gail Finney

The early-19th-century tales in this volume—those by Hoffmann and Poe—are quintessentially Romantic works. Romanticism was a cultural movement prominent in Europe and the United States from the late 1700s through the first few decades of the 1800s. Although this movement takes diverse forms in different national cultures, certain features are common throughout. Of major importance for the origins of Romanticism, for example, were the bourgeois or middle-class revolutions of the later 18th century, the American Revolution in 1776 and the French Revolution in 1789. Significantly, the watchwords of these political events—life, liberty, the pursuit of happiness, equality, and brotherhood—were promoted with reference to the individual. This focus on the individual was the basis for the democratic systems of government that the revolutions brought forth as well as for the principles of individual rights, individual freedom, individual will, and individual creativity in literature and other arts. In the arts, individualism was manifested in the freedom of the imagination and in an emphasis on the emotional expression of the individual, motivated as well by a reaction against the Enlightenment cult of reason and rationality.

The heralding of individualism brought with it, perhaps inevitably, increased attention to the self and the layers of the psyche. In fact, the Romantics can be said to have discovered the unconscious. German Romantic writers even use this term and symbolize it through subterranean imagery, above all mines. Romantic literature of fantasy and the fantastic is produced by the imagination, which is viewed as omnipotent, and by the unconscious, unbounded by the laws of everyday reality. The artist figure, whose domain is the creation of fiction and fantasy, is typically counterposed to middle-class characters with their order and regularity; an example of this opposition is found in Hoffmann's "The Sand-Man," in which the erratic behavior of the writer Nathanael contrasts sharply with that of the sensible, conventional Clara.

Freud's mapping of the mind, consisting in his view of the ego; the id or unconscious, the realm of dreams and fantasies; and the superego, or the locus of the ethical imperative, provides a useful lens through which to read Romantic works such as "The Sand-Man," which anticipates Freudian concepts like the uncanny, castration anxiety, the double, and narcissism. The last of these is characterized by a blurred conception of ego boundaries. Early German idealist thought emphasizes the limitations of empirical human perception—the fact that our five senses enable us to perceive only the appearance of things and not their essence. This thinking sometimes leads to radical subjectivism, or the notion that the world consists of our perceptions of it, that perception is reality. This idea can in turn produce narcissism or ego grandiosity—a state in which the subject, unable to distinguish between self and other, creates fantastic imagery that is actually a reflection of him- or herself. Such is the case with Nathanael's relationship to the automaton Olimpia in "The Sand-Man."

A further anticipation of Freudian thought in Romantic literature is the prevalence of the device of projection, especially the projection of fear and guilt. The projection of these emotions onto external objects, characters, and events can bring about the appearance of the supernatural, as in the tales of Poe: the guilt of the narrator in "The Tell-Tale Heart" causes him to imagine that he hears the posthumous heartbeat of the man he has killed, just as the narrator of "The Black Cat" is aghast at the howls of the titular animal whom he has accidently walled up in the tomb of the wife he has brutally murdered. Events like these are enhanced in Poe's works by gloomy, vaporous settings surrounding mysterious old houses with echoing rooms, secret passages, and ghosts in the attic. Such dark, mysterious atmospheric details are appropriate frames for Poe's explorations of mental and physical pathology.

Moving into the Victorian period, we encounter in *Alice's Adventures in Wonderland* a seemingly unambiguous example of the marvelous mode. As with fairy tales, we accept the supernatural personages and events at face value: we "suspend disbelief," in Samuel Coleridge's famous formulation. Yet the marvelous quality of the narrative belies its veiled criticism of Victorian manners, mores, and educational systems. At the same time, the Cheshire cat grin that precedes and succeeds the image of the entire cat exemplifies a theme that is prominent in much fantastic literature: partialization, or bodies in pieces. The dismembered bodies in Poe's tales, the teeth of Berenice, and the memorable motif of eyes in Hoffmann's "The Sand-Man" are characteristic of a technique that may be seen as the left hand or "other" of realism.[1] Realist narratives provide copious details of time and place, clothing, setting, characters' appearance, and so forth as a means of demonstrating the symbiosis between personage and milieu, thereby emphasizing the holistic influence of environment on the development of character. Fantastic tales also incline to the depiction of detail but, by contrast, underline fragmentation—the fragmented powers of human perception, the fragmentation of consciousness—rather than wholeness and cohesion. This fragmented sense of reality is frequently conveyed by the portrayal of bodies in pieces or of body parts that seem to function autonomously. This technique is especially pronounced in the tales of Maupassant, in which, for instance, pieces of furniture are endowed with human powers and a head of hair belonging to a deceased woman is fetishized and adored as an eroticized substitute for the woman herself. In sum, 19th-century developments such as a heightened belief in the creative powers of the individual mind, a growing sense of the subjectivity of perception, a deepened understanding of the human psyche, and a concomitant loss of belief in a cohesive relationship between self and world combine to produce rich and varied contributions to the literature of fantasy and the supernatural.

1 Deborah Harter, *Bodies in Pieces: Fantastic Narrative and the Poetics of the Fragment* (Stanford: Stanford University Press, 1996).

The Sand-Man

By E.T.A. Hoffmann

Nathanael to Lothair

I know you are all very uneasy because I have not written for such a long, long time. Mother, to be sure, is angry, and Clara, I dare say, believes I am living here in riot and revelry, and quite forgetting my sweet angel, whose image is so deeply engraved upon my heart and mind. But that is not so; daily and hourly I think of you all, and my lovely Clara's form comes to gladden me in my dreams, and smiles upon me with her bright eyes, as graciously as she used to do in the days when I used to associate daily with you.

Oh! how could I write to you in the distracted state of mind in which I have been, and which, until now, has quite bewildered me! A terrible thing has happened to me. Dark forebodings of some awful fate threatening me are spreading themselves out over my head like black clouds, impenetrable to every friendly ray of sunlight. I must now tell you what has taken place; I must, that I see well enough, but only to think of it makes the wild laughter burst from my lips. Oh! my dear, dear Lothair, what shall I say to make you feel, if only in an inadequate way, that what happened to me a few days ago could thus really exercise such a hostile and disturbing influence upon my life? I wish you were here to see for yourself! But now you will, I suppose, take me for a superstitious ghost-seer. In a word, the terrible thing which I have experienced, the fatal effect of which I in vain exert every effort to shake off, is simply that some days ago, namely, on the thirtieth of October, at twelve o'clock at noon, a peddler of weather glasses and thermometers came into my room and wanted to sell me one of his wares. I bought nothing, and threatened to kick him downstairs, whereupon he went away of his own accord.

You will conclude that it can only be very peculiar relations—relations intimately intertwined with my life—that can give significance to this event, and that it must be the peddler himself who had such a very unpleasant effect upon me. And so it really is. I will summon up all my faculties in order to narrate to you calmly and patiently enough about the early days of my youth to put matters before you in such ay that your keen sharp intellect can grasp everything clearly and distinctly, in bright and living :tures.

Just as I am beginning, I hear you laugh and Clara say, "What's all this childish nonsense about!" Well, laugh at me, laugh heartily at me, pray do. But, good God! y hair is standing on end, and I seem to be entreating you to laugh at me in the same sort of frantic despair in which Franz Moor [in Schiller's *Die Räuber]* entreated Daniel to laugh him to scorn. But to my story.

Except at dinner we, i.e., I and my brothers and sisters, saw little of our father all day long. His business no doubt took up most of his time. After our evening meal, which usually was served at seven o'clock, we all went, mother with us, into father's room, and took our places around a round table. My father smoked his pipe, drinking a large glass of beer at the same time. Often he told us many wonderful stories, and got so excited over them that his pipe would go out; I used then to light it for him with a spill, and this formed my chief amusement. Often, again, he would give us picture books to look at, while he sat silent and motionless in his easy chair, puffing out such dense clouds of smoke that we were all as it were enveloped in mist.

On such evenings mother was very sad; and as soon as it struck nine she said, "Come, children! off to bed! Come! The Sand-man is come, I see." And I always did seem to hear something trampling upstairs with slow heavy steps; that must be the Sand-man. Once in particular I was very much frightened at this dull trampling and knocking; as mother was leading us out of the room I asked her, "O mamma! who is this nasty Sand-man who always sends us away from papa? What does he look like?"

"There is no Sand-man, my dear," mother answered; "when I say the Sand-man is come, I only mean that you are sleepy and can't keep your eyes open, as if somebody had put sand in them." This answer of mother's did not satisfy me; nay, in my childish mind the thought clearly unfolded itself that mother denied there was a Sand-man only to prevent us from being afraid,—why, I always heard him come upstairs.

Full of curiosity to learn something more about this Sand-man and what he had to do with us children, I finally asked the old woman who acted as my youngest sister's nurse, what sort of man he was—the Sand-man?

"Why, 'thanael, darling, don't you know?" she replied. "Oh! he's a wicked man, who comes to little children when they won't go to bed and throws handfuls of sand in their eyes, so that they jump out of their heads all bloody; and he puts them into a bag and takes them to the half-moon as food for his little ones; and they sit there in the nest and have hooked beaks like owls, and they pick naughty little boys' and girls' eyes out with them."

After this I formed in my own mind a horrible picture of the cruel Sand-man. When anything came blundering upstairs at night I trembled with fear and dismay; and all that my mother could get out of me were the stammered words "The Sand-man! the Sand-man!" whilst the tears coursed down my cheeks. Then I ran into my bedroom, and the whole night through tormented myself with the terrible apparition of the Sand-man. I was quite old enough to perceive that the old woman's tale about the Sand-man and his little ones' nest in the half-moon couldn't be altogether true; nevertheless the Sand-man continued to be for me a fearful incubus, and I was always seized with terror—my blood always ran cold, not only when I heard anybody come up the stairs, but when I heard anybody noisily open the door to my father's room and go in. Often the Sand-man stayed away for a long time altogether; then he would come several times in close succession.

This went on for years, without my being able to accustom myself to this fearful apparition, without the image of the horrible Sand-man growing any fainter in my imagination. His intercourse with my father began to occupy my fancy ever more and more; I was restrained from asking my father about him by an unconquerable shyness; but as the years went on the desire waxed stronger and stronger within me to fathom the mystery myself and to see the fabulous Sand-man. He had been the means of disclosing to me the path of the wonderful and the adventurous, which so easily find lodgment in the mind of the child. I liked nothing better than to hear or read horrible stories of goblins, witches, dwarfs, and so on; but always at the head of them all stood the Sand-man, whose picture I scribbled in the most extraordinary and repulsive forms with both chalk and coal everywhere, on the tables, and cupboard doors, and walls.

When I was ten years old my mother removed me from the nursery into a little chamber off the corridor not far from my father's room. We still had to withdraw hastily whenever, on the stroke of nine, the mysterious unknown was heard in the house. As I lay in my little chamber I could hear him go into father's room, and soon afterwards I fancied there was a fine and peculiar smelling steam spreading itself through the house.

As my curiosity waxed stronger, my resolve to make the Sandman's acquaintance somehow or other took deeper root. Often when my mother had gone past, I slipped quickly out of my room into the corridor, but I could never see anything, for always before I could reach the place where I could get sight of him, the Sand-man was well inside the door. At last, unable to resist the impulse any longer, I determined to conceal myself in father's room and wait there for the Sand-man.

One evening I perceived from my father's silence and mother's sadness that the Sand-man would come; accordingly, pleading that I was excessively tired, I left the room before nine o'clock and concealed myself in a hiding place close beside the door. The street door creaked, and slow, heavy, echoing steps crossed the passage towards the stairs. Mother hurried past me with my brothers and sisters. Softly—softly—I opened the door to father's room. He sat as usual, silent and motionless, with his back towards the door; he did not hear me; and in a moment I was in and behind a curtain drawn before my father's open wardrobe, which stood just inside the room. Nearer and nearer and nearer came the echoing footsteps. There was a strange coughing and shuffling and mumbling outside. My heart beat with expectation and fear. A quick step now close, close beside the door, a noisy rattle of the handle, and the door flies open with a bang. Recovering my courage with an effort, I take a cautious peep out. In the middle of the room in front of my father stands the Sand-man, the bright light of the lamp falling full upon his face. The Sandman, the terrible Sand-man, is the old lawyer Coppelius who often comes to dine with us.

But the most hideous figure could not have awakened greater trepidation in my heart than this Coppelius did. Picture to yourself a large broad-shouldered man, with an immensely big head, a face the colour of yellow ochre, gray bushy eyebrows, from beneath which two piercing, greenish, cat-like eyes glittered, and a prominent Roman nose hanging over his upper lip. His distorted mouth was often screwed up into a malicious sneer; then two dark-red spots appeared on his cheeks, and a strange hissing noise proceeded from between his tightly clenched teeth. He always wore an ash-gray coat of an old-fashioned cut, a waistcoat of the same, and nether extremities to match, but black stockings and buckles set with stones on his shoes. His little wig scarcely extended beyond the crown of his head, his hair was curled round high up above his big red ears, and plastered to his temples with cosmetic, and a broad closed hair-bag stood out prominently from his neck, so that you could see the silver buckle that fastened his folded neck-cloth. Altogether he was a most disagreeable and horribly ugly figure; but what we children detested most of all was his big coarse hairy hands; we could never fancy anything that he had once touched. This he had noticed; and so, whenever our good mother quietly placed a piece of cake or sweet fruit on our plates, he delighted to touch it under some pretext or other, until the tears stood in our eyes, and from disgust and loathing we lost the enjoyment of the tit-bit that was intended to please us. And he did just the same thing when father gave us a glass of sweet wine on holidays. Then he would quickly pass his hand over it, or even sometimes raise the glass to his blue lips, and he laughed quite sardonically when all we dared do was to express our vexation in stifled sobs. He habitually called us the "little brutes"; and when he was present we might not utter a sound; and we cursed the ugly spiteful man who deliberately and intentionally spoilt all our little pleasures.

Mother seemed to dislike this hateful Coppelius as much as we did; for as soon as he appeared, her cheerfulness and bright and natural manner were transformed into sad, gloomy seriousness. Father treated him as if he were a being of some higher race, whose ill manners were to be tolerated, while no efforts ought to be spared to keep him in good humour. Coppelius had only to give a slight hint, and his favourite dishes were cooked for him and rare wine uncorked.

As soon as I saw this Coppelius, therefore, the fearful and hideous thought arose in my mind that he, and he alone, must be the Sand-man; but I no longer conceived of the Sand-man as the bugbear in the old nurse's fable, who fetched children's eyes and took them to the half-moon as food for his little ones—no! but as an ugly spectre-like fiend bringing trouble and misery and ruin, both temporal and everlasting, everywhere he appeared.

I was spellbound on the spot. At the risk of being discovered, and as I well enough knew, of being severely punished, I remained as I was, with my head thrust through the curtains listening. My father received Coppelius in a ceremonious manner.

"Come, to work!" cried the latter, in a hoarse snarling voice, throwing off his coat. Gloomily and silently my father took off his dressing gown, and both put on long black smock-frocks. Where they took them from I forgot to notice. Father opened the folding doors of a cupboard in the wall; but I saw that what I had so long taken to be a cupboard was really a dark recess, in which was a little hearth. Coppelius approached it, and a blue flame crackled upwards from it. Round about were all kinds of strange utensils.

Good God! as my father bent down over the fire how different he looked! His gentle features seemed to be drawn up by some dreadful convulsive pain into an ugly, repulsive Satanic mask. He looked like Coppelius. Coppelius plied the red-hot tongs and drew bright glowing masses out of the thick smoke and began assiduously to hammer them. I fancied that there were men's faces visible round about, but without eyes, having ghastly deep black holes where the eyes should have been.

"Eyes here! Eyes here!" cried Coppelius, in a hollow sepulchral voice. My blood ran cold with horror; I screamed and tumbled out of my hiding place onto the floor. Coppelius immediately seized me. "You little brute! You little brute!" he bleated, grinding his teeth. Then, snatching me up, he threw me on the hearth, so that the flames began to singe my hair. "Now we've got eyes—eyes—a beautiful pair of children's eyes," he whispered and, thrusting his hands into the flames he took out some red-hot grains and was about to throw them into my eyes.

Then my father clasped his hands and entreated him, saying, "Master, master, let my Nathanael keep his eyes—oh! let him keep them." Coppelius laughed shrilly and replied, "Well then, the boy may keep his eyes and whine and pule his way through the world; but we will at any rate examine the mechanism of the hand and the foot." And thereupon he roughly laid hold of me, so that my joints cracked, and twisted my hands and my feet, pulling them now this way, and now that, "That's not quite right altogether! It's better as it was!—the old fellow knew what he was about." Thus lisped and hissed Coppelius; but all around me grew black and dark; a sudden convulsive pain shot through all my nerves and bones; I knew nothing more.

I felt a soft warm breath fanning my cheek; I awakened as if out of the sleep of death; my mother was bending over me. "Is the Sand-man still here?" I stammered. "No, my dear child; he's been gone a long, long time; he'll not hurt you." Thus spoke my mother, as she kissed her recovered darling and pressed him to her heart. But why should I tire you, my dear Lothair? why do I dwell at such length on these details, when there's so much remains to be said? Enough—I was detected in my eavesdropping, and roughly handled by Coppelius. Fear and terror brought on a violent fever, of which I lay ill several weeks. "Is the Sand-man still there?" these were the first words I uttered on coming to myself again, the first sign of my recovery, of my safety. Thus, you see, I have only to relate to you the most terrible moment of my youth for you to thoroughly understand that it must not be ascribed to the weakness of my eyesight if all that I see is colourless, but to the fact that a mysterious destiny has hung a dark veil of clouds about my life, which I shall perhaps only break through when I die.

Coppelius did not show himself again; it was reported he had left the town.

It was about a year later when, in our old manner, we sat around the round table in the evening. Father was in very good spirits, and was telling us amusing tales about his youthful travels. As it was striking nine we all at once heard the street door creak on its hinges, and slow ponderous steps echoed across the passage and up the stairs. "That is Coppelius," said my mother, turning pale. "Yes, it is Coppelius," replied my father in a faint broken voice. The tears started from my mother's eyes. "But, father, father," she cried, "must it be so?" "This is the last time," he replied; "this is the last time he will come to me, I promise you. Go now, go and take the children. Go, go to bed—good night."

As for me, I felt as if I were converted into cold, heavy stone; I could not get my breath. As I stood there immovable, my mother seized me by the arm. "Come, Nathanael! come along!" I suffered myself to be led away; I went into my room. "Be a good boy and keep quiet," mother called after me; "get into bed and go to sleep." But, tortured by indescribable fear and uneasiness, I could not close my eyes. It seemed that hateful, hideous Coppelius stood before me with his glittering eyes, smiling maliciously down upon me; in vain did I strive to banish the image. Somewhere about midnight there was a terrific explosion, as if a cannon were being fired off. The whole house shook; something went rustling and clattering past my door; the house door was pulled to with a bang.

"That is Coppelius," I cried, terror-stricken, and leaped out of bed. Then I heard a wild heart-rending scream; I rushed into my father's room; the door stood open, and clouds of suffocating smoke came roiling towards me. The servant maid shouted, "Oh! my master! my master!" On the floor in front of the smoking hearth lay my father, dead, his face burned black and fearfully distorted, my sisters weeping and moaning around him, and my mother lying near them in a swoon.

"Coppelius, you atrocious fiend, you've killed my father," I shouted. My senses left me. Two days later, when my father was placed in his coffin, his features were mild and gentle again as they had been when he was alive. I found great consolation in the thought that his association with the diabolical Coppelius could not have ended in his everlasting ruin.

Our neighbours had been awakened by the explosion; the affair got talked about, and came before the magisterial authorities, who wished to cite Coppelius to clear himself. But he had disappeared from the place, leaving no traces behind him.

Now when I tell you, my dear friend, that the peddler I spoke of was the villain Coppelius, you will not blame me for seeing impending mischief in his inauspicious reappearance. He was differently dressed; but Coppelius's figure and features are too deeply impressed upon my mind for me to be capable of making a mistake in the matter. Moreover, he has not even changed his name. He proclaims himself here, I learn, to be a Piedmontese mechanician, and styles himself Giuseppe Coppola.

I am resolved to enter the lists against him and avenge my father's death, let the consequences be what they may.

Don't say a word to mother about the reappearance of this odious monster. Give my love to my darling Clara; I will write to her when I am in a somewhat calmer frame of mind. Adieu.

Clara to Nathanael

You are right, you have not written to me for a very long time, but nevertheless I believe that I still retain a place in your mind and thoughts. It is a proof that you were thinking a good deal about me when you were sending off your last letter to brother Lothair, for instead of directing it to him you directed it to me. With joy I tore open the envelope, and did not perceive the mistake until I read the words, "Oh! my dear, dear Lothair."

Now I know I ought not to have read any more of the letter, but ought to have given it to my brother. But as you have so often in innocent raillery made it a sort of reproach against me that I possessed such a calm and, for a woman, cool-headed temperament that I should be like the woman we read of—if the house was threatening to tumble down, I should stop before hastily fleeing, to smooth down a crumple in the window curtains—I need hardly tell you that the beginning of your letter quite upset me. I could scarcely breathe; there was a bright mist before my eyes.

Oh! my darling Nathanael! what could this terrible thing be that had happened? Separation from you—never to see you again, the thought was like a sharp knife in my heart. I read on and on. Your description of that horrid Coppelius made my flesh creep. I now learned for the first time what a terrible and violent death your good old father died. Brother Lothair, to whom I handed over his property, sought to comfort me, but with little success. That horrid peddler Giuseppe Coppola followed me everywhere; and I am almost ashamed to confess it, but he was able to disturb my sleep, which is usually sound and calm, with all sorts of wonderful dream shapes. But soon—the next day—I saw everything in a different light. Oh! do not be angry with me, my best beloved, if, despite your strange presentiment that Coppelius will do you some mischief, Lothair tells you I am in quite as good spirits, and just the same as ever.

I will frankly confess, it seems to me that all the horrors of which you speak, existed only in your own self, and that the real true outer world had but little to do with it. I can quite admit that old Coppelius may have been highly obnoxious to you children, but your real detestation of him arose from the fact he hated children.

Naturally enough, the gruesome Sand-man of the old nurse's story was associated in your childish mind with old Coppelius, who even though you had not believed in the Sand-man, would have been to you a ghostly bugbear, especially dangerous to children. His mysterious labours along with your father at nighttime were, I daresay, nothing more than secret experiments in alchemy, with which your mother could not be over-well pleased, owing to the large sums of money that most likely were thrown away upon them; and besides, your father, his mind full of the deceptive striving after higher knowledge, may probably have become rather indifferent to his family, as so often happens in the case of such experimentalists.

So also it is equally probable that your father brought about his death by his own imprudence, and that Coppelius is not to blame for it. I must tell you that yesterday I asked our experienced neighbour, the chemist, whether in experiments of this kind an explosion could take place which would have a momentarily fatal effect. He said, "Oh, certainly!" and described to me in his prolix and circumstantial way how it could be occasioned, mentioning at the same time so many strange and funny words that I could not remember them at all. Now I know you will be angry at your Clara, and will say, "Of the Mysterious which often clasps man in its invisible arms there's not a ray can find its way into her cold heart. She sees only the varied surface of the things of the world and, like the little child, is pleased with the golden glittering fruit, at the kernel of which lies the fatal poison."

Oh! my beloved Nathanael, do you believe then that the intuitive prescience of a dark power working within us to our own ruin cannot exist also in minds which are cheerful, natural, free from care ? But please forgive me that I, a simple girl, presume in any way to indicate to you what I really think of such an inward strife. After all, I should not find the proper words, and you would only laugh at me, not because my thoughts were stupid, but because I was so foolish as to attempt to tell them to you.

Clara = clear Guides Nathanael

If there is a dark and hostile power which traitorously fixes a thread in our hearts in order that, laying hold of it and drawing us by means of it along a dangerous road to ruin, which otherwise we should not have trod—if, I say, there is such a power, it must assume within us a form like ourselves, nay, it must be ourselves; for only in that way can we believe in it, and only so understood do we yield to it so far that it is able to accomplish its secret purpose. So long as we have sufficient firmness, fortified by cheerfulness, always to acknowledge foreign hostile influences for what they really are, while we quietly pursue the path pointed out to us by both inclination and calling, then this mysterious power perishes in its futile struggles to attain the form which is to be the reflected image of ourselves.

It is also certain, Lothair adds, that if we have once voluntarily given ourselves up to this dark physical power, it often reproduces within us the strange forms which the outer world throws in our way, so that thus it is we ourselves who engender within ourselves the spirit which by some remarkable delusion we imagine to speak in that outer form. It is the phantom of our own self whose intimate relationship with, and whose powerful influence upon our soul either plunges us into hell or elevates us to heaven.

Thus you will see, my beloved Nathanael, that I and brother Lothair have talked over the subject of dark powers and forces well; and now, after I have written down the principal results of our discussion with some difficulty, they seem to me to contain many really profound thoughts. Lothair's last words, however, I don't quite understand; I only dimly guess what he means; and yet I cannot help thinking it is all very true.

I beg you, dear, strive to forget the ugly lawyer Coppelius as well as the peddler Giuseppe Coppola. Try and convince yourself that these foreign influences can have no power over you, that it is only belief in their hostile power which can in reality make them dangerous to you.

If every line of your letter did not betray the violent excitement of your mind, and if I did not sympathize with your condition from the bottom of my heart, I could in truth jest about the lawyer Sand-man and peddler Coppelius. Pluck up your spirits! Be cheerful! I have resolved to appear to you as your guardian angel if that ugly man Coppola should dare take it into his head to bother you in your dreams, and drive him away with a good hearty laugh. I'm not afraid of him and his nasty hands, not the least little bit; I won't let him either as lawyer spoil any dainty tit-bit I've taken, or as Sand-man rob me of my eyes.

My darling, darling Nathanael,
Eternally yours..

Nathanael to Lothair

I am very sorry that Clara opened and read my last letter to you; of course the mistake is to be attributed to my own absence of mind. She has written me a very deep philosophical letter, proving conclusively that Coppelius and Coppola only exist in my own mind and are phantoms of my own self, which will at once be dissipated, as soon as I look upon them in that light. In very truth one can hardly believe that the mind which so often sparkles in those bright, beautifully smiling, childlike eyes of hers like a sweet lovely dream could draw such subtle and scholastic distinctions. She also mentions your name. You have been talking about me. I suppose you have been giving her lectures, since she sifts and refines everything so acutely. But enough of this! I must now tell you it is most certain that Giuseppe Coppola is not Coppelius. I am attending the lectures of our recently appointed Professor of Physics, who, like the distinguished naturalist, is called Spalanzani, and is of Italian origin. He has known Coppola for many years; and it is also easy to tell from Coppola's accent that he really is a Piedmontese. Coppelius was a German, though no honest German, I fancy.

Nevertheless I am not quite satisfied. You and Clara will perhaps take me for a gloomy dreamer, but in no way can I get rid of the impression which Coppelius's cursed face made upon me. I am glad to learn from Spalanzani that he has left town.

This Professor Spalanzani is a very queer fish. He is a little fat man, with prominent cheekbones, thin nose, projecting lips, and small piercing eyes. You cannot get a better picture of him than by turning over one of the Berlin pocket almanacs and looking at Gagliostro's portrait engraved by Ghodowiecki; Spalanzani looks just like him.

Once lately, as I went up the steps to his house, I perceived that beside the curtain which generally covered a glass door there was a small chink. What it was that excited my curiosity I cannot explain; but I looked through. In the room I saw a female, tall, very slender, but of perfect proportions, and splendidly dressed, sitting at a little table, on which she had placed both her arms, her hands being folded together. She sat opposite the door, so that I could easily see her angelically beautiful face. She did not appear to notice me, and there was moreover a strangely fixed look about her eyes. I might almost say they appeared as if they had no power of vision; I thought she was sleeping with her eyes open. I felt quite uncomfortable, and so I slipped away quietly into the Professor's lecture-room, which was close at hand.

Afterwards I learned that the figure which I had seen was Spalanzani's daughter, Olimpia, whom he keeps locked up in a most wicked and unaccountable way. No man is ever allowed to come near her. Perhaps, however, there is something peculiar about her after all; perhaps she's an idiot or something of that sort.

But why am I telling you all this ? I could tell you it all better and in more detail when I see you. For in a fortnight I shall be among you. I must see my dear sweet angel, my Clara, again. Then the little bit of ill-temper which, I must confess, took possession of me after her fearfully sensible letter, will be blown away. And that is the reason why I am not writing to her as well today.

With all best wishes.

Nothing more strange and extraordinary can be imagined, gracious reader, than what happened to my poor friend, the young student Nathanael, and which I have undertaken to relate to you. Have you ever experienced anything that completely took possession of your heart and mind and thoughts to the utter exclusion of everything else? All was seething and boiling within you; your blood, heated to fever pitch, leaped through your veins and inflamed your cheeks. Your gaze was so peculiar, as if seeking to grasp in empty space forms not seen by any other eye, and all your words ended in sighs betokening some mystery.

Then your friends asked you, "What is the matter with you, my dear friend? What do you see?" And, wishing to describe the inner pictures in all their vivid colours, with their lights and their shades, you struggled in vain to find words with which to express yourself. But you felt as if you must gather up all the events that had happened, wonderful, splendid, terrible, jocose, and awful, in the very first word, so that the whole might be revealed by a single electric discharge, so to speak.

Yet every word and everything that partook of the nature of communication by intelligible sounds seemed to be colourless, cold, and dead. Then you try and try again, and stutter and stammer, while your friends' prosy questions strike like icy winds upon your heart's hot fire until they extinguish it. But if, like a bold painter, you had first sketched in a few audacious strokes the outline of the picture you had in your soul, you would then easily have been able to deepen and intensify the colours one after the other, until the varied throng of living figures carried your friends away and they, like you, saw themselves in the midst of that had proceeded out of your own soul.

Strictly speaking, indulgent reader, I must indeed confess to you, nobody has asked me for the history of young Nathanael; but you are very well aware that I belong to that remarkable class of authors who, when they bear anything about in their minds in the manner I have just described, feel as if everybody who comes near them, and also the whole world to boot, were asking, "Oh! what is it? Oh! do tell us, my good sir?"

Hence I was most powerfully impelled to narrate to you Nathanael's ominous life. I was completely captivated by the elements of marvel and alienness in life; but, for this very reason, and because it was necessary in the very beginning to dispose you, indulgent reader, to bear with what is fantastic—and that is not a small matter—I racked my brain to find a way of commencing the story in a significant and original manner, calculated to arrest your attention. To begin with "Once upon a time," the best beginning for a story, seemed to me too tame; with "In the small country town S—— lived," rather better, at rate allowing plenty of room to work up to the climax; or to plunge at once *in medias res*, "'Go to the devil!' cried the student Nathanael, his eyes blazing wildly with rage and fear, when the weather-glass peddler Giuseppe Coppola"—well, that is what I really had written, when I thought I detected something of the ridiculous in Nathanael's wild glance; and the history is anything but laughable. I could not find any words which seemed fitted to reflect in even the feeblest degree the brightness of the colours of my mental vision.

I determined not to begin at all. So I pray you, gracious reader, accept the three letters which my friend Lothair has been so kind as to communicate to me as the outline of the picture, into which I will endeavour to introduce more and more colour as I proceed with my narrative. Perhaps, like a good portrait painter, I may succeed in depicting Nathanael in such a way that you will recognize it as a good likeness without being acquainted with the original, and will feel as if you had very often seen him with your own bodily eyes. Perhaps, too, you will then believe that nothing is more wonderful, nothing more fantastic than real life, and that all that a writer can do is to present it as "in a glass, darkly."

In order to make the beginning more intelligible, it is necessary to add to the letters that, soon after the death of Nathanael's father, Clara and Lothair, the children of a distant relative, who had likewise died, leaving them orphans, were taken by Nathanael's mother into her own house. Clara and Nathanael conceived a warm affection for each other, to which there could be no objection. When therefore Nathanael left home to prosecute his studies in G——, they were engaged. It is from G—— that his last letter is written, where he is attending the lectures of Spalanzani, the distinguished Professor of Physics.

I might now proceed comfortably with my narration, if at this moment Clara's image did not rise up so vividly before my eyes that I cannot turn them away from it, just as I never could when she looked upon me and smiled so sweetly. Nowhere would she have passed for beautiful; that was the unanimous opinion of everyone who professed to have any technical knowledge of beauty. But while architects praised the pure proportions of her figure and form, painters averred that her neck, shoulders, and bosom were almost too chastely modelled; and yet, on the other hand, one and all were in love with her glorious Magdalene hair, and talked a good deal of nonsense about Battoni-like colouring. One of them, a veritable romanticist, strangely enough likened her eyes to a lake by Ruisdael, in which is reflected the pure azure of the cloudless sky, the beauty of woods and flowers, and all the bright and varied life of a living landscape. Poets and musicians went still further and said, "What's all this talk about seas and reflections? How can we look upon the girl without feeling that wonderful heavenly songs and melodies beam upon us from her eyes, penetrating deep down into our hearts, till everything becomes awake and throbbing with emotion? And if we cannot sing anything at all passable then, why, we are not worth much; and this we can also plainly read in the rare smile which flits around her lips when we have the hardihood to squeak out something in her presence which we pretend to call singing, in spite of the fact that it is nothing more than a few single notes confusedly linked together."

And it really was so. Clara had the powerful fancy of a bright, innocent, unaffected child, a woman's deep and sympathetic heart, and an understanding clear, sharp, and discriminating. Dreamers and visionaries had a bad time of it with her; for without saying very much—she was not by nature of a talkative disposition—she plainly asked, by her calm steady look and rare ironical smile, "How can you imagine, my dear friends, that I can take these fleeting shadowy images for true living and breathing forms?" For this reason many found fault with her as being cold, unimaginative, and devoid of feeling;

others, however, who had reached a clearer and deeper conception of life, were extremely fond of the intelligent, childlike, large-hearted girl.

No one else had such an affection for her as Nathanael, who was a zealous and cheerful cultivator of the fields of science and art. Clara clung to her lover with all her heart; the first clouds she encountered in life were when he had to separate from her. With what delight did she fly into his arms when, as he had promised in his last letter to Lothair, he really came back to his native town and entered his mother's room! And as Nathanael had foreseen, the moment he saw Clara again he no longer thought about either the lawyer Coppelius or her sensible letter; his ill-humour had quite disappeared.

Nevertheless Nathanael was right when he told his friend Lothair that the repulsive vendor of weather glasses, Coppola, had exercised a fatal and disturbing influence upon his life. It was quite patent to all; for even during the first few days he showed that he was completely and entirely changed. He gave himself up to gloomy reveries, and moreover acted so strangely; they had never observed anything at all like it in him before. Everything, even his own life, was to him but dreams and presentiments. His constant theme was that every man who delusively imagined himself to be free was merely the plaything of the cruel sport of mysterious powers, and it was vain for man to resist them; he must humbly submit to whatever destiny had decreed for him. He went so far as to maintain that it was foolish to believe that a man could do anything in art or science of his own accord; for the inspiration in which alone any true artistic work could be done did not proceed from the spirit within outwards, but was the result of the operation directed inwards of some Higher Principle existing without and beyond ourselves.

This mystic extravagance was in the highest degree repugnant to Clara's clear intelligent mind, but it seemed vain to enter upon any attempt at refutation. Yet when Nathanael went on to prove that Coppelius was the Evil Principle which had entered into him and taken possession of him at the time he was listening behind the curtain, and that this hateful demon would in some terrible way ruin their happiness, then Clara grew grave and said, "Yes, Nathanael. You are right; Coppelius is an Evil Principle; he can do dreadful things, as bad as could a Satanic power which should assume a living physical form, but only—only if you do not banish him from your mind and thoughts. As long as you believe in him he exists and is at work; your belief in him is his only power."

Whereupon Nathanael, quite angry because Clara would only grant the existence of the demon in his own mind, began to dilate at large upon the whole mystic doctrine of devils and awful powers, but Clara abruptly broke off the theme by making, to Nathanael's very great disgust, some quite commonplace remark.

Such deep mysteries are sealed books to cold, unsusceptible characters, he thought, without its being clearly conscious to himself that he counted Clara among these inferior natures, and accordingly he did not remit his efforts to initiate her into these mysteries. In the morning, when she was helping to prepare breakfast, he would take his stand beside her, and read all sorts of mystic books to her, until she begged him—"But, my dear Nathanael, I shall have to scold you as the Evil Principle which exercises a fatal influence upon my coffee. For if I do as you wish, and let things go their own way, and look into your eyes while you read, the coffee will all boil over into the fire, and you will none of you get any breakfast." Then Nathanael hastily banged the book shut and ran away in great displeasure to his own room.

Formerly he had possessed a peculiar talent for writing pleasing, sparkling tales, which Clara took the greatest delight in hearing; but now his productions were gloomy, unintelligible, and wanting in form, so that, although Clara out of forbearance towards him did not say so, he nevertheless felt how very little interest she took in them. There was nothing that Clara disliked so much as what was tedious;

at such times her intellectual sleepiness was not to be overcome; it was betrayed both in her glances and in her words. Nathanael's effusions were, in truth, exceedingly tedious.

His ill-humour at Clara's cold prosaic temperament continued to increase; Clara could not conceal her distaste for his dark, gloomy, wearying mysticism; and thus both began to be more and more estranged from each other without exactly being aware of it themselves. The image of the ugly Coppelius had, as Nathanael was obliged to confess to himself, faded considerably in his fancy, and it often cost him great pains to present him in vivid colours in his literary efforts, in which Coppelius played the part of the ghoul of Destiny.

At length it entered into his head to make his dismal presentiment that Coppelius would ruin his happiness the subject of a poem. He made himself and Clara, united by true love, the central figures, but represented a black hand as being from time to time thrust into their life, plucking out a joy that had blossomed for them. At length, as they were standing at the altar, the terrible Coppelius appeared and touched Clara's lovely eyes, which leaped into Nathanael's own bosom, burning and hissing like bloody sparks. Then Coppelius laid hold of him, and hurled him into a blazing circle of fire, which spun round with the speed of a whirlwind, and storming and blustering, dashed away with him. The fearful noise it made was like a furious hurricane lashing the foaming sea waves until they rise up like black, white-headed giants in the midst of the raging struggle. But through the midst of the savage fury of the tempest he heard Clara's voice calling, "Can you not see me, dear? Coppelius has deceived you; they were not my eyes which burned so in your bosom; they were fiery drops of your own heart's blood. Look at me, I have got my own eyes still." Nathanael thought, "Yes, that is Clara, and I am hers forever." Then this thought laid a powerful grasp upon the fiery circle so that it stood still, and the riotous turmoil died away, rumbling down into a dark abyss. Nathanael looked into Clara's eyes; but it was death whose gaze rested so kindly upon him.

While Nathanael was writing this work he was very quiet and sober-minded; he filed and polished every line, and as he had chosen to submit himself to the limitations of meter, he did not rest until all was pure and musical. When, however, he had at length finished it and read it aloud to himself he was seized with horror and awful dread, and he screamed, "Whose hideous voice is this?" But he soon came to see in it again nothing beyond a very successful poem, and he confidently believed it would enkindle Clara's cold temperament, though to what end she should be thus aroused was not quite clear to his own mind, nor yet what would be the real purpose served by tormenting her with these dreadful pictures, which prophesied a terrible and ruinous end to her affection.

Nathanael and Clara sat in his mother's little garden. Clara was bright and cheerful, since for three entire days her lover, who had been busy writing his poem, had not teased her with his dreams or forebodings. Nathanael, too, spoke in a gay and vivacious way of things of merry import, as he formerly used to do, so that Clara said, "Ah! now I have you again. We have driven away that ugly Coppelius, you see." Then it suddenly occurred to him that he had got the poem in his pocket which he wished to read to her. He at once took out the manuscript and began to read.

Clara, anticipating something tedious as usual, prepared to submit to the infliction, and calmly resumed her knitting. But as the sombre clouds rose up darker and darker she let her knitting fall on her lap and sat with her eyes fixed in a set stare upon Nathanael's face. He was quite carried away by his own work, the fire of enthusiasm coloured his cheeks a deep red, and tears started from his eyes. At length he concluded, groaning and showing great lassitude; grasping Clara's hand, he sighed as if he were being utterly melted in inconsolable grief, "Oh! Clara! Clara!" She drew him softly to her heart and said in a low but very grave and impressive tone, "Nathanael, my darling Nathanael, throw that foolish, senseless, stupid thing into the fire."

Then Nathanael leaped indignantly to his feet, crying, as he pushed Clara from him, "You damned lifeless automaton!" and rushed away. Clara was cut to the heart, and wept bitterly. "Oh! he has never loved me, for he does not understand me," she sobbed.

Lothair entered the arbour. Clara was obliged to tell him all that had taken place. He was passionately fond of his sister; and every word of her complaint fell like a spark upon his heart, so that the displeasure which he had long entertained against his dreamy friend Nathanael was kindled into furious anger. He hastened to find Nathanael, and upbraided him in harsh words for his irrational behaviour towards his beloved sister.

The fiery Nathanael answered him in the same style. "A fantastic, crack-brained fool," was retaliated with, "A miserable, common, everyday sort of fellow." A meeting was the inevitable consequence. They agreed to meet on the following morning behind the garden wall, and fight, according to the custom of the students of the place, with sharp rapiers. They went about silent and gloomy; Clara had both heard and seen the violent quarrel, and also observed the fencing master bring the rapiers in the dusk of the evening. She had a presentiment of what was to happen. They both appeared at the appointed place wrapped up in the same gloomy silence, and threw off their coats. Their eyes flaming with the bloodthirsty light of pugnacity, they were about to begin their contest when Clara burst through the garden door. Sobbing, she screamed, "You savage, terrible men! Cut me down before you attack each other; for how can I live when my lover has slain my brother, or my brother slain my lover?"

Lothair let his weapon fall and gazed silently at the ground, while Nathanael's heart was rent with sorrow, and all the affection which he had felt for his lovely Clara in the happiest days of her golden youth was reawakened within him. His murderous weapon, too, fell from his hand; he threw himself at Clara's feet. "Oh! can you ever forgive me, my only, my dearly loved Clara? Can you, my dear brother Lothair, also forgive me?" Lothair was touched by his friend's great distress; the three young people embraced each other amid endless tears, and swore never again to break their bond of love and fidelity.

Nathanael felt as if a heavy burden that had been weighing him down to the earth was now rolled from off him, nay, as if by offering resistance to the dark power which had possessed him, he had rescued his own self from the ruin which had threatened him. Three happy days he now spent amidst the loved ones, and then returned to G——, where he had still a year to stay before settling down in his native town for life.

Everything having reference to Coppelius had been concealed from Nathanael's mother, for they knew she could not think of Coppelius without horror, since she as well as Nathanael believed him to be guilty of causing her husband's death.

When Nathanael came to the house where he lived in G——, he was greatly astonished to find it burned down to the ground, so that nothing but the bare outer walls were left standing amid a heap of ruins. Although the fire had broken out in the laboratory of the chemist who lived on the ground floor, and had therefore spread upwards, some of Nathanael's bold, active friends had succeeded in time in forcing a way into his room in the upper story and saving his books and manuscripts and instruments.

They had carried them all uninjured into another house, where they engaged a room for him; this he now at once took possession of.

That he lived opposite Professor Spalanzani did not strike him particularly, nor did it occur to him as anything more singular that he could, as he observed, by looking out of his window, see straight into the room where Olimpia often sat alone. Her figure he could plainly distinguish, although her features were uncertain and confused. It did at length occur to him, however, that she remained for hours together in the same position in which he had first discovered her through the glass door, sitting at a little table without any occupation whatever, and it was evident that she was constantly gazing across in his direction. He could not but confess to himself that he had never seen a finer figure. However, with Clara mistress of his heart, he remained perfectly unaffected by Olimpia's stiffness and apathy; and it was only occasionally that he sent a fugitive glance over his compendium across to her—that was all.

He was writing to Clara; a light tap came at the door. At his summons to "Come in," Coppola's repulsive face appeared peeping in. Nathanael felt his heart beat with trepidation; but, recollecting what Spalanzani had told him about his fellow countryman Coppola, and what he himself had so faithfully promised his beloved in respect to the Sand-man Coppelius, he was ashamed at himself for this childish fear of specters. Accordingly, he controlled himself with an effort, and said, as quietly and as calmly as he possibly could, "I don't want to buy any weather glasses, my good friend; you had better go elsewhere."

Then Coppola came right into the room, and said in a hoarse voice, screwing up his wide mouth into a hideous smile, while his little eyes flashed keenly from beneath his long gray eyelashes, "Eh! No want weather glass ? No weather glass ? I got eyes-a too. Fine eyes-a." In some fright, Nathanael cried, "You idiot, how can you have eyes?—eyes—eyes?" But Coppola, laying aside his barometers, thrust his hands into his big coat pockets and brought out several spy-glasses and spectacles, and put them on the table. "Looka! Looka! Spettacles for nose. Spettacles. Those my eyes-a." And he continued to produce more and more spectacles from his pockets until the table began to gleam and flash all over. Thousands of eyes were looking and blinking convulsively and staring up at Nathanael; he could not avert his gaze from the table. Coppola went on heaping up his spectacles, while wilder and ever wilder burning flashes crossed through and through each other and darted their blood-red rays into Nathanael's breast.

Quite overcome and frantic with terror, he shouted, "Stop! stop! you fiend!" and he seized Coppola by the arm, which Coppola had again thrust into his pocket in order to bring out still more spectacles, although the whole table was covered all over with them. With a harsh disagreeable laugh Coppola gently freed himself; and with the words "So! want none! Well, here fine glass!" he swept all his spectacles together, and put them back into his coat pockets, while from a breast pocket he produced a great number of larger and smaller perspectives. As soon as the spectacles were gone Nathanael recovered his equanimity again; and, bending his thoughts upon Clara, he clearly discerned that the gruesome incubus had proceeded only from himself, and that Coppola was an honest mechanician and optician, and far from being Coppelius's dreaded double and ghost. And then, besides, none of the glasses which Coppola now placed on the table had anything at all singular about them, at least nothing so weird as the spectacles; so, in order to square accounts with himself Nathanael now really determined to buy something of the man. He took up a small, very beautifully cut pocket perspective, and by way of proving it looked through the window.

Never before in his life had he had a glass in his hands that brought out things so clearly and sharply and distinctly. Involuntarily he directed the glass upon Spalanzani's room; Olimpia sat at the little table as usual, her arms laid upon it and her hands folded. Now he saw for the first time the regular and exquisite beauty of her features. The eyes, however, seemed to him to have a singular look of fixity and lifelessness. But as he continued to look closer and more carefully through the glass he fancied a light like humid moonbeams came into them. It seemed as if their power of vision was now being enkindled; their glances shone with ever-increasing vivacity.

Nathanael remained standing at the window as if glued to the spot by a wizard's spell, his gaze riveted unchangeably upon the divinely beautiful Olimpia. A coughing and shuffling of the feet awakened him out of his enchaining dream, as it were. Coppola stood behind him, "Tre zechini" (three ducats). Nathanael had completely forgotten the optician; he hastily paid the sum demanded. "Ain't 't? Fine-a glass? Fine-a glass?" asked Coppola in his harsh unpleasant voice, smiling sardonically. "Yes, yes, yes," rejoined Nathanael impatiently; "adieu, my good friend." But Coppola did not leave the room without casting many peculiar side glances upon Nathanael; and the young student heard him laughing loudly on the stairs. "Ah well!" thought he, "he's laughing at me because I've paid him too much for this little perspective—because I've given him too much money—that's it."

As he softly murmured these words he fancied he detected a gasping sigh as of a dying man stealing awfully through the room; his heart stopped beating with fear. But to be sure he had heaved a deep sigh himself; it was quite plain. "Clara is quite right," said he to himself, "in holding me to be an incurable ghost-seer; and yet it's very ridiculous—more ridiculous, that the stupid thought of having paid Coppola too much for his glass should cause me this strange anxiety; I can't see any reason for it."

Now he sat down to finish his letter to Clara; but a glance through the window showed him Olimpia still in her former posture. Urged by an irresistible impulse he jumped up and seized Coppola's perspective; nor could he tear himself away from the fascinating Olimpia until his friend Siegmund called for him to go to Professor Spalanzani's lecture. The curtains before the door of the all-important room were closely drawn, so that he could not see Olimpia. Nor could he even see her from his own room during the two following days, notwithstanding that he scarcely ever left his window, and maintained a scarce interrupted watch through Coppola's perspective upon her room.

On the third day curtains were drawn across the window. Plunged into the depths of despair,—goaded by longing and ardent desire, he hurried outside the walls of the town. Olimpia's image hovered about his path in the air and stepped forth out of the bushes, and peeped up at him with large and lustrous eyes from the bright surface of the brook. Clara's image was completely faded from his mind; he had no thoughts except for Olimpia. He uttered his love plaints aloud and in a lachrymose tone, "Oh! my glorious, noble star of love, have you only risen to vanish again, and leave me in the darkness and hopelessness of night?"

Returning home, he became aware that there was a good deal of noisy bustle going on in Spalanzani's house. All the doors stood wide open; men were taking in all kinds of gear and furniture; the windows of the first floor were all lifted off their hinges; busy maidservants with immense hair-brooms were driving backwards and forwards dusting and sweeping, while from inside could be heard the knocking and hammering of carpenters and upholsterers. Utterly astonished, Nathanael stood still in the street; then Siegmund joined him, laughing, and said, "Well, what do you say to our old Spalanzani?" Nathanael assured him that he could not say anything, since he did not know what it all meant. To his great astonishment, he could hear, however, that they were turning the quiet gloomy house almost inside out with their dusting and cleaning and alterations. Then he learned from Siegmund that Spalanzani intended giving a great concert and ball on the following day, and that half the university was invited. It was generally reported that Spalanzani was going to let his daughter Olimpia, whom he had so long so jealously guarded from every eye, make her first appearance.

Nathanael received an invitation. At the appointed hour, when the carriages were rolling up and the lights were gleaming brightly in the decorated halls, he went across to the Professor's, his heart beating high with expectation. The company was both numerous and brilliant.

Olimpia was richly and tastefully dressed. One could not but admire her figure and the regular beauty of her features. Yet the striking inward curve of her back, as well as the wasplike smallness of her waist, appeared to be the result of too-tight lacing, and there was something stiff and measured in her gait and bearing that made an unfavourable impression upon many. It was ascribed to the constraint imposed upon her by the company.

The concert began. Olimpia played on the piano with great skill; and sang as skillfully an *aria di bravura*, in a voice which was, if anything, almost too brilliant, but clear as glass bells. Nathanael was transported with delight; he stood in the background farthest from her, and owing to the blinding lights could not quite distinguish her features. So, without being observed, he took Coppola's glass out of his pocket, and directed it upon the beautiful Olimpia. Oh! then he perceived how her yearning eyes sought him, how every note only reached its full purity in the loving glance which penetrated to and inflamed his heart. Her roulades seemed to him to be the exultant cry towards heaven of the soul refined by love; and when at last, after the cadenza, the long trill rang loudly through the hall, he felt as if he were suddenly grasped by burning arms and could no longer control himself—he could not help shouting aloud in his mingled pain and delight, "Olimpia!" All eyes were turned upon him; many people laughed.

The concert came to an end, and the ball began. Oh! to dance with her—with her—that was now the aim of all Nathanael's wishes, of all his desires. But how should he have courage to request her, the queen of the ball, to grant him the honour of a dance? And yet he couldn't tell how it came about, just as the dance began, he found himself standing close beside her, nobody having as yet asked her to be his partner. So, with some difficulty stammering out a few words, he grasped her hand. It was cold as ice; he shook with an awful, frosty shiver. But, fixing his eyes upon her face, he saw that her glance was beaming upon him with love and longing, and at the same moment he thought that the pulse began to beat in her cold hand, and the warm life-blood to course through her veins. And passion burned more intensely in his own heart also; he threw his arm round her beautiful waist and whirled her round the hall. He had always thought that he kept good and accurate time in dancing, but from the perfectly rhythmical evenness with which Olimpia danced, and which frequently put him quite out, he perceived how very faulty his own time really was. Notwithstanding, he would not dance with any other lady; and everybody else who approached Olimpia to call upon her for a dance, he would have liked to kill on the spot. This, however, only happened twice; to his astonishment Olimpia remained after this without a partner, and he did not fail on each occasion to take her out again.

If Nathanael had been able to see anything else except the beautiful Olimpia, there would inevitably have been a good deal of unpleasant quarrelling and strife; for it was evident that Olimpia was the object of the smothered laughter suppressed only with difficulty, which was heard in various corners amongst the young people; and they followed her with very curious looks.

Nathanael, excited by dancing and the plentiful supply of wine he had consumed, had laid aside the shyness which at other times characterized him. He sat beside Olimpia, her hand in his own, and declared his love enthusiastically and passionately in words which neither of them understood, neither he nor Olimpia. And yet perhaps she did, for she sat with her eyes fixed unchangeably upon his, sighing repeatedly, "Ah! Ah! Ah!" Upon this Nathanael would answer, "Oh, you glorious heavenly lady! You ray from the promised paradise of love! Oh! what a profound soul you have! my whole being is mirrored in it!" and a good deal more in the same strain. But Olimpia only continued to sigh "Ah! Ah!" again and again.

Professor Spalanzani passed by the two happy lovers once or twice, and smiled with a look of peculiar satisfaction. All at once it seemed to Nathanael, albeit he was far away in a different world, as if it were growing perceptibly darker down below at Professor Spalanzani's. He looked about him, and to his very great alarm became aware that there were only two lights left burning in the hall, and they were on the point of going out. The music and dancing had long ago ceased. "We must part—part!" he cried, wildly and despairingly; he kissed Olimpia's hand; he bent down to her mouth, but ice-cold lips met his burning ones. As he touched her cold hand, he felt his heart thrill with awe; the legend of "The Dead Bride" shot suddenly through his mind. But Olimpia had drawn him closer to her, and the kiss appeared to warm her lips into vitality.

Professor Spalanzani strode slowly through the empty apartment, his footsteps giving a hollow echo; and his figure had, as the flickering shadows played about him, a ghostly, awful appearance. "Do you love me? Do you love me, Olimpia? Only one little word—do you love me?" whispered Nathanael, but she only sighed, "Ah! Ah!" as she rose to her feet.

"Yes, you are my lovely, glorious star of love," said Nathanael, "and will shine for ever, purifying and ennobling my heart." "Ah! Ah!" replied Olimpia, as she moved along. Nathanael followed her; they stood before the Professor. "You have had an extraordinarily animated conversation with my daughter," said he, smiling. "Well, well, my dear Mr. Nathanael, if you find pleasure in talking to the stupid girl, I am sure I shall be glad for you to come and do so." Nathanael took his leave, his heart singing and leaping in a perfect delirium of happiness.

During the next few days Spalanzani's ball was the general topic of conversation. Although the Professor had done everything to make the thing a splendid success, yet certain gay spirits related more than one thing that had occurred which was quite irregular and out of order. They were especially keen in pulling Olimpia to pieces for her taciturnity and rigid stiffness; in spite of her beautiful form they alleged that she was hopelessly stupid, and in this fact they discerned the reason why Spalanzani had so long kept her concealed from publicity Nathanael heard all this with inward wrath, but nevertheless he held his tongue; for, thought he, would it indeed be worth while to prove to these fellows that it is their own stupidity which prevents them from appreciating Olimpia's profound and brilliant parts?

One day Siegmund said to him, "Pray, brother, have the kindness to tell me how you, a clever fellow, came to lose your head over that Miss Wax-face—that wooden doll across there ? "Nathanael was about to fly into a rage, but he recollected himself and replied, "Tell me, Siegmund, how came it that Olimpia's divine charms could escape your eye, so keenly alive as it always is to beauty, and your acute perception as well? But Heaven be thanked for it, otherwise I should have had you for a rival, and then the blood of one of us would have had to be spilled."

Siegmund, perceiving how matters stood with his friend, skillfully changed his tactics and said, after remarking that all argument with one in love about the object of his affections was out of place, "Yet it's very strange that several of us have formed pretty much the same opinion about Olimpia. We think she is—you won't take it ill, brother?—that she is singularly statuesque and soulless. Her figure is regular, and so are her features, that can't be gainsaid; and if her eyes were not so utterly devoid of life, I may say, of the power of vision, she might pass for a beauty. She is strangely measured in her movements, they all seem as if they were dependent upon some wound-up clockwork. Her playing and singing have the disagreeably perfect, but insensitive timing of a singing machine, and her dancing is the same. We felt quite afraid of this Olimpia, and did not like to have anything to do with her; she seemed to us to be only acting *like* a living creature, and as if there was some secret at the bottom of it all."

Nathanael did not give way to the bitter feelings which threatened to master him at these words of Siegmund's; he fought down and got the better of his displeasure, and merely said, very earnestly, "You cold prosaic fellows may very well be afraid of her. It is only to its like that the poetically organized spirit unfolds itself. Upon me alone did her loving glances fall, and through my mind and thoughts alone did they radiate; and only in her love can I find my own self again. Perhaps, however, she doesn't do quite right not to jabber a lot of nonsense and stupid talk like other shallow people. It is true, she speaks but few words; but the few words she does speak are genuine hieroglyphs of the inner world of Love and of the higher cognition of the intellectual life revealed in the intuition of the Eternal beyond the grave. But you have no understanding for all these things, and I am only wasting words."

"God be with you, brother," said Siegmund very gently, almost sadly, "but it seems to me that you are in a very bad way. You may rely upon me, if all—No, I can't say any more." It all at once dawned upon Nathanael that his cold prosaic friend Siegmund really and sincerely wished him well, and so he warmly shook his proffered hand.

Nathanael had completely forgotten that there was a Clara in the world, whom he had once loved—and his mother and Lothair. They had all vanished from his mind; he lived for Olimpia alone.

He sat beside her every day for hours together, rhapsodizing about his love and sympathy enkindled into life, and about psychic elective affinity—all of which Olimpia listened to with great reverence.

He fished up from the very bottom of his desk all the things that he had ever written—poems, fancy sketches, visions, romances, tales, and the heap was increased daily with all kinds of aimless sonnets, stanzas, canzonets. All these he read to Olimpia hour after hour without growing tired; but then he had never had such an exemplary listener. She neither embroidered, nor knitted; she did not look out of the window, or feed a bird, or play with a little pet dog or a favourite cat, neither did she twist a piece of paper or anything of that kind round her finger; she did not forcibly convert a yawn into a low affected cough—in short, she sat hour after hour with her eyes bent unchangeably upon her lover's face, without moving or altering her position, and her gaze grew more ardent and more ardent still. And it was only when at last Nathanael rose and kissed her lips or her hand that she said, "Ah! Ah!" and then "Goodnight, dear."

Back in his own room, Nathanael would break out with, "Oh! what a brilliant—what a profound mind! Only you—you alone understand me." And his heart trembled with rapture when he reflected upon the wondrous harmony which daily revealed itself between his own and his Olimpia's character; for he fancied that she had expressed in respect to his works and his poetic genius the identical sentiments which he himself cherished deep down in his own heart, and even as if it was his own heart's voice speaking to him. And it must indeed have been so; for Olimpia never uttered any other words than those already mentioned. And when Nathanael himself in his clear and sober moments, as, for instance, directly after waking in a morning, thought about her utter passivity and taciturnity, he only said, "What are words—but words? The glance of her heavenly eyes says more than any tongue. And anyway, how can a child of heaven accustom herself to the narrow circle which the exigencies of a wretched mundane life demand?"

Professor Spalanzani appeared to be greatly pleased at the intimacy that had sprung up between his daughter Olimpia and Nathanael, and showed the young man many unmistakable proofs of his good feeling towards him. When Nathanael ventured at length to hint very delicately at an alliance with Olimpia, the Professor smiled all over his face at once, and said he should allow his daughter to make a perfectly free choice.

Encouraged by these words, and with the fire of desire burning in his heart, Nathanael resolved the very next day to implore Olimpia to tell him frankly, in plain words, what he had long read in her sweet loving glances—that she would be his for ever. He looked for the ring which his mother had given him at parting; he would present it to Olimpia as a symbol of his devotion, and of the happy life he was to lead with her from that time onwards.

While looking for it he came across his letters from Clara and Lothair; he threw them carelessly aside, found the ring, put it in his pocket, and ran across to Olimpia. While still on the stairs, in the entrance passage, he heard an extraordinary hubbub; the noise seemed to proceed from Spalanzani's study. There was a stamping—a rattling—pushing—knocking against the door, with curses and oaths intermingled. "Leave hold—leave hold—you monster—you rascal—put your life's work into it?—Ha! ha! ha! ha!—That was not our wager—I, I made the eyes—I the clockwork.—Go to the devil with your clockwork—you damned dog of a watchmaker—be off—Satan—stop—you paltry turner—you infernal beast—stop—begone—let me go." The voices which were thus making all this racket and rumpus were those of Spalanzani and the fearsome Coppelius.

Nathanael rushed in, impelled by some nameless dread. The Professor was grasping a female figure by the shoulders, the Italian Coppola held her by the feet; and they were pulling and dragging each other backwards and forwards, fighting furiously to get possession of her.

Nathanael recoiled with horror on recognizing that the figure was Olimpia. Boiling with rage, he was about to tear his beloved from the grasp of the madmen, when Coppola by an extraordinary exertion of strength twisted the figure out of the Professor's hands and gave him such a terrible blow with her, that Spalanzani reeled backwards and fell over the table among the phials and retorts, the bottles and glass cylinders, which covered it: all these things were smashed into a thousand pieces. But Coppola threw the figure across his shoulder, and, laughing shrilly and horribly, ran hastily down the stairs, the figure's ugly feet hanging down and banging and rattling like wood against the steps.

Nathanael was stupefied—he had seen only too distinctly that in Olimpia's pallid waxed face there were no eyes, merely black holes in their stead; she was an inanimate puppet. Spalanzani was rolling on the floor; the pieces of glass had cut his head and breast and arm; the blood was escaping from him in streams. But he gathered his strength together by an effort.

"After him—after him! What do you stand staring there for? Coppelius—Coppelius—he's stolen my best automaton—at which I've worked for twenty years—my life work—the clockwork—speech—movement—mine—your eyes—stolen your eyes—damn him—curse him—after him—fetch me back Olimpia—there are the eyes." And now Nathanael saw a pair of bloody eyes lying on the floor staring at him; Spalanzani seized them with his uninjured hand and threw them at him, so that they hit his breast.

Then madness dug her burning talons into Nathanael and swept down into his heart, rending his mind and thoughts to shreds. "Aha! aha! aha! Fire-wheel—fire-wheel! Spin round, lire-wheel! merrily,

merrily! Aha! wooden doll! spin round, pretty wooden doll!" and he threw himself upon the Professor, clutching him fast by the throat.

He would certainly have strangled him had not several people, attracted by the noise, rushed in and torn away the madman; and so they saved the Professor, whose wounds were immediately dressed. Siegmund, with all his strength, was not able to subdue the frantic lunatic, who continued to scream in a dreadful way, "Spin round, wooden doll!" and to strike out right and left with his doubled fists. At length the united strength of several succeeded in overpowering him by throwing him on the floor and binding him. His cries passed into a brutish bellow that was awful to hear; and thus raging with the harrowing violence of madness, he was taken away to the madhouse.

Before continuing my narration of what happened further to the unfortunate Nathanael, I will tell you, indulgent reader, in case you take any interest in that skillful mechanician and fabricator of automata Spalanzani that he recovered completely from his wounds. He had, however, to leave the university, for Nathanael's fate had created a great sensation; and the opinion was pretty generally expressed that it was an imposture altogether unpardonable to have smuggled a wooden puppet instead of a living person into intelligent tea-circles—for Olimpia had been present at several with success. Lawyers called it a cunning piece of knavery, and all the harder to punish since it was directed against the public; and it had been so craftily contrived that it had escaped unobserved by all except a few preternaturally acute students, although everybody was very wise now and remembered to have thought of several facts which occurred to them as suspicious. But these latter could not succeed in making out any sort of a consistent tale. For was it, for instance, a thing likely to occur to anyone as suspicious that, according to the declaration of an elegant beau of these tea-parties, Olimpia had, contrary to all good manners, sneezed oftener than she had yawned ? The former must have been, in the opinion of this elegant gentleman, the winding up of the concealed clockwork; it had always been accompanied by an observable creaking, and so on.

The Professor of Poetry and Eloquence took a pinch of snuff, and, slapping the lid to and clearing his throat, said solemnly, "My most honourable ladies and gentlemen, don't you see then where the rub is? The whole thing is an allegory, a continuous metaphor. You understand me? *Sapienti sat.*"

But several most honourable gentlemen did not rest satisfied with this explanation; the history of this automaton had sunk deeply into their souls, and an absurd mistrust of human figures began to prevail. Several lovers, in order to be fully convinced that they were not paying court to a wooden puppet, required that their mistress should sing and dance a little out of time, should embroider or knit or play with her little pug, &c., when being read to, but above all things else that she should do something more than merely listen—that she should frequently speak in such a way as to really show that her words presupposed as a condition some thinking and feeling. The bonds of love were in many cases drawn closer in consequence, and so of course became more engaging; in other instances they gradually relaxed and fell away. "I cannot really be made responsible for it," was the remark of more than one young gallant.

At the tea-gatherings everybody, in order to ward off suspicion, yawned to an incredible extent and never sneezed. Spalanzani was obliged, as has been said, to leave the place in order to escape a criminal charge of having fraudulently imposed an automaton upon human society. Coppola, too, had also disappeared.

When Nathanael awoke he felt as if he had been oppressed by a terrible nightmare; he opened his eyes and experienced an indescribable sensation of mental comfort, while a soft and most beautiful sensation of warmth pervaded his body. He lay on his own bed in his own room at home; Clara was bending over him, and at a little distance stood his mother and Lothair. "At last, at last, O my darling Nathanael; now we have you again; now you are cured of your grievous illness, now you are mine again." And Clara's words came from the depths of her heart; and she clasped him in her arms. The bright scalding tears streamed from his eyes, he was so overcome with mingled feelings of sorrow and delight; and he gasped forth, "My Clara, my Clara!"

Siegmund, who had staunchly stood by his friend in his hour of need, now came into the room. Nathanael gave him his hand—"My faithful brother, you have not deserted me." Every trace of insanity had left him, and in the tender hands of his mother and his beloved, and his friends, he quickly recovered his strength again. Good fortune had in the meantime visited the house; a niggardly old uncle, from whom they had never expected to get anything, had died, and left Nathanael's mother not only a considerable fortune, but also a small estate, pleasantly situated not far from the town. There they resolved to go and live, Nathanael and his mother, and Clara, to whom he was now to be married, and Lothair. Nathanael had become gentler and more childlike than he had ever been before, and now began really to understand Clara's supremely pure and noble character. None of them ever reminded him, even in the remotest degree, of the past. But when Siegmund took leave of him, Nathanael said, "By heaven, brother! I was in a bad way, but an angel came just at the right moment and led me back upon the path of light. Yes, it was Clara." Siegmund would not let him speak further, fearing lest the painful recollections of the past might arise too vividly and too intensely in his mind.

The time came for the four happy people to move to their little property. At noon they were going through the streets. After making several purchases they found that the lofty tower of the town hall was throwing its giant shadows across the market place. "Come," said Clara, "let us go up to the top once more and have a look at the distant hills." No sooner said than done. Both of them, Nathanael and Clara, went up the tower; their mother, however, went on with the servant-girl to her new home, and Lothair, not feeling inclined to climb up all the many steps, waited below. There the two lovers stood arm in arm on the topmost gallery of the tower, and gazed out into the sweet-scented wooded landscape, beyond which the blue hills rose up like a giant's city.

"Oh! do look at that strange little gray bush, it looks as if it were actually walking towards us," said Clara. Mechanically he put his hand into his side pocket; he found Coppola's perspective and looked for the bush; Clara stood in front of the glass.

Then a convulsive thrill shot through his pulse and veins; pale as a corpse, he fixed his staring eyes upon her; but soon they began to roll, and a fiery current flashed and sparkled in them, and he yelled fearfully, like a hunted animal. Leaping up high in the air and laughing horribly at the same time, he began to shout in a piercing voice, "Spin round, wooden doll! Spin round, wooden doll!" With the strength of a giant he laid hold upon Clara and tried to hurl her over, but in an agony of despair she clutched fast hold of the railing that went round the gallery.

Lothair heard the madman raging and Clara's scream of terror: a fearful presentiment flashed across his mind. He ran up the steps; the door of the second flight was locked. Clara's scream for help rang out more loudly. Mad with rage and fear, he threw himself against the door, which at length gave way. Clara's cries were growing fainter and fainter—"Help! save me! save me!" and her voice died away in the air. "She is killed—murdered by that madman," shouted Lothair. The door to the gallery was also locked.

Despair gave him the strength of a giant; he burst the door off its hinges. Good God! there was Clara in the grasp of the madman Nathanael, hanging over the gallery in the air, holding on to the iron bar with only one hand. Quick as lightning, Lothair seized his sister and pulled her back, at the same time dealing the madman a blow in the face with his doubled fist, which sent him reeling backwards, forcing him to let go his victim.

Lothair ran down with his insensible sister in his arms. She was saved. But Nathanael ran round and round the gallery, leaping up in the air and shouting, "Spin round, fire-wheel! Spin round, fire-wheel!" The people heard the wild shouting, and a crowd began to gather. In the midst of them towered the lawyer Coppelius, like a giant; he had only just arrived in the town, and had gone straight to the market place.

Some were for going up to overpower and take the madman, but Coppelius laughed and said, "Ha! ha! wait a bit; he'll come down of his own accord;" and he stood gazing up along with the rest.

All at once Nathanael stopped as if spellbound; he bent down over the railing and perceived Coppelius. With a piercing scream, "Eh! Fine eyes-a, fine eyes-a!" he leaped over the railing.

When Nathanael lay on the stone pavement with a shattered head, Coppelius had disappeared in the crush and confusion.

Several years afterwards it was reported that, outside the door of a pretty country house in a remote district, Clara had been seen sitting hand in hand with a pleasant gentleman, while two bright boys were playing at her feet. From this it may be concluded that she eventually found that quiet domestic happiness which her cheerful, blithesome character required, and which Nathanael, with his tempest-tossed soul, could never have been able to give her.

The Uncanny

By Sigmund Freud

I

It is only rarely that a psycho-analyst feels impelled to investigate the subject of aesthetics, even when aesthetics is understood to mean not merely the theory of beauty but the theory of the qualities of feeling. He works in other strata of mental life and has little to do with the subdued emotional impulses which, inhibited in their aims and dependent on a host of concurrent factors, usually furnish the material for the study of aesthetics. But it does occasionally happen that he has to interest himself in some particular province of that subject; and this province usually proves to be a rather remote one, and one which has been neglected in the specialist literature of aesthetics.

The subject of the 'uncanny'[1] is a province of this kind. It is undoubtedly related to what is frightening—to what arouses dread and horror; equally certainly, too, the word is not always used in a clearly definable sense, so that it tends to coincide with what excites fear in general. Yet we may expect that a special core of feeling is present which justifies the use of a special conceptual term. One is curious to know what this common core is which allows us to distinguish as 'uncanny' certain things which lie within the field of what is frightening.

As good as nothing is to be found upon this subject in comprehensive treatises on aesthetics, which in general prefer to concern themselves with what is beautiful, attractive and sublime—that is, with feelings of a positive nature—and with the circumstances and the objects that call them forth rather than with the opposite feelings of repulsion and distress. I know of only one attempt in medico-psychological literature, a fertile but not exhaustive paper by Jentsch (1906). But I must confess that I have not made a very thorough examination of the literature, especially the foreign literature, relating to this present

[1] [The German word, translated throughout this paper by the English 'uncanny', is *'unheimlich'*, literally 'unhomely'. The English term is not, of course, an exact equivalent of the German one.]

modest contribution of mine, for reasons which, as may easily be guessed, lie in the times in which we live;[2] so that my paper is presented to the reader without any claim to priority.

In his study of the 'uncanny' Jentsch quite rightly lays stress on the obstacle presented by the fact that people vary so very greatly in their sensitivity to this quality of feeling. The writer of the present contribution, indeed, must himself plead guilty to a special obtuseness in the matter, where extreme delicacy of perception would be more in place. It is long since he has experienced or heard of anything which has given him an uncanny impression, and he must start by translating himself into that state of feeling, by awakening in himself the possibility of experiencing it. Still, such difficulties make themselves powerfully felt in many other branches of aesthetics; we need not on that account despair of finding instances in which the quality in question will be unhesitatingly recognized by most people.

Two courses are open to us at the outset. Either we can find out what meaning has come to be attached to the word 'uncanny' in the course of its history; or we can collect all those properties of persons, things, sense-impressions, experiences and situations which arouse in us the feeling of uncanniness, and then infer the unknown nature of the uncanny from what all these examples have in common. I will say at once that both courses lead to the same result: the uncanny is that class of the frightening which leads back to what is known of old and long familiar. How this is possible, in what circumstances the familiar can become uncanny and frightening, I shall show in what follows. Let me also add that my investigation was actually begun by collecting a number of individual cases, and was only later confirmed by an examination of linguistic usage. In this discussion, however, I shall follow the reverse course.

The German word *'unheimlich'* is obviously the opposite of *'heimlich'* ['homely'], *'heimisch'* ['native']—the opposite of what is familiar; and we are tempted to conclude that what is 'uncanny' is frightening precisely because it is *not* known and familiar. Naturally not everything that is new and unfamiliar is frightening, however; the relation is not capable of inversion. We can only say that what is novel can easily become frightening and uncanny; some new things are frightening but not by any means all. Something has to be added to what is novel and unfamiliar in order to make it uncanny.

On the whole, Jentsch did not get beyond this relation of the uncanny to the novel and unfamiliar. He ascribes the essential factor in the production of the feeling of uncanniness to intellectual uncertainty; so that the uncanny would always, as it were, be something one does not know one's way about in. The better orientated in his environment a person is, the less readily will he get the impression of something uncanny in regard to the objects and events in it.

It is not difficult to see that this definition is incomplete, and we will therefore try to proceed beyond the equation 'uncanny' = 'unfamiliar'. We will first turn to other languages. But the dictionaries that we consult tell us nothing new, perhaps only because we ourselves speak a language that is foreign. Indeed, we get an impression that many languages are without a word for this particular shade of what is frightening.

I should like to express my indebtedness to Dr. Theodor Reik for the following excerpts:—

LATIN: (K. E. Georges, *Deutschlateinisches Wörterbuch,* 1898). An uncanny place: *locus suspectus;* at an uncanny time of night: *intempesta node.*

GREEK: (Rost's and Schenkl's Lexikons). ξενος (i.e. strange, foreign).

[2] [An allusion to the first World War only just concluded.]

ENGLISH: (from the dictionaries of Lucas, Bellows, Flugel and Muret-Sanders). Uncomfortable, uneasy, gloomy, dismal, uncanny, ghastly; (of a house) haunted; (of a man) a repulsive fellow.

FRENCH: (Sachs-Villatte). *Inquiétant, sinistre, lugubre, mal à son aise.*

SPANISH: (Tollhausen, 1889). *Sospechoso, de mal agüero, lúgubre, siniestro.*

The Italian and Portuguese languages seem to content themselves with words which we should describe as circumlocutions. In Arabic and Hebrew 'uncanny' means the same as 'daemonic', 'gruesome'.

Let us therefore return to the German language. In Daniel Sanders's *Wörterbuch der Deutschen Sprache* (1860, 1, 729), the following entry, which I here reproduce in full, is to be found under the word '*heimlich*'. I have laid stress on one or two passages by italicizing them.[3]

Heimlich, adj., subst. *Heimlichkeit* (pl. *Heimlichkeiten):* I. Also *heimelich, heimelig,* belonging to the house, not strange, familiar, tame, intimate, friendly, etc.

(a) (Obsolete) belonging to the house or the family, or regarded as so belonging (cf. Latin *familiaris,* familiar): *Die Heimlichen,* the members of the household; *Der heimliche Rat* (Gen. xli, 45; 2 Sam. xxiii. 23; I Chron. xii. 25; Wisd. viii. 4), now more usually *Geheimer Rat* [Privy Councillor].

(b) Of animals: tame, companionable to man. As opposed to wild, e.g. 'Animals which are neither wild nor *heimlich*', etc. 'Wild animals ... that are trained to be *heimlich* and accustomed to men.' 'If these young creatures are brought up from early days among men they become quite *heimlich,* friendly' etc.—So also: 'It (the lamb) is so *heimlich* and eats out of my hand.' 'Nevertheless, the stork is a beautiful, *heimelich* bird.'

(c) Intimate, friendly comfortable; the enjoyment of quiet content, etc., arousing a sense of agreeable restfulness and security as in one within the four walls of his house.[4] 'Is it still *heimlich* to you in your country where strangers are felling your woods?' 'She did not feel too *heimlich* with him.' 'Along a high, *heimlich,* shady path ..., beside a purling, gushing and babbling woodland brook.' 'To destroy the *Heimlichkeit* of the home.' 'I could not readily find another spot so intimate and *heimlich* as this.' 'We pictured it so comfortable, so nice, so cosy and *heimlich.*' 'In quiet *Heimlichkeit,* surrounded by close walls.' 'A careful housewife, who knows how to make a pleasing *Heimlichkeit (Häuslichkeit* [domesticity]) out of the smallest means.' 'The man who till recently had been so strange to him now seemed to him all the more *heimlich.*' 'The protestant land-owners do not feel ... *heimlich* among their catholic inferiors.' 'When it grows *heimlich* and still, and the evening quiet alone watches over your cell.' 'Quiet, lovely and *heimlich,* no place more fitted for their rest.' He did not feel at all *heimlich* about it.'—Also, [in compounds] 'The place was so peaceful, so lonely, so shadily-*heimlich.*' 'The in- and outflowing waves of the current, dreamy and lullaby-*heimlich.*' Cf. in especial *Unheimlich* [see below]. Among Swabian Swiss authors in especial, often as a trisyllable: 'How *heimelich* it seemed to Ivo again of an evening, when he was at home.' 'It was so *heimelig* in the house.' 'The warm room and the *heimelig* afternoon.' 'When a man feels in his heart that he is so small and the Lord so great—that is what is truly *heimelig.*' 'Little by little they grew at ease and *heimelig* among themselves.' 'Friendly *Heimeligkeit.*' 'I shall be nowhere more *heimelich*

---

[3] [In the translation which follows in the text above, a few details, mainly giving the sources of the quotations, have been omitted. For purposes of reference, we reprint in an Appendix the entire extract from Sanders's Dictionary exactly as it is given in German in Freud's original paper except that a few minor misprints have been put right. (Cf. p. 253.)]

[4] [It may be remarked that the English 'canny', in addition to its more usual meaning of 'shrewd', can mean 'pleasant', 'cosy'.]

than I am here.' 'That which comes from afar … assuredly does not live quite *heimelig (heimatlich* [at home], *freundnachbarlich* [in a neighbourly way]) among the people.' 'The cottage where he had once sat so often among his own people, so *heimelig*, so happy.' 'The sentinel's horn sounds so *heimelig* from the tower, and his voice invites so hospitably.' 'You go to sleep there so soft and warm, so wonderfully *heim'lig.'—This form of the word deserves to become general in order to protect this perfectly good sense of the word from becoming obsolete through an easy confusion with* II [see below]. Cf: '"*The Zecks* [a family name] *are all 'heimlich'.*" (in sense II) "*'Heimlich'? … What do you understand by 'heimlich'?" "Well, … they are like a buried spring or a dried-up pond. One cannot walk over it without always having the feeling that water might come up there again." "Oh, we call it 'unheimlich'; you call it 'heimlich'. Well, what makes you think that there is something secret and untrustworthy about this family?*"' (Gutzkow).

(d) Especially in Silesia: gay, cheerful; also of the weather.

II. Concealed, kept from sight, so that others do not get to know of or about it, withheld from others. To do something *heimlich,* i.e. behind someone's back; to steal away *heimlich; heimlich* meetings and appointments; to look on with *heimlich* pleasure at someone's discomfiture; to sigh or weep *heimlich;* to behave *heimlich,* as though there was something to conceal; *heimlich* love-affair, love, sin; *heimlich* places (which good manners oblige us to conceal) (1 Sam. v. 6). 'The *heimlich* chamber' (privy) (2 Kings x. 27.). Also, 'the *heimlich* chair'. 'To throw into pits or *Heimlichkeiten*.'—'Led the steeds *heimlich* before Laomedon.'—'As secretive, *heimlich,* deceitful and malicious towards cruel masters … as frank, open, sympathetic and helpful towards a friend in misfortune.' 'You have still to learn what is *heimlich* holiest to me.' 'The *heimlich* art' (magic).' Where public ventilation has to stop, there *heimlich* machinations begin.' 'Freedom is the whispered watchword of *heimlich* conspirators and the loud battle-cry of professed revolutionaries.' 'A holy, *heimlich* effect.' 'I have roots that are most *heimlich.* I am grown in the deep earth.' 'My *heimlich* pranks.' 'If he is not given it openly and scrupulously he may seize it *heimlich* and unscrupulously.' 'He had achromatic telescopes constructed *heimlich* and secretly.' 'Henceforth I desire that there should be nothing *heimlich* any longer between us.' 'To discover, disclose, betray someone's *Heimlichkeiten;* 'to concoct *Heimlichkeiten* behind my back'. 'In my time we studied *Heimlichkeit*' 'The hand of understanding can alone undo the powerless spell of the *Heimlichkeit* (of hidden gold).' 'Say, where is the place of concealment … in what place of hidden *Heimlichkeit?*' 'Bees, who make the lock of *Heimlichkeiten*' (i.e. sealing-wax). 'Learned in strange *Heimlichkeiten*' (magic arts).

For compounds see above, *Ic.* Note especially the negative *'un-'* : eerie, weird, arousing gruesome fear: 'Seeming quite *unheimlich* and ghostly to him.' 'The *unheimlich,* fearful hours of night.' 'I had already long since felt an *unheimlich,* even gruesome feeling.' 'Now I am beginning to have an *unheimlich* feeling.' … 'Feels an *unheimlich* horror.' *'Unheimlich* and motionless like a stone image.' 'The *unheimlich* mist called hill-fog.' 'These pale youths are *unheimlich* and are brewing heaven knows what mischief.' '*"Unheimlich" is the name for everything that ought to have remained … secret and hidden but has come to light*' (Schelling).— 'To veil the divine, to surround it with a certain *Unheimlichkeit*'—*Unheimlich* is not often used as opposite to meaning II (above).

What interests us most in this long extract is to find that among its different shades of meaning the word *'heimlich'* exhibits one which is identical with its opposite, *'unheimlich'*. What is *heimlich* thus comes to be *unheimlich.* (Cf. the quotation from Gutzkow: 'We call it *"unheimlich"*; you call it *"heimlich"*.') In general we are reminded that the word *'heimlich'* is not unambiguous, but belongs to two sets of ideas, which, without being contradictory, are yet very different: on the one hand it means what is familiar and agreeable, and on the other, what is concealed and kept out of sight.[5] *'Unheimlich'* is customarily used, we are told, as the contrary only of the first signification of *'heimlich'*, and not of the second. Sanders tells us nothing concerning a possible genetic connection between these two meanings of *heimlich.* On the other hand, we notice that Schelling says something which throws quite a new light on the concept of the *Unheimlich,* for which we were certainly not prepared. According to him, everything is *unheimlick* that ought to have remained secret and hidden but has come to light.

Some of the doubts that have thus arisen are removed if we consult Grimm's dictionary. (1877, 4, Part 2, 873 ff.)

We read:

Heimlich; adj. and adv. *vernaculus, occultus;* MHG. heimelîch, heimlîch.

(P. 874.) In a slightly different sense: 'I feel *heimlich,* well, free from fear.' …

[3] *(b) Heimlich* is also used of a place free from ghostly influences … familiar, friendly, intimate.

(P. 875: ß) Familiar, amicable, unreserved.

4. *From the idea of 'homelike', 'belonging to the house', the further idea is developed of something withdrawn from the eyes of strangers, something concealed, secret; and this idea is expanded in many ways …*

(P. 876.) 'On the left bank of the lake there lies a meadow *heimlich* in the wood.' (Schiller, *Wilhelm Tell,* I. 4.) … Poetic licence, rarely so used in modern speech … *Heimlich* is used in conjunction with a verb expressing the act of concealing: 'In the secret of his tabernacle he shall hide me *heimlich*' (Ps. xxvii. 5.) … *Heimlich* parts of the human body, *pudenda* … 'the men that died not were smitten on their *heimlich* parts.' (1 Samuel v, 12.) …

(c) Officials who give important advice which has to be kept secret in matters of state are called *heimlich* councillors; the adjective, according to modern usage, has been replaced by *geheim* [secret] … 'Pharaoh called Joseph's name "him to whom secrets are revealed" ' *(heimlich* councillor). (Gen. xli. 45)

(P. 878.) 6. *Heimlich,* as used of knowledge—mystic, allegorical: a *heimlich* meaning, *mysticus, divinus, occultus, figuratus.*

(P. 878.) *Heimlich* in a different sense, as withdrawn from knowledge, unconscious … *Heimlich* also has the meaning of that which is obscure, inaccessible to knowledge … Do you not see? They do not trust us; they fear the *heimlich* face of the Duke of Friedland.' (Schiller, *Wallensteins Lager,* Scene 2.)

9. *The notion of something hidden and dangerous, which is expressed in the last paragraph, is still further developed, so that 'heimlich' comes to have the meaning usually ascribed to 'unheimlich.'* Thus: 'At times I feel like a man who walks in the night and believes in ghosts; every corner is *heimlich* and full of terrors for him'. (Klinger, *Theater,* 3. 298.)

Thus *heimlich* is a word the meaning of which develops in the direction of ambivalence, until it finally coincides with its opposite, *unheimlich. Unheimlich* is in some way or other a sub-species of *heimlich.* Let us bear this discovery in mind, though we cannot yet rightly understand it, alongside of Schelling's[6] definition of the *Unheimlich.* If we go on to examine individual instances of uncanniness, these hints will become intelligible to us.

[5] [According to the Oxford English Dictionary, a similar ambiguity attaches to the English 'canny', which may mean not only 'cosy' but also 'endowed with occult or magical powers'.]

[6] [In the original version of the paper (1919) only, the name 'Schleiermacher' was printed here, evidently in error.]

II

When we proceed to review the things, persons, impressions, events and situations which are able to arouse in us a feeling of the uncanny in a particularly forcible and definite form, the first requirement is obviously to select a suitable example to start on. Jentsch has taken as a very good instance 'doubts whether an apparently animate being is really alive; or conversely, whether a lifeless object might not be in fact animate'; and he refers in this connection to the impression made by wax-work figures, ingeniously constructed dolls and automata. To these he adds the uncanny and of manifestations of insanity, because these excite in the spectator the impression of automatic, mechanical processes at work behind the ordinary appearance of mental activity. Without entirely accepting this author's view, we will take it as a starting-point for our own investigation because in what follows he reminds us of a writer who has succeeded in producing uncanny effects better than anyone else.

Jentsch writes: 'In telling a story, one of the most successful devices for easily creating uncanny effects is to leave the reader in uncertainty whether a particular figure in the story is a human being or an automaton, and to do it in such a way that his attention is not focused directly upon his uncertainty, so that he may not be led to go into the matter and clear it up immediately. That, as we have said, would quickly dissipate the peculiar emotional effect of the thing. E. T. A. Hoffmann has repeatedly employed this psychological artifice with success in his fantastic narratives.'

This observation, undoubtedly a correct one, refers primarily to the story of 'The Sand-Man' in Hoffmann's *Nachtstücken,*[7] which contains the original of Olympia, the doll that appears in the first act of Offenbach's opera, *Tales of Hoffmann.* But I cannot think—and I hope most readers of the story will agree with me—that the theme of the doll Olympia, who is to all appearances a living being, is by any means the only, or indeed the most important, element that must be held responsible for the quite unparalleled atmosphere of uncanniness evoked by the story. Nor is this atmosphere heightened by the fact that the author himself treats the episode of Olympia with a faint touch of satire and uses it to poke fun at the young man's idealization of his mistress. The main theme of the story is, on the contrary, something different, something which gives it its name, and which is always re-introduced at critical moments: it is the theme of the 'Sand-Man' who tears out children's eyes.

This fantastic tale opens with the childhood recollections of the student Nathaniel. In spite of his present happiness, he cannot banish the memories associated with the mysterious and terrifying death of his beloved father. On certain evenings his mother used to send the children to bed early, warning them that 'the Sand-Man was coming'; and, sure enough, Nathaniel would not fail to hear the heavy tread of a visitor, with whom his father would then be occupied for the evening. When questioned about the Sand-Man, his mother, it is true, denied that such a person existed except as a figure of speech; but his nurse could give him more definite information: 'He's a wicked man who comes when children won't go to bed, and throws handfuls of sand in their eyes so that they jump out of their heads all bleeding. Then he puts the eyes in a sack and carries them off to the half-moon to feed his children. They sit up there in their nest, and their beaks are hooked like owls' beaks, and they use them to peck up naughty boys' and girls' eyes with.'

[7] Hoffmann's *Sämtliche Werke,* Grisebach Edition, 3. [A translation of 'The Sand-Man' is included in *Eight Tales of Hoffmann,* translated by J.M. Cohen, London, Pan Books, 1952.]

Although little Nathaniel was sensible and old enough not to credit the figure of the Sand-Man with such gruesome attributes, yet the dread of him became fixed in his heart. He determined to find out what the Sand-Man looked like; and one evening, when the Sand-Man was expected again, he hid in his father's study. He recognized the visitor as the lawyer Coppelius, a repulsive person whom the children were frightened of when he occasionally came to a meal; and he now identified this Coppelius with the dreaded Sand-Man. As regards the rest of the scene, Hoffmann already leaves us in doubt whether what we are witnessing is the first delirium of the panic-stricken boy, or a succession of events which are to be regarded in the story as being real. His father and the guest are at work at a brazier with glowing flames. The little eavesdropper hears Coppelius call out: 'Eyes here! Eyes here!' and betrays himself by screaming aloud. Coppelius seizes him and is on the point of dropping bits of red-hot coal from the fire into his eyes, and then of throwing them into the brazier, but his father begs him off and saves his eyes. After this the boy falls into a deep swoon; and a long illness brings his experience to an end. Those who decide in favour of the rationalistic interpretation of the Sand-Man will not fail to recognize in the child's phantasy the persisting influence of his nurse's story. The bits of sand that are to be thrown into the child's eyes turn into bits of red-hot coal from the flames; and in both cases they are intended to make his eyes jump out. In the course of another visit of the Sand-Man's, a year later, his father is killed in his study by an explosion. The lawyer Coppelius disappears from the place without leaving a trace behind.

Nathaniel, now a student, believes that he has recognized this phantom of horror from his childhood in an itinerant optician, an Italian called Giuseppe Coppola, who at his university town, offers him weather-glasses for sale. When Nathaniel refuses, the man goes on: 'Not weather-glasses? not weather-glasses? also got fine eyes, fine eyes!' The student's terror is allayed when he finds that the proffered eyes are only harmless spectacles, and he buys a pocket spy-glass from Coppola. With its aid he looks across into Professor Spalanzani's house opposite and there spies Spalanzani's beautiful, but strangely silent and motionless daughter, Olympia. He soon falls in love with her so violently that, because of her, he quite forgets the clever and sensible girl to whom he is betrothed. But Olympia is an automaton whose clock-work has been made by Spalanzani, and whose eyes have been put in by Coppola, the Sand-Man. The student surprises the two Masters quarrelling over their handiwork. The optician carries off the wooden eyeless doll; and the mechanician, Spalanzani, picks up Olympiads bleeding eyes from the ground and throws them at Nathaniel's breast, saying that Coppola had stolen them from the student. Nathaniel succumbs to a fresh attack of madness, and in his delirium his recollection of his father's death is mingled with this new experience. 'Hurry up! hurry up! ring of fire!' he cries. 'Spin about, ring of fire—Hurrah! Hurry up, wooden doll! lovely wooden doll, spin about—.' He then falls upon the professor, Olympia's 'father', and tries to strangle him.

Rallying from a long and serious illness, Nathaniel seems at last to have recovered. He intends to marry his betrothed, with whom he has become reconciled. One day he and she are walking through the city market-place, over which the high tower of the Town Hall throws its huge shadow. On the girl's suggestion, they climb the tower, leaving her brother, who is walking with them, down below. From the top, Clara's attention is drawn to a curious object moving along the street. Nathaniel looks at this thing through Coppola's spy-glass, which he finds in his pocket, and falls into a new attack of madness. Shouting 'Spin about, wooden doll!' he tries to throw the girl into the gulf below. Her brother, brought to her side by her cries, rescues her and hastens down with her to safety. On the tower above, the madman rushes round, shrieking 'Ring of fire, spin about!'—and we know the origin of the words.

Among the people who begin to gather below there comes forward the figure of the lawyer Goppelius, who has suddenly returned. We may suppose that it was his approach, seen through the spy-glass, which threw Nathaniel into his fit of madness. As the onlookers prepare to go up and overpower the madman, Coppelius laughs and says: 'Wait a bit; he'll come down of himself.' Nathaniel suddenly stands still, catches sight of Coppelius, and with a wild shriek 'Yes! "Fine eyes—fine eyes"!' flings himself over the parapet. While he lies on the paving-stones with a shattered skull the Sand-Man vanishes in the throng.

This short summary leaves no doubt, I think, that the feeling of something uncanny is directly attached to the figure of the Sand-Man, that is, to the idea of being robbed of one's eyes, and that Jentsch's point of an intellectual uncertainty has nothing to do with the effect. Uncertainty whether an object is living or inanimate, which admittedly applied to the doll Olympia, is quite irrelevant in connection with this other, more striking instance of uncanniness. It is true that the writer creates a kind of uncertainty in us in the beginning by not letting us know, no doubt purposely, whether he is taking us into the real world or into a purely fantastic one of his own creation. He has, of course, a right to do either; and if he chooses to stage his action in a world peopled with spirits, demons and ghosts, as Shakespeare does in *Hamlet*, in *Macbeth* and, in a different sense, in *The Tempest* and *A Midsummer-Night's Dream*, we must bow to his decision and treat his setting as though it were real for as long as we put ourselves into his hands. But this uncertainty disappears in the course of Hoffmann's story, and we perceive that he intends to make us, too, look through the demon optician's spectacles or spy-glass—perhaps, indeed, that the author in his very own person once peered through such an instrument. For the conclusion of the story makes it quite clear that Coppola the optician really *is* the lawyer Coppelius[8] and also, therefore, the Sand-Man.

There is no question therefore, of any intellectual uncertainty here: we know now that we are not supposed to be looking on at the products of a madman's imagination, behind which we, with the superiority of rational minds, are able to detect the sober truth; and yet this knowledge does not lessen the impression of uncanniness in the least degree. The theory of intellectual uncertainty is thus incapable of explaining that impression.

We know from psycho-analytic experience, however, that the fear of damaging or losing one's eyes is a terrible one in children. Many adults retain their apprehensiveness in this respect, and no physical injury is so much dreaded by them as an injury to the eye. We are accustomed to say, too, that we will treasure a thing as the apple of our eye. A study of dreams, phantasies and myths has taught us that anxiety about one's eyes, the fear of going blind, is often enough a substitute for the dread of being castrated. The self-blinding of the mythical criminal, Oedipus, was simply a mitigated form of the punishment of castration—the only punishment that was adequate for him by the *lex talionis.* We may try on rationalistic grounds to deny that fears about the eye are derived from the fear of castration, and may argue that it is very natural that so precious an organ as the eye should be guarded by a proportionate dread. Indeed, we might go further and say that the fear of castration itself contains no other significance and no deeper secret than a justifiable dread of this rational kind. But this view does not account adequately for the substitutive relation between the eye and the male organ which is seen to exist in dreams and

[8] Dr. Rank has pointed out the association of the name with *'coppella'* = crucible, connecting it with the chemical operations that caused the father's death; and also with *'coppo'* = eye-socket. [Except in the first (1919) edition this footnote was attached, it seems erroneously, to the first occurrence of the name Coppelius on this page.]

myths and phantasies; nor can it dispel the impression that the threat of being castrated in especial excites a peculiarly violent and obscure emotion, and that this emotion is what first gives the idea of losing other organs its intense colouring. All further doubts are removed when we learn the details of their 'castration complex' from the analysis of neurotic patients, and realize its immense importance in their mental life.

Moreover, I would not recommend any opponent of the psycho-analytic view to select this particular story of the Sand-Man with which to support his argument that anxiety about the eyes has nothing to do with the castration complex. For why does Hoffmann bring the anxiety about eyes into such intimate connection with the father's death? And why does the Sand-Man always appear as a disturber of love? He separates the unfortunate Nathaniel from his betrothed and from her brother, his best friend; he destroys the second object of his love, Olympia, the lovely doll; and he drives him into suicide at the moment when he has won back his Clara and is about to be happily united to her. Elements in the story like these, and many others, seem arbitrary and meaningless so long as we deny all connection between fears about the eye and castration; but they become intelligible as soon as we replace the Sand-Man by the dreaded father at whose hands castration is expected.[9]

We shall venture, therefore, to refer the uncanny effect of the Sand-Man to the anxiety belonging to the castration complex of childhood. But having reached the idea that we can make an infantile factor

[9] In fact, Hoffmann's imaginative treatment of his material has not made such wild confusion of its elements that we cannot reconstruct their original arrangement. In the story of Nathaniel's childhood, the figures of his father and Coppelius represent the two opposites into which the father-imago is split by his ambivalence; whereas the one threatens to blind him—that is, to castrate him—, the other, the 'good' father, intercedes for his sight. The part of the complex which is most strongly repressed, the death-wish against the 'bad' father, finds expression in the death of the 'good' father, and Coppelius is made answerable for it. This pair of fathers is represented later, in his student days, by Professor Spalanzani and Coppola the optician. The Professor is in himself a member of the father-series, and Coppola is recognized as identical with Coppelius the lawyer. Just as they used before to work together over the secret brazier, so now they have jointly created the doll Olympia; the Professor is even called the father of Olympia. This double occurrence of activity in common betrays them as divisions of the father-imago: both the mechanician and the optician were the father of Nathaniel (and of Olympia as well). In the frightening scene in childhood, Coppelius, after sparing Nathaniel's eyes, had screwed off his arms and legs as an experiment; that is, he had worked on him as a mechanician would on a doll. This singular feature, which seems quite outside the picture of the Sand-Man, introduces a new castration equivalent; but it also points to the inner identity of Coppelius with his later counterpart, Spalanzani the mechanician, and prepares us for the interpretation of Olympia. This automatic doll can be nothing else than a materialization of Nathaniel's feminine attitude towards his father in his infancy. Her fathers, Spalanzani and Coppola, are, after all, nothing but new editions, reincarnations of Nathaniel's pair of fathers. Spalanzani's otherwise incomprehensible statement that the optician has stolen Nathaniel's eyes (see above, [p. 229]), so as to set them in the doll, now becomes significant as supplying evidence of the identity of Olympia and Nathaniel. Olympia is, as it were, a dissociated complex of Nathaniel's which confronts him aj a person, and Nathaniel's enslavement to this complex is expressed in his senseless obsessive love for Olympia. We may with justice call love of this kind narcissistic, and we can understand why someone who has fallen victim to it should relinquish the real, external object of his love. The psychological truth of the situation in which the young man, fixated upon his father by his castration complex, becomes incapable of loving a woman, is amply proved by numerous analyses of patients whose story, though less fantastic, is hardly less tragic than that of the student Nathaniel.

such as this responsible for feelings of uncanniness, we are encouraged to see whether we can apply it to other instances of the uncanny. We find in the story of the Sand-Man the other theme on which Jentsch lays stress, of a doll which appears to be alive. Jentsch believes that a particularly favourable condition for awakening uncanny feelings is created when there is intellectual uncertainty whether an object is alive or not, and when an inanimate object becomes too much like an animate one. Now, dolls are of course rather closely connected with childhood life. We remember that in their early games children do not distinguish at all sharply between living and inanimate objects, and that they are especially fond of treating their dolls like live people. In fact, I have occasionally heard a woman patient declare that even at the age of eight she had still been convinced that her dolls would be certain to come to life if she were to look at them in a particular, extremely concentrated, way. So that here, too, it is not difficult to discover a factor from childhood. But, curiously enough, while the Sand-Man story deals with the arousing of an early childhood fear, the idea of a 'living doll' excites no fear at all; children have no fear of their dolls coming to life, they may even desire it. The source of uncanny feelings would not, therefore, be an infantile fear in this case, but rather an infantile wish or even merely an infantile belief. There seems to be a contradiction here; but perhaps it is only a complication, which may be helpful to us later on.

Hoffmann is the unrivalled master of the uncanny in literature. His novel, *Die Elixire des Teufels* [*The Devil's Elixir*], contains a whole mass of themes to which one is tempted to ascribe the uncanny effect of the narrative;[10] but it is too obscure and intricate a story for us to venture upon a summary of it. Towards the end of the book the reader is told the facts, hitherto concealed from him, from which the action springs; with the result, not that he is at last enlightened, but that he falls into a state of complete bewilderment. The author has piled up too much material of the same kind. In consequence one's grasp of the story as a whole suffers, though not the impression it makes. We must content ourselves with selecting those themes of uncanniness which are most prominent, and with seeing whether they too can fairly be traced back to infantile sources. These themes are all concerned with the phenomenon of the 'doubled which appears in every shape and in every degree of development. Thus we have characters who are to be considered identical because they look alike. This relation is accentuated by mental processes leaping from one of these characters to another—by what we should call telepathy—, so that the one possesses knowledge, feelings and experience in common with the other. Or it is marked by the fact that the

Hoffmann was the child of an unhappy marriage. When he was three years old, his father left his small family, and was never united to them again. According to Grisebach, in his biographical introduction to Hoffmann's works, the writer's relation to his father was always a most sensitive subject with him.

[10] [Under the rubric 'Varia' in one of the issues of the *Internationale Zeitschrift fur Psychoanalyse* for 1919 (5, 308), the year in which the present paper was first published, there appears over the initials 'S.F.' a short note which it is not unreasonable to attribute to Freud. Its insertion here, though strictly speaking irrelevant, may perhaps be excused. The note is headed: 'E. T. A. Hoffmann on the Function of Consciousness' and it proceeds: 'In *Die Elixire des Teufels* (Part II, p. 210, in Hesse's edition)—a novel rich in masterly descriptions of pathological mental states—Schonfeld comforts the hero, whose consciousness is temporarily disturbed, with the following words: "And what do you get out of it? I mean out of the particular mental function which we call consciousness, and which is nothing but the confounded activity of a damned toll-collector—excise-man—deputy-chief customs officer, who has set up his infamous bureau in our top storey and who exclaims, whenever any goods try to get out: 'Hi! hi! exports are prohibited … they must stay here … here, in this country.…'"']

subject identifies himself with someone else, so that he is in doubt as to which his self is, or substitutes the extraneous self for his own. In other words, there is a doubling, dividing and interchanging of the self. And finally there is the constant recurrence of the same thing[11]—the repetition of the same features or character-traits or vicissitudes, of the same crimes, or even the same names through several consecutive generations.

The theme of the 'double' has been very thoroughly treated by Otto Rank (1914). He has gone into the connections which the 'double' has with reflections in mirrors, with shadows, with guardian spirits, with the belief in the soul and with the fear of death; but he also lets in a flood of light on the surprising evolution of the idea. For the 'double' was originally an insurance against the destruction of the ego, an 'energetic denial of the power of death', as Rank says; and probably the 'immortal' soul was the first 'double' of the body. This invention of doubling as a preservation against extinction has its counterpart in the language of dreams, which is fond of representing castration by a doubling or multiplication of a genital symbol.[12] The same desire led the Ancient Egyptians to develop the art of making images of the dead in lasting materials. Such ideas, however, have sprung from the soil of unbounded self-love, from the primary narcissism which dominates the mind of the child and of primitive man. But when this stage has been surmounted, the 'double' reverses its aspect. From having been an assurance of immortality, it becomes the uncanny harbinger of death.

The idea of the 'double' does not necessarily disappear with the passing of primary narcissism, for it can receive fresh meaning from the later stages of the ego's development. A special agency is slowly formed there, which is able to stand over against the rest of the ego, which has the function of observing and criticizing the self and of exercising a censorship within the mind, and which we become aware of as our 'conscience'. In the pathological case of delusions of being watched, this mental agency becomes isolated, dissociated from the ego, and discernible to the physician's eye. The fact that an agency of this kind exists, which is able to treat the rest of the ego like an object—the fact, that is, that man is capable of self-observation—renders it possible to invest the old idea of a 'double' with a new meaning and to ascribe a number of things to it—above all, those things which seem to self-criticism to belong to the old surmounted narcissism of earliest times.[13]

But it is not only this latter material, offensive as it is to the criticism of the ego, which may be incorporated in the idea of a double. There are also all the unfulfilled but possible futures to which we still

---

[11] [This phrase seems to be an echo from Nietzsche (e.g. from the last part of *Also Sprach Zarathustra*). In Chapter III of *Beyond the Pleasure Principle* (1920*g*), *Standard Ed.*, 18, 22, Freud puts a similar phrase 'the perpetual recurrence of the same thing' into inverted commas.]

[12] [Cf. *The Interpretation of Dreams, Standard Ed.*, 5, 357.]

[13] I believe that when poets complain that two souls dwell in the human breast, and when popular psychologists talk of the splitting of people's egos, what they are thinking of is this division (in the sphere of ego-psychology) between the critical agency and the rest of the ego, and not the antithesis discovered by psycho-analysis between the ego and what is unconscious and repressed. It is true that the distinction between these two antitheses is to some extent effaced by the circumstance that foremost among the things that are rejected by the criticism of the ego are derivatives of the repressed.—[Freud had already discussed this critical agency at length in Section III of his paper on narcissism (1914*c*), and it was soon to be further expanded into the 'ego-ideal' and 'superego' in Chapter XI of his *Group Psychology* (1921*c*) and Chapter III of *The Ego and the Id* (1923*b*) respectively.]

like to cling in phantasy, all the strivings of the ego which adverse external circumstances have crushed, and all our suppressed acts of volition which nourish in us the illusion of Free Will.[14] [Cf. Freud, 1901*b*, Chapter XII (B).]

But after having thus considered the *manifest* motivation of the figure of a 'double', we have to admit that none of this helps us to understand the extraordinarily strong feeling of something uncanny that pervades the conception; and our knowledge of pathological mental processes enables us to add that nothing in this more superficial material could account for the urge towards defence which has caused the ego to project that material outward as something foreign to itself. When all is said and done, the quality of uncanniness can only come from the fact of the 'double' being a creation dating back to a very early mental stage, long since surmounted—a stage, incidentally, at which it wore a more friendly aspect. The 'double' has become a thing of terror, just as, after the collapse of their religion, the gods turned into demons.[15]

The other forms of ego-disturbance exploited by Hoffmann can easily be estimated along the same lines as the theme of the 'double'. They are a harking-back to particular phases in the evolution of the self-regarding feeling, a regression to a time when the ego had not yet marked itself off sharply from the external world and from other people. I believe that these factors are partly responsible for the impression of uncanniness, although it is not easy to isolate and determine exactly their share of it.

The factor of the repetition of the same thing will perhaps not appeal to everyone as a source of uncanny feeling. From what I have observed, this phenomenon does undoubtedly, subject to certain conditions and combined with certain circumstances, arouse an uncanny feeling, which, furthermore, recalls the sense of helplessness experienced in some dream-states. As I was walking, one hot summer afternoon, through the deserted streets of a provincial town in Italy which was unknown to me, I found myself in a quarter of whose character I could not long remain in doubt. Nothing but painted women were to be seen at the windows of the small houses, and I hastened to leave the narrow street at the next turning. But after having wandered about for a time without enquiring my way, I suddenly found myself back in the same street, where my presence was now beginning to excite attention. I hurried away once more, only to arrive by another *détour* at the same place yet a third time. Now, however, a feeling overcame me which I can only describe as uncanny, and I was glad enough to find myself back at the piazza I had left a short while before, without any further voyages of discovery. Other situations which have in common with my adventure an unintended recurrence of the same situation, but which differ radically from it in other respects, also result in the same feeling of helplessness and of uncanniness. So, for instance, when, caught in a mist perhaps, one has lost one's way in a mountain forest, every attempt to find the marked or familiar path may bring one back again and again to one and the same spot, which one can identify by some particular landmark. Or one may wander about in a dark, strange room, looking for the door or the electric switch, and collide time after time with the same piece of furniture—though it is true that Mark Twain succeeded by wild exaggeration in turning this latter situation into

[14] In Ewers's *Der Student von Prag,* which serves as the starting-point of Rank's study on the 'double', the hero has promised his beloved not to kill his antagonist in a duel. But on his way to the duelling-ground he meets his 'double', who has already killed his rival.

[15] Heine, *Die Götter im Exil.*

something irresistibly comic.[16] If we take another class of things, it is easy to see that there, too, it is only this factor of involuntary repetition which surrounds what would otherwise be innocent enough with an uncanny atmosphere, and forces upon us the idea of something fateful and inescapable when otherwise we should have spoken only of 'chance'. For instance, we naturally attach no importance to the event when we hand in an overcoat and get a cloakroom ticket with the number, let us say, 62; or when we find that our cabin on a ship bears that number. But the impression is altered if two such events, each in itself indifferent, happen close together—if we come across the number 62 several times in a single day, or if we begin to notice that everything which has a number—addresses, hotel rooms, compartments in railway trains—invariably has the same one, or at all events one which contains the same figures. We do feel this to be uncanny. And unless a man is utterly hardened and proof against the lure of superstition, he will be tempted to ascribe a secret meaning to this obstinate recurrence of a number; he will take it, perhaps, as an indication of the span of life allotted to him.[17] Or suppose one is engaged in reading the works of the famous physiologist, Hering, and within the space of a few days receives two letters from two different countries, each from a person called Hering, though one has never before had any dealings with anyone of that name. Not long ago an ingenious scientist (Kammerer, 1919) attempted to reduce coincidences of this kind to certain laws, and so deprive them of their uncanny effect. I will not venture to decide whether he has succeeded or not.

How exactly we can trace back to infantile psychology the uncanny effect of such similar recurrences is a question I can only lightly touch on in these pages; and I must refer the reader instead to another work,[18] already completed, in which this has been gone into in detail, but in a different connection. For it is possible to recognize the dominance in the unconscious mind of a 'compulsion to repeat' proceeding from the instinctual impulses and probably inherent in the very nature of the instincts—a compulsion powerful enough to overrule the pleasure principle, lending to certain aspects of the mind their daemonic character, and still very clearly expressed in the impulses of small children; a compulsion, too, which is responsible for a part of the course taken by the analyses of neurotic patients. All these considerations prepare us for the discovery that whatever reminds us of this inner 'compulsion to repeat' is perceived as uncanny.

Now, however, it is time to turn from these aspects of the matter, which are in any case difficult to judge, and look for some undeniable instances of the uncanny, in the hope that an analysis of them will decide whether our hypothesis is a valid one.

In the story of 'The Ring of Polycrates',[19] the King of Egypt turns away in horror from his host, Polycrates, because he sees that his friend's every wish is at once fulfilled, his every care promptly removed by kindly fate. His host has become Uncanny' to him. His own explanation, that the too fortunate man has to fear the envy of the gods, seems obscure to us; its meaning is veiled in mythological language. We will therefore turn to another example in a less grandiose setting. In the case history of

---

[16] [Mark Twain, *A Tramp Abroad,* London, 1880, 1, 107.]

[17] [Freud had himself reached the age of 62 a year earlier, in 1918.]

[18] [This was published a year later as *Beyond the Pleasure Principle* (1920*g*). The various manifestations of the 'compulsion to repeat' enumerated here are enlarged upon in Chapters II and III of that work. The 'compulsion to repeat' had already been described by Freud as a clinical phenomenon, in a technical paper published five years earlier (1914*g*).]

[19] [Schiller's poem based on Herodotus.]

an obsessional neurotic,[20] I have described how the patient once stayed in a hydropathic establishment and benefited greatly by it. He had the good sense, however, to attribute his improvement not to the therapeutic properties of the water, but to the situation of his room, which immediately adjoined that of a very accommodating nurse. So on his second visit to the establishment he asked for the same room, but was told that it was already occupied by an old gentleman, whereupon he gave vent to his annoyance in the words: 'I wish he may be struck dead for it.' A fortnight later the old gentleman really did have a stroke. My patient thought this an 'uncanny' experience. The impression of uncanniness would have been stronger still if less time had elapsed between his words and the untoward event, or if he had been able to report innumerable similar coincidences. As a matter of fact, he had no difficulty in producing coincidences of this sort; but then not only he but every obsessional neurotic I have observed has been able to relate analogous experiences. They are never surprised at their invariably running up against someone they have just been thinking of, perhaps for the first time for a long while. If they say one day 'I haven't had any news of so-and-so for a long time', they will be sure to get a letter from him the next morning, and an accident or a death will rarely take place without having passed through their mind a little while before. They are in the habit of referring to this state of affairs in the most modest manner, saying that they have 'presentiments' which 'usually' come true.

One of the most uncanny and wide-spread forms of superstition is the dread of the evil eye, which has been exhaustively studied by the Hamburg oculist Seligmann (1910-11). There never seems to have been any doubt about the source of this dread. Whoever possesses something that is at once valuable and fragile is afraid of other people's envy, in so far as he projects on to them the envy he would have felt in their place. A feeling like this betrays itself by a look[21] even though it is not put into words; and when a man is prominent owing to noticeable, and particularly owing to unattractive, attributes, other people are ready to believe that his envy is rising to a more than usual degree of intensity and that this intensity will convert it into effective action. What is feared is thus a secret intention of doing harm, and certain signs are taken to mean that that intention has the necessary power at its command.

These last examples of the uncanny are to be referred to the principle which I have called 'omnipotence of thoughts', taking the name from an expression used by one of my patients.[22] And now we find ourselves on familiar ground. Our analysis of instances of the uncanny has led us back to the old, animistic conception of the universe. This was characterized by the idea that the world was peopled with the spirits of human beings; by the subject's narcissistic overvaluation of his own mental processes; by the belief in the omnipotence of thoughts and the technique of magic based on that belief; by the attribution to various outside persons and things of carefully graded magical powers, or '*mana*'; as well as by all the other creations with the help of which man, in the unrestricted narcissism of that stage of development, strove to fend off the manifest prohibitions of reality. It seems as if each one of us has been through a phase of individual development corresponding to this animistic stage in primitive men, that none of us has passed through it without preserving certain residues and traces of it which are still capable of

[20] 'Notes upon a Case of Obsessional Neurosis' (1909*d*) [*Standard Ed.*, 10, 234].

[21] ['The evil eye' *in* German is '*der böse Blick*.' literally 'the evil look'.]

[22] [The obsessional patient referred to just above—the 'Rat Man' (1909*d*), *Standard Ed.*, 10, 233f.]

manifesting themselves, and that everything which now strikes us as 'uncanny' fulfils the condition of touching those residues of animistic mental activity within us and bringing them to expression.[23]

At this point I will put forward two considerations which, I think, contain the gist of this short study. In the first place, if psycho-analytic theory is correct in maintaining that every affect belonging to an emotional impulse, whatever its kind, is transformed, if it is repressed, into anxiety, then among instances of frightening things there must be one class in which the frightening element can be shown to be something repressed which *recurs*, This class of frightening things would then constitute the uncanny; and it must be a matter of indifference whether what is uncanny was itself originally frightening or whether it carried some *other* affect. In the second place, if this is indeed the secret nature of the uncanny, we can understand why linguistic usage has extended *das Heimliche* ['homely'] into its opposite, *das Unheimliche* (p. 226); for this uncanny is in reality nothing new or alien, but something which is familiar and old-established in the mind and which has become alienated from it only through the process of repression. This reference to the factor of repression enables us, furthermore, to understand Schelling's definition [p. 224] of the uncanny as something which ought to have remained hidden but has come to light.

It only remains for us to test our new hypothesis on one or two more examples of the uncanny.

Many people experience the feeling in the highest degree in relation to death and dead bodies, to the return of the dead, and to spirits and ghosts. As we have seen [p. 221] some languages in use today can only render the German expression 'an *unheimlich* house' by 'a *haunted* house'. We might indeed have begun our investigation with this example, perhaps the most striking of all, of something uncanny, but we refrained from doing so because the uncanny in it is too much intermixed with what is purely gruesome and is in part overlaid by it. There is scarcely any other matter, however, upon which our thoughts and feelings have changed so little since the very earliest times, and in which discarded forms have been so completely preserved under a thin disguise, as our relation to death. Two things account for our conservatism: the strength of our original emotional reaction to death and the insufficiency of our scientific knowledge about it. Biology has not yet been able to decide whether death is the inevitable fate of every living being or whether it is only a regular but yet perhaps avoidable event in life.[24] It is true that the statement 'All men are mortal' is paraded in text-books of logic as an example of a general proposition; but no human being really grasps it, and our unconscious has as little use now as it ever had for the idea of its own mortality.[25] Religions continue to dispute the importance of the undeniable fact of individual death and to postulate a life after death; civil governments still believe that they cannot maintain moral order among the living if they do not uphold the prospect of a better life hereafter as a recompense for mundane existence. In our great cities, placards announce lectures that undertake to

[23] *Cf.* my book *Totem and Taboo* (1912-13), Essay III, 'Animism, Magic and the Omnipotence of Thoughts', where the following footnote will be found: 'We appear to attribute an "uncanny" quality to impressions that seek to confirm the omnipotence of thoughts and the animistic mode of thinking in general, after we have reached a stage at which, in our *judgement*, we have abandoned such beliefs.' *[Standard Ed.,* 13, 86.]

[24] [This problem figures prominently in *Beyond the Pleasure Principle* (1920*g*), on which Freud was engaged while writing the present paper. See *Standard Ed.,* 18, 44 ff.]

[25] [Freud had discussed the individual's attitude to death at greater length in the second part of his paper 'Thoughts for the Times on War and Death' (1915*b*).]

tell us how to get into touch with the souls of the departed; and it cannot be denied that not a few of the most able and penetrating minds among our men of science have come to the conclusion, especially towards the close of their own lives, that a contact of this kind is not impossible. Since almost all of us still think as savages do on this topic, it is no matter for surprise that the primitive fear of the dead is still so strong within us and always ready to come to the surface on any provocation. Most likely our fear still implies the old belief that the dead man becomes the enemy of his survivor and seeks to carry him off to share his new life with him. Considering our unchanged attitude towards death, we might rather enquire what has become of the repression, which is the necessary condition of a primitive feeling recurring in the shape of something uncanny. But repression is there, too. All supposedly educated people have ceased to believe officially that the dead can become visible as spirits, and have made any such appearances dependent on improbable and remote conditions; their emotional attitude towards their dead, moreover, once a highly ambiguous and ambivalent one, has been toned down in the higher strata of the mind into an unambiguous feeling of piety.[26]

We have now only a few remarks to add—for animism, magic and sorcery, the omnipotence of thoughts, man's attitude to death, involuntary repetition and the castration complex comprise practically all the factors which turn something frightening into something uncanny.

We can also speak of a living person as uncanny, and we do so when we ascribe evil intentions to him. But that is not all; in addition to this we must feel that his intentions to harm us are going to be carried out with the help of special powers. A good instance of this is the '*Gettatore*',[27] that uncanny figure of Romanic superstition which Schaeffer, with intuitive poetic feeling and profound psycho-analytic understanding, has transformed into a sympathetic character in his *Josef Montfort.* But the question of these secret powers brings us back again to the realm of animism. It was the pious Gretchen's intuition that Mephistopheles possessed secret powers of this kind that made him so uncanny to her.

Sie fühlt dass ich ganz sicher ein Genie,
Vielleicht sogar der Teufel bin.[28]

The uncanny effect of epilepsy and of madness has the same origin. The layman sees in them the working of forces hitherto unsuspected in his fellow-men, but at the same time he is dimly aware of them in remote corners of his own being. The Middle Ages quite consistently ascribed all such maladies to the influence of demons and in this their psychology was almost correct. Indeed, I should not be surprised to hear that psychoanalysis, which is concerned with laying bare these hidden forces, has itself become uncanny to many people for that very reason. In one case, after I had succeeded—though none too rapidly—in effecting a cure in a girl who had been an invalid for many years, I myself heard this view expressed by the patient's mother long after her recovery.

---

[26] Cf. *Totem and Taboo [Standard Ed.,* 13, 66].

[27] [Literally 'thrower' (of bad luck), or 'one who casts' (the evil eye).—Schaeffer's novel was published in 1918.]

[28] [She feels that surely I'm a genius now,— Perhaps the very Devil indeed! Goethe, *Faust,* Part I (Scene 16), (Bayard Taylor's translation).]

Dismembered limbs, a severed head, a hand cut off at the wrist, as in a fairy tale of Hauff's,[29] feet which dance by themselves, as in the book by Schaeffer which I mentioned above— all these have something peculiarly uncanny about them, especially when, as in the last instance, they prove capable of independent activity in addition. As we already know, this kind of uncanniness springs from its proximity to the castration complex. To some people the idea of being buried alive by mistake is the most uncanny thing of all. And yet psycho-analysis has taught us that this terrifying phantasy is only a transformation of another phantasy which had originally nothing terrifying about it at all, but was qualified by a certain lasciviousness—the phantasy, I mean, of intra-uterine existence.[30]

There is one more point of general application which I should like to add, though, strictly speaking, it has been included in what has already been said about animism and modes of working of the mental apparatus that have been surmounted; for I think it deserves special emphasis. This is that an uncanny effect is often and easily produced when the distinction between imagination and reality is effaced, as when something that we have hitherto regarded as imaginary appears before us in reality, or when a symbol takes over the full functions of the thing it symbolizes, and so on. It is this factor which contributes not a little to the uncanny effect attaching to magical practices. The infantile element in this, which also dominates the minds of neurotics, is the over-accentuation of psychical reality in comparison with material reality—a feature closely allied to the belief in the omnipotence of thoughts. In the middle of the isolation of war-time a number of the English *Strand Magazine* fell into my hands; and, among other somewhat redundant matter, I read a story about a young married couple who move into a furnished house in which there is a curiously shaped table with carvings of crocodiles on it. Towards evening an intolerable and very specific smell begins to pervade the house; they stumble over something in the dark; they seem to see a vague form gliding over the stairs—in short, we are given to understand that the presence of the table causes ghostly crocodiles to haunt the place, or that the wooden monsters come to life in the dark, or something of the sort. It was a naive enough story, but the uncanny feeling it produced was quite remarkable.

To conclude this collection of examples, which is certainly not complete, I will relate an instance taken from psychoanalytic experience; if it does not rest upon mere coincidence, it furnishes a beautiful confirmation of our theory of the uncanny. It often happens that neurotic men declare that they feel there is something uncanny about the female genital organs, This *unheimlich* place, however, is the entrance to the former *Heim* [home] of all human beings, to the place where each one of us lived once upon a time and in the beginning. There is a joking saying that 'Love is home-sickness'; and whenever a man dreams of a place or a country and says to himself, while he is still dreaming: 'this place is familiar to me, I've been here before', we may interpret the place as being his mother's genitals or her body.[31] In this case too, then, the *unheimlich* is what was once *heimisch,* familiar; the prefix *'un'* ['un-'] is the token of repression.[32]

---

[29] *[Die Geschichte von der abgehauenen Hand* ('The Story of the Severed Hand').]

[30] [See Section VIII of Freud's analysis of the 'Wolf Man' (1918*b*), above p. 101 ff.]

[31] [Cf. *The Interpretation of Dreams* (1900*a*), *Standard Ed., 5,* 399.]

[32] [See Freud's paper on 'Negation' (1925A).]

III

In the course of this discussion the reader will have felt certain doubts arising in his mind; and he must now have an opportunity of collecting them and bringing them forward.

It may be true that the uncanny [*unheimlich*] is something which is secretly familiar [*heimlich-heimisch*], which has undergone repression and then returned from it, and that everything that is uncanny fulfils this condition. But the selection of material on this basis does not enable us to solve the problem of the uncanny. For our proposition is clearly not convertible. Not everything that fulfils this condition—not everything that recalls repressed desires and surmounted modes of thinking belonging to the prehistory of the individual and of the race—is on that account uncanny.

Nor shall we conceal the fact that for almost every example adduced in support of our hypothesis one may be found which rebuts it. The story of the severed hand in Hauff's fairy tale [p. 244] certainly has an uncanny effect, and we have traced that effect back to the castration complex; but most readers will probably agree with me in judging that no trace of uncanniness is provoked by Herodotus's story of the treasure of Rhampsinitus, in which the master-thief, whom the princess tries to hold fast by the hand, leaves his brother's severed hand behind with her instead. Again, the prompt fulfilment of the wishes of Polycrates [p. 239] undoubtedly affects us in the same uncanny way as it did the king of Egypt; yet our own fairy stories are crammed with instantaneous wish-fulfilments which produce no uncanny effect whatever. In the story of 'The Three Wishes', the woman is tempted by the savoury smell of a sausage to wish that she might have one too, and in an instant it lies on a plate before her. In his annoyance at her hastiness her husband wishes it may hang on her nose. And there it is, dangling from her nose. All this is very striking but not in the least uncanny. Fairy tales quite frankly adopt the animistic standpoint of the omnipotence of thoughts and wishes, and yet I cannot think of any genuine fairy story which has anything uncanny about it. We have heard that it is in the highest degree uncanny when an inanimate object—a picture or a doll—comes to life; nevertheless in Hans Andersen's stories the household utensils, furniture and tin soldiers are alive, yet nothing could well be more remote from the uncanny. And we should hardly call it uncanny when Pygmalion's beautiful statue comes to life.

Apparent death and the re-animation of the dead have been represented as most uncanny themes. But things of this sort too are very common in fairy stories. Who would be so bold as to call it uncanny, for instance, when Snow-White opens her eyes once more? And the resuscitation of the dead in accounts of miracles, as in the New Testament, elicits feelings quite unrelated to the uncanny. Then, too, the theme that achieves such an indubitably uncanny effect, the unintended recurrence of the same thing, serves other and quite different purposes in another class of cases. We have already come across one example [p. 237] in which it is employed to call up a feeling of the comic; and we could multiply instances of this kind. Or again, it works as a means of emphasis, and so on. And once more: what is the origin of the uncanny effect of silence, darkness and solitude?

Do not these factors point to the part played by danger in the genesis of what is uncanny, notwithstanding that in children these same factors are the most frequent determinants of the expression of fear [rather than of the uncanny]? And are we after all justified in entirely ignoring intellectual uncertainty as a factor, seeing that we have admitted its importance in relation to death [p. 242]?

It is evident therefore, that we must be prepared to admit that there are other elements besides those which we have so far laid down as determining the production of uncanny feelings. We might say that these preliminary results have satisfied *psycho-analytic* interest in the problem of the uncanny, and that what remains probably calls for an *aesthetic* enquiry. But that would be to open the door to doubts about what exactly is the value of our general contention that the uncanny proceeds from something familiar which has been repressed.

We have noticed one point which may help us to resolve these uncertainties: nearly all the instances that contradict our hypothesis are taken from the realm of fiction, of imaginative writing. This suggests that we should differentiate between the uncanny that we actually experience and the uncanny that we merely picture or read about.

What is *experienced* as uncanny is much more simply conditioned but comprises far fewer instances. We shall find, I think, that it fits in perfectly with our attempt at a solution, and can be traced back without exception to something familiar that has been repressed. But here, too, we must make a certain important and psychologically significant differentiation in our material, which is best illustrated by turning to suitable examples.

Let us take the uncanny associated with the omnipotence of thoughts, with the prompt fulfilment of wishes, with secret injurious powers and with the return of the dead. The condition under which the feeling of uncanniness arises here is unmistakable. We—or our primitive forefathers—once believed that these possibilities were realities, and were convinced that they actually happened. Nowadays we no longer believe in them, we have *surmounted* these modes of thought; but we do not feel quite sure of our new beliefs, and the old ones still exist within us ready to seize upon any confirmation. As soon as something *actually happens* in our lives which seems to confirm the old, discarded beliefs we get a feeling of the uncanny; it is as though we were making a judgement something like this: 'So, after all, it is *true* that one can kill a person by the mere wish!' or, 'So the dead *do* live on and appear on the scene of their former activities!' and so on. Conversely, anyone who has completely and finally rid himself of animistic beliefs will be insensible to this type of the uncanny. The most remarkable coincidences of wish and fulfilment, the most mysterious repetition of similar experiences in a particular place or on a particular date, the most deceptive sights and suspicious noises—none of these things will disconcert him or raise the kind of fear which can be described as 'a fear of something uncanny'. The whole thing is purely an affair of 'reality-testing', a question of the material reality of the phenomena.[33]

---

[33] Since the uncanny effect of a 'double' also belongs to this same group it is interesting to observe what the effect is of meeting one's own image unbidden and unexpected. Ernst Mach has related two such observations in his *Analyse der Empfindungen* (1900, 3). On the first occasion he was not a little startled when he realized that the face before him was his own. The second time he formed a very unfavourable opinion about the supposed stranger who entered the omnibus, and thought 'What a shabby-looking school-master that man is who is getting in!'—I can report a similar adventure. I was sitting alone in my *wagon-lit* compartment when a more than usually violent jolt of the train swung back the door of the adjoining washing-cabinet, and an elderly gentleman in a dressing-gown and a travelling cap came in. I assumed that in leaving the washing-cabinet, which lay between the two compartments, he had taken the wrong direction and come into my compartment by mistake. Jumping up with the intention of putting him right, I at once realized to my dismay that the intruder was nothing but my own reflection in the looking-glass on the open door. I can still recollect that I thoroughly disliked his appearance. Instead, therefore, of being *frightened* by our 'doubles', both Mach and I simply failed to recognize them as such. Is it not possible, though, that our dislike of them was a vestigial trace of the archaic reaction which feels the 'double' to be something uncanny?

The state of affairs is different when the uncanny proceeds from repressed infantile complexes, from the castration complex, womb-phantasies, etc.; but experiences which arouse this kind of uncanny feeling are not of very frequent occurrence in real life. The uncanny which proceeds from actual experience belongs for the most part to the first group [the group dealt with in the previous paragraph]. Nevertheless the distinction between the two is theoretically very important. Where the uncanny comes from infantile complexes the question of material reality does not arise; its place is taken by psychical reality. What is involved is an actual repression of some content of thought and a return of this repressed content, not a cessation of *belief in the reality* of such a content. We might say that in the one case what had been repressed is a particular ideational content, and in the other the belief in its (material) reality. But this last phrase no doubt extends the term 'repression' beyond its legitimate meaning. It would be more correct to take into account a psychological distinction which can be detected here, and to say that the animistic beliefs of civilized people are in a state of having been (to a greater or lesser extent) *surmounted* [rather than repressed]. Our conclusion could then be stated thus: an uncanny experience occurs either when infantile complexes which have been repressed are once more revived by some impression, or when primitive beliefs which have been surmounted seem once more to be confirmed. Finally, we must not let our predilection for smooth solutions and lucid exposition blind us to the fact that these two classes of uncanny experience are not always sharply distinguishable. When we consider that primitive beliefs are most intimately connected with infantile complexes, and are, in fact, based on them, we shall not be greatly astonished to find that the distinction is often a hazy one.

The uncanny as it is depicted in *literature,* in stories and imaginative productions, merits in truth a separate discussion. Above all, it is a much more fertile province than the uncanny in real life, for it contains the whole of the latter and something more besides, something that cannot be found in real life. The contrast between what has been repressed and what has been surmounted cannot be transposed on to the uncanny in fiction without profound modification; for the realm of phantasy depends for its effect on the fact that its content is not submitted to reality-testing. The somewhat paradoxical result is that *in the first place a great deal that is not uncanny in fiction would be so if it happened in real life; and in the second place that there are many more means of creating uncanny effects in fiction than there are in real life.*

The imaginative writer has this licence among many others, that he can select his world of representation so that it either coincides with the realities we are familiar with or departs from them in what particulars he pleases. We accept his ruling in every case. In fairy tales, for instance, the world of reality is left behind from the very start, and the animistic system of beliefs is frankly adopted. Wish-fulfilments, secret powers, omnipotence of thoughts, animation of inanimate objects, all the elements so common in fairy stories, can exert no uncanny influence here; for, as we have learnt, that feeling cannot arise unless there is a conflict of judgement as to whether things which have been 'surmounted' and are regarded as incredible may not, after all, be possible; and this problem is eliminated from the outset by the postulates of the world of fairy tales. Thus we see that fairy stories, which have furnished us with most of the contradictions to our hypothesis of the uncanny, confirm the first part of our proposition—that in the realm of fiction many things are not uncanny which would be so if they happened in real life. In the case of these stories there are other contributory factors, which we shall briefly touch upon later.

The creative writer can also choose a setting which though less imaginary than the world of fairy tales, does yet differ from the real world by admitting superior spiritual beings such as daemonic spirits or ghosts of the dead. So long as they remain within their setting of poetic reality, such figures lose any uncanniness which they might possess. The souls in Dante's *Inferno,* or the supernatural apparitions in Shakespeare's *Hamlet, Macbeth* or *Julius Caesar,* may be gloomy and terrible enough, but they are no more really uncanny than Homer's jovial world of gods. We adapt our judgement to the imaginary reality imposed on us by the writer, and regard souls, spirits and ghosts as though their existence had the same validity as our own has in material reality. In this case too we avoid all trace of the uncanny.

The situation is altered as soon as the writer pretends to move in the world of common reality. In this case he accepts as well all the conditions operating to produce uncanny feelings in real life; and everything that would have an uncanny effect in reality has it in his story. But in this case he can even increase his effect and multiply it far beyond what could happen in reality, by bringing about events which never or very rarely happen in fact. In doing this he is in a sense betraying us to the superstitiousness which we have ostensibly surmounted; he deceives us by promising to give us the sober truth, and then after all overstepping it. We react to his inventions as we would have reacted to real experiences; by the time we have seen through his trick it is already too late and the author has achieved his object. But it must be added that his success is not unalloyed. We retain a feeling of dissatisfaction, a kind of grudge against the attempted deceit. I have noticed this particularly after reading Schnitzler's *Die Weissagung* [*The Prophecy*] and similar stories which flirt with the supernatural. However, the writer has one more means which he can use in order to avoid our recalcitrance and at the same time to improve his chances of success. He can keep us in the dark for a long time about the precise nature of the presuppositions on which the world he writes about is based, or he can cunningly and ingeniously avoid any definite information on the point to the last. Speaking generally, however, we find a confirmation of the second part of our proposition—that fiction presents more opportunities for creating uncanny feelings than are possible in real life.

Strictly speaking, all these complications relate only to that class of the uncanny which proceeds from forms of thought that have been surmounted. The class which proceeds from repressed complexes is more resistant and remains as powerful in fiction as in real experience, subject to one exception [see p. 252]. The uncanny belonging to the first class—that proceeding from forms of thought that have been surmounted— retains its character not only in experience but in fiction as well, so long as the setting is one of material reality; but where it is given an arbitrary and artificial setting in fiction, it is apt to lose that character.

We have clearly not exhausted the possibilities of poetic licence and the privileges enjoyed by story-writers in evoking or in excluding an uncanny feeling. In the main we adopt an unvarying passive attitude towards real experience and are subject to the influence of our physical environment. But the storyteller has a *peculiarly* directive power over us; by means of the moods he can put us into, he is able to guide the current of our emotions, to dam it up in one direction and make it flow in another, and he often obtains a great variety of effects from the same material. All this is nothing new, and has doubtless long since been fully taken into account by students of aesthetics. We have drifted into this field of research half involuntarily, through the temptation to explain certain instances which contradicted our theory of the causes of the uncanny. Accordingly we will now return to the examination of a few of those instances.

We have already asked [p. 246] why it is that the severed hand in the story of the treasure of Rhampsinitus has no uncanny effect in the way that the severed hand has in Hauff's story. The question seems to have gained in importance now that we have recognized that the class of the uncanny which proceeds from repressed complexes is the more resistant of the two. The answer is easy. In the Herodotus story our thoughts are concentrated much more on the superior cunning of the master-thief than on the feelings of the princess. The princess may very well have had an uncanny feeling, indeed she very probably fell into a swoon; but *we* have no such sensations, for we put ourselves in the thief's place, not in hers. In Nestroy's farce, *Der Zerrissene* [*The Torn Man*], another means is used to avoid any impression of the uncanny in the scene in which the fleeing man, convinced that he is a murderer, lifts up one trap-door after another and each time sees what he takes to be the ghost of his victim rising up out of it. He calls out in despair, 'But I've only killed *one* man. Why this ghastly multiplication?' We know what went before this scene and do not share his error, so what must be uncanny to him has an irresistibly comic effect on us. Even a 'real' ghost, as in Oscar Wilde's *Canterville Ghost*, loses all power of at least arousing *gruesome* feelings in us as soon as the author begins to amuse himself by being ironical about it and allows liberties to be taken with it. Thus we see how inde-pendent emotional effects can be of the actual subject-matter in the world of fiction. In fairy stories feelings of fear—including therefore uncanny feelings—are ruled out altogether. We understand this, and that is why we ignore any opportunities we find in them for developing such feelings.

Concerning the factors of silence, solitude and darkness [pp. 246-7], we can only say that they are actually elements in the production of the infantile anxiety from which the majority of human beings have never become quite free. This problem has been discussed from a psycho-analytic point of view elsewhere.[34]

[34] [See the discussion of children's fear of the dark in Section V of the third of Freud's *Three Essays* (1905*d*), *Standard Ed.*, 7, 224 *n*.]

Berenice

By Edgar Allan Poe

MISERY is manifold. The wretchedness of earth is multiform. Overreaching the wide horizon as the rainbow, its hues are as various as the hues of that arch—as distinct too, yet as intimately blended. Overreaching the wide horizon as the rainbow! How is it that from beauty I have derived a type of unloveliness?—from the covenant of peace, a simile of sorrow? But as, in ethics, evil is a consequence of good, so, in fact, out of joy is sorrow born. Either the memory of past bliss is the anguish of today, or the agonies which are, have their origin in the ecstasies which might have been.

My baptismal name is Egaeus; that of my family I will not mention. Yet there are no towers in the land more time-honored than my gloomy, gray, hereditary halls. Our line has been called a race of visionaries; and in many striking particulars—in the character of the family mansion—in the frescos of the chief saloon—in the tapestries of the dormitories—in the chiselling of some buttresses in the armory—but more especially in the gallery of antique paintings—in the fashion of the library chamber—and, lastly, in the very peculiar nature of the library's contents—there is more than sufficient evidence to warrant the belief.

The recollections of my earliest years are connected with that chamber, and with its volumes—of which latter I will say no more. Here died my mother. Herein was I born. But it is mere idleness to say that I had not lived before—that the soul has no previous existence. You deny it?—let us not argue the matter. Convinced myself, I seek not to convince. There is, however, a remembrance of aerial forms—of spiritual and meaning eyes—of sounds, musical yet sad—a remembrance which will not be excluded; a memory like a shadow—vague, variable, indefinite, unsteady; and like a shadow, too, in the impossibility of my getting rid of it while the sunlight of my reason shall exist.

In that chamber was I born. Thus awaking from the long night of what seemed, but was not, nonentity, at once into the very regions of fairy land—into a palace of imagination—into the wild dominions of monastic thought and erudition—it is not singular that I gazed around me with a startled and ardent eye—that I loitered away my boyhood in books, and dissipated my youth in reverie; but it is singular that as years rolled away, and the noon of manhood found me still in the mansion of my fathers—it is wonderful what stagnation there fell upon the springs of my life—wonderful how total an inversion took place in the character of my commonest thought. The realities of the world affected me as visions, and as visions only, while the wild ideas of the land of dreams became, in turn, not the material of my every-day existence, but in very deed that existence utterly and solely in itself.

* * * * * * *

Berenice and I were cousins, and we grew up together in my paternal halls. Yet differently we grew—I, ill of health, and buried in gloom—she, agile, graceful, and overflowing with energy; hers, the ramble on the hill-side—mine the studies of the cloister; I, living within my own heart, and addicted, body and soul, to the most intense and painful meditation—she, roaming carelessly through life, with no thought of the shadows in her path, or the silent flight of the raven-winged hours. Berenice!—I call upon her name—Berenice!—and from the gray ruins of memory a thousand tumultuous recollections are startled at the sound! Ah, vividly is her image before me now, as in the early days of her light-heartedness and joy! Oh, gorgeous yet fantastic beauty! Oh, sylph amid the shrubberies of Arnheim! Oh, Naiad among its fountains! And then—then all is mystery and terror, and a tale which should not be told. Disease—a fatal disease, fell like the simoon upon her frame; and, even while I gazed upon her, the spirit of change swept over her, pervading her mind, her habits, and her character, and, in a manner the most subtle and terrible, disturbing even the identity of her person! Alas! the destroyer came and went!—and the victim—where is she? I knew her not—or knew her no longer as Berenice.

Among the numerous train of maladies superinduced by that fatal and primary one which effected a revolution of so horrible a kind in the moral and physical being of my cousin, may be mentioned as the most distressing and obstinate in its nature, a species of epilepsy not unfrequently terminating in trance itself—trance very nearly resembling positive dissolution, and from which her manner of recovery was in most instances, startlingly abrupt. In the mean time my own disease—for I have been told that I should call it by no other appellation—my own disease, then, grew rapidly upon me, and assumed finally a monomaniac character of a novel and extraordinary form—hourly and momently gaining vigor—and at length obtaining over me the most incomprehensible ascendancy. This monomania, if I must so term it, consisted in a morbid irritability of those properties of the mind in metaphysical science termed the attentive. It is more than probable that I am not understood; but I fear, indeed, that it is in no manner possible to convey to the mind of the merely general reader, an adequate idea of that nervous intensity of interest with which, in my case, the powers of meditation (not to speak technically) busied and buried themselves, in the contemplation of even the most ordinary objects of the universe.

To muse for long unwearied hours, with my attention riveted to some frivolous device on the margin, or in the typography of a book; to become absorbed, for the better part of a summer's day, in a quaint shadow falling aslant upon the tapestry or upon the floor; to lose myself, for an entire night, in watching the steady flame of a lamp, or the embers of a fire; to dream away whole days over the perfume of a flower; to repeat, monotonously, some common word, until the sound, by dint of frequent repetition, ceased to convey any idea whatever to the mind; to lose all sense of motion or physical existence, by means of absolute bodily quiescence long and obstinately persevered in: such were a few of the most common and least pernicious vagaries induced by a condition of the mental faculties, not, indeed, altogether unparalleled, but certainly bidding defiance to anything like analysis or explanation.

Yet let me not be misapprehended. The undue, earnest, and morbid attention thus excited by objects in their own nature frivolous, must not be confounded in character with that ruminating propensity common to all mankind, and more especially indulged in by persons of ardent imagination. It was not even, as might be at first supposed, an extreme condition, or exaggeration of such propensity, but primarily and essentially distinct and different. In the one instance, the dreamer, or enthusiast, being interested by an object usually not frivolous, imperceptibly loses sight of this object in a wilderness of deductions and suggestions issuing therefrom, until, at the conclusion of a day dream often replete with luxury, he finds the incitamentum, or first cause of his musings, entirely vanished and forgotten. In my case, the primary object was invariably frivolous , although assuming, through the medium of my distempered vision, a refracted and unreal importance. Few deductions, if any, were made; and those few pertinaciously returning in upon the original object as a centre. The meditations were never pleasurable; and, at the termination of the reverie, the first cause, so far from being out of sight, had attained that supernaturally exaggerated interest which was the prevailing feature of the disease. In a word, the powers of mind more particularly exercised were, with me, as I have said before, the attentive, and are, with the day-dreamer, the speculative.

My books, at this epoch, if they did not actually serve to irritate the disorder, partook, it will be perceived, largely, in their imaginative and inconsequential nature, of the characteristic qualities of the disorder itself. I well remember, among others, the treatise of the noble Italian, Coelius Secundus Curio, "De Amplitudine Beati Regni Dei;" St. Austin's great work, the "City of God;" and Tertullian's "De Carne Christi," in which the paradoxical sentence "*Mortuus est Dei filius; credible est quia ineptum est: et sepultus resurrexit; certum est quia impossibile est,*" occupied my undivided time, for many weeks of laborious and fruitless investigation.

Thus it will appear that, shaken from its balance only by trivial things, my reason bore resemblance to that ocean-crag spoken of by Ptolemy Hephestion, which steadily resisting the attacks of human violence, and the fiercer fury of the waters and the winds, trembled only to the touch of the flower called Asphodel. And although, to a careless thinker, it might appear a matter beyond doubt, that the alteration produced by her unhappy malady, in the moral condition of Berenice, would afford me many objects for the exercise of that intense and abnormal meditation whose nature I have been at some trouble in explaining, yet such was not in any degree the case. In the lucid intervals of my infirmity, her calamity, indeed, gave me pain, and, taking deeply to heart that total wreck of her fair and gentle life, I did not fall to ponder, frequently and bitterly, upon the wonder-working means by which so strange a revolution had been so suddenly brought to pass. But these reflections partook not of the idiosyncrasy of my disease, and were such as would have occurred, under similar circumstances, to the ordinary mass of mankind. True to its own character, my disorder revelled in the less important but more startling changes wrought in the physical frame of Berenice—in the singular and most appalling distortion of her personal identity.

During the brightest days of her unparalleled beauty, most surely I had never loved her. In the strange anomaly of my existence, feelings with me, had never been of the heart, and my passions always were of the mind. Through the gray of the early morning—among the trellised shadows of the forest at noon-day—and in the silence of my library at night—she had flitted by my eyes, and I had seen her—not as the living and breathing Berenice, but as the Berenice of a dream; not as a being of the earth, earthy, but as the abstraction of such a being; not as a thing to admire, but to analyze; not as an object of love, but as the theme of the most abstruse although desultory speculation. And now—now I shuddered in her presence, and grew pale at her approach; yet, bitterly lamenting her fallen and desolate condition, I called to mind that she had loved me long, and, in an evil moment, I spoke to her of marriage.

And at length the period of our nuptials was approaching, when, upon an afternoon in the winter of the year—one of those unseasonably warm, calm, and misty days which are the nurse of the beautiful Halcyon,—I sat, (and sat, as I thought, alone,) in the inner apartment of the library. But, uplifting my eyes, I saw that Berenice stood before me.

Was it my own excited imagination—or the misty influence of the atmosphere—or the uncertain twilight of the chamber—or the gray draperies which fell around her figure—that caused in it so vacillating and indistinct an outline? I could not tell. She spoke no word; and I—not for worlds could I have uttered a syllable. An icy chill ran through my frame; a sense of insufferable anxiety oppressed me; a consuming curiosity pervaded my soul; and sinking back upon the chair, I remained for some time breathless and motionless, with my eyes riveted upon her person. Alas! its emaciation was excessive, and not one vestige of the former being lurked in any single line of the contour. My burning glances at length fell upon the face.

The forehead was high, and very pale, and singularly placid; and the once jetty hair fell partially over it, and overshadowed the hollow temples with innumerable ringlets, now of a vivid yellow, and jarring discordantly, in their fantastic character, with the reigning melancholy of the countenance. The eyes were lifeless, and lustreless, and seemingly pupilless, and I shrank involuntarily from their glassy stare to he contemplation of the thin and shrunken lips. They parted; and in a smile of peculiar meaning, the teeth of the changed Berenice disclosed themselves slowly to my view. Would to God that I had never beheld them, or that, having done so, I had died!

* * * * * * *

The shutting of a door disturbed me, and, looking up, I found that my cousin had departed from the chamber. But from the disordered chamber of my brain, had not, alas! departed, and would not be driven away, the white and ghastly spectrum of the teeth. Not a speck on their surface—not a shade on their enamel—not an indenture in their edges—but what that period of her smile had sufficed to brand in upon my memory. I saw them now even more unequivocally than I beheld them then. The teeth!—the teeth!—they were here, and there, and everywhere, and visibly and palpably before me; long, narrow, and excessively white, with the pale lips writhing about them, as in the very moment of their first terrible development. Then came the full fury of my monomania, and I struggled in vain against its strange and irresistible influence. In the multiplied objects of the external world I had no thoughts but for the teeth. For these I longed with a phrenzied desire. All other matters and all different interests became absorbed in their single contemplation. They—they alone were present to the mental eye, and they, in their sole individuality, became the essence of my mental life. I held them in every light. I turned them in every attitude. I surveyed their characteristics. I dwelt upon their peculiarities. I pondered upon their conformation. I mused upon the alteration in their nature. I shuddered as I assigned to them in imagination a sensitive and sentient power, and even when unassisted by the lips, a capability of moral expression. Of Mademoiselle Salle it has been well said, "*Que tous ses pas etaient des sentiments*," and

"All her teeth were ideas"

of Berenice I more seriously believed *que toutes ses dents etaient des idees. Des idees*!—ah here was the idiotic thought that destroyed me! *Des idees*!—ah therefore it was that I coveted them so madly! I felt that their possession could alone ever restore me to peace, in giving me back to reason.

And the evening closed in upon me thus—and then the darkness came, and tarried, and went—and the day again dawned—and the mists of a second night were now gathering around—and still I sat motionless in that solitary room—and still I sat buried in meditation—and still the phantasma of the teeth maintained its terrible ascendancy, as, with the most vivid hideous distinctness, it floated about amid the changing lights and shadows of the chamber. At length there broke in upon my dreams a cry as of horror and dismay; and thereunto, after a pause, succeeded the sound of troubled voices, intermingled with many low moanings of sorrow or of pain. I arose from my seat, and throwing open one of the doors of the library, saw standing out in the ante-chamber a servant maiden, all in tears, who told me that Berenice was—no more! She had been seized with epilepsy in the early morning, and now, at the closing in of the night, the grave was ready for its tenant, and all the preparations for the burial were completed.

*   *   *   *   *   *   *

I found myself sitting in the library, and again sitting there alone. It seemed that I had newly awakened from a confused and exciting dream. I knew that it was now midnight, and I was well aware, that since the setting of the sun, Berenice had been interred. But of that dreary period which intervened I had no positive, at least no definite comprehension. Yet its memory was replete with horror—horror more horrible from being vague, and terror more terrible from ambiguity. It was a fearful page in the record my existence, written all over with dim, and hideous, and unintelligible recollections. I strived to decypher them, but in vain; while ever and anon, like the spirit of a departed sound, the shrill and piercing shriek of a female voice seemed to be ringing in my ears. I had done a deed—what was it? I asked myself the question aloud, and the whispering echoes of the chamber answered me,—"what was it?"

On the table beside me burned a lamp, and near it lay a little box. It was of no remarkable character, and I had seen it frequently before, for it was the property of the family physician; but how came it there, upon my table, and why did I shudder in regarding it? These things were in no manner to be accounted for, and my eyes at length dropped to the open pages of a book, and to a sentence underscored therein. The words were the singular but simple ones of the poet Ebn Zaiat:—"*Dicebant mihi sodales si sepulchrum amicae visitarem, curas meas aliquantulum fore levatas.*" Why then, as I perused them, did the hairs of my head erect themselves on end, and the blood of my body become congealed within my veins?

There came a light tap at the library door—and, pale as the tenant of a tomb, a menial entered upon tiptoe. His looks were wild with terror, and he spoke to me in a voice tremulous, husky, and very low. What said he?—some broken sentences I heard. He told of a wild cry disturbing the silence of the night—of the gathering together of the household—of a search in the direction of the sound; and then his tones grew thrillingly distinct as he whispered me of a violated grave—of a disfigured body enshrouded, yet still breathing—still palpitating—still alive!

He pointed to garments;—they were muddy and clotted with gore. I spoke not, and he took me gently by the hand: it was indented with the impress of human nails. He directed my attention to some object against the wall. I looked at it for some minutes: it was a spade. With a shriek I bounded to the table, and grasped the box that lay upon it. But I could not force it open; and in my tremor, it slipped from my hands, and fell heavily, and burst into pieces; and from it, with a rattling sound, there rolled out some instruments of dental surgery, intermingled with thirty-two small, white and ivory-looking substances that were scattered to and fro about the floor.

The Fall of the House of Usher

By Edgar Allan Poe

DURING the whole of a dull, dark, and soundless day in the autumn of the year, when the clouds hung oppressively low in the heavens, I had been passing alone, on horseback, through a singularly dreary tract of country; and at length found myself, as the shades of the evening drew on, within view of the melancholy House of Usher. I know not how it was—but, with the first glimpse of the building, a sense of insufferable gloom pervaded my spirit. I say insufferable; for the feeling was unrelieved by any of that half-pleasurable, because poetic, sentiment, with which the mind usually receives even the sternest natural images of the desolate or terrible. I looked upon the scene before me—upon the mere house, and the simple landscape features of the domain—upon the bleak walls—upon the vacant eye-like windows—upon a few rank sedges—and upon a few white trunks of decayed trees—with an utter depression of soul which I can compare to no earthly sensation more properly than to the after-dream of the reveller upon opium—the bitter lapse into everyday life—the hideous dropping off of the veil. There was an iciness, a sinking, a sickening of the heart—an unredeemed dreariness of thought which no goading of the imagination could torture into aught of the sublime. What was it—I paused to think—what was it that so unnerved me in the contemplation of the House of Usher? It was a mystery all insoluble; nor could I grapple with the shadowy fancies that crowded upon me as I pondered. I was forced to fall back upon the unsatisfactory conclusion, that while, beyond doubt, there are combinations of very simple natural objects which have the power of thus affecting us, still the analysis of this power lies among considerations beyond our depth. It was possible, I reflected, that a mere different arrangement of the particulars of the scene, of the details of the picture, would be sufficient to modify, or perhaps to annihilate its capacity for sorrowful impression; and, acting upon this idea, I reined my horse to the precipitous brink of a black and lurid tarn that lay in unruffled lustre by the dwelling, and gazed down—but with a shudder even more thrilling than before—upon the remodelled and inverted images of the gray sedge, and the ghastly tree-stems, and the vacant and eye-like windows.

Nevertheless, in this mansion of gloom I now proposed to myself a sojourn of some weeks. Its proprietor, Roderick Usher, had been one of my boon companions in boyhood; but many years had elapsed since our last meeting. A letter, however, had lately reached me in a distant part of the country—a letter from him—which, in its wildly importunate nature, had admitted of no other than a personal reply. The MS. gave evidence of nervous agitation. The writer spoke of acute bodily illness—of a mental disorder which oppressed him—and of an earnest desire to see me, as his best, and indeed his only personal friend, with a view of attempting, by the cheerfulness of my society, some alleviation of his malady. It was the manner in which all this, and much more, was said—it was the apparent heart that went with his request—which allowed me no room for hesitation; and I accordingly obeyed forthwith what I still considered a very singular summons.

Although, as boys, we had been even intimate associates, yet I really knew little of my friend. His reserve had been always excessive and habitual. I was aware, however, that his very ancient family had been noted, time out of mind, for a peculiar sensibility of temperament, displaying itself, through long ages, in many works of exalted art, and manifested, of late, in repeated deeds of munificent yet unobtrusive charity, as well as in a passionate devotion to the intricacies, perhaps even more than to the orthodox and easily recognisable beauties, of musical science. I had learned, too, the very remarkable fact, that the stem of the Usher race, all time-honored as it was, had put forth, at no period, any enduring branch; in other words, that the entire family lay in the direct line of descent, and had always, with very trifling and very temporary variation, so lain. It was this deficiency, I considered, while running over in thought the perfect keeping of the character of the premises with the accredited character of the people, and while speculating upon the possible influence which the one, in the long lapse of centuries, might have exercised upon the other—it was this deficiency, perhaps, of collateral issue, and the consequent undeviating transmission, from sire to son, of the patrimony with the name, which had, at length, so identified the two as to merge the original title of the estate in the quaint and equivocal appellation of the "House of Usher"—an appellation which seemed to include, in the minds of the peasantry who used it, both the family and the family mansion.

I have said that the sole effect of my somewhat childish experiment—that of looking down within the tarn—had been to deepen the first singular impression. There can be no doubt that the consciousness of the rapid increase of my superstition—for why should I not so term it?—served mainly to accelerate the increase itself. Such, I have long known, is the paradoxical law of all sentiments having terror as a basis. And it might have been for this reason only, that, when I again uplifted my eyes to the house itself, from its image in the pool, there grew in my mind a strange fancy—a fancy so ridiculous, indeed, that I but mention it to show the vivid force of the sensations which oppressed me. I had so worked upon my imagination as really to believe that about the whole mansion and domain there hung an atmosphere peculiar to themselves and their immediate vicinity—an atmosphere which had no affinity with the air of heaven, but which had reeked up from the decayed trees, and the gray wall, and the silent tarn—a pestilent and mystic vapor, dull, sluggish, faintly discernible, and leaden-hued.

Shaking off from my spirit what must have been a dream, I scanned more narrowly the real aspect of the building. Its principal feature seemed to be that of an excessive antiquity. The discoloration of ages had been great. Minute fungi overspread the whole exterior, hanging in a fine tangled web-work from the eaves. Yet all this was apart from any extraordinary dilapidation. No portion of the masonry had fallen; and there appeared to be a wild inconsistency between its still perfect adaptation of parts, and the crumbling condition of the individual stones. In this there was much that reminded me of the specious totality of old wood-work which has rotted for long years in some neglected vault, with no disturbance from the breath of the external air. Beyond this indication of extensive decay, however, the fabric gave little token of instability. Perhaps the eye of a scrutinizing observer might have discovered a barely perceptible fissure, which, extending from the roof of the building in front, made its way down the wall in a zigzag direction, until it became lost in the sullen waters of the tarn.

Noticing these things, I rode over a short causeway to the house. A servant in waiting took my horse, and I entered the Gothic archway of the hall. A valet, of stealthy step, thence conducted me, in silence, through many dark and intricate passages in my progress to the studio of his master. Much that I encountered on the way contributed, I know not how, to heighten the vague sentiments of which I have already spoken. While the objects around me—while the carvings of the ceilings, the sombre tapestries of the walls, the ebon blackness of the floors, and the phantasmagoric armorial trophies which rattled as I strode, were but matters to which, or to such as which, I had been accustomed from my infancy—while I hesitated not to acknowledge how familiar was all this—I still wondered to find how unfamiliar were the fancies which ordinary images were stirring up. On one of the staircases, I met the physician of the family. His countenance, I thought, wore a mingled expression of low cunning and perplexity. He accosted me with trepidation and passed on. The valet now threw open a door and ushered me into the presence of his master.

The room in which I found myself was very large and lofty. The windows were long, narrow, and pointed, and at so vast a distance from the black oaken floor as to be altogether inaccessible from within. Feeble gleams of encrimsoned light made their way through the trellissed panes, and served to render sufficiently distinct the more prominent objects around; the eye, however, struggled in vain to reach the remoter angles of the chamber, or the recesses of the vaulted and fretted ceiling. Dark draperies hung upon the walls. The general furniture was profuse, comfortless, antique, and tattered. Many books and musical instruments lay scattered about, but failed to give any vitality to the scene. I felt that I breathed an atmosphere of sorrow. An air of stern, deep, and irredeemable gloom hung over and pervaded all.

Upon my entrance, Usher arose from a sofa on which he had been lying at full length, and greeted me with a vivacious warmth which had much in it, I at first thought, of an overdone cordiality—of the constrained effort of the ennuyé; man of the world. A glance, however, at his countenance, convinced me of his perfect sincerity. We sat down; and for some moments, while he spoke not, I gazed upon him with a feeling half of pity, half of awe. Surely, man had never before so terribly altered, in so brief a period, as had Roderick Usher! It was with difficulty that I could bring myself to admit the identity of the wan being before me with the companion of my early boyhood. Yet the character of his face had been at all times remarkable. A cadaverousness of complexion; an eye large, liquid, and luminous beyond comparison; lips somewhat thin and very pallid, but of a surpassingly beautiful curve; a nose of a delicate Hebrew model, but with a breadth of nostril unusual in similar formations; a finely moulded chin, speaking, in its want of prominence, of a want of moral energy; hair of a more than web-like softness and tenuity; these features, with an inordinate expansion above the regions of the temple, made up altogether a countenance not easily to be forgotten. And now in the mere exaggeration of the prevailing character of these features, and of the expression they were wont to convey, lay so much of change that I doubted to whom I spoke. The now ghastly pallor of the skin, and the now miraculous lustre of the eye, above all things startled and even awed me. The silken hair, too, had been suffered to grow all unheeded, and as, in its wild gossamer texture, it floated rather than fell about the face, I could not, even with effort, connect its Arabesque expression with any idea of simple humanity.

In the manner of my friend I was at once struck with an incoherence—an inconsistency; and I soon found this to arise from a series of feeble and futile struggles to overcome an habitual trepidancy—an excessive nervous agitation. For something of this nature I had indeed been prepared, no less by his letter, than by reminiscences of certain boyish traits, and by conclusions deduced from his peculiar physical conformation and temperament. His action was alternately vivacious and sullen. His voice varied rapidly from a tremulous indecision (when the animal spirits seemed utterly in abeyance) to that species of energetic concision—that abrupt, weighty, unhurried, and hollow-sounding enunciation—that leaden, self-balanced and perfectly modulated guttural utterance, which may be observed in the lost drunkard, or the irreclaimable eater of opium, during the periods of his most intense excitement.

It was thus that he spoke of the object of my visit, of his earnest desire to see me, and of the solace he expected me to afford him. He entered, at some length, into what he conceived to be the nature of his malady. It was, he said, a constitutional and a family evil, and one for which he despaired to find a remedy—a mere nervous affection, he immediately added, which would undoubtedly soon pass off. It displayed itself in a host of unnatural sensations. Some of these, as he detailed them, interested and bewildered me; although, perhaps, the terms, and the general manner of the narration had their weight. He suffered much from a morbid acuteness of the senses; the most insipid food was alone endurable; he could wear only garments of certain texture; the odors of all flowers were oppressive; his eyes were tortured by even a faint light; and there were but peculiar sounds, and these from stringed instruments, which did not inspire him with horror.

To an anomalous species of terror I found him a bounden slave. "I shall perish," said he, "I must perish in this deplorable folly. Thus, thus, and not otherwise, shall I be lost. I dread the events of the future, not in themselves, but in their results. I shudder at the thought of any, even the most trivial, incident, which may operate upon this intolerable agitation of soul. I have, indeed, no abhorrence of danger, except in its absolute effect—in terror. In this unnerved—in this pitiable condition—I feel that the period will sooner or later arrive when I must abandon life and reason together, in some struggle with the grim phantasm, FEAR."

I learned, moreover, at intervals, and through broken and equivocal hints, another singular feature of his mental condition. He was enchained by certain superstitious impressions in regard to the dwelling which he tenanted, and whence, for many years, he had never ventured forth—in regard to an influence whose supposititious force was conveyed in terms too shadowy here to be re-stated—an influence which some peculiarities in the mere form and substance of his family mansion, had, by dint of long sufferance, he said, obtained over his spirit—an effect which the physique of the gray walls and turrets, and of the dim tarn into which they all looked down, had, at length, brought about upon the morale of his existence.

He admitted, however, although with hesitation, that much of the peculiar gloom which thus afflicted him could be traced to a more natural and far more palpable origin—to the severe and long-continued illness—indeed to the evidently approaching dissolution—of a tenderly beloved sister—his sole companion for long years—his last and only relative on earth. "Her decease," he said, with a bitterness which I can never forget, "would leave him (him the hopeless and the frail) the last of the ancient race of the Ushers." While he spoke, the lady Madeline (for so was she called) passed slowly through a remote portion of the apartment, and, without having noticed my presence, disappeared. I regarded her with an utter astonishment not unmingled with dread—and yet I found it impossible to account for such feelings. A sensation of stupor oppressed me, as my eyes followed her retreating steps. When a door, at length, closed upon her, my glance sought instinctively and eagerly the countenance of the brother—but he had buried his face in his hands, and I could only perceive that a far more than ordinary wanness had overspread the emaciated fingers through which trickled many passionate tears.

The disease of the lady Madeline had long baffled the skill of her physicians. A settled apathy, a gradual wasting away of the person, and frequent although transient affections of a partially cataleptical character, were the unusual diagnosis. Hitherto she had steadily borne up against the pressure of her malady, and had not betaken herself finally to bed; but, on the closing in of the evening of my arrival at the house, she succumbed (as her brother told me at night with inexpressible agitation) to the prostrating power of the destroyer; and I learned that the glimpse I had obtained of her person would thus probably be the last I should obtain—that the lady, at least while living, would be seen by me no more.

For several days ensuing, her name was unmentioned by either Usher or myself: and during this period I was busied in earnest endeavors to alleviate the melancholy of my friend. We painted and read together; or I listened, as if in a dream, to the wild improvisations of his speaking guitar. And thus, as a closer and still closer intimacy admitted me more unreservedly into the recesses of his spirit, the more bitterly did I perceive the futility of all attempt at cheering a mind from which darkness, as if an inherent positive quality, poured forth upon all objects of the moral and physical universe, in one unceasing radiation of gloom.

I shall ever bear about me a memory of the many solemn hours I thus spent alone with the master of the House of Usher. Yet I should fail in any attempt to convey an idea of the exact character of the studies, or of the occupations, in which he involved me, or led me the way. An excited and highly distempered ideality threw a sulphureous lustre over all. His long improvised dirges will ring forever in my ears. Among other things, I hold painfully in mind a certain singular perversion and amplification of the wild air of the last waltz of Von Weber. From the paintings over which his elaborate fancy brooded, and which grew, touch by touch, into vaguenesses at which I shuddered the more thrillingly, because I shuddered knowing not why;—from these paintings (vivid as their images now are before me) I would in vain endeavor to educe more than a small portion which should lie within the compass of merely written words. By the utter simplicity, by the nakedness of his designs, he arrested and overawed attention. If ever mortal painted an idea, that mortal was Roderick Usher. For me at least—in the circumstances then surrounding me—there arose out of the pure abstractions which the hypochondriac contrived to throw upon his canvass, an intensity of intolerable awe, no shadow of which felt I ever yet in the contemplation of the certainly glowing yet too concrete reveries of Fuseli.

One of the phantasmagoric conceptions of my friend, partaking not so rigidly of the spirit of abstraction, may be shadowed forth, although feebly, in words. A small picture presented the interior of an immensely long and rectangular vault or tunnel, with low walls, smooth, white, and without interruption or device. Certain accessory points of the design served well to convey the idea that this excavation lay at an exceeding depth below the surface of the earth. No outlet was observed in any portion of its vast extent, and no torch, or other artificial source of light was discernible; yet a flood of intense rays rolled throughout, and bathed the whole in a ghastly and inappropriate splendor.

I have just spoken of that morbid condition of the auditory nerve which rendered all music intolerable to the sufferer, with the exception of certain effects of stringed instruments. It was, perhaps, the narrow limits to which he thus confined himself upon the guitar, which gave birth, in great measure, to the fantastic character of his performances. But the fervid facility of his impromptus could not be so accounted for. They must have been, and were, in the notes, as well as in the words of his wild fantasias (for he not unfrequently accompanied himself with rhymed verbal improvisations), the result of that intense mental collectedness and concentration to which I have previously alluded as observable only in particular moments of the highest artificial excitement. The words of one of these rhapsodies I have easily remembered. I was, perhaps, the more forcibly impressed with it, as he gave it, because, in the under or mystic current of its meaning, I fancied that I perceived, and for the first time, a full consciousness on the part of Usher, of the tottering of his lofty reason upon her throne. The verses, which were entitled "The Haunted Palace," ran very nearly, if not accurately, thus:

I.

In the greenest of our valleys,
By good angels tenanted,
Once a fair and stately palace—
Radiant palace—reared its head.
In the monarch Thought's dominion—
It stood there!
Never seraph spread a pinion
Over fabric half so fair.

II.

Banners yellow, glorious, golden,
On its roof did float and flow;
(This—all this—was in the olden
Time long ago)
And every gentle air that dallied,
In that sweet day,
Along the ramparts plumed and pallid,
A winged odor went away.

III.

Wanderers in that happy valley
Through two luminous windows saw
Spirits moving musically
To a lute's well-tunéd law,
Round about a throne, where sitting
(Porphyrogene!)
In state his glory well befitting,
The ruler of the realm was seen.

IV.
And all with pearl and ruby glowing
Was the fair palace door,
Through which came flowing, flowing, flowing,
And sparkling evermore,
A troop of Echoes whose sweet duty
Was but to sing,
In voices of surpassing beauty,
The wit and wisdom of their king.

V.
But evil things, in robes of sorrow,
Assailed the monarch's high estate;
(Ah, let us mourn, for never morrow
Shall dawn upon him, desolate!)
And, round about his home, the glory
That blushed and bloomed
Is but a dim-remembered story
Of the old time entombed.

VI.
And travellers now within that valley,
Through the red-litten windows, see
Vast forms that move fantastically
To a discordant melody;
While, like a rapid ghastly river,
Through the pale door,
A hideous throng rush out forever,
And laugh—but smile no more.

I well remember that suggestions arising from this ballad, led us into a train of thought wherein there became manifest an opinion of Usher's which I mention not so much on account of its novelty, (for other men have thought thus,) as on account of the pertinacity with which he maintained it. This opinion, in its general form, was that of the sentience of all vegetable things. But, in his disordered fancy, the idea had assumed a more daring character, and trespassed, under certain conditions, upon the kingdom of inorganization. I lack words to express the full extent, or the earnest abandon of his persuasion. The belief, however, was connected (as I have previously hinted) with the gray stones of the home of his forefathers. The conditions of the sentience had been here, he imagined, fulfilled in the method of collocation of these stones—in the order of their arrangement, as well as in that of the many fungi which overspread them, and of the decayed trees which stood around—above all, in the long undisturbed endurance of this arrangement, and in its reduplication in the still waters of the tarn. Its evidence—the evidence of the sentience—was to be seen, he said, (and I here started as he spoke,) in the gradual yet certain condensation of an atmosphere of their own about the waters and the walls. The result was discoverable, he added, in that silent, yet importunate and terrible influence which for centuries had moulded the destinies of his family, and which made him what I now saw him—what he was. Such opinions need no comment, and I will make none.

Our books—the books which, for years, had formed no small portion of the mental existence of the invalid—were, as might be supposed, in strict keeping with this character of phantasm. We pored together over such works as the Ververt et Chartreuse of Gresset; the Belphegor of Machiavelli; the Heaven and Hell of Swedenborg; the Subterranean Voyage of Nicholas Klimm by Holberg; the Chiromancy of Robert Flud, of Jean D'Indaginé, and of De la Chambre; the Journey into the Blue Distance of Tieck; and the City of the Sun of Campanella. One favorite volume was a small octavo edition of the Directorium Inquisitorium , by the Dominican Eymeric de Gironne; and there were passages in Pomponius Mela, about the old African Satyrs and Oegipans, over which Usher would sit dreaming for hours. His chief delight, however, was found in the perusal of an exceedingly rare and curious book in quarto Gothic—the manual of a forgotten church—the Vigiliae Mortuorum secundum Chorum Ecclesiae Maguntinae.

I could not help thinking of the wild ritual of this work, and of its probable influence upon the hypochondriac, when, one evening, having informed me abruptly that the lady Madeline was no more, he stated his intention of preserving her corpse for a fortnight, (previously to its final interment,) in one of the numerous vaults within the main walls of the building. The worldly reason, however, assigned for this singular proceeding, was one which I did not feel at liberty to dispute. The brother had been led to his resolution (so he told me) by consideration of the unusual character of the malady of the deceased, of certain obtrusive and eager inquiries on the part of her medical men, and of the remote and exposed situation of the burial-ground of the family. I will not deny that when I called to mind the sinister countenance of the person whom I met upon the staircase, on the day of my arrival at the house, I had no desire to oppose what I regarded as at best but a harmless, and by no means an unnatural, precaution.

At the request of Usher, I personally aided him in the arrangements for the temporary entombment. The body having been encoffined, we two alone bore it to its rest. The vault in which we placed it (and which had been so long unopened that our torches, half smothered in its oppressive atmosphere, gave us little opportunity for investigation) was small, damp, and entirely without means of admission for light; lying, at great depth, immediately beneath that portion of the building in which was my own sleeping apartment. It had been used, apparently, in remote feudal times, for the worst purposes of a donjon-keep, and, in later days, as a place of deposit for powder, or some other highly combustible substance, as a portion of its floor, and the whole interior of a long archway through which we reached it, were carefully sheathed with copper. The door, of massive iron, had been, also, similarly protected. Its immense weight caused an unusually sharp grating sound, as it moved upon its hinges.

Having deposited our mournful burden upon tressels within this region of horror, we partially turned aside the yet unscrewed lid of the coffin, and looked upon the face of the tenant. A striking similitude between the brother and sister now first arrested my attention; and Usher, divining, perhaps, my thoughts, murmured out some few words from which I learned that the deceased and himself had been twins, and that sympathies of a scarcely intelligible nature had always existed between them. Our glances, however, rested not long upon the dead—for we could not regard her unawed. The disease which had thus entombed the lady in the maturity of youth, had left, as usual in all maladies of a strictly cataleptical character, the mockery of a faint blush upon the bosom and the face, and that suspiciously lingering smile upon the lip which is so terrible in death. We replaced and screwed down the lid, and, having secured the door of iron, made our way, with toil, into the scarcely less gloomy apartments of the upper portion of the house.

And now, some days of bitter grief having elapsed, an observable change came over the features of the mental disorder of my friend. His ordinary manner had vanished. His ordinary occupations were neglected or forgotten. He roamed from chamber to chamber with hurried, unequal, and objectless step. The pallor of his countenance had assumed, if possible, a more ghastly hue—but the luminousness of his eye had utterly gone out. The once occasional huskiness of his tone was heard no more; and a tremulous quaver, as if of extreme terror, habitually characterized his utterance. There were times, indeed, when I thought his unceasingly agitated mind was laboring with some oppressive secret, to divulge which he struggled for the necessary courage. At times, again, I was obliged to resolve all into the mere inexplicable vagaries of madness, for I beheld him gazing upon vacancy for long hours, in an attitude of the profoundest attention, as if listening to some imaginary sound. It was no wonder that his condition terrified—that it infected me. I felt creeping upon me, by slow yet certain degrees, the wild influences of his own fantastic yet impressive superstitions.

It was, especially, upon retiring to bed late in the night of the seventh or eighth day after the placing of the lady Madeline within the donjon, that I experienced the full power of such feelings. Sleep came not near my couch—while the hours waned and waned away. I struggled to reason off the nervousness which had dominion over me. I endeavored to believe that much, if not all of what I felt, was due to the bewildering influence of the gloomy furniture of the room—of the dark and tattered draperies, which, tortured into motion by the breath of a rising tempest, swayed fitfully to and fro upon the walls, and rustled uneasily about the decorations of the bed. But my efforts were fruitless. An irrepressible tremor gradually pervaded my frame; and, at length, there sat upon my very heart an incubus of utterly causeless alarm. Shaking this off with a gasp and a struggle, I uplifted myself upon the pillows, and, peering earnestly within the intense darkness of the chamber, harkened—I know not why, except that an instinctive spirit prompted me—to certain low and indefinite sounds which came, through the pauses of the storm, at long intervals, I knew not whence. Overpowered by an intense sentiment of horror, unaccountable yet unendurable, I threw on my clothes with haste (for I felt that I should sleep no more during the night), and endeavored to arouse myself from the pitiable condition into which I had fallen, by pacing rapidly to and fro through the apartment.

I had taken but few turns in this manner, when a light step on an adjoining staircase arrested my attention. I presently recognised it as that of Usher. In an instant afterward he rapped, with a gentle touch, at my door, and entered, bearing a lamp. His countenance was, as usual, cadaverously wan—but, moreover, there was a species of mad hilarity in his eyes—an evidently restrained hysteria in his whole demeanor. His air appalled me—but anything was preferable to the solitude which I had so long endured, and I even welcomed his presence as a relief. affected by this.

"And you have not seen it?" he said abruptly, after having stared about him for some moments in silence—"you have not then seen it?—but, stay! you shall." Thus speaking, and having carefully shaded his lamp, he hurried to one of the casements, and threw it freely open to the storm.

The impetuous fury of the entering gust nearly lifted us from our feet. It was, indeed, a tempestuous yet sternly beautiful night, and one wildly singular in its terror and its beauty. A whirlwind had apparently collected its force in our vicinity; for there were frequent and violent alterations in the direction of the wind; and the exceeding density of the clouds (which hung so low as to press upon the turrets of the house) did not prevent our perceiving the life-like velocity with which they flew careering from all points against each other, without passing away into the distance. I say that even their exceeding density did not prevent our perceiving this—yet we had no glimpse of the moon or stars—nor was there any flashing forth of the lightning. But the under surfaces of the huge masses of agitated vapor, as well as all terrestrial objects immediately around us, were glowing in the unnatural light of a faintly luminous and distinctly visible gaseous exhalation which hung about and enshrouded the mansion.

"You must not—you shall not behold this!" said I, shudderingly, to Usher, as I led him, with a gentle violence, from the window to a seat. "These appearances, which bewilder you, are merely electrical phenomena not uncommon—or it may be that they have their ghastly origin in the rank miasma of the tarn. Let us close this casement;—the air is chilling and dangerous to your frame. Here is one of your favorite romances. I will read, and you shall listen;—and so we will pass away this terrible night together."

The antique volume which I had taken up was the "Mad Trist" of Sir Launcelot Canning; but I had called it a favorite of Usher's more in sad jest than in earnest; for, in truth, there is little in its uncouth and unimaginative prolixity which could have had interest for the lofty and spiritual ideality of my friend. It was, however, the only book immediately at hand; and I indulged a vague hope that the excitement which now agitated the hypochondriac, might find relief (for the history of mental disorder is full of similar anomalies) even in the extremeness of the folly which I should read. Could I have judged, indeed, by the wild overstrained air of vivacity with which he harkened, or apparently harkened, to the words of the tale, I might well have congratulated myself upon the success of my design.

I had arrived at that well-known portion of the story where Ethelred, the hero of the Trist, having sought in vain for peaceable admission into the dwelling of the hermit, proceeds to make good an entrance by force. Here, it will be remembered, the words of the narrative run thus:

"And Ethelred, who was by nature of a doughty heart, and who was now mighty withal, on account of the powerfulness of the wine which he had drunken, waited no longer to hold parley with the hermit, who, in sooth, was of an obstinate and maliceful turn, but, feeling the rain upon his shoulders, and fearing the rising of the tempest, uplifted his mace outright, and, with blows, made quickly room in the plankings of the door for his gauntleted hand; and now pulling therewith sturdily, he so cracked, and ripped, and tore all asunder, that the noise of the dry and hollow-sounding wood alarummed and reverberated throughout the forest."

At the termination of this sentence I started, and for a moment, paused; for it appeared to me (although I at once concluded that my excited fancy had deceived me)—it appeared to me that, from some very remote portion of the mansion, there came, indistinctly, to my ears, what might have been, in its exact similarity of character, the echo (but a stifled and dull one certainly) of the very cracking and ripping sound which Sir Launcelot had so particularly described. It was, beyond doubt, the coincidence alone which had arrested my attention; for, amid the rattling of the sashes of the casements, and the ordinary commingled noises of the still increasing storm, the sound, in itself, had nothing, surely, which should have interested or disturbed me. I continued the story:

"But the good champion Ethelred, now entering within the door, was sore enraged and amazed to perceive no signal of the maliceful hermit; but, in the stead thereof, a dragon of a scaly and prodigious demeanor, and of a fiery tongue, which sate in guard before a palace of gold, with a floor of silver; and upon the wall there hung a shield of shining brass with this legend enwritten—

Who entereth herein, a conqueror hath bin;
Who slayeth the dragon, the shield he shall win;

And Ethelred uplifted his mace, and struck upon the head of the dragon, which fell before him, and gave up his pesty breath, with a shriek so horrid and harsh, and withal so piercing, that Ethelred had fain to close his ears with his hands against the dreadful noise of it, the like whereof was never before heard."

Here again I paused abruptly, and now with a feeling of wild amazement—for there could be no doubt whatever that, in this instance, I did actually hear (although from what direction it proceeded I found it impossible to say) a low and apparently distant, but harsh, protracted, and most unusual screaming or grating sound—the exact counterpart of what my fancy had already conjured up for the dragon's unnatural shriek as described by the romancer.

Oppressed, as I certainly was, upon the occurrence of this second and most extraordinary coincidence, by a thousand conflicting sensations, in which wonder and extreme terror were predominant, I still retained sufficient presence of mind to avoid exciting, by any observation, the sensitive nervousness of my companion. I was by no means certain that he had noticed the sounds in question; although, assuredly, a strange alteration had, during the last few minutes, taken place in his demeanor. From a position fronting my own, he had gradually brought round his chair, so as to sit with his face to the door of the chamber; and thus I could but partially perceive his features, although I saw that his lips trembled as if he were murmuring inaudibly. His head had dropped upon his breast—yet I knew that he was not asleep, from the wide and rigid opening of the eye as I caught a glance of it in profile. The motion of his body, too, was at variance with this idea—for he rocked from side to side with a gentle yet constant and uniform sway. Having rapidly taken notice of all this, I resumed the narrative of Sir Launcelot, which thus proceeded:

"And now, the champion, having escaped from the terrible fury of the dragon, bethinking himself of the brazen shield, and of the breaking up of the enchantment which was upon it, removed the carcass from out of the way before him, and approached valorously over the silver pavement of the castle to where the shield was upon the wall; which in sooth tarried not for his full coming, but fell down at his feet upon the silver floor, with a mighty great and terrible ringing sound."

No sooner had these syllables passed my lips, than—as if a shield of brass had indeed, at the moment, fallen heavily upon a floor of silver—I became aware of a distinct, hollow, metallic, and clangorous, yet apparently muffled reverberation. Completely unnerved, I leaped to my feet; but the measured rocking movement of Usher was undisturbed. I rushed to the chair in which he sat. His eyes were bent fixedly before him, and throughout his whole countenance there reigned a stony rigidity. But, as I placed my hand upon his shoulder, there came a strong shudder over his whole person; a sickly smile quivered about his lips; and I saw that he spoke in a low, hurried, and gibbering murmur, as if unconscious of my presence. Bending closely over him, I at length drank in the hideous import of his words.

"Not hear it?—yes, I hear it, and have heard it. Long—long—long—many minutes, many hours, many days, have I heard it—yet I dared not—oh, pity me, miserable wretch that I am!—I dared not—I dared not speak! We have put her living in the tomb! Said I not that my senses were acute? I now tell you that I heard her first feeble movements in the hollow coffin. I heard them—many, many days ago—yet I dared not—I dared not speak! And now—tonight—Ethelred—ha! ha!—the breaking of the hermit's door, and the death-cry of the dragon, and the clangor of the shield!—say, rather, the rending of her coffin, and the grating of the iron hinges of her prison, and her struggles within the coppered archway of the vault! Oh whither shall I fly? Will she not be here anon? Is she not hurrying to upbraid me for my haste? Have I not heard her footstep on the stair? Do I not distinguish that heavy and horrible beating of her heart? Madman!"—here he sprang furiously to his feet, and shrieked out his syllables, as if in the effort he were giving up his soul—"Madman! I tell you that she now stands without the door!"

As if in the superhuman energy of his utterance there had been found the potency of a spell—the huge antique pannels to which the speaker pointed, threw slowly back, upon the instant, their ponderous and ebony jaws. It was the work of the rushing gust—but then without those doors there did stand the lofty and enshrouded figure of the lady Madeline of Usher. There was blood upon her white robes, and the evidence of some bitter struggle upon every portion of her emaciated frame. For a moment she remained trembling and reeling to and fro upon the threshold—then, with a low moaning cry, fell heavily inward upon the person of her brother, and in her violent and now final death-agonies, bore him to the floor a corpse, and a victim to the terrors he had anticipated.

From that chamber, and from that mansion, I fled aghast. The storm was still abroad in all its wrath as I found myself crossing the old causeway. Suddenly there shot along the path a wild light, and I turned to see whence a gleam so unusual could have issued; for the vast house and its shadows were alone behind me. The radiance was that of the full, setting, and blood-red moon, which now shone vividly through that once barely-discernible fissure, of which I have before spoken as extending from the roof of the building, in a zigzag direction, to the base. While I gazed, this fissure rapidly widened—there came a fierce breath of the whirlwind—the entire orb of the satellite burst at once upon my sight—my brain reeled as I saw the mighty walls rushing asunder—there was a long tumultuous shouting sound like the voice of a thousand waters—and the deep and dank tarn at my feet closed sullenly and silently over the fragments of the "House of Usher."

The Pit and the Pendulum

By Edgar Allan Poe

Impia tortorum longas hic turba furores Sanguinis innocui non satiata, aluit. Sospite nunc patria, fracto nunc funeris antro, Mors ubi dira fuit vita salusque patent.—Quatrain composed for the gates of a market to be erected upon the site of the Jacobin Club House in Paris.

I WAS sick, sick unto death, with that long agony, and when they at length unbound me, and I was permitted to sit, I felt that my senses were leaving me. The sentence, the dread sentence of death, was the last of distinct accentuation which reached my ears. After that, the sound of the inquisitorial voices seemed merged in one dreamy indeterminate hum. It conveyed to my soul the idea of REVOLUTION, perhaps from its association in fancy with the burr of a mill-wheel. This only for a brief period, for presently I heard no more. Yet, for a while, I saw, but with how terrible an exaggeration! I saw the lips of the black-robed judges. They appeared to me white—whiter than the sheet upon which I trace these words—and thin even to grotesqueness; thin with the intensity of their expression of firmness, of immovable resolution, of stern contempt of human torture. I saw that the decrees of what to me was fate were still issuing from those lips. I saw them writhe with a deadly locution. I saw them fashion the syllables of my name, and I shuddered, because no sound succeeded. I saw, too, for a few moments of delirious horror, the soft and nearly imperceptible waving of the sable draperies which enwrapped the walls of the apartment; and then my vision fell upon the seven tall candles upon the table. At first they wore the aspect of charity, and seemed white slender angels who would save me: but then all at once there came a most deadly nausea over my spirit, and I felt every fibre in my frame thrill, as if I had touched the wire of a galvanic battery, while the angel forms became meaningless spectres, with heads of flame, and I saw that from them there would be no help. And then there stole into my fancy, like a rich musical note, the thought of what sweet rest there must be in the grave. The thought came gently and stealthily, and it seemed long before it attained full appreciation; but just as my spirit came at length properly to feel and entertain it, the figures of the judges vanished, as if magically, from before me; the tall candles sank into nothingness; their flames went out utterly; the blackness of darkness superened; all sensations appeared swallowed up in a mad rushing descent as of the soul into Hades. Then silence, and stillness, and night were the universe.

I had swooned; but still will not say that all of consciousness was lost. What of it there remained I will not attempt to define, or even to describe; yet all was not lost. In the deepest slumber—no! In delirium—no! In a swoon—no! In death—no! Even in the grave all was not lost. Else there is no immortality for man. Arousing from the most profound of slumbers, we break the gossamer web of some dream. Yet in a second afterwards (so frail may that web have been) we remember not that we have dreamed. In the return to life from the swoon there are two stages; first, that of the sense of mental or spiritual; secondly, that of the sense of physical existence. It seems probable that if, upon reaching the second stage, we could recall the impressions of the first, we should find these impressions eloquent in memories of the gulf beyond. And that gulf is, what? How at least shall we distinguish its shadows from those of the tomb? But if the impressions of what I have termed the first stage are not at will recalled, yet, after long interval, do they not come unbidden, while we marvel whence they come? He who has never swooned is not he who finds strange palaces and wildly familiar faces in coals that glow; is not he who beholds floating in mid-air the sad visions that the many may not view; is not he who ponders over the perfume of some novel flower; is not he whose brain grows bewildered with the meaning of some musical cadence which has never before arrested his attention.

Amid frequent and thoughtful endeavours to remember , amid earnest struggles to regather some token of the state of seeming nothingness into which my soul had lapsed, there have been moments when I have dreamed of success; there have been brief, very brief periods when I have conjured up remembrances which the lucid reason of a later epoch assures me could have had reference only to that condition of seeming unconsciousness. These shadows of memory tell indistinctly of tall figures that lifted and bore me in silence down—down—still down—till a hideous dizziness oppressed me at the mere idea of the interminableness of the descent. They tell also of a vague horror at my heart on account of that heart's unnatural stillness. Then comes a sense of sudden motionlessness throughout all things; as if those who bore me (a ghastly train!) had outrun, in their descent, the limits of the limitless , and paused from the wearisomeness of their toil. After this I call to mind flatness and dampness; and then all is MADNESS—the madness of a memory which busies itself among forbidden things.

Very suddenly there came back to my soul motion and sound—the tumultuous motion of the heart, and in my ears the sound of its beating. Then a pause in which all is blank. Then again sound, and motion, and touch, a tingling sensation pervading my frame. Then the mere consciousness of existence, without thought, a condition which lasted long. Then, very suddenly, THOUGHT, and shuddering terror, and earnest endeavour to comprehend my true state. Then a strong desire to lapse into insensibility. Then a rushing revival of soul and a successful effort to move. And now a full memory of the trial, of the judges, of the sable draperies, of the sentence, of the sickness, of the swoon. Then entire forgetfulness of all that followed; of all that a later day and much earnestness of endeavour have enabled me vaguely to recall.

So far I had not opened my eyes. I felt that I lay upon my back unbound. I reached out my hand, and it fell heavily upon something damp and hard. There I suffered it to remain for many minutes, while I strove to imagine where and what I could be. I longed, yet dared not, to employ my vision. I dreaded the first glance at objects around me. It was not that I feared to look upon things horrible, but that I grew aghast lest there should be NOTHING to see. At length, with a wild desperation at heart,

I quickly unclosed my eyes. My worst thoughts, then, were confirmed. The blackness of eternal night encompassed me. I struggled for breath. The intensity of the darkness seemed to oppress and stifle me. The atmosphere was intolerably close. I still lay quietly, and made effort to exercise my reason. I brought to mind the inquisitorial proceedings, and attempted from that point to deduce my real condition. The sentence had passed, and it appeared to me that a very long interval of time had since elapsed. Yet not for a moment did I suppose myself actually dead. Such a supposition, notwithstanding what we read in fiction , is altogether inconsistent with real existence;—but where and in what state was I? The condemned to death, I knew, perished usually at the auto-da-fes, and one of these had been held on the very night of the day of my trial. Had I been remanded to my dungeon, to await the next sacrifice, which would not take place for many months? This I at once saw could not be. Victims had been in immediate demand. Moreover my dungeon, as well as all the condemned cells at Toledo, had stone floors, and light was not altogether excluded.

A fearful idea now suddenly drove the blood in torrents upon my heart, and for a brief period I once more relapsed into insensibility. Upon recovering, I at once started to my feet, trembling convulsively in every fibre. I thrust my arms wildly above and around me in all directions. I felt nothing; yet dreaded to move a step, lest I should be impeded by the walls of a TOMB. Perspiration burst from every pore, and stood in cold big beads upon my forehead. The agony of suspense grew at length intolerable, and I cautiously moved forward, with my arms extended, and my eyes straining from their sockets, in the hope of catching some faint ray of light. I proceeded for many paces, but still all was blackness and vacancy. I breathed more freely. It seemed evident that mine was not, at least, the most hideous of fates.

And now, as I still continued to step cautiously onward, there came thronging upon my recollection a thousand vague rumours of the horrors of Toledo. Of the dungeons there had been strange things narrated—fables I had always deemed them—but yet strange, and too ghastly to repeat, save in a whisper. Was I left to perish of starvation in this subterranean world of darkness; or what fate perhaps even more fearful awaited me? That the result would be death, and a death of more than customary bitterness, I knew too well the character of my judges to doubt. The mode and the hour were all that occupied or distracted me.

My outstretched hands at length encountered some solid obstruction. It was a wall, seemingly of stone masonry—very smooth, slimy, and cold. I followed it up; stepping with all the careful distrust with which certain antique narratives had inspired me. This process, however, afforded me no means of ascertaining the dimensions of my dungeon; as I might make its circuit, and return to the point whence I set out, without being aware of the fact, so perfectly uniform seemed the wall. I therefore sought the knife which had been in my pocket when led into the inquisitorial chamber, but it was gone; my clothes had been exchanged for a wrapper of coarse serge. I had thought of forcing the blade in some minute crevice of the masonry, so as to identify my point of departure. The difficulty, nevertheless, was but trivial, although, in the disorder of my fancy, it seemed at first insuperable. I tore a part of the hem from the robe, and placed the fragment at full length, and at right angles to the wall. In groping my way around the prison, I could not fail to encounter this rag upon completing the circuit. So, at least, I thought, but I had not counted upon the extent of the dungeon, or upon my own weakness. The ground was moist and slippery. I staggered onward for some time, when I stumbled and fell. My excessive fatigue induced me to remain prostrate, and sleep soon overtook me as I lay.

Upon awaking, and stretching forth an arm, I found beside me a loaf and a pitcher with water. I was too much exhausted to reflect upon this circumstance , but ate and drank with avidity. Shortly afterwards I resumed my tour around the prison, and with much toil came at last upon the fragment of the serge. Up to the period when I fell I had counted fifty-two paces, and upon resuming my walk I had counted forty-eight more, when I arrived at the rag. There were in all, then, a hundred paces; and, admitting two paces to the yard, I presumed the dungeon to be fifty yards in circuit. I had met, however, with many angles in the wall, and thus I could form no guess at the shape of the vault, for vault I could not help supposing it to be.

I had little object—certainly no hope—in these researches, but a vague curiosity prompted me to continue them. Quitting the wall, I resolved to cross the area of the enclosure. At first I proceeded with extreme caution, for the floor although seemingly of solid material was treacherous with slime. At length, however, I took courage and did not hesitate to step firmly—endeavouring to cross in as direct a line as possible. I had advanced some ten or twelve paces in this manner, when the remnant of the torn hem of my robe became entangled between my legs. I stepped on it, and fell violently on my face.

In the confusion attending my fall, I did not immediately apprehend a somewhat startling circumstance, which yet, in a few seconds afterward, and while I still lay prostrate, arrested my attention. It was this: my chin rested upon the floor of the prison, but my lips, and the upper portion of my head, although seemingly at a less elevation than the chin, touched nothing. At the same time, my forehead seemed bathed in a clammy vapour, and the peculiar smell of decayed fungus arose to my nostrils. I put forward my arm, and shuddered to find that I had fallen at the very brink of a circular pit, whose extent of course I had no means of ascertaining at the moment. Groping about the masonry just below the margin, I succeeded in dislodging a small fragment, and let it fall into the abyss. For many seconds I hearkened to its reverberations as it dashed against the sides of the chasm in its descent; at length there was a sullen plunge into water, succeeded by loud echoes. At the same moment there came a sound resembling the quick opening, and as rapid closing of a door overhead, while a faint gleam of light flashed suddenly through the gloom, and as suddenly faded away.

I saw clearly the doom which had been prepared for me, and congratulated myself upon the timely accident by which I had escaped. Another step before my fall, and the world had seen me no more and the death just avoided was of that very character which I had regarded as fabulous and frivolous in the tales respecting the Inquisition. To the victims of its tyranny, there was the choice of death with its direst physical agonies, or death with its most hideous moral horrors. I had been reserved for the latter. By long suffering my nerves had been unstrung, until I trembled at the sound of my own voice, and had become in every respect a fitting subject for the species of torture which awaited me.

Shaking in every limb, I groped my way back to the wall—resolving there to perish rather than risk the terrors of the wells, of which my imagination now pictured many in various positions about the dungeon. In other conditions of mind I might have had courage to end my misery at once by a plunge into one of these abysses; but now I was the veriest of cowards. Neither could I forget what I had read of these pits—that the SUDDEN extinction of life formed no part of their most horrible plan.

Agitation of spirit kept me awake for many long hours; but at length I again slumbered. Upon arousing, I found by my side, as before, a loaf and a pitcher of water. A burning thirst consumed me, and I emptied the vessel at a draught. It must have been drugged, for scarcely had I drunk before I became irresistibly drowsy. A deep sleep fell upon me—a sleep like that of death. How long it lasted of course

I know not; but when once again I unclosed my eyes the objects around me were visible. By a wild sulphurous lustre, the origin of which I could not at first determine, I was enabled to see the extent and aspect of the prison.

In its size I had been greatly mistaken. The whole circuit of its walls did not exceed twenty-five yards. For some minutes this fact occasioned me a world of vain trouble; vain indeed—for what could be of less importance, under the terrible circumstances which environed me than the mere dimensions of my dungeon? But my soul took a wild interest in trifles, and I busied myself in endeavours to account for the error I had committed in my measurement. The truth at length flashed upon me. In my first attempt at exploration I had counted fifty-two paces up to the period when I fell; I must then have been within a pace or two of the fragment of serge; in fact I had nearly performed the circuit of the vault. I then slept, and upon awaking, I must have returned upon my steps, thus supposing the circuit nearly double what it actually was. My confusion of mind prevented me from observing that I began my tour with the wall to the left, and ended it with the wall to the right.

I had been deceived too in respect to the shape of the enclosure. In feeling my way I had found many angles, and thus deduced an idea of great irregularity, so potent is the effect of total darkness upon one arousing from lethargy or sleep! The angles were simply those of a few slight depressions or niches at odd intervals. The general shape of the prison was square. What I had taken for masonry seemed now to be iron, or some other metal in huge plates, whose sutures or joints occasioned the depression. The entire surface of this metallic enclosure was rudely daubed in all the hideous and repulsive devices to which the charnel superstition of the monks has given rise. The figures of fiends in aspects of menace, with skeleton forms and other more really fearful images, overspread and disfigured the walls. I observed that the outlines of these monstrosities were sufficiently distinct, but that the colours seemed faded and blurred, as if from the effects of a damp atmosphere. I now noticed the floor, too, which was of stone. In the centre yawned the circular pit from whose jaws I had escaped; but it was the only one in the dungeon.

All this I saw indistinctly and by much effort, for my personal condition had been greatly changed during slumber. I now lay upon my back, and at full length, on a species of low framework of wood. To this I was securely bound by a long strap resembling a surcingle. It passed in many convolutions about my limbs and body, leaving at liberty only my head, and my left arm to such extent that I could by dint of much exertion supply myself with food from an earthen dish which lay by my side on the floor. I saw to my horror that the pitcher had been removed. I say to my horror, for I was consumed with intolerable thirst. This thirst it appeared to be the design of my persecutors to stimulate, for the food in the dish was meat pungently seasoned.

Looking upward, I surveyed the ceiling of my prison. It was some thirty or forty feet overhead, and constructed much as the side walls. In one of its panels a very singular figure riveted my whole attention. It was the painted figure of Time as he is commonly represented, save that in lieu of a scythe he held what at a casual glance I supposed to be the pictured image of a huge pendulum, such as we see on antique clocks. There was something, however, in the appearance of this machine which caused me to regard it more attentively. While I gazed directly upward at it (for its position was immediately over my own), I fancied that I saw it in motion. In an instant afterward the fancy was confirmed. Its sweep was brief, and of course slow. I watched it for some minutes, somewhat in fear but more in wonder. Wearied at length with observing its dull movement, I turned my eyes upon the other objects in the cell.

A slight noise attracted my notice, and looking to the floor, I saw several enormous rats traversing it. They had issued from the well which lay just within view to my right. Even then while I gazed, they came up in troops hurriedly, with ravenous eyes, allured by the scent of the meat. From this it required much effort and attention to scare them away.

It might have been half-an-hour, perhaps even an hour (for I could take but imperfect note of time) before I again cast my eyes upward. What I then saw confounded and amazed me. The sweep of the pendulum had increased in extent by nearly a yard. As a natural consequence, its velocity was also much greater. But what mainly disturbed me was the idea that it had perceptibly DESCENDED. I now observed, with what horror it is needless to say, that its nether extremity was formed of a crescent of glittering steel, about a foot in length from horn to horn; the horns upward, and the under edge evidently as keen as that of a razor. Like a razor also it seemed massy and heavy, tapering from the edge into a solid and broad structure above. It was appended to a weighty rod of brass, and the whole HISSED as it swung through the air.

I could no longer doubt the doom prepared for me by monkish ingenuity in torture. My cognisance of the pit had become known to the inquisitorial agents—THE PIT, whose horrors had been destined for so bold a recusant as myself, THE PIT, typical of hell, and regarded by rumour as the Ultima Thule of all their punishments. The plunge into this pit I had avoided by the merest of accidents, and I knew that surprise or entrapment into torment formed an important portion of all the grotesquerie of these dungeon deaths. Having failed to fall, it was no part of the demon plan to hurl me into the abyss, and thus (there being no alternative) a different and a milder destruction awaited me. Milder! I half smiled in my agony as I thought of such application of such a term.

What boots it to tell of the long, long hours of horror more than mortal, during which I counted the rushing oscillations of the steel! Inch by inch—line by line—with a descent only appreciable at intervals that seemed ages—down and still down it came! Days passed—it might have been that many days passed—ere it swept so closely over me as to fan me with its acrid breath. The odour of the sharp steel forced itself into my nostrils. I prayed—I wearied heaven with my prayer for its more speedy descent. I grew frantically mad, and struggled to force myself upward against the sweep of the fearful scimitar. And then I fell suddenly calm and lay smiling at the glittering death as a child at some rare bauble.

There was another interval of utter insensibility; it was brief, for upon again lapsing into life there had been no perceptible descent in the pendulum. But it might have been long—for I knew there were demons who took note of my swoon, and who could have arrested the vibration at pleasure. Upon my recovery, too, I felt very—oh! inexpressibly—sick and weak, as if through long inanition. Even amid the agonies of that period the human nature craved food. With painful effort I outstretched my left arm as far as my bonds permitted, and took possession of the small remnant which had been spared me by the rats. As I put a portion of it within my lips there rushed to my mind a half-formed thought of joy—of hope. Yet what business had I with hope? It was, as I say, a half-formed thought—man has many such, which are never completed. I felt that it was of joy—of hope; but I felt also that it had perished in its formation. In vain I struggled to perfect—to regain it. Long suffering had nearly annihilated all my ordinary powers of mind. I was an imbecile—an idiot.

The vibration of the pendulum was at right angles to my length. I saw that the crescent was designed to cross the region of the heart. It would fray the serge of my robe; it would return and repeat its operations—again—and again. Notwithstanding its terrifically wide sweep (some thirty feet or more) and the hissing vigour of its descent, sufficient to sunder these very walls of iron, still the fraying of my robe would be all that, for several minutes, it would accomplish; and at this thought I paused. I dared not go farther than this reflection. I dwelt upon it with a pertinacity of attention—as if, in so dwelling, I could arrest HERE the descent of the steel. I forced myself to ponder upon the sound of the crescent as it should pass across the garment—upon the peculiar thrilling sensation which the friction of cloth produces on the nerves. I pondered upon all this frivolity until my teeth were on edge.

Down—steadily down it crept. I took a frenzied pleasure in contrasting its downward with its lateral velocity. To the right—to the left—far and wide—with the shriek of a damned spirit! to my heart with the stealthy pace of the tiger! I alternately laughed and howled, as the one or the other idea grew predominant.

Down—certainly, relentlessly down! It vibrated within three inches of my bosom! I struggled violently—furiously—to free my left arm. This was free only from the elbow to the hand. I could reach the latter, from the platter beside me to my mouth with great effort, but no farther. Could I have broken the fastenings above the elbow, I would have seized and attempted to arrest the pendulum. I might as well have attempted to arrest an avalanche!

Down—still unceasingly—still inevitably down! I gasped and struggled at each vibration. I shrunk convulsively at its very sweep. My eyes followed its outward or upward whirls with the eagerness of the most unmeaning despair; they closed themselves spasmodically at the descent, although death would have been a relief, O, how unspeakable! Still I quivered in every nerve to think how slight a sinking of the machinery would precipitate that keen glistening axe upon my bosom. It was hope that prompted the nerve to quiver—the frame to shrink. It was HOPE—the hope that triumphs on the rack—that whispers to the death-condemned even in the dungeons of the Inquisition.

I saw that some ten or twelve vibrations would bring the steel in actual contact with my robe, and with this observation there suddenly came over my spirit all the keen, collected calmness of despair. For the first time during many hours, or perhaps days, I THOUGHT. It now occurred to me that the bandage or surcingle which enveloped me was UNIQUE. I was tied by no separate cord. The first stroke of the razor-like crescent athwart any portion of the band would so detach it that it might be unwound from my person by means of my left hand. But how fearful, in that case, the proximity of the steel! The result of the slightest struggle, how deadly! Was it likely, moreover, that the minions of the torturer had not foreseen and provided for this possibility! Was it probable that the bandage crossed my bosom in the track of the pendulum? Dreading to find my faint, and, as it seemed, my last hope frustrated, I so far elevated my head as to obtain a distinct view of my breast. The surcingle enveloped my limbs and body close in all directions save SAVE IN THE PATH OF THE DESTROYING CRESCENT.

Scarcely had I dropped my head back into its original position when there flashed upon my mind what I cannot better describe than as the unformed half of that idea of deliverance to which I have previously alluded, and of which a moiety only floated indeterminately through my brain when I raised food to my burning lips. The whole thought was now present—feeble, scarcely sane, scarcely definite, but still entire. I proceeded at once, with the nervous energy of despair, to attempt its execution.

For many hours the immediate vicinity of the low framework upon which I lay had been literally swarming with rats. They were wild, bold, ravenous , their red eyes glaring upon me as if they waited but for motionlessness on my part to make me their prey. "To what food," I thought, "have they been accustomed in the well?"

They had devoured, in spite of all my efforts to prevent them, all but a small remnant of the contents of the dish. I had fallen into an habitual see-saw or wave of the hand about the platter; and at length the unconscious uniformity of the movement deprived it of effect. In their voracity the vermin frequently fastened their sharp fangs in my fingers. With the particles of the oily and spicy viand which now remained, I thoroughly rubbed the bandage wherever I could reach it; then, raising my hand from the floor, I lay breathlessly still.

At first the ravenous animals were startled and terrified at the change—at the cessation of movement. They shrank alarmedly back; many sought the well. But this was only for a moment. I had not counted in vain upon their voracity. Observing that I remained without motion, one or two of the boldest leaped upon the frame-work and smelt at the surcingle. This seemed the signal for a general rush. Forth from the well they hurried in fresh troops. They clung to the wood, they overran it, and leaped in hundreds upon my person. The measured movement of the pendulum disturbed them not at all. Avoiding its strokes, they busied themselves with the annointed bandage. They pressed, they swarmed upon me in ever accumulating heaps. They writhed upon my throat; their cold lips sought my own; I was half stifled by their thronging pressure; disgust, for which the world has no name, swelled my bosom, and chilled with heavy clamminess my heart. Yet one minute and I felt that the struggle would be over. Plainly I perceived the loosening of the bandage. I knew that in more than one place it must be already severed. With a more than human resolution I lay STILL.

Nor had I erred in my calculations, nor had I endured in vain. I at length felt that I was FREE. The surcingle hung in ribands from my body. But the stroke of the pendulum already pressed upon my bosom. It had divided the serge of the robe. It had cut through the linen beneath. Twice again it swung, and a sharp sense of pain shot through every nerve. But the moment of escape had arrived. At a wave of my hand my deliverers hurried tumultously away. With a steady movement, cautious, sidelong, shrinking, and slow, I slid from the embrace of the bandage and beyond the reach of the scimitar. For the moment, at least I WAS FREE.

Free! and in the grasp of the Inquisition! I had scarcely stepped from my wooden bed of horror upon the stone floor of the prison, when the motion of the hellish machine ceased and I beheld it drawn up by some invisible force through the ceiling. This was a lesson which I took desperately to heart. My every motion was undoubtedly watched. Free! I had but escaped death in one form of agony to be delivered unto worse than death in some other. With that thought I rolled my eyes nervously around on the barriers of iron that hemmed me in. Something unusual—some change which at first I could not appreciate distinctly—it was obvious had taken place in the apartment. For many minutes of a dreamy and trembling abstraction I busied myself in vain, unconnected conjecture. During this period I became aware, for the first time, of the origin of the sulphurous light which illumined the cell. It proceeded from a fissure about half-an-inch in width extending entirely around the prison at the base of the walls which thus appeared, and were completely separated from the floor. I endeavoured, but of course in vain, to look through the aperture.

As I arose from the attempt, the mystery of the alteration in the chamber broke at once upon my understanding. I have observed that although the outlines of the figures upon the walls were sufficiently distinct, yet the colours seemed blurred and indefinite. These colours had now assumed, and were momentarily assuming, a startling and most intense brilliancy, that give to the spectral and fiendish portraitures an aspect that might have thrilled even firmer nerves than my own. Demon eyes, of a wild and ghastly vivacity, glared upon me in a thousand directions where none had been visible before, and gleamed with the lurid lustre of a fire that I could not force my imagination to regard as unreal.

UNREAL!—Even while I breathed there came to my nostrils the breath of the vapour of heated iron! A suffocating odour pervaded the prison! A deeper glow settled each moment in the eyes that glared at my agonies! A richer tint of crimson diffused itself over the pictured horrors of blood. I panted 'I gasped for breath! There could be no doubt of the design of my tormentors—oh most unrelenting! oh, most demoniac of men! I shrank from the glowing metal to the centre of the cell. Amid the thought of the fiery destruction that impended, the idea of the coolness of the well came over my soul like balm. I rushed to its deadly brink. I threw my straining vision below. The glare from the enkindled roof illumined its inmost recesses. Yet, for a wild moment, did my spirit refuse to comprehend the meaning of what I saw. At length it forced—it wrestled its way into my soul—it burned itself in upon my shuddering reason. O for a voice to speak!—oh, horror!—oh, any horror but this! With a shriek I rushed from the margin and buried my face in my hands—weeping bitterly.

The heat rapidly increased, and once again I looked up, shuddering as if with a fit of the ague. There had been a second change in the cell—and now the change was obviously in the FORM. As before , it was in vain that I at first endeavoured to appreciate or understand what was taking place. But not long was I left in doubt. The inquisitorial vengeance had been hurried by my two-fold escape, and there was to be no more dallying with the King of Terrors. The room had been square. I saw that two of its iron angles were now acute—two consequently, obtuse. The fearful difference quickly increased with a low rumbling or moaning sound. In an instant the apartment had shifted its form into that of a lozenge. But the alteration stopped not here—I neither hoped nor desired it to stop. I could have clasped the red walls to my bosom as a garment of eternal peace. "Death," I said "any death but that of the pit!" Fool! might I not have known that INTO THE PIT it was the object of the burning iron to urge me? Could I resist its glow? or if even that, could I withstand its pressure? And now, flatter and flatter grew the lozenge, with a rapidity that left me no time for contemplation. Its centre, and of course, its greatest width, came just over the yawning gulf. I shrank back—but the closing walls pressed me resistlessly onward. At length for my seared and writhing body there was no longer an inch of foothold on the firm floor of the prison. I struggled no more, but the agony of my soul found vent in one loud, long, and final scream of despair. I felt that I tottered upon the brink—I averted my eyes—

There was a discordant hum of human voices! There was a loud blast as of many trumpets! There was a harsh grating as of a thousand thunders! The fiery walls rushed back! An outstretched arm caught my own as I fell fainting into the abyss. It was that of General Lasalle. The French army had entered Toledo. The Inquisition was in the hands of its enemies.

The Black Cat

By Edgar Allan Poe

FOR the most wild, yet most homely narrative which I am about to pen, I neither expect nor solicit belief. Mad indeed would I be to expect it, in a case where my very senses reject their own evidence. Yet, mad am I not—and very surely do I not dream. But tomorrow I die, and today I would unburthen my soul. My immediate purpose is to place before the world, plainly, succinctly, and without comment, a series of mere household events. In their consequences, these events have terrified—have tortured—have destroyed me. Yet I will not attempt to expound them. To me, they have presented little but Horror—to many they will seem less terrible than barroques. Hereafter, perhaps, some intellect may be found which will reduce my phantasm to the common-place—some intellect more calm, more logical, and far less excitable than my own, which will perceive, in the circumstances I detail with awe, nothing more than an ordinary succession of very natural causes and effects.

From my infancy I was noted for the docility and humanity of my disposition. My tenderness of heart was even so conspicuous as to make me the jest of my companions. I was especially fond of animals, and was indulged by my parents with a great variety of pets. With these I spent most of my time, and never was so happy as when feeding and caressing them. This peculiarity of character grew with my growth, and in my manhood, I derived from it one of my principal sources of pleasure. To those who have cherished an affection for a faithful and sagacious dog, I need hardly be at the trouble of explaining the nature or the intensity of the gratification thus derivable. There is something in the unselfish and self-sacrificing love of a brute, which goes directly to the heart of him who has had frequent occasion to test the paltry friendship and gossamer fidelity of mere Man.

I married early, and was happy to find in my wife a disposition not uncongenial with my own. Observing my partiality for domestic pets, she lost no opportunity of procuring those of the most agreeable kind. We had birds, gold-fish, a fine dog, rabbits, a small monkey, and a cat.

This latter was a remarkably large and beautiful animal, entirely black, and sagacious to an astonishing degree. In speaking of his intelligence, my wife, who at heart was not a little tinctured with superstition, made frequent allusion to the ancient popular notion, which regarded all black cats as witches in disguise. Not that she was ever serious upon this point—and I mention the matter at all for no better reason than that it happens, just now, to be remembered.

Pluto—this was the cat's name—was my favorite pet and playmate. I alone fed him, and he attended me wherever I went about the house. It was even with difficulty that I could prevent him from following me through the streets.

Our friendship lasted, in this manner, for several years, during which my general temperament and character—through the instrumentality of the Fiend Intemperance—had (I blush to confess it) experienced a radical alteration for the worse. I grew, day by day, more moody, more irritable, more regardless of the feelings of others. I suffered myself to use intemperate language to my wife. At length, I even offered her personal violence. My pets, of course, were made to feel the change in my disposition. I not only neglected, but ill-used them. For Pluto, however, I still retained sufficient regard to restrain me from maltreating him, as I made no scruple of maltreating the rabbits, the monkey, or even the dog, when by accident, or through affection, they came in my way. But my disease grew upon me—for what disease is like Alcohol!—and at length even Pluto, who was now becoming old, and consequently somewhat peevish—even Pluto began to experience the effects of my ill temper.

One night, returning home, much intoxicated, from one of my haunts about town, I fancied that the cat avoided my presence. I seized him; when, in his fright at my violence, he inflicted a slight wound upon my hand with his teeth. The fury of a demon instantly possessed me. I knew myself no longer. My original soul seemed, at once, to take its flight from my body and a more than fiendish malevolence, gin-nurtured, thrilled every fibre of my frame. I took from my waistcoat-pocket a pen-knife, opened it, grasped the poor beast by the throat, and deliberately cut one of its eyes from the socket! I blush, I burn, I shudder, while I pen the damnable atrocity.

When reason returned with the morning—when I had slept off the fumes of the night's debauch—I experienced a sentiment half of horror, half of remorse, for the crime of which I had been guilty; but it was, at best, a feeble and equivocal feeling, and the soul remained untouched. I again plunged into excess, and soon drowned in wine all memory of the deed.

In the meantime the cat slowly recovered. The socket of the lost eye presented, it is true, a frightful appearance, but he no longer appeared to suffer any pain. He went about the house as usual, but, as might be expected, fled in extreme terror at my approach. I had so much of my old heart left, as to be at first grieved by this evident dislike on the part of a creature which had once so loved me. But this feeling soon gave place to irritation. And then came, as if to my final and irrevocable overthrow, the spirit of PERVERSENESS. Of this spirit philosophy takes no account. Yet I am not more sure that my soul lives, than I am that perverseness is one of the primitive impulses of the human heart—one of the indivisible primary faculties, or sentiments, which give direction to the character of Man. Who has not, a hundred times, found himself committing a vile or a silly action, for no other reason than because he knows he should not? Have we not a perpetual inclination, in the teeth of our best judgment, to violate that which is Law , merely because we understand it to be such? This spirit of perverseness, I say, came to my final overthrow. It was this unfathomable longing of the soul to vex itself—to offer violence to its own nature—to do wrong for the wrong's sake only—that urged me to continue and finally to consummate the injury I had inflicted upon the unoffending brute. One morning, in cool blood, I slipped a noose about its neck and hung it to the limb of a tree;—hung it with the tears streaming from my eyes, and with the bitterest remorse at my heart;—hung it because I knew that it had loved me, and because I felt it had given me no reason of offence;—hung it because I knew that in so doing I was committing a sin—a deadly sin that would so jeopardize my immortal soul as to place it—if such a thing wore possible—even beyond the reach of the infinite mercy of the Most Merciful and Most Terrible God.

On the night of the day on which this cruel deed was done, I was aroused from sleep by the cry of fire. The curtains of my bed were in flames. The whole house was blazing. It was with great difficulty that my wife, a servant, and myself, made our escape from the conflagration. The destruction was complete. My entire worldly wealth was swallowed up, and I resigned myself thenceforward to despair.

I am above the weakness of seeking to establish a sequence of cause and effect, between the disaster and the atrocity. But I am detailing a chain of facts—and wish not to leave even a possible link imperfect. On the day succeeding the fire, I visited the ruins. The walls, with one exception, had fallen in. This exception was found in a compartment wall, not very thick, which stood about the middle of the house, and against which had rested the head of my bed. The plastering had here, in great measure, resisted the action of the fire—a fact which I attributed to its having been recently spread. About this wall a dense crowd were collected, and many persons seemed to be examining a particular portion of it with very minute and eager attention. The words "strange!" "singular!" and other similar expressions, excited my curiosity. I approached and saw, as if graven in bas relief upon the white surface, the figure of a gigantic cat. The impression was given with an accuracy truly marvellous. There was a rope about the animal's neck.

When I first beheld this apparition—for I could scarcely regard it as less—my wonder and my terror were extreme. But at length reflection came to my aid. The cat, I remembered, had been hung in a garden adjacent to the house. Upon the alarm of fire, this garden had been immediately filled by the crowd—by some one of whom the animal must have been cut from the tree and thrown, through an open window, into my chamber. This had probably been done with the view of arousing me from sleep. The falling of other walls had compressed the victim of my cruelty into the substance of the freshly-spread plaster; the lime of which, with the flames, and the ammonia from the carcass, had then accomplished the portraiture as I saw it.

Although I thus readily accounted to my reason, if not altogether to my conscience, for the startling fact just detailed, it did not the less fail to make a deep impression upon my fancy. For months I could not rid myself of the phantasm of the cat; and, during this period, there came back into my spirit a half-sentiment that seemed, but was not, remorse. I went so far as to regret the loss of the animal, and to look about me, among the vile haunts which I now habitually frequented, for another pet of the same species, and of somewhat similar appearance, with which to supply its place.

One night as I sat, half stupified, in a den of more than infamy, my attention was suddenly drawn to some black object, reposing upon the head of one of the immense hogsheads of Gin, or of Rum, which constituted the chief furniture of the apartment. I had been looking steadily at the top of this hogshead for some minutes, and what now caused me surprise was the fact that I had not sooner perceived the object thereupon. I approached it, and touched it with my hand. It was a black cat—a very large one—fully as large as Pluto, and closely resembling him in every respect but one. Pluto had not a white hair upon any portion of his body; but this cat had a large, although indefinite splotch of white, covering nearly the whole region of the breast. Upon my touching him, he immediately arose, purred loudly, rubbed against my hand, and appeared delighted with my notice. This, then, was the very creature of which I was in search. I at once offered to purchase it of the landlord; but this person made no claim to it—knew nothing of it—had never seen it before.

I continued my caresses, and, when I prepared to go home, the animal evinced a disposition to accompany me. I permitted it to do so; occasionally stooping and patting it as I proceeded. When it reached the house it domesticated itself at once, and became immediately a great favorite with my wife.

For my own part, I soon found a dislike to it arising within me. This was just the reverse of what I had anticipated; but—I know not how or why it was—its evident fondness for myself rather disgusted and annoyed. By slow degrees, these feelings of disgust and annoyance rose into the bitterness of hatred. I avoided the creature; a certain sense of shame, and the remembrance of my former deed of cruelty, preventing me from physically abusing it. I did not, for some weeks, strike, or otherwise violently ill use it; but gradually—very gradually—I came to look upon it with unutterable loathing, and to flee silently from its odious presence, as from the breath of a pestilence.

What added, no doubt, to my hatred of the beast, was the discovery, on the morning after I brought it home, that, like Pluto, it also had been deprived of one of its eyes. This circumstance, however, only endeared it to my wife, who, as I have already said, possessed, in a high degree, that humanity of feeling which had once been my distinguishing trait, and the source of many of my simplest and purest pleasures.

With my aversion to this cat, however, its partiality for myself seemed to increase. It followed my footsteps with a pertinacity which it would be difficult to make the reader comprehend. Whenever I sat, it would crouch beneath my chair, or spring upon my knees, covering me with its loathsome caresses. If I arose to walk it would get between my feet and thus nearly throw me down, or, fastening its long and sharp claws in my dress, clamber, in this manner, to my breast. At such times, although I longed to destroy it with a blow, I was yet withheld from so doing, partly by a memory of my former crime, but chiefly—let me confess it at once—by absolute dread of the beast.

This dread was not exactly a dread of physical evil—and yet I should be at a loss how otherwise to define it. I am almost ashamed to own—yes, even in this felon's cell, I am almost ashamed to own—that the terror and horror with which the animal inspired me, had been heightened by one of the merest chimaeras it would be possible to conceive. My wife had called my attention, more than once, to the character of the mark of white hair, of which I have spoken, and which constituted the sole visible difference between the strange beast and the one I had destroyed. The reader will remember that this mark, although large, had been originally very indefinite; but, by slow degrees—degrees nearly imperceptible, and which for a long time my Reason struggled to reject as fanciful—it had, at length, assumed a rigorous distinctness of outline. It was now the representation of an object that I shudder to name—and for this, above all, I loathed, and dreaded, and would have rid myself of the monster had I dared—it was now, I say, the image of a hideous—of a ghastly thing—of the GALLOWS!—oh, mournful and terrible engine of Horror and of Crime—of Agony and of Death!

And now was I indeed wretched beyond the wretchedness of mere Humanity. And a brute beast—whose fellow I had contemptuously destroyed—a brute beast to work out for me—for me a man, fashioned in the image of the High God—so much of insufferable wo! Alas! neither by day nor by night knew I the blessing of Rest any more! During the former the creature left me no moment alone; and, in the latter, I started, hourly, from dreams of unutterable fear, to find the hot breath of the thing upon my face, and its vast weight—an incarnate Night-Mare that I had no power to shake off—incumbent eternally upon my heart!

Beneath the pressure of torments such as these, the feeble remnant of the good within me succumbed. Evil thoughts became my sole intimates—the darkest and most evil of thoughts. The moodiness of my usual temper increased to hatred of all things and of all mankind; while, from the sudden, frequent, and ungovernable outbursts of a fury to which I now blindly abandoned myself, my uncomplaining wife, alas! was the most usual and the most patient of sufferers.

One day she accompanied me, upon some household errand, into the cellar of the old building which our poverty compelled us to inhabit. The cat followed me down the steep stairs, and, nearly throwing me headlong, exasperated me to madness. Uplifting an axe, and forgetting, in my wrath, the childish dread which had hitherto stayed my hand, I aimed a blow at the animal which, of course, would have proved instantly fatal had it descended as I wished. But this blow was arrested by the hand of my wife. Goaded, by the interference, into a rage more than demoniacal, I withdrew my arm from her grasp and buried the axe in her brain. She fell dead upon the spot, without a groan.

This hideous murder accomplished, I set myself forthwith, and with entire deliberation, to the task of concealing the body. I knew that I could not remove it from the house, either by day or by night, without the risk of being observed by the neighbors. Many projects entered my mind. At one period I thought of cutting the corpse into minute fragments, and destroying them by fire. At another, I resolved to dig a grave for it in the floor of the cellar. Again, I deliberated about casting it in the well in the yard—about packing it in a box, as if merchandize, with the usual arrangements, and so getting a porter to take it from the house. Finally I hit upon what I considered a far better expedient than either of these. I determined to wall it up in the cellar—as the monks of the middle ages are recorded to have walled up their victims.

For a purpose such as this the cellar was well adapted. Its walls were loosely constructed, and had lately been plastered throughout with a rough plaster, which the dampness of the atmosphere had prevented from hardening. Moreover, in one of the walls was a projection, caused by a false chimney, or fireplace, that had been filled up, and made to resemble the red of the cellar. I made no doubt that I could readily displace the bricks at this point, insert the corpse, and wall the whole up as before, so that no eye could detect any thing suspicious. And in this calculation I was not deceived. By means of a crow-bar I easily dislodged the bricks, and, having carefully deposited the body against the inner wall, I propped it in that position, while, with little trouble, I re-laid the whole structure as it originally stood. Having procured mortar, sand, and hair, with every possible precaution, I prepared a plaster which could not be distinguished from the old, and with this I very carefully went over the new brickwork. When I had finished, I felt satisfied that all was right. The wall did not present the slightest appearance of having been disturbed. The rubbish on the floor was picked up with the minutest care. I looked around triumphantly, and said to myself—"Here at least, then, my labor has not been in vain."

My next step was to look for the beast which had been the cause of so much wretchedness; for I had, at length, firmly resolved to put it to death. Had I been able to meet with it, at the moment, there could have been no doubt of its fate; but it appeared that the crafty animal had been alarmed at the violence of my previous anger, and forebore to present itself in my present mood. It is impossible to describe, or to imagine, the deep, the blissful sense of relief which the absence of the detested creature occasioned in my bosom. It did not make its appearance during the night—and thus for one night at least, since its introduction into the house, I soundly and tranquilly slept; aye, slept even with the burden of murder upon my soul!

The second and the third day passed, and still my tormentor came not. Once again I breathed as a freeman. The monster, in terror, had fled the premises forever! I should behold it no more! My happiness was supreme! The guilt of my dark deed disturbed me but little. Some few inquiries had been made, but these had been readily answered. Even a search had been instituted—but of course nothing was to be discovered. I looked upon my future felicity as secured.

Upon the fourth day of the assassination, a party of the police came, very unexpectedly, into the house, and proceeded again to make rigorous investigation of the premises. Secure, however, in the inscrutability of my place of concealment, I felt no embarrassment whatever. The officers bade me accompany them in their search. They left no nook or corner unexplored. At length, for the third or fourth time, they descended into the cellar. I quivered not in a muscle. My heart beat calmly as that of one who slumbers in innocence. I walked the cellar from end to end. I folded my arms upon my bosom, and roamed easily to and fro. The police were thoroughly satisfied and prepared to depart. The glee at my heart was too strong to be restrained. I burned to say if but one word, by way of triumph, and to render doubly sure their assurance of my guiltlessness.

"Gentlemen," I said at last, as the party ascended the steps, "I delight to have allayed your suspicions. I wish you all health, and a little more courtesy. By the bye, gentlemen, this—this is a very well constructed house." [In the rabid desire to say something easily, I scarcely knew what I uttered at all.]—"I may say an excellently well constructed house. These walls are you going, gentlemen?—these walls are solidly put together;" and here, through the mere phrenzy of bravado, I rapped heavily, with a cane which I held in my hand, upon that very portion of the brick-work behind which stood the corpse of the wife of my bosom.

But may God shield and deliver me from the fangs of the Arch-Fiend! No sooner had the reverberation of my blows sunk into silence, than I was answered by a voice from within the tomb!—by a cry, at first muffled and broken, like the sobbing of a child, and then quickly swelling into one long, loud, and continuous scream, utterly anomalous and inhuman—a howl—a wailing shriek, half of horror and half of triumph, such as might have arisen only out of hell, conjointly from the throats of the dammed in their agony and of the demons that exult in the damnation.

Of my own thoughts it is folly to speak. Swooning, I staggered to the opposite wall. For one instant the party upon the stairs remained motionless, through extremity of terror and of awe. In the next, a dozen stout arms were toiling at the wall. It fell bodily. The corpse, already greatly decayed and clotted with gore, stood erect before the eyes of the spectators. Upon its head, with red extended mouth and solitary eye of fire, sat the hideous beast whose craft had seduced me into murder, and whose informing voice had consigned me to the hangman. I had walled the monster up within the tomb!

The Tell-Tale Heart

By Edgar Allan Poe

TRUE! nervous, very, very dreadfully nervous I had been and am; but why WILL you say that I am mad? The disease had sharpened my senses, not destroyed, not dulled them. Above all was the sense of hearing acute. I heard all things in the heaven and in the earth. I heard many things in hell. How then am I mad? Hearken! and observe how healthily, how calmly, I can tell you the whole story.

It is impossible to say how first the idea entered my brain, but, once conceived, it haunted me day and night. Object there was none. Passion there was none. I loved the old man. He had never wronged me. He had never given me insult. For his gold I had no desire. I think it was his eye! Yes, it was this! One of his eyes resembled that of a vulture—a pale blue eye with a film over it. Whenever it fell upon me my blood ran cold, and so by degrees, very gradually, I made up my mind to take the life of the old man, and thus rid myself of the eye for ever.

Now this is the point. You fancy me mad. Madmen know nothing. But you should have seen me. You should have seen how wisely I proceeded—with what caution—with what foresight, with what dissimulation, I went to work! I was never kinder to the old man than during the whole week before I killed him. And every night about midnight I turned the latch of his door and opened it oh, so gently! And then, when I had made an opening sufficient for my head, I put in a dark lantern all closed, closed so that no light shone out, and then I thrust in my head. Oh, you would have laughed to see how cunningly I thrust it in! I moved it slowly, very, very slowly, so that I might not disturb the old man's sleep. It took me an hour to place my whole head within the opening so far that I could see him as he lay upon his bed. Ha! would a madman have been so wise as this? And then when my head was well in the room I undid the lantern cautiously—oh, so cautiously—cautiously (for the hinges creaked), I undid it just so much that a single thin ray fell upon the vulture eye. And this I did for seven long nights, every night just at midnight, but I found the eye always closed, and so it was impossible to do the work, for it was not the old man who vexed me but his Evil Eye. And every morning, when the day broke, I went boldly into the chamber and spoke courageously to him, calling him by name in a hearty tone, and inquiring how he had passed the night. So you see he would have been a very profound old man, indeed , to suspect that every night, just at twelve, I looked in upon him while he slept.

Upon the eighth night I was more than usually cautious in opening the door. A watch's minute hand moves more quickly than did mine. Never before that night had I felt the extent of my own powers, of my sagacity. I could scarcely contain my feelings of triumph. To think that there I was opening the door little by little, and he not even to dream of my secret deeds or thoughts. I fairly chuckled at the idea, and perhaps he heard me, for he moved on the bed suddenly as if startled. Now you may think that I drew back—but no. His room was as black as pitch with the thick darkness (for the shutters were close fastened through fear of robbers), and so I knew that he could not see the opening of the door, and I kept pushing it on steadily, steadily.

I had my head in, and was about to open the lantern, when my thumb slipped upon the tin fastening, and the old man sprang up in the bed, crying out, "Who's there?"

I kept quite still and said nothing. For a whole hour I did not move a muscle, and in the meantime I did not hear him lie down. He was still sitting up in the bed, listening; just as I have done night after night hearkening to the death watches in the wall.

Presently, I heard a slight groan, and I knew it was the groan of mortal terror. It was not a groan of pain or of grief—oh, no! It was the low stifled sound that arises from the bottom of the soul when overcharged with awe. I knew the sound well. Many a night, just at midnight, when all the world slept, it has welled up from my own bosom, deepening, with its dreadful echo, the terrors that distracted me. I say I knew it well. I knew what the old man felt, and pitied him although I chuckled at heart. I knew that he had been lying awake ever since the first slight noise when he had turned in the bed. His fears had been ever since growing upon him. He had been trying to fancy them causeless, but could not. He had been saying to himself, "It is nothing but the wind in the chimney, it is only a mouse crossing the floor," or, "It is merely a cricket which has made a single chirp." Yes he has been trying to comfort himself with these suppositions; but he had found all in vain. ALL IN VAIN, because Death in approaching him had stalked with his black shadow before him and enveloped the victim. And it was the mournful influence of the unperceived shadow that caused him to feel, although he neither saw nor heard, to feel the presence of my head within the room.

When I had waited a long time very patiently without hearing him lie down, I resolved to open a little—a very, very little crevice in the lantern. So I opened it—you cannot imagine how stealthily, stealthily—until at length a single dim ray like the thread of the spider shot out from the crevice and fell upon the vulture eye.

It was open, wide, wide open, and I grew furious as I gazed upon it. I saw it with perfect distinctness—all a dull blue with a hideous veil over it that chilled the very marrow in my bones, but I could see nothing else of the old man's face or person, for I had directed the ray as if by instinct precisely upon the damned spot.

And now have I not told you that what you mistake for madness is but over-acuteness of the senses? now, I say, there came to my ears a low, dull, quick sound, such as a watch makes when enveloped in cotton. I knew that sound well too. It was the beating of the old man's heart. It increased my fury as the beating of a drum stimulates the soldier into courage.

But even yet I refrained and kept still. I scarcely breathed. I held the lantern motionless. I tried how steadily I could maintain the ray upon the eye. Meantime the hellish tattoo of the heart increased. It grew quicker and quicker, and louder and louder, every instant. The old man's terror must have been extreme! It grew louder, I say, louder every moment!—do you mark me well? I have told you that I am nervous: so I am. And now at the dead hour of the night, amid the dreadful silence of that old house, so strange a noise as this excited me to uncontrollable terror. Yet, for some minutes longer I refrained and stood still. But the beating grew louder, louder! I thought the heart must burst. And now a new anxiety seized me—the sound would be heard by a neighbour! The old man's hour had come! With a loud yell, I threw open the lantern and leaped into the room. He shrieked once—once only. In an instant I dragged him to the floor, and pulled the heavy bed over him. I then smiled gaily, to find the deed so far done. But for many minutes the heart beat on with a muffled sound. This, however, did not vex me; it would not be heard through the wall. At length it ceased. The old man was dead. I removed the bed and examined the corpse. Yes, he was stone, stone dead. I placed my hand upon the heart and held it there many minutes. There was no pulsation. He was stone dead. His eye would trouble me no more.

If still you think me mad, you will think so no longer when I describe the wise precautions I took for the concealment of the body. The night waned, and I worked hastily, but in silence.

I took up three planks from the flooring of the chamber, and deposited all between the scantlings. I then replaced the boards so cleverly so cunningly, that no human eye—not even his—could have detected anything wrong. There was nothing to wash out—no stain of any kind—no blood-spot whatever. I had been too wary for that.

When I had made an end of these labours, it was four o'clock—still dark as midnight. As the bell sounded the hour, there came a knocking at the street door. I went down to open it with a light heart,—for what had I now to fear? There entered three men, who introduced themselves, with perfect suavity, as officers of the police. A shriek had been heard by a neighbour during the night; suspicion of foul play had been aroused; information had been lodged at the police office, and they (the officers) had been deputed to search the premises.

I smiled,—for what had I to fear? I bade the gentlemen welcome. The shriek, I said, was my own in a dream. The old man, I mentioned, was absent in the country. I took my visitors all over the house. I bade them search—search well. I led them, at length, to his chamber. I showed them his treasures, secure, undisturbed. In the enthusiasm of my confidence, I brought chairs into the room, and desired them here to rest from their fatigues, while I myself, in the wild audacity of my perfect triumph, placed my own seat upon the very spot beneath which reposed the corpse of the victim.

The officers were satisfied. My MANNER had convinced them. I was singularly at ease. They sat and while I answered cheerily, they chatted of familiar things. But, ere long, I felt myself getting pale and wished them gone. My head ached, and I fancied a ringing in my ears; but still they sat, and still chatted. The ringing became more distinct: I talked more freely to get rid of the feeling: but it continued and gained definitiveness—until, at length, I found that the noise was NOT within my ears.

No doubt I now grew VERY pale; but I talked more fluently, and with a heightened voice. Yet the sound increased—and what could I do? It was A LOW, DULL, QUICK SOUND—MUCH SUCH A SOUND AS A WATCH MAKES WHEN ENVELOPED IN COTTON. I gasped for breath, and yet the officers heard it not. I talked more quickly, more vehemently but the noise steadily increased. I arose and argued about trifles, in a high key and with violent gesticulations; but the noise steadily increased. Why WOULD they not be gone? I paced the floor to and fro with heavy strides, as if excited to fury by the observations of the men, but the noise steadily increased. O God! what COULD I do? I foamed—I raved—I swore! I swung the chair upon which I had been sitting, and grated it upon the boards, but the noise arose over all and continually increased. It grew louder—louder—louder! And still the men chatted pleasantly , and smiled. Was it possible they heard not? Almighty God!—no, no? They heard!—they suspected!—they KNEW!—they were making a mockery of my horror!—this I thought, and this I think. But anything was better than this agony! Anything was more tolerable than this derision! I could bear those hypocritical smiles no longer! I felt that I must scream or die!—and now—again—hark! louder! louder! louder! louder! LOUDER!—

"Villains!" I shrieked, "dissemble no more! I admit the deed!—tear up the planks!—here, here!—it is the beating of his hideous heart!"

Shock ending

reveals possession & power

Common theme: burial in Poe

Relationship b/w narrator & old man?
Significance of old man for narrator?

He only doesn't like the 'Evil Eye'

Fear he would become like the old man

Eye associated w/ sight & perception
→ narrator's subjective perspective
metaphorically sees into depth of the narrator

Alice's Adventures in Wonderland

By Lewis Carroll

Lewis Carroll, *Alice's Adventures in Wonderland*. Copyright in the Public Domain.

Chapter I - Down the Rabbit-Hole

Alice was beginning to get very tired of sitting by her sister on the bank, and of having nothing to do: once or twice she had peeped into the book her sister was reading, but it had no pictures or conversations in it, 'and what is the use of a book,' thought Alice 'without pictures or conversation?'

So she was considering in her own mind (as well as she could, for the hot day made her feel very sleepy and stupid), whether the pleasure of making a daisy-chain would be worth the trouble of getting up and picking the daisies, when suddenly a White Rabbit with pink eyes ran close by her.

There was nothing so *very* remarkable in that; nor did Alice think it so *very* much out of the way to hear the Rabbit say to itself, 'Oh dear! Oh dear! I shall be late!' (when she thought it over afterwards, it occurred to her that she ought to have wondered at this, but at the time it all seemed quite natural); but when the Rabbit actually *took a watch out of its waistcoat-pocket,* and looked at it, and then hurried on, Alice started to her feet, for it flashed across her mind that she had never before seen a rabbit with either a waistcoat-pocket, or a watch to take out of it, and burning with curiosity, she ran across the field after it, and fortunately was just in time to see it pop down a large rabbit-hole under the hedge.

In another moment down went Alice after it, never once considering how in the world she was to get out again.

The rabbit-hole went straight on like a tunnel for some way, and then dipped suddenly down, so suddenly that Alice had not a moment to think about stopping herself before she found herself falling down a very deep well.

Either the well was very deep, or she fell very slowly, for she had plenty of time as she went down to look about her and to wonder what was going to happen next. First, she tried to look down and make out what she was coming to, but it was too dark to see anything; then she looked at the sides of the well, and noticed that they were filled with cupboards and book-shelves; here and there she saw maps and pictures hung upon pegs. She took down a jar from one of the shelves as she passed; it was labelled 'ORANGE MARMALADE', but to her great disappointment it was empty: she did not like to drop the jar for fear of killing somebody, so managed to put it into one of the cupboards as she fell past it.

'Well!' thought Alice to herself, 'after such a fall as this, I shall think nothing of tumbling down stairs! How brave they'll all think me at home! Why, I wouldn't say anything about it, even if I fell off the top of the house!' (Which was very likely true.)

Down, down, down. Would the fall *never* come to an end! 'I wonder how many miles I've fallen by this time?' she said aloud. 'I must be getting somewhere near the centre of the earth. Let me see: that would be four thousand miles down , I think—' (for, you see, Alice had learnt several things of this sort in her lessons in the schoolroom, and though this was not a *very* good opportunity for showing off her knowledge, as there was no one to listen to her, still it was good practice to say it over) '—yes, that's about the right distance—but then I wonder what Latitude or Longitude I've got to?' (Alice had no idea what Latitude was, or Longitude either, but thought they were nice grand words to say.)

Presently she began again. 'I wonder if I shall fall right *through* the earth! How funny it'll seem to come out among the people that walk with their heads downward! The Antipathies, I think—' (she was rather glad there *was* no one listening, this time, as it didn't sound at all the right word) '—but I shall have to ask them what the name of the country is, you know. Please, Ma' am, is this New Zealand or Australia?' (and she tried to curtsey as she spoke—fancy *curtseying* as you're falling through the air! Do you think you could manage it?) 'And what an ignorant little girl she'll think me for asking! No, it'll never do to ask: perhaps I shall see it written up somewhere.'

Down, down, down. There was nothing else to do, so Alice soon began talking again. 'Dinah'll miss me very much to-night, I should think!' (Dinah was the cat.) 'I hope they'll remember her saucer of milk at tea-time. Dinah my dear! I wish you were down here with me! There are no mice in the air, I'm afraid, but you might catch a bat, and that's very like a mouse, you know. But do cats eat bats, I wonder?' And here Alice began to get rather sleepy, and went on saying to herself, in a dreamy sort of way, 'Do cats eat bats? Do cats eat bats?' and sometimes, 'Do bats eat cats?' for, you see, as she couldn't answer either question, it didn't much matter which way she put it. She felt that she was dozing off, and had just begun to dream that she was walking hand in hand with Dinah, and saying to her very earnestly, 'Now, Dinah, tell me the truth: did you ever eat a bat?' when suddenly, thump! thump! down she came upon a heap of sticks and dry leaves, and the fall was over.

Alice was not a bit hurt, and she jumped up on to her feet in a moment: she looked up, but it was all dark overhead; before her was another long passage, and the White Rabbit was still in sight, hurrying down it. There was not a moment to be lost: away went Alice like the wind, and was just in time to hear it say, as it turned a corner, 'Oh my ears and whiskers, how late it's getting!' She was close behind it when she turned the corner, but the Rabbit was no longer to be seen: she found herself in a long, low hall, which was lit up by a row of lamps hanging from the roof.

There were doors all round the hall, but they were all locked; and when Alice had been all the way down one side and up the other, trying every door, she walked sadly down the middle, wondering how she was ever to get out again.

Suddenly she came upon a little three-legged table, all made of solid glass; there was nothing on it except a tiny golden key, and Alice's first thought was that it might belong to one of the doors of the hall; but, alas! either the locks were too large, or the key was too small, but at any rate it would not open any of them. However, on the second time round, she came upon a low curtain she had not noticed before, and behind it was a little door about fifteen inches high: she tried the little golden key in the lock, and to her great delight it fitted!

Alice opened the door and found that it led into a small passage, not much larger than a rat-hole: she knelt down and looked along the passage into the loveliest garden you ever saw. How she longed to get out of that dark hall, and wander about among those beds of bright flowers and those cool fountains, but she could not even get her head though the doorway; 'and even if my head would go through,' thought poor Alice, 'it would be of very little use without my shoulders. Oh, how I wish I could shut up like a telescope! I think I could, if I only know how to begin.' For, you see, so many out-of-the-way things had happened lately, that Alice had begun to think that very few things indeed were really impossible.

There seemed to be no use in waiting by the little door, so she went back to the table, half hoping she might find another key on it, or at any rate a book of rules for shutting people up like telescopes: this time she found a little bottle on it, ('which certainly was not here before,' said Alice,) and round the neck of the bottle was a paper label, with the words 'DRINK ME' beautifully printed on it in large letters.

It was all very well to say 'Drink me,' but the wise little Alice was not going to do *that* in a hurry. 'No, I'll look first,' she said, 'and see whether it's marked "*poison*" or not'; for she had read several nice little histories about children who had got burnt, and eaten up by wild beasts and other unpleasant things, all because they *would* not remember the simple rules their friends had taught them: such as, that a red-hot poker will burn you if you hold it too long; and that if you cut your finger *very* deeply with a knife, it usually bleeds; and she had never forgotten that, if you drink much from a bottle marked 'poison,' it is almost certain to disagree with you, sooner or later.

However, this bottle was NOT marked 'poison,' so Alice ventured to taste it, and finding it very nice, (it had, in fact, a sort of mixed flavour of cherry-tart, custard, pine-apple, roast turkey, toffee, and hot buttered toast,) she very soon finished it off.

* * * * * *

'What a curious feeling!' said Alice; 'I must be shutting up like a telescope.'

And so it was indeed: she was now only ten inches high, and her face brightened up at the thought that she was now the right size for going though the little door into that lovely garden. First, however, she waited for a few minutes to see if she was going to shrink any further: she felt a little nervous about this; 'for it might end, you know,' said Alice to herself, 'in my going out altogether, like a candle. I wonder what I should be like then?' And she tried to fancy what the flame of a candle is like after the candle is blown out, for she could not remember ever having seen such a thing.

After a while, finding that nothing more happened, she decided on going into the garden at once; but, alas for poor Alice! when she got to the door, she found he had forgotten the little golden key, and when she went back to the table for it, she found she could not possibly reach it: she could see it quite plainly through the glass, and she tried her best to climb up one of the legs of the table, but it was too slippery; and when she had tired herself out with trying, the poor little thing sat down and cried.

'Come, there's no use in crying like that!' said Alice to herself, rather sharply; 'I advise you to leave off this minute!' She generally gave herself very good advice, (though she very seldom followed it), and sometimes she scolded herself so severely as to bring tears into her eyes; and once she remembered trying to box her own ears for having cheated herself in a game of croquet she was playing against herself, for this curious child was very fond of pretending to be two people. 'But it's no use now,' thought poor Alice, 'to pretend to be two people! Why, there's hardly enough of me left to make ONE respectable person!'

Soon her eye fell on a little glass box that was lying under the table: she opened it, and found in it a very small cake, on which the words 'EAT ME' were beautifully marked in currants. 'Well, I'll eat it,' said Alice, 'and if it makes me grow larger, I can reach the key; and if it makes me grow smaller, I can creep under the door; so either way I'll get into the garden, and I don't care which happens!'

She ate a little bit, and said anxiously to herself, 'Which way? Which way?', holding her hand on the top of her head to feel which way it was growing, and she was quite surprised to find that she remained the same size: to be sure, this generally happens when one eats cake, but Alice had got so much into the way of expecting nothing but out-of-the-way things to happen, that it seemed quite dull and stupid for life to go on in the common way.

So she set to work, and very soon finished off the cake.

* * * * * *

Chapter 2 - The Pool of Tears

'Curiouser and curiouser!' cried Alice (she was so much surprised, that for the moment she quite forgot how to speak good English); 'now I'm opening out like the largest telescope that ever was! Good-bye, feet!' (for when she looked down at her feet, they seemed to be almost out of sight, they were getting so far off). 'Oh, my poor little feet, I wonder who will put on your shoes and stockings for you now, dears? I'm sure _I_ shan't be able! I shall be a great deal too far off to trouble myself about you: you must manage the best way you can;—but I must be kind to them,' thought Alice, 'or perhaps they won't walk the way I want to go! Let me see: I'll give them a new pair of boots every Christmas.'

And she went on planning to herself how she would manage it. 'They must go by the carrier,' she thought; 'and how funny it'll seem, sending presents to one's own feet! And how odd the directions will look!

ALICE'S RIGHT FOOT, ESQ.
HEARTHRUG,
NEAR THE FENDER,
(WITH ALICE'S LOVE).

Oh dear, what nonsense I'm talking!'

Just then her head struck against the roof of the hall: in fact she was now more than nine feet high, and she at once took up the little golden key and hurried off to the garden door.

Poor Alice! It was as much as she could do, lying down on one side, to look through into the garden with one eye; but to get through was more hopeless than ever: she sat down and began to cry again.

'You ought to be ashamed of yourself,' said Alice, 'a great girl like you,' (she might well say this), 'to go on crying in this way! Stop this moment, I tell you!' But she went on all the same, shedding gallons of tears, until there was a large pool all round her, about four inches deep and reaching half down the hall.

After a time she heard a little pattering of feet in the distance, and she hastily dried her eyes to see what was coming. It was the White Rabbit returning , splendidly dressed, with a pair of white kid gloves in one hand and a large fan in the other: he came trotting along in a great hurry, muttering to himself as he came, 'Oh! the Duchess, the Duchess! Oh! won't she be savage if I've kept her waiting!' Alice felt so desperate that she was ready to ask help of any one; so, when the Rabbit came near her, she began, in a low, timid voice, 'If you please, sir—' The Rabbit started violently, dropped the white kid gloves and the fan, and skurried away into the darkness as hard as he could go.

Alice took up the fan and gloves, and, as the hall was very hot, she kept fanning herself all the time she went on talking: 'Dear, dear! How queer everything is to-day! And yesterday things went on just as usual. I wonder if I've been changed in the night? Let me think: was I the same when I got up this morning? I almost think I can remember feeling a little different. But if I'm not the same, the next question is, Who in the world am I? Ah, THAT'S the great puzzle!' And she began thinking over all the children she knew that were of the same age as herself, to see if she could have been changed for any of them.

'I'm sure I'm not Ada,' she said, 'for her hair goes in such long ringlets, and mine doesn't go in ringlets at all; and I'm sure I can't be Mabel, for I know all sorts of things, and she, oh! she knows such a very little! Besides, SHE'S she, and I'm I, and—oh dear, how puzzling it all is! I'll try if I know all the things I used to know. Let me see: four times five is twelve, and four times six is thirteen, and four times seven is—oh dear! I shall never get to twenty at that rate! However, the Multiplication Table doesn't signify: let's try Geography. London is the capital of Paris, and Paris is the capital of Rome, and Rome—no, THAT'S all wrong, I'm certain! I must have been changed for Mabel! I'll try and say "How doth the little—"' and she crossed her hands on her lap as if she were saying lessons, and began to repeat it, but her voice sounded hoarse and strange, and the words did not come the same as they used to do:—

'How doth the little crocodile Improve his shining tail, And pour the waters of the Nile On every golden scale!

'How cheerfully he seems to grin, How neatly spread his claws, And welcome little fishes in With gently smiling jaws!'

'I'm sure those are not the right words,' said poor Alice, and her eyes filled with tears again as she went on, 'I must be Mabel after all, and I shall have to go and live in that poky little house, and have next to no toys to play with, and oh! ever so many lessons to learn! No, I've made up my mind about it; if I'm Mabel, I'll stay down here! It'll be no use their putting their heads down and saying "Come up again, dear!" I shall only look up and say "Who am I then? Tell me that first, and then, if I like being that person, I'll come up: if not, I'll stay down here till I'm somebody else"—but, oh dear!' cried Alice, with a sudden burst of tears, 'I do wish they WOULD put their heads down! I am so VERY tired of being all alone here!'

As she said this she looked down at her hands, and was surprised to see that she had put on one of the Rabbit's little white kid gloves while she was talking. 'How CAN I have done that?' she thought. 'I must be growing small again.' She got up and went to the table to measure herself by it, and found that, as nearly as she could guess, she was now about two feet high, and was going on shrinking rapidly: she soon found out that the cause of this was the fan she was holding, and she dropped it hastily, just in time to avoid shrinking away altogether.

'That WAS a narrow escape!' said Alice, a good deal frightened at the sudden change, but very glad to find herself still in existence; 'and now for the garden!' and she ran with all speed back to the little door: but, alas! the little door was shut again, and the little golden key was lying on the glass table as before, 'and things are worse than ever,' thought the poor child, 'for I never was so small as this before, never! And I declare it's too bad, that it is!'

As she said these words her foot slipped, and in another moment, splash! she was up to her chin in salt water. He first idea was that she had somehow fallen into the sea, 'and in that case I can go back by railway,' she said to herself. (Alice had been to the seaside once in her life, and had come to the general conclusion, that wherever you go to on the English coast you find a number of bathing machines in the sea, some children digging in the sand with wooden spades, then a row of lodging houses, and behind them a railway station.) However, she soon made out that she was in the pool of tears which she had wept when she was nine feet high.

'I wish I hadn't cried so much!' said Alice, as she swam about, trying to find her way out. 'I shall be punished for it now, I suppose, by being drowned in my own tears! That WILL be a queer thing, to be sure! However, everything is queer to-day.'

Just then she heard something splashing about in the pool a little way off, and she swam nearer to make out what it was: at first she thought it must be a walrus or hippopotamus, but then she remembered how small she was now, and she soon made out that it was only a mouse that had slipped in like herself.

'Would it be of any use, now,' thought Alice, 'to speak to this mouse? Everything is so out-of-the-way down here, that I should think very likely it can talk: at any rate, there's no harm in trying.' So she began: 'O Mouse, do you know the way out of this pool? I am very tired of swimming about here, O Mouse!' (Alice thought this must be the right way of speaking to a mouse: she had never done such a thing before, but she remembered having seen in her brother's Latin Grammar, 'A mouse—of a mouse—to a mouse—a mouse—O mouse!' The Mouse looked at her rather inquisitively, and seemed to her to wink with one of its little eyes, but it said nothing.

'Perhaps it doesn't understand English,' thought Alice; 'I daresay it's a French mouse, come over with William the Conqueror.' (For, with all her knowledge of history, Alice had no very clear notion how long ago anything had happened.) So she began again: '*Ou est ma chatte*?' which was the first sentence in her French lesson-book. The Mouse gave a sudden leap out of the water, and seemed to quiver all over with fright. 'Oh, I beg your pardon!' cried Alice hastily, afraid that she had hurt the poor animal's feelings. 'I quite forgot you didn't like cats.'

'Not like cats!' cried the Mouse, in a shrill, passionate voice. 'Would YOU like cats if you were me?'

'Well, perhaps not,' said Alice in a soothing tone: 'don't be angry about it. And yet I wish I could show you our cat Dinah: I think you'd take a fancy to cats if you could only see her. She is such a dear quiet thing,' Alice went on, half to herself, as she swam lazily about in the pool, 'and she sits purring so nicely by the fire, licking her paws and washing her face—and she is such a nice soft thing to nurse—and she's such a capital one for catching mice—oh, I beg your pardon!' cried Alice again, for this time the Mouse was bristling all over, and she felt certain it must be really offended. 'We won't talk about her any more if you'd rather not.'

'We indeed!' cried the Mouse, who was trembling down to the end of his tail. 'As if I would talk on such a subject! Our family always HATED cats: nasty, low, vulgar things! Don't let me hear the name again!'

'I won't indeed!' said Alice, in a great hurry to change the subject of conversation. 'Are you—are you fond—of—of dogs?' The Mouse did not answer, so Alice went on eagerly: 'There is such a nice little dog near our house I should like to show you! A little bright-eyed terrier, you know, with oh, such long curly brown hair! And it'll fetch things when you throw them, and it'll sit up and beg for its dinner, and all sorts of things—I can't remember half of them— and it belongs to a farmer, you know, and he says it's so useful, it's worth a hundred pounds! He says it kills all the rats and—oh dear!' cried Alice in a sorrowful tone, 'I'm afraid I've offended it again!' For the Mouse was swimming away from her as hard as it could go, and making quite a commotion in the pool as it went.

So she called softly after it, 'Mouse dear! Do come back again, and we won't talk about cats or dogs either, if you don't like them!' When the Mouse heard this, it turned round and swam slowly back to her: its face was quite pale (with passion, Alice thought), and it said in a low trembling voice, 'Let us get to the shore, and then I'll tell you my history, and you'll understand why it is I hate cats and dogs.'

It was high time to go, for the pool was getting quite crowded with the birds and animals that had fallen into it: there were a Duck and a Dodo, a Lory and an Eaglet, and several other curious creatures. Alice led the way, and the whole party swam to the shore.

Chapter 3 - A Caucus-Race and a Long Tale

They were indeed a queer-looking party that assembled on the bank—the birds with draggled feathers, the animals with their fur clinging close to them, and all dripping wet, cross, and uncomfortable.

The first question of course was, how to get dry again: they had a consultation about this, and after a few minutes it seemed quite natural to Alice to find herself talking familiarly with them, as if she had known them all her life. Indeed, she had quite a long argument with the Lory, who at last turned sulky, and would only say, 'I am older than you, and must know better'; and this Alice would not allow without knowing how old it was, and, as the Lory positively refused to tell its age, there was no more to be said.

At last the Mouse, who seemed to be a person of authority among them, called out, 'Sit down, all of you, and listen to me! I'LL soon make you dry enough!' They all sat down at once, in a large ring, with the Mouse in the middle. Alice kept her eyes anxiously fixed on it, for she felt sure she would catch a bad cold if she did not get dry very soon.

'Ahem!' said the Mouse with an important air, 'are you all ready? This is the driest thing I know. Silence all round, if you please! "William the Conqueror, whose cause was favoured by the pope, was soon submitted to by the English, who wanted leaders, and had been of late much accustomed to usurpation and conquest. Edwin and Morcar, the earls of Mercia and Northumbria—"'

'Ugh!' said the Lory, with a shiver.

'I beg your pardon!' said the Mouse, frowning, but very politely: 'Did you speak?'

'Not I!' said the Lory hastily.

'I thought you did,' said the Mouse. '—I proceed. "Edwin and Morcar, the earls of Mercia and Northumbria, declared for him: and even Stigand, the patriotic archbishop of Canterbury, found it advisable—"'

'Found WHAT?' said the Duck.

'Found IT,' the Mouse replied rather crossly: 'of course you know what "it" means.'

'I know what "it" means well enough, when I find a thing,' said the Duck: 'it's generally a frog or a worm. The question is, what did the archbishop find?'

The Mouse did not notice this question, but hurriedly went on, '"—found it advisable to go with Edgar Atheling to meet William and offer him the crown. William's conduct at first was moderate. But the insolence of his Normans—" How are you getting on now, my dear?' it continued, turning to Alice as it spoke.

'As wet as ever,' said Alice in a melancholy tone: 'it doesn't seem to dry me at all.'

'In that case,' said the Dodo solemnly, rising to its feet, 'I move that the meeting adjourn, for the immediate adoption of more energetic remedies—'

'Speak English!' said the Eaglet. 'I don't know the meaning of half those long words, and, what's more, I don't believe you do either!' And the Eaglet bent down its head to hide a smile: some of the other birds tittered audibly.

'What I was going to say,' said the Dodo in an offended tone, 'was, that the best thing to get us dry would be a Caucus-race.'

'What IS a Caucus-race?' said Alice; not that she wanted much to know, but the Dodo had paused as if it thought that SOMEBODY ought to speak, and no one else seemed inclined to say anything.

'Why,' said the Dodo, 'the best way to explain it is to do it.' (And, as you might like to try the thing yourself, some winter day, I will tell you how the Dodo managed it.)

First it marked out a race-course, in a sort of circle, ('the exact shape doesn't matter,' it said,) and then all the party were placed along the course, here and there. There was no 'One, two, three, and away,' but they began running when they liked, and left off when they liked, so that it was not easy to know when the race was over. However, when they had been running half an hour or so, and were quite dry again, the Dodo suddenly called out 'The race is over!' and they all crowded round it, panting, and asking, 'But who has won?'

This question the Dodo could not answer without a great deal of thought, and it sat for a long time with one finger pressed upon its forehead (the position in which you usually see Shakespeare, in the pictures of him), while the rest waited in silence. At last the Dodo said, 'EVERYBODY has won, and all must have prizes.'

'But who is to give the prizes?' quite a chorus of voices asked.

'Why, SHE, of course,' said the Dodo, pointing to Alice with one finger; and the whole party at once crowded round her, calling out in a confused way, 'Prizes! Prizes!'

Alice had no idea what to do, and in despair she put her hand in her pocket, and pulled out a box of comfits, (luckily the salt water had not got into it), and handed them round as prizes. There was exactly one a-piece all round.

'But she must have a prize herself, you know,' said the Mouse.

'Of course,' the Dodo replied very gravely. 'What else have you got in your pocket?' he went on, turning to Alice.

'Only a thimble,' said Alice sadly.

'Hand it over here,' said the Dodo.

Then they all crowded round her once more, while the Dodo solemnly presented the thimble, saying 'We beg your acceptance of this elegant thimble'; and, when it had finished this short speech, they all cheered.

Alice thought the whole thing very absurd, but they all looked so grave that she did not dare to laugh; and, as she could not think of anything to say, she simply bowed, and took the thimble, looking as solemn as she could.

The next thing was to eat the comfits: this caused some noise and confusion, as the large birds complained that they could not taste theirs, and the small ones choked and had to be patted on the back. However, it was over at last, and they sat down again in a ring, and begged the Mouse to tell them something more.

'You promised to tell me your history, you know,' said Alice, 'and why it is you hate—C and D,' she added in a whisper, half afraid that it would be offended again.

'Mine is a long and a sad tale!' said the Mouse, turning to Alice, and sighing.

'It IS a long tail, certainly,' said Alice, looking down with wonder at the Mouse's tail; 'but why do you call it sad?' And she kept on puzzling about it while the Mouse was speaking, so that her idea of the tale was something like this:—

'Fury said to a
mouse, That he
met in the
house,
"Let us
both go to
law: *I* will
prosecute
you. —Come,
I'll take no
denial; We
must have a
trial: For
really this
morning I've
nothing
to do."
Said the
mouse to the
cur, "Such
a trial,
dear Sir,
With
no jury
or judge,
would be
wasting
our
breath."
"I'll be
judge, I'll
be jury,"
Said
cunning
old Fury:
"I'll
try the
whole
cause,
and
condemn
you
to
death."'

'You are not attending!' said the Mouse to Alice severely. 'What are you thinking of?'

'I beg your pardon,' said Alice very humbly: 'you had got to the fifth bend, I think?'

'I had NOT!' cried the Mouse, sharply and very angrily.

'A knot!' said Alice, always ready to make herself useful, and looking anxiously about her. 'Oh, do let me help to undo it!'

'I shall do nothing of the sort,' said the Mouse, getting up and walking away. 'You insult me by talking such nonsense!'

'I didn't mean it!' pleaded poor Alice. 'But you're so easily offended, you know!'

The Mouse only growled in reply.

'Please come back and finish your story!' Alice called after it; and the others all joined in chorus, 'Yes, please do!' but the Mouse only shook its head impatiently, and walked a little quicker.

'What a pity it wouldn't stay!' sighed the Lory, as soon as it was quite out of sight; and an old Crab took the opportunity of saying to her daughter 'Ah, my dear! Let this be a lesson to you never to lose YOUR temper!' 'Hold your tongue, Ma!' said the young Crab, a little snappishly. 'You're enough to try the patience of an oyster!'

'I wish I had our Dinah here, I know I do!' said Alice aloud, addressing nobody in particular. 'She'd soon fetch it back!'

'And who is Dinah, if I might venture to ask the question?' said the Lory.

Alice replied eagerly, for she was always ready to talk about her pet: 'Dinah 's our cat. And she's such a capital one for catching mice you can't think! And oh, I wish you could see her after the birds! Why, she'll eat a little bird as soon as look at it!'

This speech caused a remarkable sensation among the party. Some of the birds hurried off at once: one the old Magpie began wrapping itself up very carefully, remarking, 'I really must be getting home; the night-air doesn't suit my throat!' and a Canary called out in a trembling voice to its children, 'Come away, my dears! It's high time you were all in bed!' On various pretexts they all moved off, and Alice was soon left alone.

'I wish I hadn't mentioned Dinah!' she said to herself in a melancholy tone. 'Nobody seems to like her, down here, and I'm sure she's the best cat in the world! Oh, my dear Dinah! I wonder if I shall ever see you any more!' And here poor Alice began to cry again, for she felt very lonely and low-spirited. In a little while, however, she again heard a little pattering of footsteps in the distance, and she looked up eagerly, half hoping that the Mouse had changed his mind, and was coming back to finish his story.

Chapter 4 - The Rabbit Sends in a Little Bill

It was the White Rabbit, trotting slowly back again, and looking anxiously about as it went, as if it had lost something; and she heard it muttering to itself 'The Duchess! The Duchess! Oh my dear paws! Oh my fur and whiskers! She'll get me executed, as sure as ferrets are ferrets! Where CAN I have dropped them, I wonder?' Alice guessed in a moment that it was looking for the fan and the pair of white kid gloves, and she very good-naturedly began hunting about for them, but they were nowhere to be seen—everything seemed to have changed since her swim in the pool, and the great hall, with the glass table and the little door, had vanished completely.

Very soon the Rabbit noticed Alice, as she went hunting about, and called out to her in an angry tone, 'Why, Mary Ann, what ARE you doing out here? Run home this moment, and fetch me a pair of gloves and a fan! Quick, now!' And Alice was so much frightened that she ran off at once in the direction it pointed to, without trying to explain the mistake it had made.

'He took me for his housemaid,' she said to herself as she ran. 'How surprised he'll be when he finds out who I am! But I'd better take him his fan and gloves—that is, if I can find them.' As she said this, she came upon a neat little house, on the door of which was a bright brass plate with the name 'W. RABBIT' engraved upon it. She went in without knocking, and hurried upstairs, in great fear lest she should meet the real Mary Ann, and be turned out of the house before she had found the fan and gloves.

'How queer it seems,' Alice said to herself, 'to be going messages for a rabbit! I suppose Dinah'll be sending me on messages next!' And she began fancying the sort of thing that would happen: '"Miss Alice! Come here directly, and get ready for your walk!" "Coming in a minute, nurse! But I've got to see that the mouse doesn't get out." Only I don't think,' Alice went on, 'that they' d let Dinah stop in the house if it began ordering people about like that!'

By this time she had found her way into a tidy little room with a table in the window, and on it (as she had hoped) a fan and two or three pairs of tiny white kid gloves: she took up the fan and a pair of the gloves, and was just going to leave the room, when her eye fell upon a little bottle that stood near the looking-glass. There was no label this time with the words 'DRINK ME,' but nevertheless she uncorked it and put it to her lips. 'I know SOMETHING interesting is sure to happen,' she said to herself, 'whenever I eat or drink anything; so I'll just see what this bottle does. I do hope it'll make me grow large again, for really I'm quite tired of being such a tiny little thing!'

It did so indeed, and much sooner than she had expected: before she had drunk half the bottle, she found her head pressing against the ceiling, and had to stoop to save her neck from being broken. She hastily put down the bottle, saying to herself 'That's quite enough—I hope I shan't grow any more—As it is, I can't get out at the door—I do wish I hadn't drunk quite so much!'

Alas! it was too late to wish that! She went on growing, and growing, and very soon had to kneel down on the floor: in another minute there was not even room for this, and she tried the effect of lying down with one elbow against the door, and the other arm curled round her head. Still she went on growing, and, as a last resource, she put one arm out of the window, and one foot up the chimney, and said to herself 'Now I can do no more, whatever happens. What WILL become of me?'

Luckily for Alice, the little magic bottle had now had its full effect, and she grew no larger: still it was very uncomfortable, and, as there seemed to be no sort of chance of her ever getting out of the room again, no wonder she felt unhappy.

'It was much pleasanter at home,' thought poor Alice, 'when one wasn't always growing larger and smaller, and being ordered about by mice and rabbits. I almost wish I hadn't gone down that rabbit-hole—and yet—and yet—it's rather curious, you know, this sort of life! I do wonder what CAN have happened to me! When I used to read fairy-tales, I fancied that kind of thing never happened, and now here I am in the middle of one! There ought to be a book written about me, that there ought! And when I grow up, I'll write one—but I'm grown up now,' she added in a sorrowful tone; 'at least there's no room to grow up any more HERE.'

'But then,' thought Alice, 'shall I NEVER get any older than I am now? That'll be a comfort, one way—never to be an old woman—but then—always to have lessons to learn! Oh, I shouldn't like THAT!'

'Oh, you foolish Alice!' she answered herself. 'How can you learn lessons in here? Why, there's hardly room for YOU, and no room at all for any lesson-books!'

And so she went on, taking first one side and then the other, and making quite a conversation of it altogether; but after a few minutes she heard a voice outside, and stopped to listen.

'Mary Ann! Mary Ann!' said the voice. 'Fetch me my gloves this moment!' Then came a little pattering of feet on the stairs. Alice knew it was the Rabbit coming to look for her, and she trembled till she shook the house, quite forgetting that she was now about a thousand times as large as the Rabbit, and had no reason to be afraid of it.

Presently the Rabbit came up to the door, and tried to open it; but, as the door opened inwards, and Alice's elbow was pressed hard against it, that attempt proved a failure. Alice heard it say to itself 'Then I'll go round and get in at the window.'

'THAT you won't' thought Alice, and, after waiting till she fancied she heard the Rabbit just under the window, she suddenly spread out her hand, and made a snatch in the air. She did not get hold of anything, but she heard a little shriek and a fall, and a crash of broken glass, from which she concluded that it was just possible it had fallen into a cucumber-frame, or something of the sort.

Next came an angry voice—the Rabbit's—'Pat! Pat! Where are you?' And then a voice she had never heard before, 'Sure then I'm here! Digging for apples, yer honour!'

'Digging for apples, indeed!' said the Rabbit angrily. 'Here! Come and help me out of THIS!' (Sounds of more broken glass.)

'Now tell me, Pat, what's that in the window?'

'Sure, it's an arm, yer honour!' (He pronounced it 'arrum.')

'An arm, you goose! Who ever saw one that size? Why, it fills the whole window!'

'Sure, it does, yer honour: but it's an arm for all that.'

'Well, it's got no business there, at any rate: go and take it away!'

There was a long silence after this, and Alice could only hear whispers now and then; such as, 'Sure, I don't like it, yer honour, at all, at all!' 'Do as I tell you, you coward!' and at last she spread out her hand again, and made another snatch in the air. This time there were TWO little shrieks, and more sounds of broken glass. 'What a number of cucumber-frames there must be!' thought Alice. 'I wonder what they'll do next! As for pulling me out of the window, I only wish they COULD! I'm sure I don't want to stay in here any longer!'

She waited for some time without hearing anything more: at last came a rumbling of little cartwheels, and the sound of a good many voice all talking together: she made out the words: 'Where's the other ladder?—Why, I hadn't to bring but one; Bill's got the other—Bill! fetch it here, lad!—Here, put 'em up at this corner—No, tie 'em together first—they don't reach half high enough yet—Oh! they'll do well enough; don't be particular—Here, Bill! catch hold of this rope—Will the roof bear?—Mind that loose slate—Oh, it's coming down! Heads below!' (a loud crash)—'Now, who did that?—It was Bill, I fancy—Who's to go down the chimney?—Nay, I shan't! YOU do it!—That I won't, then!—Bill's to go down—Here, Bill! the master says you're to go down the chimney!'

'Oh! So Bill's got to come down the chimney, has he?' said Alice to herself. 'Shy, they seem to put everything upon Bill! I wouldn't be in Bill's place for a good deal: this fireplace is narrow, to be sure; but I THINK I can kick a little!'

She drew her foot as far down the chimney as she could, and waited till she heard a little animal (she couldn't guess of what sort it was) scratching and scrambling about in the chimney close above her: then, saying to herself 'This is Bill,' she gave one sharp kick, and waited to see what would happen next.

The first thing she heard was a general chorus of 'There goes Bill!' then the Rabbit's voice along—'Catch him, you by the hedge!' then silence, and then another confusion of voices—'Hold up his head—Brandy now—Don't choke him—How was it, old fellow? What happened to you? Tell us all about it!'

Last came a little feeble, squeaking voice, ('That's Bill,' thought Alice,) 'Well, I hardly know—No more, thank ye; I'm better now—but I'm a deal too flustered to tell you—all I know is, something comes at me like a Jack-in-the-box, and up I goes like a sky-rocket!'

'So you did, old fellow!' said the others.

'We must burn the house down!' said the Rabbit's voice; and Alice called out as loud as she could, 'If you do. I'll set Dinah at you!'

There was a dead silence instantly, and Alice thought to herself, 'I wonder what they WILL do next! If they had any sense, they'd take the roof off.' After a minute or two, they began moving about again, and Alice heard the Rabbit say, 'A barrowful will do, to begin with.'

'A barrowful of WHAT?' thought Alice; but she had not long to doubt, for the next moment a shower of little pebbles came rattling in at the window, and some of them hit her in the face. 'I'll put a stop to this,' she said to herself, and shouted out, 'You'd better not do that again!' which produced another dead silence.

Alice noticed with some surprise that the pebbles were all turning into little cakes as they lay on the floor, and a bright idea came into her head. 'If I eat one of these cakes,' she thought, 'it's sure to make SOME change in my size; and as it can't possibly make me larger, it must make me smaller, I suppose.'

So she swallowed one of the cakes, and was delighted to find that she began shrinking directly. As soon as she was small enough to get through the door, she ran out of the house, and found quite a crowd of little animals and birds waiting outside. The poor little Lizard, Bill, was in the middle, being held up by two guinea-pigs, who were giving it something out of a bottle. They all made a rush at Alice the moment she appeared; but she ran off as hard as she could, and soon found herself safe in a thick wood.

'The first thing I've got to do,' said Alice to herself, as she wandered about in the wood, 'is to grow to my right size again; and the second thing is to find my way into that lovely garden. I think that will be the best plan.'

It sounded an excellent plan, no doubt, and very neatly and simply arranged; the only difficulty was, that she had not the smallest idea how to set about it; and while she was peering about anxiously among the trees, a little sharp bark just over her head made her look up in a great hurry.

An enormous puppy was looking down at her with large round eyes, and feebly stretching out one paw, trying to touch her. 'Poor little thing!' said Alice, in a coaxing tone, and she tried hard to whistle to it; but she was terribly frightened all the time at the thought that it might be hungry, in which case it would be very likely to eat her up in spite of all her coaxing.

Hardly knowing what she did, she picked up a little bit of stick, and held it out to the puppy; whereupon the puppy jumped into the air off all its feet at once, with a yelp of delight, and rushed at the stick, and made believe to worry it; then Alice dodged behind a great thistle, to keep herself from being run over; and the moment she appeared on the other side, the puppy made another rush at the stick, and tumbled head over heels in its hurry to get hold of it; then Alice, thinking it was very like having a game of play with a cart-horse, and expecting every moment to be trampled under its feet, ran round the thistle again; then the puppy began a series of short charges at the stick, running a very little way forwards each time and a long way back, and barking hoarsely all the while, till at last it sat down a good way off, panting, with its tongue hanging out of its mouth, and its great eyes half shut.

This seemed to Alice a good opportunity for making her escape; so she set off at once, and ran till she was quite tired and out of breath, and till the puppy' s bark sounded quite faint in the distance.

'And yet what a dear little puppy it was!' said Alice, as she leant against a buttercup to rest herself, and fanned herself with one of the leaves: 'I should have liked teaching it tricks very much, if—if I'd only been the right size to do it! Oh dear! I'd nearly forgotten that I've got to grow up again! Let me see—how IS it to be managed? I suppose I ought to eat or drink something or other; but the great question is, what?'

The great question certainly was, what? Alice looked all round her at the flowers and the blades of grass, but she did not see anything that looked like the right thing to eat or drink under the circumstances. There was a large mushroom growing near her, about the same height as herself; and when she had looked under it, and on both sides of it, and behind it, it occurred to her that she might as well look and see what was on the top of it.

She stretched herself up on tiptoe, and peeped over the edge of the mushroom, and her eyes immediately met those of a large caterpillar, that was sitting on the top with its arms folded, quietly smoking a long hookah, and taking not the smallest notice of her or of anything else.

Chapter 5 - Advice from a Caterpillar

The Caterpillar and Alice looked at each other for some time in silence: at last the Caterpillar took the hookah out of its mouth, and addressed her in a languid, sleepy voice.

'Who are YOU?' said the Caterpillar.

This was not an encouraging opening for a conversation. Alice replied, rather shyly, 'I—I hardly know, sir, just at present—at least I know who I WAS when I got up this morning, but I think I must have been changed several times since then.'

'What do you mean by that?' said the Caterpillar sternly. 'Explain yourself!'

'I can't explain MYSELF, I'm afraid, sir' said Alice, 'because I'm not myself, you see.'

'I don't see,' said the Caterpillar.

'I'm afraid I can't put it more clearly,' Alice replied very politely, 'for I can't understand it myself to begin with; and being so many different sizes in a day is very confusing.'

'It isn't,' said the Caterpillar.

'Well, perhaps you haven't found it so yet,' said Alice; 'but when you have to turn into a chrysalis—you will some day, you know—and then after that into a butterfly, I should think you'll feel it a little queer, won't you?'

'Not a bit,' said the Caterpillar.

'Well, perhaps your feelings may be different,' said Alice; 'all I know is, it would feel very queer to ME.'

'You!' said the Caterpillar contemptuously. 'Who are YOU?'

Which brought them back again to the beginning of the conversation. Alice felt a little irritated at the Caterpillar's making such VERY short remarks, and she drew herself up and said, very gravely, 'I think, you ought to tell me who YOU are, first.'

'Why?' said the Caterpillar.

Here was another puzzling question; and as Alice could not think of any good reason, and as the Caterpillar seemed to be in a VERY unpleasant state of mind, she turned away.

'Come back!' the Caterpillar called after her. 'I've something important to say!'

This sounded promising, certainly: Alice turned and came back again.

'Keep your temper,' said the Caterpillar.

'Is that all?' said Alice, swallowing down her anger as well as she could.

'No,' said the Caterpillar.

Alice thought she might as well wait, as she had nothing else to do, and perhaps after all it might tell her something worth hearing. For some minutes it puffed away without speaking, but at last it unfolded its arms, took the hookah out of its mouth again, and said, 'So you think you're changed, do you?'

'I'm afraid I am, sir,' said Alice; 'I can't remember things as I used—and I don't keep the same size for ten minutes together!'

'Can't remember WHAT things?' said the Caterpillar.

'Well, I've tried to say "HOW DOTH THE LITTLE BUSY BEE," but it all came different!' Alice replied in a very melancholy voice.

'Repeat, "YOU ARE OLD, FATHER WILLIAM,"' said the Caterpillar.

Alice folded her hands, and began:—

'You are old, Father William,' the young man said,
'And your hair has become very white;
And yet you incessantly stand on your head—
Do you think, at your age, it is right?'

'In my youth,' Father William replied to his son,
'I feared it might injure the brain;
But, now that I'm perfectly sure I have none,
Why, I do it again and again.'

'You are old,' said the youth, 'as I mentioned before,
And have grown most uncommonly fat;
Yet you turned a back-somersault in at the door—
Pray, what is the reason of that?'

'In my youth,' said the sage, as he shook his grey locks,
'I kept all my limbs very supple;
By the use of this ointment—one shilling the box—
Allow me to sell you a couple?'

'You are old,' said the youth, 'and your jaws are too weak
For anything tougher than suet;
Yet you finished the goose, with the bones and the beak—
Pray how did you manage to do it?'

'In my youth,' said his father, 'I took to the law,
And argued each case with my wife;
And the muscular strength, which it gave to my jaw,
Has lasted the rest of my life.'

'You are old,' said the youth, 'one would hardly suppose
That your eye was as steady as ever;
Yet you balanced an eel on the end of your nose—
What made you so awfully clever?'

'I have answered three questions, and that is enough,'
Said his father; 'don't give yourself airs!
Do you think I can listen all day to such stuff?
Be off, or I'll kick you down stairs!'

'That is not said right,' said the Caterpillar.

'Not QUITE right, I'm afraid,' said Alice, timidly; 'some of the words have got altered.'

'It is wrong from beginning to end,' said the Caterpillar decidedly, and there was silence for some minutes.

The Caterpillar was the first to speak.

'What size do you want to be?' it asked.

'Oh, I'm not particular as to size,' Alice hastily replied; 'only one doesn't like changing so often, you know.'

'I DON'T know,' said the Caterpillar.

Alice said nothing: she had never been so much contradicted in her life before, and she felt that she was losing her temper.

'Are you content now?' said the Caterpillar.

'Well, I should like to be a LITTLE larger, sir, if you wouldn't mind,' said Alice: 'three inches is such a wretched height to be.'

'It is a very good height indeed!' said the Caterpillar angrily, rearing itself upright as it spoke (it was exactly three inches high).

'But I'm not used to it!' pleaded poor Alice in a piteous tone. And she thought of herself, 'I wish the creatures wouldn't be so easily offended!'

'You'll get used to it in time,' said the Caterpillar; and it put the hookah into its mouth and began smoking again.

This time Alice waited patiently until it chose to speak again. In a minute or two the Caterpillar took the hookah out of its mouth and yawned once or twice, and shook itself. Then it got down off the mushroom, and crawled away in the grass, merely remarking as it went, 'One side will make you grow taller, and the other side will make you grow shorter.'

'One side of WHAT? The other side of WHAT?' thought Alice to herself.

'Of the mushroom,' said the Caterpillar, just as if she had asked it aloud; and in another moment it was out of sight.

Alice remained looking thoughtfully at the mushroom for a minute, trying to make out which were the two sides of it; and as it was perfectly round, she found this a very difficult question. However, at last she stretched her arms round it as far as they would go, and broke off a bit of the edge with each hand.

'And now which is which?' she said to herself, and nibbled a little of the right-hand bit to try the effect: the next moment she felt a violent blow underneath her chin: it had struck her foot!

She was a good deal frightened by this very sudden change, but she felt that there was no time to be lost, as she was shrinking rapidly; so she set to work at once to eat some of the other bit. Her chin was pressed so closely against her foot, that there was hardly room to open her mouth; but she did it at last, and managed to swallow a morsel of the lefthand bit.

* * * * * *

'Come, my head's free at last!' said Alice in a tone of delight, which changed into alarm in another moment, when she found that her shoulders were nowhere to be found: all she could see, when she looked down, was an immense length of neck, which seemed to rise like a stalk out of a sea of green leaves that lay far below her.

'What CAN all that green stuff be?' said Alice. 'And where HAVE my shoulders got to? And oh, my poor hands, how is it I can't see you?' She was moving them about as she spoke, but no result seemed to follow, except a little shaking among the distant green leaves.

As there seemed to be no chance of getting her hands up to her head, she tried to get her head down to them, and was delighted to find that her neck would bend about easily in any direction, like a serpent. She had just succeeded in curving it down into a graceful zigzag, and was going to dive in among the leaves, which she found to be nothing but the tops of the trees under which she had been wandering, when a sharp hiss made her draw back in a hurry: a large pigeon had flown into her face, and was beating her violently with its wings.

'Serpent!' screamed the Pigeon.

'I'm NOT a serpent!' said Alice indignantly. 'Let me alone!'

'Serpent, I say again!' repeated the Pigeon, but in a more subdued tone, and added with a kind of sob, 'I've tried every way, and nothing seems to suit them!'

'I haven't the least idea what you're talking about,' said Alice.

'I've tried the roots of trees, and I've tried banks, and I've tried hedges,' the Pigeon went on, without attending to her; 'but those serpents! There's no pleasing them!'

Alice was more and more puzzled, but she thought there was no use in saying anything more till the Pigeon had finished.

'As if it wasn't trouble enough hatching the eggs,' said the Pigeon; 'but I must be on the look-out for serpents night and day! Why, I haven't had a wink of sleep these three weeks!'

'I'm very sorry you've been annoyed,' said Alice, who was beginning to see its meaning.

'And just as I'd taken the highest tree in the wood,' continued the Pigeon, raising its voice to a shriek, 'and just as I was thinking I should be free of them at last, they must needs come wriggling down from the sky! Ugh, Serpent!'

'But I'm NOT a serpent, I tell you!' said Alice. 'I'm a—I'm a—'

'Well! WHAT are you?' said the Pigeon. 'I can see you're trying to invent something!'

'I—I'm a little girl,' said Alice, rather doubtfully, as she remembered the number of changes she had gone through that day.

'A likely story indeed!' said the Pigeon in a tone of the deepest contempt. 'I've seen a good many little girls in my time, but never ONE with such a neck as that! No, no! You're a serpent; and there's no use denying it. I suppose you'll be telling me next that you never tasted an egg!'

'I HAVE tasted eggs, certainly,' said Alice, who was a very truthful child; 'but little girls eat eggs quite as much as serpents do, you know.'

'I don't believe it,' said the Pigeon; 'but if they do, why then they're a kind of serpent, that's all I can say.'

This was such a new idea to Alice, that she was quite silent for a minute or two, which gave the Pigeon the opportunity of adding, 'You're looking for eggs, I know THAT well enough; and what does it matter to me whether you're a little girl or a serpent?'

'It matters a good deal to ME,' said Alice hastily; 'but I'm not looking for eggs, as it happens; and if I was, I shouldn't want YOURS: I don't like them raw.'

'Well, be off, then!' said the Pigeon in a sulky tone, as it settled down again into its nest. Alice crouched down among the trees as well as she could, for her neck kept getting entangled among the branches, and every now and then she had to stop and untwist it. After a while she remembered that she still held the pieces of mushroom in her hands, and she set to work very carefully, nibbling first at one and then at the other, and growing sometimes taller and sometimes shorter, until she had succeeded in bringing herself down to her usual height.

It was so long since she had been anything near the right size, that it felt quite strange at first; but she got used to it in a few minutes, and began talking to herself, as usual. 'Come, there's half my plan done now! How puzzling all these changes are! I'm never sure what I'm going to be, from one minute to another! However, I've got back to my right size: the next thing is, to get into that beautiful garden—how IS that to be done, I wonder?' As she said this, she came suddenly upon an open place, with a little house in it about four feet high. 'Whoever lives there,' thought Alice, 'it'll never do to come upon them THIS size: why, I should frighten them out of their wits!' So she began nibbling at the righthand bit again, and did not venture to go near the house till she had brought herself down to nine inches high.

Chapter 6 - Pig and Pepper

For a minute or two she stood looking at the house, and wondering what to do next, when suddenly a footman in livery came running out of the wood—(she considered him to be a footman because he was in livery: otherwise, judging by his face only, she would have called him a fish)—and rapped loudly at the door with his knuckles. It was opened by another footman in livery, with a round face, and large eyes like a frog; and both footmen, Alice noticed, had powdered hair that curled all over their heads. She felt very curious to know what it was all about, and crept a little way out of the wood to listen.

The Fish-Footman began by producing from under his arm a great letter, nearly as large as himself, and this he handed over to the other, saying, in a solemn tone, 'For the Duchess. An invitation from the Queen to play croquet.' The Frog-Footman repeated, in the same solemn tone, only changing the order of the words a little, 'From the Queen. An invitation for the Duchess to play croquet.'

Then they both bowed low, and their curls got entangled together.

Alice laughed so much at this, that she had to run back into the wood for fear of their hearing her; and when she next peeped out the Fish-Footman was gone, and the other was sitting on the ground near the door, staring stupidly up into the sky.

Alice went timidly up to the door, and knocked.

'There's no sort of use in knocking,' said the Footman, 'and that for two reasons. First, because I'm on the same side of the door as you are; secondly, because they're making such a noise inside, no one could possibly hear you.' And certainly there was a most extraordinary noise going on within—a constant howling and sneezing, and every now and then a great crash, as if a dish or kettle had been broken to pieces.

'Please, then,' said Alice, 'how am I to get in?'

'There might be some sense in your knocking,' the Footman went on without attending to her, 'if we had the door between us. For instance, if you were INSIDE, you might knock, and I could let you out, you know.' He was looking up into the sky all the time he was speaking, and this Alice thought decidedly uncivil. 'But perhaps he can't help it,' she said to herself; 'his eyes are so VERY nearly at the top of his head. But at any rate he might answer questions.—How am I to get in?' she repeated, aloud.

'I shall sit here,' the Footman remarked, 'till tomorrow—'

At this moment the door of the house opened, and a large plate came skimming out, straight at the Footman's head: it just grazed his nose, and broke to pieces against one of the trees behind him.

'—or next day, maybe,' the Footman continued in the same tone, exactly as if nothing had happened.

'How am I to get in?' asked Alice again, in a louder tone.

'ARE you to get in at all?' said the Footman. 'That's the first question, you know.'

It was, no doubt: only Alice did not like to be told so. 'It's really dreadful,' she muttered to herself, 'the way all the creatures argue. It's enough to drive one crazy!'

The Footman seemed to think this a good opportunity for repeating his remark, with variations. 'I shall sit here,' he said, 'on and off, for days and days.'

'But what am I to do?' said Alice.

'Anything you like,' said the Footman, and began whistling.

'Oh, there's no use in talking to him,' said Alice desperately: 'he's perfectly idiotic!' And she opened the door and went in.

The door led right into a large kitchen, which was full of smoke from one end to the other: the Duchess was sitting on a three-legged stool in the middle, nursing a baby; the cook was leaning over the fire, stirring a large cauldron which seemed to be full of soup.

'There's certainly too much pepper in that soup!' Alice said to herself, as well as she could for sneezing.

There was certainly too much of it in the air. Even the Duchess sneezed occasionally; and as for the baby, it was sneezing and howling alternately without a moment's pause. The only things in the kitchen that did not sneeze, were the cook, and a large cat which was sitting on the hearth and grinning from ear to ear.

'Please would you tell me,' said Alice, a little timidly, for she was not quite sure whether it was good manners for her to speak first, 'why your cat grins like that?'

'It's a Cheshire cat,' said the Duchess, 'and that's why. Pig!'

She said the last word with such sudden violence that Alice quite jumped; but she saw in another moment that it was addressed to the baby, and not to her, so she took courage, and went on again:—

'I didn't know that Cheshire cats always grinned; in fact, I didn't know that cats COULD grin.'

'They all can,' said the Duchess; 'and most of 'em do.'

'I don't know of any that do,' Alice said very politely, feeling quite pleased to have got into a conversation.

'You don't know much,' said the Duchess; 'and that's a fact.'

Alice did not at all like the tone of this remark, and thought it would be as well to introduce some other subject of conversation. While she was trying to fix on one, the cook took the cauldron of soup off the fire, and at once set to work throwing everything within her reach at the Duchess and the baby—the fire-irons came first; then followed a shower of saucepans, plates, and dishes. The Duchess took no notice of them even when they hit her; and the baby was howling so much already, that it was quite impossible to say whether the blows hurt it or not.

'Oh, PLEASE mind what you're doing!' cried Alice, jumping up and down in an agony of terror. 'Oh, there goes his PRECIOUS nose'; as an unusually large saucepan flew close by it, and very nearly carried it off.

'If everybody minded their own business,' the Duchess said in a hoarse growl, 'the world would go round a deal faster than it does.'

'Which would NOT be an advantage,' said Alice, who felt very glad to get an opportunity of showing off a little of her knowledge. 'Just think of what work it would make with the day and night! You see the earth takes twenty-four hours to turn round on its axis—'

'Talking of axes,' said the Duchess, 'chop off her head!'

Alice glanced rather anxiously at the cook, to see if she meant to take the hint; but the cook was busily stirring the soup, and seemed not to be listening, so she went on again: 'Twenty-four hours, I THINK; or is it twelve? I—'

'Oh, don't bother ME,' said the Duchess; 'I never could abide figures!' And with that she began nursing her child again, singing a sort of lullaby to it as she did so, and giving it a violent shake at the end of every line:

'Speak roughly to your little boy,
And beat him when he sneezes:
He only does it to annoy,
Because he knows it teases.'
CHORUS.
(In which the cook and the baby joined):—
'Wow! wow! wow!'

While the Duchess sang the second verse of the song, she kept tossing the baby violently up and down, and the poor little thing howled so, that Alice could hardly hear the words:—

'I speak severely to my boy,
I beat him when he sneezes;
For he can thoroughly enjoy
The pepper when he pleases!'
CHORUS.
'Wow! wow! wow!'

'Here! you may nurse it a bit, if you like!' the Duchess said to Alice, flinging the baby at her as she spoke. 'I must go and get ready to play croquet with the Queen,' and she hurried out of the room. The cook threw a frying-pan after her as she went out, but it just missed her.

Alice caught the baby with some difficulty, as it was a queer-shaped little creature, and held out its arms and legs in all directions, 'just like a star-fish,' thought Alice. The poor little thing was snorting like a steam-engine when she caught it, and kept doubling itself up and straightening itself out again, so that altogether, for the first minute or two, it was as much as she could do to hold it.

As soon as she had made out the proper way of nursing it, (which was to twist it up into a sort of knot, and then keep tight hold of its right ear and left foot, so as to prevent its undoing itself,) she carried it out into the open air. 'IF I don't take this child away with me,' thought Alice, 'they're sure to kill it in a day or two: wouldn't it be murder to leave it behind?' She said the last words out loud, and the little thing grunted in reply (it had left off sneezing by this time). 'Don't grunt,' said Alice; 'that's not at all a proper way of expressing yourself.'

The baby grunted again, and Alice looked very anxiously into its face to see what was the matter with it. There could be no doubt that it had a VERY turn-up nose, much more like a snout than a real nose; also its eyes were getting extremely small for a baby: altogether Alice did not like the look of the thing at all. 'But perhaps it was only sobbing,' she thought, and looked into its eyes again, to see if there were any tears.

No, there were no tears. 'If you're going to turn into a pig, my dear,' said Alice, seriously, 'I'll have nothing more to do with you. Mind now!' The poor little thing sobbed again (or grunted, it was impossible to say which), and they went on for some while in silence.

Alice was just beginning to think to herself, 'Now, what am I to do with this creature when I get it home?' when it grunted again, so violently, that she looked down into its face in some alarm. This time there could be NO mistake about it: it was neither more nor less than a pig, and she felt that it would be quite absurd for her to carry it further.

So she set the little creature down, and felt quite relieved to see it trot away quietly into the wood. 'If it had grown up,' she said to herself, 'it would have made a dreadfully ugly child: but it makes rather a handsome pig, I think.' And she began thinking over other children she knew, who might do very well as pigs, and was just saying to herself, 'if one only knew the right way to change them—' when she was a little startled by seeing the Cheshire Cat sitting on a bough of a tree a few yards off.

The Cat only grinned when it saw Alice. It looked good-natured, she thought: still it had VERY long claws and a great many teeth, so she felt that it ought to be treated with respect.

'Cheshire Puss,' she began, rather timidly, as she did not at all know whether it would like the name: however, it only grinned a little wider. 'Come, it's pleased so far,' thought Alice, and she went on. 'Would you tell me, please, which way I ought to go from here?'

'That depends a good deal on where you want to get to,' said the Cat.

'I don't much care where—' said Alice.

'Then it doesn't matter which way you go,' said the Cat.

'—so long as I get SOMEWHERE,' Alice added as an explanation.

'Oh, you're sure to do that,' said the Cat, 'if you only walk long enough.'

Alice felt that this could not be denied, so she tried another question. 'What sort of people live about here?'

'In THAT direction,' the Cat said, waving its right paw round, 'lives a Hatter: and in THAT direction,' waving the other paw, 'lives a March Hare. Visit either you like: they're both mad.'

'But I don't want to go among mad people,' Alice remarked.

'Oh, you can't help that,' said the Cat: 'we're all mad here. I'm mad. You're mad.'

'How do you know I'm mad?' said Alice.

'You must be,' said the Cat, 'or you wouldn't have come here.'

Alice didn't think that proved it at all; however, she went on 'And how do you know that you're mad?'

'To begin with,' said the Cat, 'a dog's not mad. You grant that?'

'I suppose so,' said Alice.

'Well, then,' the Cat went on, 'you see, a dog growls when it's angry, and wags its tail when it's pleased. Now I growl when I'm pleased, and wag my tail when I'm angry. Therefore I'm mad.'

'I call it purring, not growling,' said Alice.

'Call it what you like,' said the Cat. 'Do you play croquet with the Queen to-day?'

'I should like it very much,' said Alice, 'but I haven't been invited yet.'

'You'll see me there,' said the Cat, and vanished.

Alice was not much surprised at this, she was getting so used to queer things happening. While she was looking at the place where it had been, it suddenly appeared again.

'By-the-bye, what became of the baby?' said the Cat. 'I'd nearly forgotten to ask.'

'It turned into a pig,' Alice quietly said, just as if it had come back in a natural way.

'I thought it would,' said the Cat, and vanished again.

Alice waited a little, half expecting to see it again, but it did not appear, and after a minute or two she walked on in the direction in which the March Hare was said to live. 'I've seen hatters before,' she said to herself; 'the March Hare will be much the most interesting, and perhaps as this is May it won't be raving mad—at least not so mad as it was in March.' As she said this, she looked up, and there was the Cat again, sitting on a branch of a tree.

'Did you say pig, or fig?' said the Cat.

'I said pig,' replied Alice; 'and I wish you wouldn't keep appearing and vanishing so suddenly: you make one quite giddy.'

'All right,' said the Cat; and this time it vanished quite slowly, beginning with the end of the tail, and ending with the grin, which remained some time after the rest of it had gone.

'Well! I've often seen a cat without a grin,' thought Alice; 'but a grin without a cat! It's the most curious thing I ever say in my life!'

She had not gone much farther before she came in sight of the house of the March Hare: she thought it must be the right house, because the chimneys were shaped like ears and the roof was thatched with fur. It was so large a house, that she did not like to go nearer till she had nibbled some more of the lefthand bit of mushroom, and raised herself to about two feet high: even then she walked up towards it rather timidly, saying to herself 'Suppose it should be raving mad after all! I almost wish I'd gone to see the Hatter instead!'

Chapter 7 - A Mad Tea-Party

There was a table set out under a tree in front of the house, and the March Hare and the Hatter were having tea at it: a Dormouse was sitting between them, fast asleep, and the other two were using it as a cushion, resting their elbows on it, and the talking over its head. 'Very uncomfortable for the Dormouse,' thought Alice; 'only, as it's asleep, I suppose it doesn't mind.'

The table was a large one, but the three were all crowded together at one corner of it: 'No room! No room!' they cried out when they saw Alice coming. 'There's PLENTY of room!' said Alice indignantly, and she sat down in a large arm-chair at one end of the table.

'Have some wine,' the March Hare said in an encouraging tone.

Alice looked all round the table, but there was nothing on it but tea. 'I don't see any wine,' she remarked.

'There isn't any,' said the March Hare.

'Then it wasn't very civil of you to offer it,' said Alice angrily.

'It wasn't very civil of you to sit down without being invited,' said the March Hare.

'I didn't know it was YOUR table,' said Alice; 'it's laid for a great many more than three.'

'Your hair wants cutting,' said the Hatter. He had been looking at Alice for some time with great curiosity, and this was his first speech.

'You should learn not to make personal remarks,' Alice said with some severity; 'it's very rude.'

The Hatter opened his eyes very wide on hearing this; but all he SAID was, 'Why is a raven like a writing-desk?'

'Come, we shall have some fun now!' thought Alice. 'I'm glad they've begun asking riddles.—I believe I can guess that,' she added aloud.

'Do you mean that you think you can find out the answer to it?' said the March Hare.

'Exactly so,' said Alice.

'Then you should say what you mean,' the March Hare went on.

'I do,' Alice hastily replied; 'at least—at least I mean what I say—that's the same thing, you know.'

'Not the same thing a bit!' said the Hatter. 'You might just as well say that "I see what I eat" is the same thing as "I eat what I see"!'

'You might just as well say,' added the March Hare, 'that "I like what I get" is the same thing as "I get what I like"!'

'You might just as well say,' added the Dormouse, who seemed to be talking in his sleep, 'that "I breathe when I sleep" is the same thing as "I sleep when I breathe"!'

‘It IS the same thing with you,’ said the Hatter, and here the conversation dropped, and the party sat silent for a minute, while Alice thought over all she could remember about ravens and writing-desks, which wasn’t much.

The Hatter was the first to break the silence. ‘What day of the month is it?’ he said, turning to Alice: he had taken his watch out of his pocket, and was looking at it uneasily, shaking it every now and then, and holding it to his ear.

Alice considered a little, and then said ‘The fourth.’

‘Two days wrong!’ sighed the Hatter. ‘I told you butter wouldn’t suit the works!’ he added looking angrily at the March Hare.

‘It was the BEST butter,’ the March Hare meekly replied.

‘Yes, but some crumbs must have got in as well,’ the Hatter grumbled: ‘you shouldn’t have put it in with the bread-knife.’

The March Hare took the watch and looked at it gloomily: then he dipped it into his cup of tea, and looked at it again: but he could think of nothing better to say than his first remark, ‘It was the BEST butter, you know.’

Alice had been looking over his shoulder with some curiosity. ‘What a funny watch!’ she remarked. ‘It tells the day of the month, and doesn’t tell what o’clock it is!’

‘Why should it?’ muttered the Hatter. ‘Does YOUR watch tell you what year it is?’

‘Of course not,’ Alice replied very readily: ‘but that’s because it stays the same year for such a long time together.’

‘Which is just the case with MINE,’ said the Hatter.

Alice felt dreadfully puzzled. The Hatter’s remark seemed to have no sort of meaning in it, and yet it was certainly English. ‘I don’t quite understand you,’ she said, as politely as she could.

‘The Dormouse is asleep again,’ said the Hatter, and he poured a little hot tea upon its nose.

The Dormouse shook its head impatiently, and said, without opening its eyes, ‘Of course, of course; just what I was going to remark myself.’

‘Have you guessed the riddle yet?’ the Hatter said, turning to Alice again.

‘No, I give it up,’ Alice replied: ‘what’s the answer?’

‘I haven’t the slightest idea,’ said the Hatter.

‘Nor I,’ said the March Hare.

Alice sighed wearily. ‘I think you might do something better with the time,’ she said, ‘than waste it in asking riddles that have no answers.’

‘If you knew Time as well as I do,’ said the Hatter, ‘you wouldn’t talk about wasting IT. It’s HIM.’

‘I don’t know what you mean,’ said Alice.

‘Of course you don’t!’ the Hatter said, tossing his head contemptuously. ‘I dare say you never even spoke to Time!’

‘Perhaps not,’ Alice cautiously replied: ‘but I know I have to beat time when I learn music.’

‘Ah! that accounts for it,’ said the Hatter. ‘He won’t stand beating. Now, if you only kept on good terms with him, he’d do almost anything you liked with the clock. For instance, suppose it were nine o’clock in the morning, just time to begin lessons: you’d only have to whisper a hint to Time, and round goes the clock in a twinkling! Half-past one, time for dinner!’

(‘I only wish it was,’ the March Hare said to itself in a whisper.)

‘That would be grand, certainly,’ said Alice thoughtfully: ‘but then—I shouldn’t be hungry for it, you know.’

‘Not at first, perhaps,’ said the Hatter: ‘but you could keep it to half-past one as long as you liked.’

‘Is that the way YOU manage?’ Alice asked.

The Hatter shook his head mournfully. ‘Not I!’ he replied. ‘We quarrelled last March—just before HE went mad, you know—’ (pointing with his tea spoon at the March Hare,) ‘—it was at the great concert given by the Queen of Hearts, and I had to sing

“Twinkle, twinkle, little bat!
How I wonder what you’re at!”

You know the song, perhaps?’

‘I’ve heard something like it,’ said Alice.

‘It goes on, you know,’ the Hatter continued, ‘in this way:—

“Up above the world you fly,
Like a tea-tray in the sky.
Twinkle, twinkle—”’

Here the Dormouse shook itself, and began singing in its sleep ‘Twinkle, twinkle, twinkle, twinkle—’ and went on so long that they had to pinch it to make it stop.

‘Well, I’d hardly finished the first verse,’ said the Hatter, ‘when the Queen jumped up and bawled out, “He’s murdering the time! Off with his head!”’

‘How dreadfully savage!’ exclaimed Alice.

'And ever since that,' the Hatter went on in a mournful tone, 'he won't do a thing I ask! It's always six o'clock now.'

A bright idea came into Alice's head. 'Is that the reason so many tea-things are put out here?' she asked.

'Yes, that's it,' said the Hatter with a sigh: 'it's always tea-time, and we've no time to wash the things between whiles.'

'Then you keep moving round, I suppose?' said Alice.

'Exactly so,' said the Hatter: 'as the things get used up.'

'But what happens when you come to the beginning again?' Alice ventured to ask.

'Suppose we change the subject,' the March Hare interrupted, yawning. 'I'm getting tired of this. I vote the young lady tells us a story.'

'I'm afraid I don't know one,' said Alice, rather alarmed at the proposal.

'Then the Dormouse shall!' they both cried. 'Wake up, Dormouse!' And they pinched it on both sides at once.

The Dormouse slowly opened his eyes. 'I wasn't asleep,' he said in a hoarse, feeble voice: 'I heard every word you fellows were saying.'

'Tell us a story!' said the March Hare.

'Yes, please do!' pleaded Alice.

'And be quick about it,' added the Hatter, 'or you'll be asleep again before it's done.'

'Once upon a time there were three little sisters,' the Dormouse began in a great hurry; 'and their names were Elsie, Lacie, and Tillie; and they lived at the bottom of a well—'

'What did they live on?' said Alice, who always took a great interest in questions of eating and drinking.

'They lived on treacle,' said the Dormouse, after thinking a minute or two.

'They couldn't have done that, you know,' Alice gently remarked; 'they'd have been ill.'

'So they were,' said the Dormouse; 'VERY ill.'

Alice tried to fancy to herself what such an extraordinary ways of living would be like, but it puzzled her too much, so she went on: 'But why did they live at the bottom of a well?'

'Take some more tea,' the March Hare said to Alice, very earnestly.

'I've had nothing yet,' Alice replied in an offended tone, 'so I can't take more.'

'You mean you can't take LESS,' said the Hatter: 'it's very easy to take MORE than nothing.'

'Nobody asked YOUR opinion,' said Alice.

'Who's making personal remarks now?' the Hatter asked triumphantly.

Alice did not quite know what to say to this: so she helped herself to some tea and bread-and-butter, and then turned to the Dormouse, and repeated her question. 'Why did they live at the bottom of a well?'

The Dormouse again took a minute or two to think about it, and then said, 'It was a treacle-well.'

'There's no such thing!' Alice was beginning very angrily, but the Hatter and the March Hare went 'Sh! sh!' and the Dormouse sulkily remarked, 'If you can't be civil, you'd better finish the story for yourself.'

'No, please go on!' Alice said very humbly; 'I won't interrupt again. I dare say there may be ONE.'

'One, indeed!' said the Dormouse indignantly. However, he consented to go on. 'And so these three little sisters—they were learning to draw, you know—'

'What did they draw?' said Alice, quite forgetting her promise.

'Treacle,' said the Dormouse, without considering at all this time.

'I want a clean cup,' interrupted the Hatter: 'let's all move one place on.'

He moved on as he spoke, and the Dormouse followed him: the March Hare moved into the Dormouse's place, and Alice rather unwillingly took the place of the March Hare. The Hatter was the only one who got any advantage from the change: and Alice was a good deal worse off than before, as the March Hare had just upset the milk-jug into his plate.

Alice did not wish to offend the Dormouse again, so she began very cautiously: 'But I don't understand. Where did they draw the treacle from?'

'You can draw water out of a water-well,' said the Hatter; 'so I should think you could draw treacle out of a treacle-well—eh, stupid?'

'But they were IN the well,' Alice said to the Dormouse, not choosing to notice this last remark.

'Of course they were', said the Dormouse; '—well in.'

This answer so confused poor Alice, that she let the Dormouse go on for some time without interrupting it.

'They were learning to draw,' the Dormouse went on, yawning and rubbing its eyes, for it was getting very sleepy; 'and they drew all manner of things—everything that begins with an M—'

'Why with an M?' said Alice.

'Why not?' said the March Hare.

Alice was silent.

The Dormouse had closed its eyes by this time, and was going off into a doze; but, on being pinched by the Hatter, it woke up again with a little shriek, and went on: '—that begins with an M, such as mouse-traps, and the moon, and memory, and muchness—you know you say things are "much of a muchness"—did you ever see such a thing as a drawing of a muchness?'

'Really, now you ask me,' said Alice, very much confused, 'I don't think—'

'Then you shouldn't talk,' said the Hatter.

This piece of rudeness was more than Alice could bear: she got up in great disgust, and walked off; the Dormouse fell asleep instantly, and neither of the others took the least notice of her going, though she looked back once or twice, half hoping that they would call after her: the last time she saw them, they were trying to put the Dormouse into the teapot.

‘At any rate I’ll never go THERE again!’ said Alice as she picked her way through the wood. ‘It’s the stupidest tea-party I ever was at in all my life!’

Just as she said this, she noticed that one of the trees had a door leading right into it. ‘That’s very curious!’ she thought. ‘But everything’s curious today. I think I may as well go in at once.’ And in she went.

Once more she found herself in the long hall, and close to the little glass table. ‘Now, I’ll manage better this time,’ she said to herself, and began by taking the little golden key, and unlocking the door that led into the garden. Then she went to work nibbling at the mushroom (she had kept a piece of it in her pocked) till she was about a foot high: then she walked down the little passage: and THEN—she found herself at last in the beautiful garden, among the bright flower-beds and the cool fountains.

Chapter 8 - The Queen’s Croquet-Ground

A large rose-tree stood near the entrance of the garden: the roses growing on it were white, but there were three gardeners at it, busily painting them red. Alice thought this a very curious thing, and she went nearer to watch them, and just as she came up to them she heard one of them say, ‘Look out now, Five! Don’t go splashing paint over me like that!’

‘I couldn’t help it,’ said Five, in a sulky tone; ‘Seven jogged my elbow.’

On which Seven looked up and said, ‘That’s right, Five! Always lay the blame on others!’

‘YOU’D better not talk!’ said Five. ‘I heard the Queen say only yesterday you deserved to be beheaded!’

‘What for?’ said the one who had spoken first.

‘That’s none of YOUR business, Two!’ said Seven.

‘Yes, it IS his business!’ said Five, ‘and I’ll tell him—it was for bringing the cook tulip-roots instead of onions.’

Seven flung down his brush, and had just begun ‘Well, of all the unjust things—’ when his eye chanced to fall upon Alice, as she stood watching them, and he checked himself suddenly: the others looked round also, and all of them bowed low.

‘Would you tell me,’ said Alice, a little timidly, ‘why you are painting those roses?’

Five and Seven said nothing, but looked at Two. Two began in a low voice, ‘Why the fact is, you see, Miss, this here ought to have been a RED rose-tree, and we put a white one in by mistake; and if the Queen was to find it out, we should all have our heads cut off, you know. So you see, Miss, we’re doing our best, afore she comes, to—’ At this moment Five, who had been anxiously looking across the garden, called out ‘The Queen! The Queen!’ and the three gardeners instantly threw themselves flat upon their faces. There was a sound of many footsteps, and Alice looked round, eager to see the Queen.

First came ten soldiers carrying clubs; these were all shaped like the three gardeners, oblong and flat, with their hands and feet at the corners: next the ten courtiers; these were ornamented all over with diamonds, and walked two and two, as the soldiers did. After these came the royal children; there were ten of them, and the little dears came jumping merrily along hand in hand, in couples: they were all ornamented with hearts. Next came the guests, mostly Kings and Queens, and among them Alice recognised the White Rabbit: it was talking in a hurried nervous manner, smiling at everything that was said, and went by without noticing her. Then followed the Knave of Hearts, carrying the King’s crown on a crimson velvet cushion; and, last of all this grand procession, came THE KING AND QUEEN OF HEARTS.

Alice was rather doubtful whether she ought not to lie down on her face like the three gardeners, but she could not remember every having heard of such a rule at processions; 'and besides, what would be the use of a procession,' thought she, 'if people had all to lie down upon their faces, so that they couldn't see it?' So she stood still where she was, and waited.

When the procession came opposite to Alice, they all stopped and looked at her, and the Queen said severely 'Who is this?' She said it to the Knave of Hearts, who only bowed and smiled in reply.

'Idiot!' said the Queen, tossing her head impatiently; and, turning to Alice, she went on, 'What's your name, child?'

'My name is Alice, so please your Majesty,' said Alice very politely; but she added, to herself, 'Why, they're only a pack of cards, after all. I needn't be afraid of them!'

'And who are THESE?' said the Queen, pointing to the three gardeners who were lying round the rose-tree; for, you see, as they were lying on their faces, and the pattern on their backs was the same as the rest of the pack, she could not tell whether they were gardeners, or soldiers, or courtiers, or three of her own children.

'How should I know?' said Alice, surprised at her own courage. 'It's no business of MINE.'

The Queen turned crimson with fury, and, after glaring at her for a moment like a wild beast, screamed 'Off with her head! Off—'

'Nonsense!' said Alice, very loudly and decidedly, and the Queen was silent.

The King laid his hand upon her arm, and timidly said 'Consider, my dear: she is only a child!'

The Queen turned angrily away from him, and said to the Knave 'Turn them over!'

The Knave did so, very carefully, with one foot.

'Get up!' said the Queen, in a shrill, loud voice, and the three gardeners instantly jumped up, and began bowing to the King, the Queen, the royal children, and everybody else.

'Leave off that!' screamed the Queen. 'You make me giddy.' And then, turning to the rose-tree, she went on, 'What HAVE you been doing here?'

'May it please your Majesty,' said Two, in a very humble tone, going down on one knee as he spoke, 'we were trying—'

'I see!' said the Queen, who had meanwhile been examining the roses. 'Off with their heads!' and the procession moved on, three of the soldiers remaining behind to execute the unfortunate gardeners, who ran to Alice for protection.

'You shan't be beheaded!' said Alice, and she put them into a large flower-pot that stood near. The three soldiers wandered about for a minute or two, looking for them, and then quietly marched off after the others.

'Are their heads off?' shouted the Queen.

'Their heads are gone, if it please your Majesty!' the soldiers shouted in reply.

'That's right!' shouted the Queen. 'Can you play croquet?'

The soldiers were silent, and looked at Alice, as the question was evidently meant for her.

'Yes!' shouted Alice.

'Come on, then!' roared the Queen, and Alice joined the procession, wondering very much what would happen next.

'It's—it's a very fine day!' said a timid voice at her side. She was walking by the White Rabbit, who was peeping anxiously into her face.

'Very,' said Alice: '—where's the Duchess?'

'Hush! Hush!' said the Rabbit in a low, hurried tone. He looked anxiously over his shoulder as he spoke, and then raised himself upon tiptoe, put his mouth close to her ear, and whispered 'She's under sentence of execution.'

'What for?' said Alice.

'Did you say "What a pity!"?' the Rabbit asked.

'No, I didn't,' said Alice: 'I don't think it's at all a pity. I said "What for?"'

'She boxed the Queen's ears—' the Rabbit began. Alice gave a little scream of laughter. 'Oh, hush!' the Rabbit whispered in a frightened tone. 'The Queen will hear you! You see, she came rather late, and the Queen said—'

'Get to your places!' shouted the Queen in a voice of thunder, and people began running about in all directions, tumbling up against each other; however, they got settled down in a minute or two, and the game began. Alice thought she had never seen such a curious croquet-ground in her life; it was all ridges and furrows; the balls were live hedgehogs, the mallets live flamingoes, and the soldiers had to double themselves up and to stand on their hands and feet, to make the arches.

The chief difficulty Alice found at first was in managing her flamingo: she succeeded in getting its body tucked away, comfortably enough, under her arm, with its legs hanging down, but generally, just as she had got its neck nicely straightened out, and was going to give the hedgehog a blow with its head, it WOULD twist itself round and look up in her face, with such a puzzled expression that she could not help bursting out laughing: and when she had got its head down, and was going to begin again, it was very provoking to find that the hedgehog had unrolled itself, and was in the act of crawling away: besides all this, there was generally a ridge or furrow in the way wherever she wanted to send the hedgehog to, and, as the doubled-up soldiers were always getting up and walking off to other parts of the ground, Alice soon came to the conclusion that it was a very difficult game indeed.

The players all played at once without waiting for turns, quarrelling all the while, and fighting for the hedgehogs; and in a very short time the Queen was in a furious passion, and went stamping about, and shouting 'Off with his head!' or 'Off with her head!' about once in a minute.

Alice began to feel very uneasy: to be sure, she had not as yet had any dispute with the Queen, but she knew that it might happen any minute, 'and then,' thought she, 'what would become of me? They're dreadfully fond of beheading people here; the great wonder is, that there's any one left alive!'

She was looking about for some way of escape, and wondering whether she could get away without being seen, when she noticed a curious appearance in the air: it puzzled her very much at first, but, after watching it a minute or two, she made it out to be a grin, and she said to herself 'It's the Cheshire Cat: now I shall have somebody to talk to.'

'How are you getting on?' said the Cat, as soon as there was mouth enough for it to speak with.

Alice waited till the eyes appeared, and then nodded. 'It's no use speaking to it,' she thought, 'till its ears have come, or at least one of them.' In another minute the whole head appeared, and then Alice put down her flamingo, and began an account of the game, feeling very glad she had someone to listen to her. The Cat seemed to think that there was enough of it now in sight, and no more of it appeared.

'I don't think they play at all fairly,' Alice began, in rather a complaining tone, 'and they all quarrel so dreadfully one can't hear oneself speak—and they don't seem to have any rules in particular; at least, if there are, nobody attends to them—and you've no idea how confusing it is all the things being alive; for instance, there's the arch I've got to go through next walking about at the other end of the ground—and I should have croqueted the Queen's hedgehog just now, only it ran away when it saw mine coming!'

'How do you like the Queen?' said the Cat in a low voice.

'Not at all,' said Alice: 'she's so extremely—' Just then she noticed that the Queen was close behind her, listening: so she went on, '—likely to win, that it's hardly worth while finishing the game.'

The Queen smiled and passed on.

'Who ARE you talking to?' said the King, going up to Alice, and looking at the Cat's head with great curiosity.

'It's a friend of mine—a Cheshire Cat,' said Alice: 'allow me to introduce it.'

'I don't like the look of it at all,' said the King: 'however, it may kiss my hand if it likes.'

'I'd rather not,' the Cat remarked.

'Don't be impertinent,' said the King, 'and don't look at me like that!' He got behind Alice as he spoke.

'A cat may look at a king,' said Alice. 'I've read that in some book, but I don't remember where.'

'Well, it must be removed,' said the King very decidedly, and he called the Queen, who was passing at the moment, 'My dear! I wish you would have this cat removed!'

The Queen had only one way of settling all difficulties, great or small. 'Off with his head!' she said, without even looking round.

'I'll fetch the executioner myself,' said the King eagerly, and he hurried off.

Alice thought she might as well go back, and see how the game was going on, as she heard the Queen's voice in the distance, screaming with passion. She had already heard her sentence three of the players to be executed for having missed their turns, and she did not like the look of things at all, as the game was in such confusion that she never knew whether it was her turn or not. So she went in search of her hedgehog.

The hedgehog was engaged in a fight with another hedgehog, which seemed to Alice an excellent opportunity for croqueting one of them with the other: the only difficulty was, that her flamingo was gone across to the other side of the garden, where Alice could see it trying in a helpless sort of way to fly up into a tree.

By the time she had caught the flamingo and brought it back, the fight was over, and both the hedgehogs were out of sight: 'but it doesn't matter much,' thought Alice, 'as all the arches are gone from this side of the ground.' So she tucked it away under her arm, that it might not escape again, and went back for a little more conversation with her friend.

When she got back to the Cheshire Cat, she was surprised to find quite a large crowd collected round it: there was a dispute going on between the executioner, the King, and the Queen, who were all talking at once, while all the rest were quite silent, and looked very uncomfortable.

The moment Alice appeared, she was appealed to by all three to settle the question, and they repeated their arguments to her, though, as they all spoke at once, she found it very hard indeed to make out exactly what they said.

The executioner's argument was, that you couldn't cut off a head unless there was a body to cut it off from: that he had never had to do such a thing before, and he wasn't going to begin at HIS time of life.

The King's argument was, that anything that had a head could be beheaded, and that you weren't to talk nonsense.

The Queen's argument was, that if something wasn't done about it in less than no time she'd have everybody executed, all round. (It was this last remark that had made the whole party look so grave and anxious.)

Alice could think of nothing else to say but 'It belongs to the Duchess: you'd better ask HER about it.'

'She's in prison,' the Queen said to the executioner: 'fetch her here.' And the executioner went off like an arrow.

The Cat's head began fading away the moment he was gone, and, by the time he had come back with the Duchess, it had entirely disappeared; so the King and the executioner ran wildly up and down looking for it, while the rest of the party went back to the game.

Chapter 9 - The Mock Turtle's Story

'You can't think how glad I am to see you again, you dear old thing!' said the Duchess, as she tucked her arm affectionately into Alice's, and they walked off together.

Alice was very glad to find her in such a pleasant temper, and thought to herself that perhaps it was only the pepper that had made her so savage when they met in the kitchen.

'When I'M a Duchess,' she said to herself, (not in a very hopeful tone though), 'I won't have any pepper in my kitchen AT ALL. Soup does very well without—Maybe it's always pepper that makes people hot-tempered,' she went on, very much pleased at having found out a new kind of rule, 'and vinegar that makes them sour—and camomile that makes them bitter—and—and barley-sugar and such things that make children sweet-tempered. I only wish people knew that: then they wouldn't be so stingy about it, you know—'

She had quite forgotten the Duchess by this time, and was a little startled when she heard her voice close to her ear. 'You're thinking about something, my dear, and that makes you forget to talk. I can't tell you just now what the moral of that is, but I shall remember it in a bit.'

'Perhaps it hasn't one,' Alice ventured to remark.

'Tut, tut, child!' said the Duchess. 'Everything's got a moral, if only you can find it.' And she squeezed herself up closer to Alice's side as she spoke.

Alice did not much like keeping so close to her: first, because the Duchess was VERY ugly; and secondly, because she was exactly the right height to rest her chin upon Alice's shoulder, and it was an uncomfortably sharp chin. However, she did not like to be rude, so she bore it as well as she could.

'The game's going on rather better now,' she said, by way of keeping up the conversation a little.

"Tis so,' said the Duchess: 'and the moral of that is—" Oh, 'tis love, 'tis love, that makes the world go round!"'

'Somebody said,' Alice whispered, 'that it's done by everybody minding their own business!'

'Ah, well! It means much the same thing,' said the Duchess, digging her sharp little chin into Alice's shoulder as she added, 'and the moral of THAT is—"Take care of the sense, and the sounds will take care of themselves."'

'How fond she is of finding morals in things!' Alice thought to herself.

'I dare say you're wondering why I don't put my arm round your waist,' the Duchess said after a pause: 'the reason is, that I'm doubtful about the temper of your flamingo. Shall I try the experiment?'

'HE might bite,' Alice cautiously replied, not feeling at all anxious to have the experiment tried.

'Very true,' said the Duchess: 'flamingoes and mustard both bite. And the moral of that is—"Birds of a feather flock together."'

'Only mustard isn't a bird,' Alice remarked.

'Right, as usual,' said the Duchess: 'what a clear way you have of putting things!'

'It's a mineral, I THINK,' said Alice.

'Of course it is,' said the Duchess, who seemed ready to agree to everything that Alice said; 'there's a large mustard-mine near here. And the moral of that is—"The more there is of mine, the less there is of yours."'

'Oh, I know!' exclaimed Alice, who had not attended to this last remark, 'it's a vegetable. It doesn't look like one, but it is.'

'I quite agree with you,' said the Duchess; 'and the moral of that is—"Be what you would seem to be"—or if you'd like it put more simply—"Never imagine yourself not to be otherwise than what it might appear to others that what you were or might have been was not otherwise than what you had been would have appeared to them to be otherwise."'

'I think I should understand that better,' Alice said very politely, 'if I had it written down: but I can't quite follow it as you say it.'

'That's nothing to what I could say if I chose,' the Duchess replied, in a pleased tone.

'Pray don't trouble yourself to say it any longer than that,' said Alice.

'Oh, don't talk about trouble!' said the Duchess. 'I make you a present of everything I've said as yet.'

'A cheap sort of present!' thought Alice. 'I'm glad they don't give birthday presents like that!' But she did not venture to say it out loud.

'Thinking again?' the Duchess asked, with another dig of her sharp little chin.

'I've a right to think,' said Alice sharply, for she was beginning to feel a little worried.

'Just about as much right,' said the Duchess, 'as pigs have to fly; and the m—'

But here, to Alice's great surprise, the Duchess's voice died away, even in the middle of her favourite word 'moral,' and the arm that was linked into hers began to tremble. Alice looked up, and there stood the Queen in front of them, with her arms folded, frowning like a thunderstorm.

'A fine day, your Majesty!' the Duchess began in a low, weak voice.

'Now, I give you fair warning,' shouted the Queen, stamping on the ground as she spoke; 'either you or your head must be off, and that in about half no time! Take your choice!'

The Duchess took her choice, and was gone in a moment.

'Let's go on with the game,' the Queen said to Alice; and Alice was too much frightened to say a word, but slowly followed her back to the croquet-ground.

The other guests had taken advantage of the Queen's absence, and were resting in the shade: however, the moment they saw her, they hurried back to the game, the Queen merely remarking that a moment's delay would cost them their lives.

All the time they were playing the Queen never left off quarrelling with the other players, and shouting 'Off with his head!' or 'Off with her head!' Those whom she sentenced were taken into custody by the soldiers, who of course had to leave off being arches to do this, so that by the end of half an hour or so there were no arches left, and all the players, except the King, the Queen, and Alice, were in custody and under sentence of execution.

Then the Queen left off, quite out of breath, and said to Alice, 'Have you seen the Mock Turtle yet?'

'No,' said Alice. 'I don't even know what a Mock Turtle is.'

'It's the thing Mock Turtle Soup is made from,' said the Queen.

'I never saw one, or heard of one,' said Alice.

'Come on, then,' said the Queen, 'and he shall tell you his history,'

As they walked off together, Alice heard the King say in a low voice, to the company generally, 'You are all pardoned.' 'Come, THAT'S a good thing!' she said to herself, for she had felt quite unhappy at the number of executions the Queen had ordered.

They very soon came upon a Gryphon, lying fast asleep in the sun. (IF you don't know what a Gryphon is, look at the picture.) 'Up, lazy thing!' said the Queen, 'and take this young lady to see the Mock Turtle, and to hear his history. I must go back and see after some executions I have ordered'; and she walked off, leaving Alice alone with the Gryphon. Alice did not quite like the look of the creature, but on the whole she thought it would be quite as safe to stay with it as to go after that savage Queen: so she waited.

The Gryphon sat up and rubbed its eyes: then it watched the Queen till she was out of sight: then it chuckled. 'What fun!' said the Gryphon, half to itself, half to Alice.

'What IS the fun?' said Alice.

'Why, SHE,' said the Gryphon. 'It's all her fancy, that: they never executes nobody, you know. Come on!'

'Everybody says "come on!" here,' thought Alice, as she went slowly after it: 'I never was so ordered about in all my life, never!'

They had not gone far before they saw the Mock Turtle in the distance, sitting sad and lonely on a little ledge of rock, and, as they came nearer, Alice could hear him sighing as if his heart would break. She pitied him deeply. 'What is his sorrow?' she asked the Gryphon, and the Gryphon answered, very nearly in the same words as before, 'It's all his fancy, that: he hasn't got no sorrow, you know. Come on!'

So they went up to the Mock Turtle, who looked at them with large eyes full of tears, but said nothing.

'This here young lady,' said the Gryphon, 'she wants for to know your history, she do.'

'I'll tell it her,' said the Mock Turtle in a deep, hollow tone: 'sit down, both of you, and don't speak a word till I've finished.'

So they sat down, and nobody spoke for some minutes. Alice thought to herself, 'I don't see how he can EVEN finish, if he doesn't begin.' But she waited patiently.

'Once,' said the Mock Turtle at last, with a deep sigh, 'I was a real Turtle.'

These words were followed by a very long silence, broken only by an occasional exclamation of 'Hjckrrh!' from the Gryphon, and the constant heavy sobbing of the Mock Turtle. Alice was very nearly getting up and saying, 'Thank you, sir, for your interesting story,' but she could not help thinking there MUST be more to come, so she sat still and said nothing.

'When we were little,' the Mock Turtle went on at last, more calmly, though still sobbing a little now and then, 'we went to school in the sea. The master was an old Turtle—we used to call him Tortoise—'

'Why did you call him Tortoise, if he wasn't one?' Alice asked.

'We called him Tortoise because he taught us,' said the Mock Turtle angrily: 'really you are very dull!'

'You ought to be ashamed of yourself for asking such a simple question,' added the Gryphon; and then they both sat silent and looked at poor Alice, who felt ready to sink into the earth. At last the Gryphon said to the Mock Turtle, 'Drive on, old fellow! Don't be all day about it!' and he went on in these words:

'Yes, we went to school in the sea, though you mayn't believe it—'

'I never said I didn't!' interrupted Alice.

'You did,' said the Mock Turtle.

'Hold your tongue!' added the Gryphon, before Alice could speak again. The Mock Turtle went on.

'We had the best of educations—in fact, we went to school every day—'

'I'VE been to a day-school, too,' said Alice; 'you needn't be so proud as all that.'

'With extras?' asked the Mock Turtle a little anxiously.

'Yes,' said Alice, 'we learned French and music.'

'And washing?' said the Mock Turtle.

'Certainly not!' said Alice indignantly.

'Ah! then yours wasn't a really good school,' said the Mock Turtle in a tone of great relief. 'Now at OURS they had at the end of the bill, "French, music, AND WASHING—extra."'

'You couldn't have wanted it much,' said Alice; 'living at the bottom of the sea.'

'I couldn't afford to learn it.' said the Mock Turtle with a sigh. 'I only took the regular course.'

'What was that?' inquired Alice.

'Reeling and Writhing, of course, to begin with,' the Mock Turtle replied; 'and then the different branches of Arithmetic—Ambition, Distraction, Uglification, and Derision.'

'I never heard of "Uglification,"' Alice ventured to say. 'What is it?'

The Gryphon lifted up both its paws in surprise. 'What! Never heard of uglifying!' it exclaimed. 'You know what to beautify is, I suppose?'

'Yes,' said Alice doubtfully: 'it means—to—make—anything—prettier.'

'Well, then,' the Gryphon went on, 'if you don't know what to uglify is, you ARE a simpleton.'

Alice did not feel encouraged to ask any more questions about it, so she turned to the Mock Turtle, and said 'What else had you to learn?'

'Well, there was Mystery,' the Mock Turtle replied, counting off the subjects on his flappers, '—Mystery, ancient and modern, with Seaography: then Drawling—the Drawling-master was an old conger-eel, that used to come once a week: HE taught us Drawling, Stretching, and Fainting in Coils.'

'What was THAT like?' said Alice.

'Well, I can't show it you myself,' the Mock Turtle said: 'I'm too stiff. And the Gryphon never learnt it.'

'Hadn't time,' said the Gryphon: 'I went to the Classics master, though. He was an old crab, HE was.'

'I never went to him,' the Mock Turtle said with a sigh: 'he taught Laughing and Grief, they used to say.'

'So he did, so he did,' said the Gryphon, sighing in his turn; and both creatures hid their faces in their paws.

'And how many hours a day did you do lessons?' said Alice, in a hurry to change the subject.

'Ten hours the first day,' said the Mock Turtle: 'nine the next, and so on.'

'What a curious plan!' exclaimed Alice.

'That's the reason they're called lessons,' the Gryphon remarked: 'because they lessen from day to day.'

This was quite a new idea to Alice, and she thought it over a little before she made her next remark. 'Then the eleventh day must have been a holiday?'

'Of course it was,' said the Mock Turtle.

'And how did you manage on the twelfth?' Alice went on eagerly.

'That's enough about lessons,' the Gryphon interrupted in a very decided tone: 'tell her something about the games now.'

Chapter 10 - The Lobster Quadrille

The Mock Turtle sighed deeply, and drew the back of one flapper across his eyes. He looked at Alice, and tried to speak, but for a minute or two sobs choked his voice. 'Same as if he had a bone in his throat,' said the Gryphon: and it set to work shaking him and punching him in the back. At last the Mock Turtle recovered his voice, and, with tears running down his cheeks, he went on again:—

'You may not have lived much under the sea—' ('I haven't,' said Alice)—'and perhaps you were never even introduced to a lobster—' (Alice began to say 'I once tasted—' but checked herself hastily, and said 'No, never') '—so you can have no idea what a delightful thing a Lobster Quadrille is!'

'No, indeed,' said Alice. 'What sort of a dance is it?'

'Why,' said the Gryphon, 'you first form into a line along the sea-shore—'

'Two lines!' cried the Mock Turtle. 'Seals, turtles, salmon, and so on; then, when you've cleared all the jelly-fish out of the way—'

'THAT generally takes some time,' interrupted the Gryphon.

'—you advance twice—'

'Each with a lobster as a partner!' cried the Gryphon.

'Of course,' the Mock Turtle said: 'advance twice, set to partners—'

'—change lobsters, and retire in same order,' continued the Gryphon.

'Then, you know,' the Mock Turtle went on, 'you throw the—'

'The lobsters!' shouted the Gryphon, with a bound into the air.

'—as far out to sea as you can—'

'Swim after them!' screamed the Gryphon.

'Turn a somersault in the sea!' cried the Mock Turtle, capering wildly about.

'Back to land again, and that's all the first figure,' said the Mock Turtle, suddenly dropping his voice; and the two creatures, who had been jumping about like mad things all this time, sat down again very sadly and quietly, and looked at Alice.

'It must be a very pretty dance,' said Alice timidly.

'Would you like to see a little of it?' said the Mock Turtle.

'Very much indeed,' said Alice.

'Come, let's try the first figure!' said the Mock Turtle to the Gryphon. 'We can do without lobsters, you know. Which shall sing?'

'Oh, YOU sing,' said the Gryphon. 'I've forgotten the words.'

So they began solemnly dancing round and round Alice, every now and then treading on her toes when they passed too close, and waving their forepaws to mark the time, while the Mock Turtle sang this, very slowly and sadly:—

'"Will you walk a little faster?" said a whiting to a snail.
"There's a porpoise close behind us, and he's treading on my tail.

See how eagerly the lobsters and the turtles all advance!

They are waiting on the shingle—will you come and join the dance?
Will you, won't you, will you, won't you, will you join the dance?
Will you, won't you, will you, won't you, won't you join the dance?

"You can really have no notion how delightful it will be
When they take us up and throw us, with the lobsters, out to sea!"
But the snail replied "Too far, too far!" and gave a look askance—
Said he thanked the whiting kindly, but he would not join the dance.
Would not, could not, would not, could not, would not join the dance.
Would not, could not, would not, could not, could not join the dance.

"'What matters it how far we go?" his scaly friend replied. "
There is another shore, you know, upon the other side.
The further off from England the nearer is to France—
Then turn not pale, beloved snail, but come and join the dance.
Will you, won't you, will you, won't you, will you join the dance?
Will you, won't you, will you, won't you, won't you join the dance?'"

'Thank you, it's a very interesting dance to watch,' said Alice, feeling very glad that it was over at last: 'and I do so like that curious song about the whiting!'

'Oh, as to the whiting,' said the Mock Turtle, 'they—you've seen them, of course?'

'Yes,' said Alice, 'I've often seen them at dinn—' she checked herself hastily.

'I don't know where Dinn may be,' said the Mock Turtle, 'but if you've seen them so often, of course you know what they're like.'

'I believe so,' Alice replied thoughtfully. 'They have their tails in their mouths—and they're all over crumbs.'

'You're wrong about the crumbs,' said the Mock Turtle: 'crumbs would all wash off in the sea. But they HAVE their tails in their mouths; and the reason is—' here the Mock Turtle yawned and shut his eyes.—'Tell her about the reason and all that,' he said to the Gryphon.

'The reason is,' said the Gryphon, 'that they WOULD go with the lobsters to the dance. So they got thrown out to sea. So they had to fall a long way. So they got their tails fast in their mouths. So they couldn't get them out again. That's all.'

'Thank you,' said Alice, 'it's very interesting. I never knew so much about a whiting before.'

'I can tell you more than that, if you like,' said the Gryphon. 'Do you know why it's called a whiting?'

'I never thought about it,' said Alice. 'Why?'

'IT DOES THE BOOTS AND SHOES.' the Gryphon replied very solemnly.

Alice was thoroughly puzzled. 'Does the boots and shoes!' she repeated in a wondering tone.

'Why, what are YOUR shoes done with?' said the Gryphon. 'I mean, what makes them so shiny?'

Alice looked down at them, and considered a little before she gave her answer. 'They're done with blacking, I believe.'

'Boots and shoes under the sea,' the Gryphon went on in a deep voice, 'are done with a whiting. Now you know.'

'And what are they made of?' Alice asked in a tone of great curiosity.

'Soles and eels, of course,' the Gryphon replied rather impatiently: 'any shrimp could have told you that.'

'If I'd been the whiting,' said Alice, whose thoughts were still running on the song, 'I'd have said to the porpoise, "Keep back, please: we don't want YOU with us!"'

'They were obliged to have him with them,' the Mock Turtle said: 'no wise fish would go anywhere without a porpoise.'

'Wouldn't it really?' said Alice in a tone of great surprise.

'Of course not,' said the Mock Turtle: 'why, if a fish came to ME, and told me he was going a journey, I should say "With what porpoise?"'

'Don't you mean "purpose"?' said Alice.

'I mean what I say,' the Mock Turtle replied in an offended tone. And the Gryphon added 'Come, let's hear some of YOUR adventures.'

'I could tell you my adventures—beginning from this morning,' said Alice a little timidly: 'but it's no use going back to yesterday, because I was a different person then.'

'Explain all that,' said the Mock Turtle.

'No, no! The adventures first,' said the Gryphon in an impatient tone: 'explanations take such a dreadful time.'

So Alice began telling them her adventures from the time when she first saw the White Rabbit. She was a little nervous about it just at first, the two creatures got so close to her, one on each side, and opened their eyes and mouths so VERY wide, but she gained courage as she went on. Her listeners were perfectly quiet till she got to the part about her repeating 'YOU ARE OLD, FATHER WILLIAM,' to the Caterpillar, and the words all coming different, and then the Mock Turtle drew a long breath, and said 'That's very curious.'

'It's all about as curious as it can be,' said the Gryphon.

'It all came different!' the Mock Turtle repeated thoughtfully. 'I should like to hear her try and repeat something now. Tell her to begin.' He looked at the Gryphon as if he thought it had some kind of authority over Alice.

'Stand up and repeat "'TIS THE VOICE OF THE SLUGGARD,"' said the Gryphon.

'How the creatures order one about, and make one repeat lessons!' thought Alice; 'I might as well be at school at once.' However, she got up, and began to repeat it, but her head was so full of the Lobster Quadrille, that she hardly knew what she was saying, and the words came very queer indeed:—

''Tis the voice of the Lobster; I heard him declare,
"You have baked me too brown, I must sugar my hair."
As a duck with its eyelids, so he with his nose
Trims his belt and his buttons, and turns out his toes.'

[later editions continued as follows

When the sands are all dry, he is gay as a lark,
And will talk in contemptuous tones of the Shark,
But, when the tide rises and sharks are around,
His voice has a timid and tremulous sound.]

'That's different from what I used to say when I was a child,' said the Gryphon.

'Well, I never heard it before,' said the Mock Turtle; 'but it sounds uncommon nonsense.'

Alice said nothing; she had sat down with her face in her hands, wondering if anything would EVER happen in a natural way again.

'I should like to have it explained,' said the Mock Turtle.

'She can't explain it,' said the Gryphon hastily. 'Go on with the next verse.'

'But about his toes?' the Mock Turtle persisted. 'How COULD he turn them out with his nose, you know?'

'It's the first position in dancing.' Alice said; but was dreadfully puzzled by the whole thing, and longed to change the subject.

'Go on with the next verse,' the Gryphon repeated impatiently: 'it begins "I passed by his garden."'

Alice did not dare to disobey, though she felt sure it would all come wrong, and she went on in a trembling voice:—

'I passed by his garden, and marked, with one eye,
How the Owl and the Panther were sharing a pie—'
[later editions continued as follows
The Panther took pie-crust, and gravy, and meat,
While the Owl had the dish as its share of the treat.
When the pie was all finished, the Owl, as a boon,
Was kindly permitted to pocket the spoon:
While the Panther received knife and fork with a growl,
And concluded the banquet—]

'What IS the use of repeating all that stuff,' the Mock Turtle interrupted, 'if you don't explain it as you go on? It's by far the most confusing thing I ever heard!'

'Yes, I think you'd better leave off,' said the Gryphon: and Alice was only too glad to do so.

'Shall we try another figure of the Lobster Quadrille?' the Gryphon went on. 'Or would you like the Mock Turtle to sing you a song?'

'Oh, a song, please, if the Mock Turtle would be so kind,' Alice replied, so eagerly that the Gryphon said, in a rather offended tone, 'Hm! No accounting for tastes! Sing her "Turtle Soup," will you, old fellow?'

The Mock Turtle sighed deeply, and began, in a voice sometimes choked with sobs, to sing this:—

'Beautiful Soup, so rich and green,

Waiting in a hot tureen!
Who for such dainties would not stoop?
Soup of the evening, beautiful Soup!
Soup of the evening, beautiful Soup!
Beau—ootiful Soo—oop!
Beau—ootiful Soo—oop!
Soo—oop of the e—e—evening,

Beautiful, beautiful Soup!
'Beautiful Soup! Who cares for fish,
Game, or any other dish?
Who would not give all else for two
pennyworth only of beautiful Soup?
Pennyworth only of beautiful Soup?
Beau—ootiful Soo—oop!
Beau—ootiful Soo—oop!
Soo—oop of the e—e—evening,
Beautiful, beauti—FUL SOUP!'

'Chorus again!' cried the Gryphon, and the Mock Turtle had just begun to repeat it, when a cry of 'The trial's beginning!' was heard in the distance.

'Come on!' cried the Gryphon, and, taking Alice by the hand, it hurried off, without waiting for the end of the song.

'What trial is it?' Alice panted as she ran; but the Gryphon only answered 'Come on!' and ran the faster, while more and more faintly came, carried on the breeze that followed them, the melancholy words:—

'Soo—oop of the e—e—evening,
Beautiful, beautiful Soup!'

Chapter 11 - Who Stole the Tarts?

The King and Queen of Hearts were seated on their throne when they arrived, with a great crowd assembled about them—all sorts of little birds and beasts, as well as the whole pack of cards: the Knave was standing before them, in chains, with a soldier on each side to guard him; and near the King was the White Rabbit, with a trumpet in one hand, and a scroll of parchment in the other. In the very middle of the court was a table, with a large dish of tarts upon it: they looked so good, that it made Alice quite hungry to look at them—'I wish they'd get the trial done,' she thought, 'and hand round the refreshments!' But there seemed to be no chance of this, so she began looking at everything about her, to pass away the time.

Alice had never been in a court of justice before, but she had read about them in books, and she was quite pleased to find that she knew the name of nearly everything there. 'That's the judge,' she said to herself, 'because of his great wig.'

The judge, by the way, was the King; and as he wore his crown over the wig, (look at the frontispiece if you want to see how he did it,) he did not look at all comfortable, and it was certainly not becoming.

'And that's the jury-box,' thought Alice, 'and those twelve creatures,' (she was obliged to say 'creatures,' you see, because some of them were animals, and some were birds,) 'I suppose they are the jurors.' She said this last word two or three times over to herself, being rather proud of it: for she thought, and rightly too, that very few little girls of her age knew the meaning of it at all. However, 'jury-men' would have done just as well.

The twelve jurors were all writing very busily on slates. 'What are they doing?' Alice whispered to the Gryphon. 'They can't have anything to put down yet, before the trial's begun.'

'They're putting down their names,' the Gryphon whispered in reply, 'for fear they should forget them before the end of the trial.'

'Stupid things!' Alice began in a loud, indignant voice, but she stopped hastily, for the White Rabbit cried out, 'Silence in the court!' and the King put on his spectacles and looked anxiously round, to make out who was talking.

Alice could see, as well as if she were looking over their shoulders, that all the jurors were writing down 'stupid things!' on their slates, and she could even make out that one of them didn't know how to spell 'stupid,' and that he had to ask his neighbour to tell him. 'A nice muddle their slates'll be in before the trial's over!' thought Alice.

One of the jurors had a pencil that squeaked. This of course, Alice could not stand, and she went round the court and got behind him, and very soon found an opportunity of taking it away. She did it so quickly that the poor little juror (it was Bill, the Lizard) could not make out at all what had become of it; so, after hunting all about for it, he was obliged to write with one finger for the rest of the day; and this was of very little use, as it left no mark on the slate.

'Herald, read the accusation!' said the King.

On this the White Rabbit blew three blasts on the trumpet, and then unrolled the parchment scroll, and read as follows:—

'The Queen of Hearts, she made some tarts,
All on a summer day:
The Knave of Hearts, he stole those tarts,
And took them quite away!'

'Consider your verdict,' the King said to the jury.

'Not yet, not yet!' the Rabbit hastily interrupted. 'There's a great deal to come before that!'

'Call the first witness,' said the King; and the White Rabbit blew three blasts on the trumpet, and called out, 'First witness!'

The first witness was the Hatter. He came in with a teacup in one hand and a piece of bread-and-butter in the other. 'I beg pardon, your Majesty,' he began, 'for bringing these in: but I hadn't quite finished my tea when I was sent for.'

'You ought to have finished,' said the King. 'When did you begin?'

The Hatter looked at the March Hare, who had followed him into the court, arm-in-arm with the Dormouse. 'Fourteenth of March, I think it was,' he said.

'Fifteenth,' said the March Hare.

'Sixteenth,' added the Dormouse.

'Write that down,' the King said to the jury, and the jury eagerly wrote down all three dates on their slates, and then added them up, and reduced the answer to shillings and pence.

'Take off your hat,' the King said to the Hatter.

'It isn't mine,' said the Hatter.

'Stolen!' the King exclaimed, turning to the jury, who instantly made a memorandum of the fact.

'I keep them to sell,' the Hatter added as an explanation; 'I've none of my own. I'm a hatter.'

Here the Queen put on her spectacles, and began staring at the Hatter, who turned pale and fidgeted.

'Give your evidence,' said the King; 'and don't be nervous, or I'll have you executed on the spot.'

This did not seem to encourage the witness at all: he kept shifting from one foot to the other, looking uneasily at the Queen, and in his confusion he bit a large piece out of his teacup instead of the bread-and-butter.

Just at this moment Alice felt a very curious sensation, which puzzled her a good deal until she made out what it was: she was beginning to grow larger again, and she thought at first she would get up and leave the court; but on second thoughts she decided to remain where she was as long as there was room for her.

'I wish you wouldn't squeeze so.' said the Dormouse, who was sitting next to her. 'I can hardly breathe.'

'I can't help it,' said Alice very meekly: 'I'm growing.'

'You've no right to grow here,' said the Dormouse.

'Don't talk nonsense,' said Alice more boldly: 'you know you're growing too.'

'Yes, but I grow at a reasonable pace,' said the Dormouse: 'not in that ridiculous fashion.' And he got up very sulkily and crossed over to the other side of the court.

All this time the Queen had never left off staring at the Hatter, and, just as the Dormouse crossed the court, she said to one of the officers of the court, 'Bring me the list of the singers in the last concert!' on which the wretched Hatter trembled so, that he shook both his shoes off.

'Give your evidence,' the King repeated angrily, 'or I'll have you executed, whether you're nervous or not.'

'I'm a poor man, your Majesty,' the Hatter began, in a trembling voice, '—and I hadn't begun my tea—not above a week or so—and what with the bread-and-butter getting so thin—and the twinkling of the tea—'

'The twinkling of the what?' said the King.

'It began with the tea,' the Hatter replied.

'Of course twinkling begins with a T!' said the King sharply. 'Do you take me for a dunce? Go on!'

'I'm a poor man,' the Hatter went on, 'and most things twinkled after that—only the March Hare said—'

'I didn't!' the March Hare interrupted in a great hurry.

'You did!' said the Hatter.

'I deny it!' said the March Hare.

'He denies it,' said the King: 'leave out that part.'

'Well, at any rate, the Dormouse said—' the Hatter went on, looking anxiously round to see if he would deny it too: but the Dormouse denied nothing, being fast asleep.

'After that,' continued the Hatter, 'I cut some more bread-and-butter—'

'But what did the Dormouse say?' one of the jury asked.

'That I can't remember,' said the Hatter.

'You MUST remember,' remarked the King, 'or I'll have you executed.'

The miserable Hatter dropped his teacup and bread-and-butter, and went down on one knee. 'I'm a poor man, your Majesty,' he began.

'You're a very poor speaker,' said the King.

Here one of the guinea-pigs cheered, and was immediately suppressed by the officers of the court. (As that is rather a hard word, I will just explain to you how it was done. They had a large canvas bag, which tied up at the mouth with strings: into this they slipped the guinea-pig, head first, and then sat upon it.)

'I'm glad I've seen that done,' thought Alice. 'I've so often read in the newspapers, at the end of trials, "There was some attempts at applause, which was immediately suppressed by the officers of the court," and I never understood what it meant till now.'

'If that's all you know about it, you may stand down,' continued the King.

'I can't go no lower,' said the Hatter: 'I'm on the floor, as it is.'

'Then you may SIT down,' the King replied.

Here the other guinea-pig cheered, and was suppressed.

'Come, that finished the guinea-pigs!' thought Alice. 'Now we shall get on better.'

'I'd rather finish my tea,' said the Hatter, with an anxious look at the Queen, who was reading the list of singers.

'You may go,' said the King, and the Hatter hurriedly left the court, without even waiting to put his shoes on.

'—and just take his head off outside,' the Queen added to one of the officers: but the Hatter was out of sight before the officer could get to the door.

'Call the next witness!' said the King.

The next witness was the Duchess's cook. She carried the pepper-box in her hand, and Alice guessed who it was, even before she got into the court, by the way the people near the door began sneezing all at once.

'Give your evidence,' said the King.

'Shan't,' said the cook.

The King looked anxiously at the White Rabbit, who said in a low voice, 'Your Majesty must cross-examine THIS witness.'

'Well, if I must, I must,' the King said, with a melancholy air, and, after folding his arms and frowning at the cook till his eyes were nearly out of sight, he said in a deep voice, 'What are tarts made of?'

'Pepper, mostly,' said the cook.

'Treacle,' said a sleepy voice behind her.

'Collar that Dormouse,' the Queen shrieked out. 'Behead that Dormouse! Turn that Dormouse out of court! Suppress him! Pinch him! Off with his whiskers!'

For some minutes the whole court was in confusion, getting the Dormouse turned out, and, by the time they had settled down again, the cook had disappeared.

'Never mind!' said the King, with an air of great relief. 'Call the next witness.' And he added in an undertone to the Queen, 'Really, my dear, YOU must cross-examine the next witness. It quite makes my forehead ache!'

Alice watched the White Rabbit as he fumbled over the list, feeling very curious to see what the next witness would be like, '—for they haven't got much evidence YET,' she said to herself. Imagine her surprise, when the White Rabbit read out, at the top of his shrill little voice, the name 'Alice!'

Chapter 12 - Alice's Evidence

'Here!' cried Alice, quite forgetting in the flurry of the moment how large she had grown in the last few minutes, and she jumped up in such a hurry that she tipped over the jury-box with the edge of her skirt, upsetting all the jurymen on to the heads of the crowd below, and there they lay sprawling about, reminding her very much of a globe of goldfish she had accidentally upset the week before.

'Oh, I BEG your pardon!' she exclaimed in a tone of great dismay, and began picking them up again as quickly as she could, for the accident of the goldfish kept running in her head, and she had a vague sort of idea that they must be collected at once and put back into the jury-box, or they would die.

'The trial cannot proceed,' said the King in a very grave voice, 'until all the jurymen are back in their proper places—ALL,' he repeated with great emphasis, looking hard at Alice as he said do.

Alice looked at the jury-box, and saw that, in her haste, she had put the Lizard in head downwards, and the poor little thing was waving its tail about in a melancholy way, being quite unable to move. She soon got it out again, and put it right; 'not that it signifies much,' she said to herself; 'I should think it would be QUITE as much use in the trial one way up as the other.'

As soon as the jury had a little recovered from the shock of being upset, and their slates and pencils had been found and handed back to them, they set to work very diligently to write out a history of the accident, all except the Lizard, who seemed too much overcome to do anything but sit with its mouth open, gazing up into the roof of the court.

'What do you know about this business?' the King said to Alice.

'Nothing,' said Alice.

'Nothing WHATEVER?' persisted the King.

'Nothing whatever,' said Alice.

'That's very important,' the King said, turning to the jury. They were just beginning to write this down on their slates, when the White Rabbit interrupted: 'UNimportant, your Majesty means, of course,' he said in a very respectful tone, but frowning and making faces at him as he spoke.

'UNimportant, of course, I meant,' the King hastily said, and went on to himself in an undertone, 'important—unimportant—unimportant—important—' as if he were trying which word sounded best.

Some of the jury wrote it down 'important,' and some 'unimportant.' Alice could see this, as she was near enough to look over their slates; 'but it doesn't matter a bit,' she thought to herself.

At this moment the King, who had been for some time busily writing in his note-book, cackled out 'Silence!' and read out from his book, 'Rule Forty-two. ALL PERSONS MORE THAN A MILE HIGH TO LEAVE THE COURT.'

Everybody looked at Alice.

'I'M not a mile high,' said Alice.

'You are,' said the King.

'Nearly two miles high,' added the Queen.

'Well, I shan't go, at any rate,' said Alice: 'besides, that's not a regular rule: you invented it just now.'

'It's the oldest rule in the book,' said the King.

'Then it ought to be Number One,' said Alice.

The King turned pale, and shut his note-book hastily. 'Consider your verdict,' he said to the jury, in a low, trembling voice.

'There's more evidence to come yet, please your Majesty,' said the White Rabbit, jumping up in a great hurry; 'this paper has just been picked up.'

'What's in it?' said the Queen.

'I haven't opened it yet,' said the White Rabbit, 'but it seems to be a letter, written by the prisoner to—to somebody.'

'It must have been that,' said the King, 'unless it was written to nobody, which isn't usual, you know.'

'Who is it directed to?' said one of the jurymen.

'It isn't directed at all,' said the White Rabbit; 'in fact, there's nothing written on the OUTSIDE.' He unfolded the paper as he spoke, and added 'It isn't a letter, after all: it's a set of verses.'

'Are they in the prisoner's handwriting?' asked another of they jurymen.

'No, they're not,' said the White Rabbit, 'and that's the queerest thing about it.' (The jury all looked puzzled.)

'He must have imitated somebody else's hand,' said the King. (The jury all brightened up again.)

'Please your Majesty,' said the Knave, 'I didn't write it, and they can't prove I did: there's no name signed at the end.'

'If you didn't sign it,' said the King, 'that only makes the matter worse. You MUST have meant some mischief, or else you'd have signed your name like an honest man.'

There was a general clapping of hands at this: it was the first really clever thing the King had said that day.

'That PROVES his guilt,' said the Queen.

'It proves nothing of the sort!' said Alice. 'Why, you don't even know what they're about!'

'Read them,' said the King.

The White Rabbit put on his spectacles. 'Where shall I begin, please your Majesty?' he asked.

'Begin at the beginning,' the King said gravely, 'and go on till you come to the end: then stop.'

These were the verses the White Rabbit read:—

'They told me you had been to her,
And mentioned me to him:
She gave me a good character,
But said I could not swim.

He sent them word I had not gone
(We know it to be true):
If she should push the matter on,
What would become of you?

I gave her one, they gave him two,
You gave us three or more;
They all returned from him to you,
Though they were mine before.

If I or she should chance to be
Involved in this affair,
He trusts to you to set them free,
Exactly as we were.

My notion was that you had been
(Before she had this fit)
An obstacle that came between
Him, and ourselves, and it.

Don't let him know she liked them best,
For this must ever be
A secret, kept from all the rest,
Between yourself and me.'

'That's the most important piece of evidence we've heard yet,' said the King, rubbing his hands; 'so now let the jury—'

'If any one of them can explain it,' said Alice, (she had grown so large in the last few minutes that she wasn't a bit afraid of interrupting him,) 'I'll give him sixpence. _I_ don't believe there's an atom of meaning in it.'

The jury all wrote down on their slates, '*She* doesn't believe there's an atom of meaning in it,' but none of them attempted to explain the paper.

'If there's no meaning in it,' said the King, 'that saves a world of trouble, you know, as we needn't try to find any. And yet I don't know,' he went on, spreading out the verses on his knee, and looking at them with one eye; 'I seem to see some meaning in them, after all. "*—said I could not swim—*" you can't swim, can you?' he added, turning to the Knave.

The Knave shook his head sadly. 'Do I look like it?' he said. (Which he certainly did *not*, being made entirely of cardboard.)

'All right, so far,' said the King, and he went on muttering over the verses to himself: '"*We know it to be true—*" that's the jury, of course— "*I gave her one, they gave him two—*" why, that must be what he did with the tarts, you know—'

'But, it goes on "*They all returned from him to you,*"' said Alice.

'Why, there they are!' said the King triumphantly, pointing to the tarts on the table. 'Nothing can be clearer than *that*. Then again— "*Before she had this fit—*" you never had fits, my dear, I think?' he said to the Queen.

'Never!' said the Queen furiously, throwing an inkstand at the Lizard as she spoke. (The unfortunate little Bill had left off writing on his slate with one finger, as he found it made no mark; but he now hastily began again, using the ink, that was trickling down his face, as long as it lasted.)

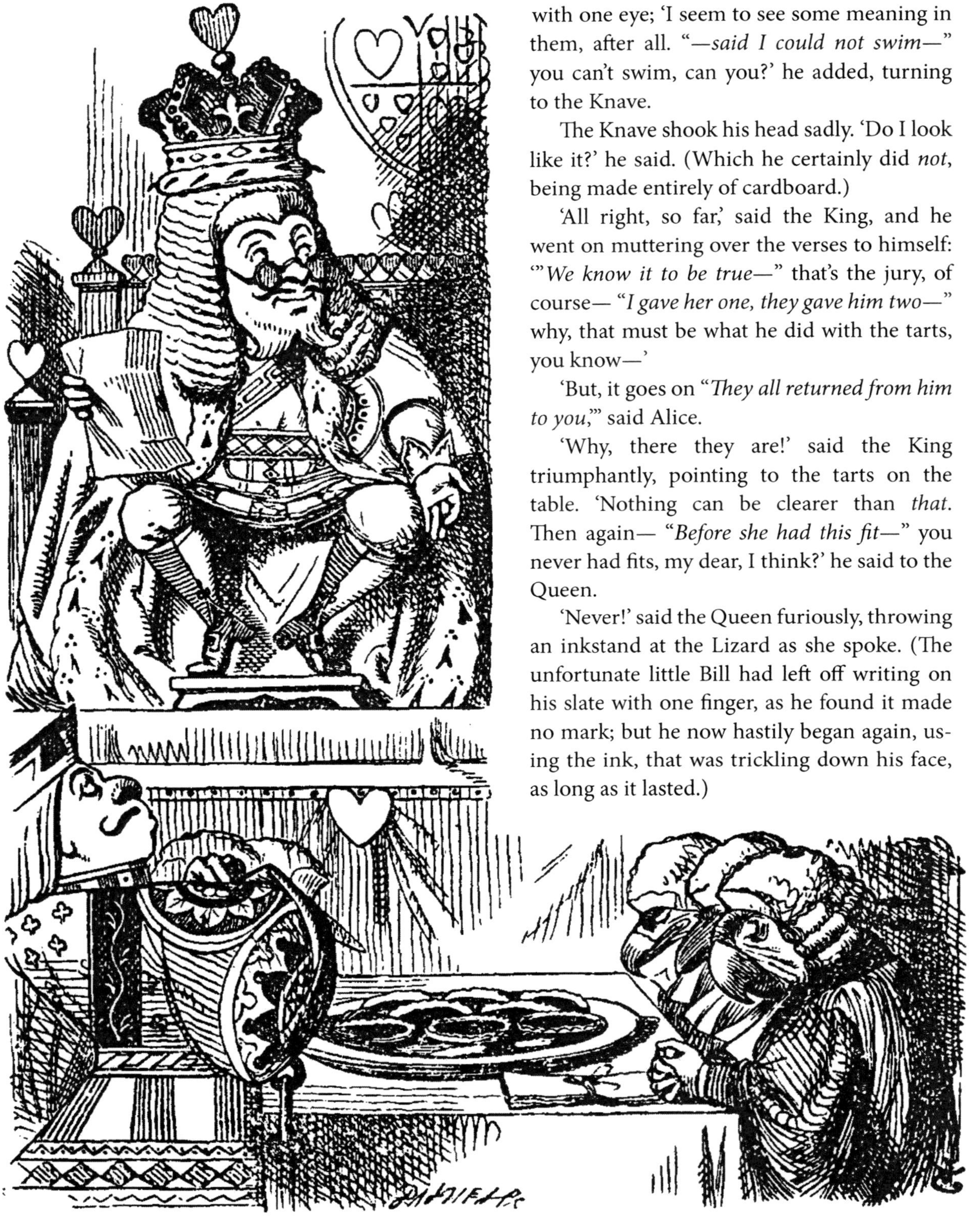

'Then the words don't *fit* you,' said the King, looking round the court with a smile. There was a dead silence.

'It's a pun!' the King added in an offended tone, and everybody laughed, 'Let the jury consider their verdict,' the King said, for about the twentieth time that day.

'No, no!' said the Queen. 'Sentence first—verdict afterwards.' makes fun of Justice

'Stuff and nonsense!' said Alice loudly. 'The idea of having the sentence first!'

'Hold your tongue!' said the Queen, turning purple.

'I won't!' said Alice.

'Off with her head!' the Queen shouted at the top of her voice. Nobody moved.

'Who cares for you?' said Alice, (she had grown to her full size by this time.) 'You're nothing but a pack of cards!'

At this the whole pack rose up into the air, and came flying down upon her: she gave a little scream, half of fright and half of anger, and tried to beat them off, and found herself lying on the bank, with her head in the lap of her sister, who was gently brushing away some dead leaves that had fluttered down from the trees upon her face. dead leaves = cards (element of dream)

'Wake up, Alice dear!' said her sister; 'Why, what a long sleep you've had!'

Sister redreams Alice's dream
Parallel to Wizard of Oz.

'Oh, I've had such a curious dream!' said Alice, and she told her sister, as well as she could remember them, all these strange Adventures of hers that you have just been reading about; and when she had finished, her sister kissed her, and said, 'It WAS a curious dream, dear, certainly: but now run in to your tea; it's getting late.' So Alice got up and ran off, thinking while she ran, as well she might, what a wonderful dream it had been.

But her sister sat still just as she left her, leaning her head on her hand, watching the setting sun, and thinking of little Alice and all her wonderful Adventures, till she too began dreaming after a fashion, and this was her dream:—

First, she dreamed of little Alice herself, and once again the tiny hands were clasped upon her knee, and the bright eager eyes were looking up into hers—she could hear the very tones of her voice, and see that queer little toss of her head to keep back the wandering hair that WOULD always get into her eyes—and still as she listened, or seemed to listen, the whole place around her became alive the strange creatures of her little sister's dream.

The long grass rustled at her feet as the White Rabbit hurried by—the frightened Mouse splashed his way through the neighbouring pool—she could hear the rattle of the teacups as the March Hare and his friends shared their never-ending meal, and the shrill voice of the Queen ordering off her unfortunate guests to execution—once more the pig-baby was sneezing on the Duchess's knee, while plates and dishes crashed around it—once more the shriek of the Gryphon, the squeaking of the Lizard's slate-pencil, and the choking of the suppressed guinea-pigs, filled the air, mixed up with the distant sobs of the miserable Mock Turtle.

So she sat on, with closed eyes, and half believed herself in Wonderland, though she knew she had but to open them again, and all would change to dull reality—the grass would be only rustling in the wind, and the pool rippling to the waving of the reeds—the rattling teacups would change to tinkling sheep-bells, and the Queen's shrill cries to the voice of the shepherd boy—and the sneeze of the baby, the shriek of the Gryphon, and all thy other queer noises, would change (she knew) to the confused clamour of the busy farm-yard—while the lowing of the cattle in the distance would take the place of the Mock Turtle's heavy sobs.

Lastly, she pictured to herself how this same little sister of hers would, in the after-time, be herself a grown woman; and how she would keep, through all her riper years, the simple and loving heart of her childhood: and how she would gather about her other little children, and make *their* eyes bright and eager with many a strange tale, perhaps even with the dream of Wonderland of long ago: and how she would feel with all their simple sorrows, and find a pleasure in all their simple joys, remembering her own child-life, and the happy summer days.

The Head of Hair

By Guy de Maupassant

The walls of the cell were whitewashed and completely bare. This bright but sinister little room received its light through a narrow, barred window, high up and well out of reach. The madman, sitting on a wicker chair, was staring at us with a vague, terror-stricken look in his eyes.

He was very thin, with sunken cheeks. His hair was almost white—and you had the impression that it must have gone white within the space of a few months. His clothes seemed too big for his bony limbs and his hunched and shrunken body. You had the feeling that this man was being eaten alive, that there was some single thought gnawing away at him, just as a grub gnaws away at a fruit. His madness, his obsession was there in that head, relentless, aggressive, all-consuming, eating away his body, little by little. A single idea—a thing invisible, intangible, imperceptible—was burrowing into his flesh, drinking up his blood, destroying his life …

What a mysterious business it was—a man being destroyed by a dream! To see him sitting there, possessed of a devil, filled you with an uncomfortable mixture of fear and pity. What strange, terrifying, mortal delusion occupied that brow of his, furrowed by deep wrinkles which were continually twitching and shifting.

'He has terrible fits of rage,' said the doctor. 'He's one of the strangest cases I have ever seen. His affliction is a form of insanity which is both erotic and macabre. He's a sort of necrophiliac … What's more, he's kept a diary which depicts his mental illness for us with remarkable clarity. So his madness, in a sense, is something we can get to grips with … If you're interested you can look through what he's written.'

I followed the doctor into his office, and he handed me the diary kept by this poor wretch.

'Read it,' he said, 'and then you can tell me your opinion.'

This is what was written in the note-book …

Up to the age of thirty-two I led a very quiet life, and had never been in love. Life seemed to me to be very good. It was uncomplicated, easy to live. I had plenty of money. I was interested in so many different things that I never developed an overwhelming passion for any one of them. In those days it was good to be alive! Every morning I used to wake up happy, ready to do whatever took my fancy, and I used to go to bed content, calmly looking forward to the next day and to a future free from care.

I had had a few mistresses, but I never knew the madness of desire or the torments of love. It's good to live like that. It's better to be in love—but love can be a terrible thing. I suppose that the average person in love must experience a wonderful happiness, but it is probably a happiness not as great as mine, for love came upon me in an incredible way ...

Having plenty of money I used to collect antiques, especially old furniture. And I often used to think about the unknown hands which had touched these articles, about the eyes which had gazed on them in admiration, about the hearts which had loved them—for people *do* love mere things!

I used to spend hour after hour staring at a little watch from the eighteenth century. It was so dainty, so pretty, with its enamel and its delicately-worked gold. And it was still going, just as it had done on the day when a woman had bought it and experienced the delight of owning a fine piece of jewellery. It had never stopped pulsating away as it lived out its mechanical life, and it had ticked away smoothly for a whole century.

Who, I wonder, was the first woman to wear it on her bosom, keeping it warm and cosy in the folds of her dress—the heart of the little watch beating close against the heart of a woman? What hand had enclosed it, had turned it over and over again with the tips of warm fingers, and then had wiped clean the porcelain shepherds whose image had been momentarily dulled by the moistness of human skin? What eye had gazed upon this little face decorated with flowers, watching for the long-awaited hour, the dear, divine hour of love?

How I wish I had known her, or even seen her, the woman who once chose this rare and exquisite object! Alas, she is dead! And I am possessed by the desire for women of long ago ... I love—from a distance—all those women who once were in love! The thought of all these bygone passions fills my heart with longing. Oh! To think of all the beauty, all the smiles, all the caresses and hopes of youth! Should not such things live for ever?!

How I have wept—for a whole night, sometimes—over the poor women of olden days, women who were so beautiful, so tender, so gentle, women who opened wide their arms ready to receive a kiss—and now they are dead! The kiss itself is immortal. It travels from mouth to mouth, from century to century, from age to age. Men and women receive kisses, give kisses—and die.

I am attracted by the past, and terrified by the present, because all that the future holds is death. I long for everything that has already taken place, I weep for those who have already lived. I wish I could stop the passage of time, stay the fleeting hour. But on and on it goes ... Time rushes by and, second by second, it steals a little bit of myself for the nothingness of tomorrow ... And I shall never pass this way again.

Farewell, ladies of yesteryear! I love you all!

But I do not ask for pity. I have found the woman I have been waiting for, and through her I have tasted unimagined delights ...

One sunny morning I was strolling through Paris in a very cheerful mood, walking along with a light step, and casually glancing into the shop windows. Suddenly I noticed in an antique shop an Italian bureau from the seventeenth century. It was very handsome, and very rare. I felt sure it was the work of a Venetian craftsman by the name of Vitelli who was very famous in his day.

Having looked at it, I walked on. Why did the image of this piece of furniture pursue me with such power that I had to turn round and retrace my steps? I stopped once again outside the shop, and as I stood looking at it, I felt that it was tempting me.

What a strange thing this kind of temptation is! You look at an object, and gradually it seduces you, disturbs you, invades your very being—just as a woman's face can do. You are penetrated by its charm, a peculiar charm which is composed of its shape, its colour, the countenance it possesses, even though it is a mere thing. And already you are in love with it, you want it, you must have it. You are overcome by a desire for possession, a desire which is sweet at first, like something timid, but then it increases and becomes violent, irresistible.

And shopkeepers seem to be able to sense this secret, growing desire—when they see the—gleam in the eyes of their customers …

I bought this piece of furniture and had it delivered to my home straight away. I put it in my bedroom.

Oh, I feel sorry for those people who do not know the honeymoon which the collector enjoys with an item he has just purchased! You let your eyes and your fingers run over it, just as if it were human flesh. You are constantly coming back to it, always thinking about it, wherever you go, whatever you do. The thought of this beloved object accompanies you when you walk down the street, when you mingle with the crowds, everywhere you go. And when you get back home, before you even take off your gloves and your hat, you go and gaze at it as tenderly as any lover.

For a whole week I really adored this piece of furniture. Every now and then I would open the doors and the drawers, handling it with sheer delight, savouring all the intimate joys of possession.

Now, one evening, as I was feeling the thickness of one of the sides I realized that it must contain a secret recess. My heart started pounding with excitement, and I spent the whole night in a vain attempt to find the hiding-place.

I managed it the next day by pushing the blade of a knife into a crack in the woodwork. A panel slid back, and I saw, lying on a background of black velvet, a magnificent head of hair—a woman's hair!

Yes, a head of hair, a great mass of braided hair! It was blond, with an auburn sheen, bound with a thread of gold, and it was so long that it must have been cut off close against the skin.

I stared at it in amazement, trembling and feeling uneasy. A perfume which was barely perceptible—so ancient that it seemed like the ghost of a perfume—was coming from this mysterious recess and the remarkable relic it contained.

I took hold of it, gently, almost reverently, and I drew it from its place of concealment. Immediately it uncoiled itself, spilling out in a golden wave which almost reached to the floor. It was thick, yet light, as supple and as brilliant as the fiery tail of a comet.

I felt myself in the grip of a strange emotion. What did this mean? When did it happen? How did it happen? Why had this hair been locked away in this piece of furniture? What adventure, what drama, could this memento reveal?

Who had cut off this hair? A lover on the day he said farewell?

A husband, on the day of vengeance? Or did the woman who had worn this hair cut it off herself, on a day of despair?

Or was it when she had taken her vows and become a nun that it had been tossed away like some love-token, bequeathed to the outside world? Or was it when they nailed her into her coffin, this beautiful girl who had died so young? Was it then that the one who loved her had kept the glorious adornment of her head, the only part of her which he could possibly keep, the only living part of her which would never decay in death, the only part of her which he could still love and caress and embrace in the frenzy of his grief?

Was it not strange that the hair had survived like this, when there remained not the merest fragment of the body to which it had belonged?

I let my fingers run through it and felt it brushing against my skin with a unique caress—the caress of a dead woman. I felt so overcome with emotion that I nearly started weeping.

For a long, long time I held it in my hands. Then I became convinced that it was exciting me, as though something of the woman's soul remained concealed within it. And I placed it back on the velvet which had become dull with age, and I slid back the panel and locked the bureau, then went out to walk through the city and think things over …

I walked on, feeling very melancholy—and very uneasy too, with the kind of uneasiness people experience when they have exchanged a passionate kiss. I had the impression that I had already lived in a previous age, that I must have known this woman in real life.

And I found my lips sobbing out some lines from the fifteenth-century poet Francois Villon:

Dictes-moy, où ne en quel pays
Est Flora, la belle Romaine …?
Et Jehanne, la bonne Lorraine
Que Anglais brûlèrent a Rouen?
Où sont-ils, Vierge souveraine?
Mais où sont les neiges d'antan?

Tell me, in which country now
Is Flora, the Roman beauty …?
And Joan, the good lass from Lorraine
Whom the English burnt in Rouen?
Where are they now, Virgin supreme?
Where are the snows of yesteryear?

When I got back home I experienced an overwhelming need to have another look at my strange find. I took hold of it and, as soon as I touched it, I felt a shudder run through the whole of my body.

For the next few days, however, I continued to live in my usual way, in my normal state of mine—though I was never free from the nagging thought of this head of hair.

Each time I returned home the moment I entered I simply had to see it and handle it. I used to turn the key in the bureau with the same thrill of expectancy a man has when he opens the door to the house of his beloved mistress, for in my hands and my heart I felt a constant need—a confused, peculiar, sensual need—to dip my fingers into that delightful stream of dead hair.

Then, when I had finished stroking it and locked it away in the bureau again, I used to experience a powerful impression of its presence in there, as though it were some human being I had hidden away and kept a prisoner. I lusted for it again, and felt a renewal of the overwhelming impulse to take it out, to fondle it, to excite myself almost to the point of exhaustion by handling this object which was cold, sleek, exciting, maddening—sheer delight!

I must have lived in this state for another month or two, though I can't remember just how long it lasted. All I know is that I became obsessed with the hair, and that it somehow took possession of me. I was happy, yet tormented, as though I was unable to express my love fully, as though I had declared my love and was now waiting for the physical embrace.

I used to shut myself up in my room with it so I could press it against my skin and bury my lips in it, kissing it and biting it. I would smother my face in it, drinking it in, drowning my eyes in its rippling waves of gold …

I was in love with it! Yes, I was in love with it! I could no longer do without it, nor go a single hour without seeing it.

And I was waiting … waiting for something …What was I waiting for? For *her*!

One night I suddenly woke up with the conviction that I was not alone in my room.

Of course, when I looked, there was no-one there. Yet I couldn't get back to sleep again, and after tossing and turning in a feverish insomnia I got out of bed in order to fondle the hair. It seemed to be more delightful than ever—and more full of life … Do the dead return?

The hot and passionate kisses I lavished upon it made me almost faint with bliss, and I took it back to bed with me, and lay there pressing my lips to it as if it were a mistress I was about to possess …

Ah, the dead do return! *She* has returned! Yes, I have seen her, I have held her in my arms, I have possessed her, just as she was in real life in the olden days—tall, blond, plump, with breasts which felt cold and hips which were shaped like a lyre. And as I caressed her my fingers ran over those divine undulations which go from the bosom to the feet, following all the curves of her flesh.

Yes, she was mine—every day, every night. She came back, the Dead Woman, the beautiful Dead Woman, the Adorable, the Mysterious, the Unknown—every night!

My happiness was so great that I could no longer conceal it. In her presence I experienced a superhuman ecstacy, the profound, inexplicable bliss of possessing the Intangible, the Invisible, the Dead Woman! No lover tasted more ardent or more terrible delights!

I could not find a way of concealing my happiness. I loved her so passionately that I could no longer bear to be without her. I took her with me wherever I went and whatever I did. I escorted her when I walked through the city, just as if she were my wife. I took her with me to the theatre and sat in a box with her, just as if she were my mistress …

But they saw her … They guessed my secret … And they have taken her from me! … They have thrown me into prison, like a common criminal … they have taken her from me! … Oh, how desperately unhappy I am! …

This was as far as the manuscript went … I was just turning to the doctor with a look of bewilderment on my face when, suddenly there rang out through the asylum a terrible cry—a howl of helpless rage and the anguish of frustrated desire.

'Just listen to him!' said the doctor. 'We have to cool this obscene madman down by giving him a cold shower—five times a day.'

I was so astonished and upset, so moved with the horror and pity of it all, that I simply blurted out: 'But … what about this hair? Does it actually exist?'

The doctor got up, opened a cupboard full of bottles and surgical instruments, and threw over to me a mass of gleaming blond hair which seemed to fly across the room like a golden bird.

I gave a shudder as I felt on my hands its delicate, tender caress. And I stood there with my heart beating faster, filled with disgust—and envy … With disgust, because I felt I was handling an object associated with something criminal … With envy, because I felt the powerful temptation of a thing outrageous and mysterious …

The doctor remarked, with a shrug of his shoulders:

'Ah, well. The mind of man is capable of everything.'

Who Knows?

By Guy de Maupassant

I

My God! I can't believe it! At last, at long last, I am actually going to put down in black and white what happened to me! That's if I am able! If I dare! The whole story is so weird, so impossible to explain, so … crazy!

If I were not absolutely certain of what I saw and sure that there is no gap in the chain of events I am about to relate, if I were not totally convinced that there is no possibility of a mistake about what happened, I would simply think it was a hallucination or that I had been fooled by some sort of strange illusion. And when all is said and done, who knows anyway?

I am at present in a psychiatric clinic but I came here voluntarily as a precautionary measure because I was afraid. Only one other human being knows my history and that is the doctor here. I am going to write it down, though quite why, I am not sure. Perhaps to get it off my chest. The weight of it on my mind all the time is practically unbearable. It's a waking nightmare. These are the facts.

I have always been something of a loner, a bit dreamy, you might say but well-meaning unambitious with no particular animosity towards my fellow human beings and fairly content with my lot. I have always lived alone because of a certain creeping unease I feel in the presence of other people. I don't know how to explain it. I am not averse to seeing people—I mean, I go out and eat with friends and so forth but if I feel they have been near me for any prolonged period of time, even the closest begin to get so much on my nerves that I have this overwhelming, increasingly urgent desire to see them gone or to go off and be by myself.

It is actually more than a desire. It is a real need, something absolutely essential to me. If I were forced to stay in company, and if I had to stay not so much listening as simply hearing the conversation of other people, I know that some kind of accident would happen to me. I'm not sure what exactly. Who knows, after all? I'd probably faint, I suppose, yes, that's it, I'd pass out!

I love my solitude so much that I cannot even bear to have others sleeping under the same roof as me. I could never live in Paris, for example. I die a slow death when I'm there. It's a kind of annihilation of the spirit for me; both my mind and my body are tortured by the consciousness of a vast, seething mass of humanity living around me there, awake or asleep. I tell you, other people's sleep is even more painful to me than their speech! I can never rest while I know, while I can feel behind that wall, say, the existence of others whose powers of reasoning are temporarily and regularly shut down.

Why am I like this? Who knows? Perhaps the reason is very simple. Maybe I just tire very quickly of anything that is not happening to myself. And there must be thousands like me. There are two kinds of people in the world. First there are those who need others and who are entertained, distracted, even soothed by company. Solitude for this kind of person is a huge, unremitting burden to bear, something as difficult and daunting as crossing a desert or climbing a dangerous glacier. Then there's the second type of person who gets tired, irritated and finally bored stiff in the company of others. For this kind of person, solitude is a balm, something they can lie back and bask in while their thoughts are allowed to roam free.

In other words we're talking about a perfectly normal psychological given. Some people are good at living extrovertly, others introvertly. I happen to be one of those whose capacity for attention to the outside world is very small and quickly exhausted. As soon as it reaches its limit I feel this intolerable unease throughout both my mind and my body.

As a result of this I have become, or rather had become, very attached to inanimate objects which were as important to me as human beings. My house has, or had, become a world in which I lived a solitary yet active life, surrounded by familiar objects, furniture and *bibelots* as lovable to me as human faces. Little by little I filled my house with these things and lived in their midst as happily as in the arms of a beloved woman whose warm, familiar embrace has become a prerequisite to a calm, untroubled existence.

I had had the house built within an attractive garden by which it was set back a little way from the road. It was situated on the outskirts of a town to which I could go whenever I felt like a little social life. All my servants lived in a building some way off at the end of a vegetable garden surrounded by a high wall. So beautifully soothing to me was the dark enfolding of the night in the silence of my secluded home, nestling as it did under the leaves of the huge surrounding trees, that every evening I used to put off going to bed the longer to savour it.

This particular night, they were putting on a production of *Sigurd* at the local theatre. It was the first time I had heard this beautiful, fairytale opera and I enjoyed it enormously. I was walking happily home, my ears full of the lovely arias, in my mind's eye seeing again the magical scenery. It was very, very dark indeed, so dark, in fact, that I could hardly see the road, and several times nearly fell into the ditch. From the tollgate to my house it's about a kilometre, maybe more—in other words, about a twenty-minute gentle walk. It was between one and half past one in the morning. The sky cleared a little above me and the sad old crescent moon of the last quarter appeared. The new crescent moon, the one which rises at about four or five in the afternoon, is bright and cheerful like polished silver but the one rising after midnight is a dismal, reddish, rather gloomy one, a real Sabbath moon. Anybody with nocturnal habits will tell you that, I'm sure. The first, however slender, however threadlike, throws a shining brilliance that fills the heart with delight and casts sharp shadows on the earth. The last hardly sheds more than a dying glow and that so dull as to make hardly any shadow at all.

I could see in the distance the dense mass which was my garden when, out of nowhere, it seemed, a sort of unease began to creep over me at the thought of entering it. I slackened my pace. The air was balmy. The great clump of trees ahead looked like a tomb beneath which my house lay buried.

I opened my gate and began to walk up the long avenue of sycamores leading to the house, arched to make a vault-like tunnel, with banks of flowers on either side, then lawns where flowerbeds formed vague ovals among the pale shadows. As I approached the house, I was gripped by a strange feeling of foreboding. I stopped in my tracks. There was not a sound to be heard. Not a leaf rustled. What on earth was the matter with me, I wondered. I had been coming home like this for ten years with never a hint of any anxiety in my mind. I was not frightened. I have never been afraid of the night. Had I spotted some prowler or burglar, anger would have translated itself into physical action and I would have hurled myself at him without the slightest hesitation. Besides, I was armed. I had my revolver on me. But I never touched it. I knew that I needed to control by myself the fear I could feel stirring into life within me.

What was it? Some premonition? The mysterious kind of premonition which grips a man's senses when they are about to witness something inexplicable? Perhaps so. Who knows? As I moved forward, my flesh began to creep. When I reached the outside walls of my vast house with its closed shutters I felt I needed to wait a few minutes before opening the front door and going in. I sat on a garden seat under my drawing room windows. Trembling a little, I leaned my head against the wall and focused on the shadowy bushes beyond. For the first few moments I noticed nothing unusual. I had a little roaring in the ears but I get that often. It's as if I can hear trains passing, bells ringing, or the stamp of a crowd on the march.

Soon, however, this roaring became more distinct, sharper in tone and more specific. I had been wrong in thinking this was the usual sound of-blood coursing through my arteries. This was a very particular sound which, however difficult to define, was coming, there was no doubt about this now, from within my house itself.

Through the wall I could hear it continuously, more of a tremor than a noise, the vague shifting of a host of things, as if all the furniture were being picked up, shaken, then dragged quietly off. Well! As you can imagine, for a very long time I wondered whether I was hearing things. But having glued my ear to the shutter to try and find out what this disturbance inside my home was, I came to the firm conclusion that something incomprehensible and abnormal was going on. I was not so much frightened as ... how can I put it? ... terrified with astonishment. I did not load my revolver, guessing quite correctly, as it turned out, that there was no earthly reason to do so. I waited.

For a long time I continued to wait, not knowing what to do, with a mind perfectly clear though full of trepidation. By now I was standing listening to the noise increase at times to an ear-shattering pitch. At other times, too, this mysterious upheaval sounded like a growl of impatience or even of anger. Suddenly ashamed of being such a coward, I got hold of my bunch of keys, chose the one I needed, rammed it into the lock, turned it twice, then flung the door open with such force I sent it crashing against the interior wall.

It sounded like gunshot as the noise echoed from top to bottom of my entire house, from which came now a thunderous reverberation. It was so sudden and so deafening that I recoiled a few paces in horror. Although I knew it was still useless, this time I did take my revolver out of its holster.

Again, I waited for ... I don't know how long ... a little while I suppose. What I could now hear was the extraordinary sound of steps coming down the stairway and on to the parquet and the carpets—the sound not of shoes or of human footwear but the clatter of wooden and iron crutches clashing like cymbals, or so it seemed. Suddenly, what should I see waddling over the threshold of my own room but the big armchair in which I used to sit to read. It came out into the garden. Others from the drawing room followed it and were followed in turn by low settees crawling crocodile-like along on their squat little legs. All my other chairs leapt out like goats, with footstools lolloping alongside.

You can imagine what I felt like! I slid behind some shrubbery and remained crouching there watching the procession continue to pass by, for they were all leaving, one after the other, quickly or slowly, according to size and weight. My piano, my full-size grand piano galloped wildly past me with a musical murmur in its flank; the smallest objects such as hairbrushes and crystal chandelier droplets crawled like ants on the ground accompanied by glass goblets on which the moonlight cast little glowworms of phosphorescence; curtains, hangings, tapestries spread like pools and stretched out octopus-like tentacles of fabric as they swam past. My desk hove into view, a rare eighteenth-century piece now containing some photographs and all the letters tracing the sad history of my painful love-life.

I suddenly lost my fear. I threw myself on it and held it down as if it had been a burglar or a woman attempting to flee. However, there was no stopping it and despite all my angry efforts I could not even slow down its inexorable progress. In my desperate struggle against this appalling power I was thrown to the ground, then rolled over and dragged along the gravel. In no time, the rest of the furniture in its train began to trample all over me, bruising my legs in the process. When I let go of the desk the rest of the pieces careered over my body as a cavalry charge mows down a fallen rider.

Frightened witless, I managed to drag myself away from the avenue and hide myself again behind the trees, from which position I watched everything down to the smallest, the most modest of my former possessions, including some of whose existence I was not even aware, all disappear.

Then in the distance, from within my home now echoing as empty houses do, I heard a tremendous noise of doors shutting. My house from attic to cellar rang with the sound of slamming until the door which I myself had just recently opened in terror finally also closed.

I too now fled and ran towards the town. I did not regain any degree of composure until I was again in the streets where late-night revellers were making their way home. I went to a hotel where I was known and rang the bell. I dusted myself down before going in to explain that I had lost my keys, among them the one for the garden gate where my servants slept in the separate house within the fence protecting my fruit and vegetables from thieves.

I dived into the bed they gave me and covered myself up to the eyes. I could not sleep, however, and as I lay waiting for daylight I could hear my heart pounding. I had ordered my servants to be alerted at dawn, and at seven o'clock my manservant came knocking at the door.

He looked devastated.

'Something dreadful happened in the night, Monsieur,' he said.

'Oh? What was that?'

'Monsieur has been robbed of every single article in the house, every single one, down to the very smallest piece.'

This news pleased me. I have no idea why. Who knows? I felt perfectly in control, certain that I could pretend and that I need tell no one what I had seen. I was sure I could keep this terrible secret hidden in my subconscious. I replied: 'It must be the same people who stole my keys. We must let the police know at once. I shall join you in a few minutes after I've got dressed.'

The inquiry lasted five months. Nothing was discovered. Not a single piece of mine was recovered and not the slightest trace of robbers ever found. My God! Imagine if I'd said what I knew! If I'd said a word about that, it would have been myself rather than any robbers who would have been locked up for believing such a thing! Oh yes, I kept my mouth shut all right! But I never refurnished the house. That would have been pointless. The whole business would have started up again. I wished never to return there. I stayed away therefore and never saw the place again.

I came and lived in a hotel in Paris where I consulted doctors about the state of my nerves which had been giving me a lot of trouble ever since that appalling night. They recommended that I do some travelling and I followed their advice.

II

I started with a trip to Italy, where the sun did me good. For six months I wandered about between Venice, Florence, Rome and Naples. Then I toured through Sicily admiring its wildlife and the monuments left by the Greeks and others. I went on to Africa and made a leisurely crossing of the great, calm, yellow desert. Here I saw camels roam, as well as gazelles and Arab vagabonds, and on its light, transparent air no trace of animosity ever seems to be felt, either by day or by night.

I returned to France via Marseille where, despite traditional Provencal gaiety, the relative diminution in light cast a tinge of sadness over me. Returning to this continent I felt strangely like an invalid who, though allegedly cured of his illness, knows from the dull ache that he feels that it is merely dormant within him.

Then I came back to Paris. After a month I was bored with it. It was autumn, and before winter set in I wanted to make a tour of Normandy, then still unfamiliar territory to me. I started in Rouen, of course, and for a week wandered around enthusiastically, finding fresh delights in the medieval city of Gothic monuments which is such an astonishing and wonderful museum in itself.

One afternoon at around four o'clock I turned in to an incredible street where a river called Eau de Robec flowed with water as black as ink. While I was looking with great interest at the bizarre architecture of the houses there, my attention was drawn to a series of antique shops set all in a row, one next door to the other. Those crooked old dealers in antiquity had certainly picked the right place. The street was eerie, with its pointed tile and slate roofs where ancient weather vanes still creaked on high. Stored in the dark interiors of these shops could be seen carved sideboards piled high, one on top of the other, Nevers pottery, Moustiers ware, painted statuettes, carved oak figures, crucifixes, Madonnas, saints, church ornaments, chasubles, copes and even one or two holy vases, as well as a tabernacle conveniently vacated by the Godhead. What amazing places they were, these huge, tall houses like Aladdin's caves crammed to bursting with all kinds of objects of seemingly finite use, but which had long survived their first owners and endured through their century, their times and fashions, to be bought as curiosities by the generations that followed!

My fondness for such things was revived in this enclave of the ancient. I went from shop to shop, crossing in two strides the little bridges made of four worm-eaten planks thrown across the evil-smelling Eau de Robec. God help me! What a frightful shock I was soon to get! On one side of a vault packed tightly with stuff and looking like the entrance to the catacombs of some furniture cemetery, what should appear before my eyes but one of my own most beautiful cupboards! I approached, trembling in every limb, so much so in fact that at first I dared not touch it. Tentatively I stretched out my hand. Yes, it was mine all right; a unique, Louis XIII piece, once seen never forgotten. Suddenly, peering into the darkest depths of this gallery I saw three of my armchairs covered in petit point, and farther on still, my two Henri II tables, such rare examples that people used to come from Paris to look at them.

Imagine! Just imagine what I felt like!

On I went nevertheless. Half-dead with fright, still I advanced. I'm brave, I'll say that for me! Nearly paralysed with dread by now, I inched forward like a knight from the dark ages making his way through the enchanted forest. As I moved on, with every step I gradually found everything that had once belonged to me—my chandeliers, my books, my pictures, my curtains, rugs, armour, everything except the desk full of love-letters, of which there was no sign anywhere.

Farther in still I went descending into the deepest of the dark galleries below, then climbing up to the upper storeys. I was alone. I called but never an answer came. I was alone. There was no one else in the vast, winding labyrinth of a house. Night fell and, reluctant to leave, I sat down in the shadows on one of the chairs formerly my own. From time to time I shouted, 'Hallo! Hallo! Anybody there?'

I must have been there for more than an hour when I heard footsteps; soft, slow footsteps coming from I knew not where. I nearly ran away but, bracing myself, I called out once more and noticed a gleam of light coming from the next room.

'Who's there?' called a voice.

'A customer,' I replied.

'Don't you think it's a bit late to just wander into somebody's shop like this?'

'I've been waiting over an hour to see you,' I went on.

'You could have come back tomorrow.'

'I shall have left Rouen tomorrow.'

I dared not go forward and he showed no sign of coming to me. I could still see the gleam of light shining on a tapestry which showed two angels flying over a battlefield. That was mine also.

'Well? Are you coming or not?' I said.

'I'm waiting for you,' he replied.

I rose and went in his direction.

Standing in the middle of a large room was a very small man, phenomenally fat, and extremely ugly. He had a meagre, ill-trimmed, yellowing beard and not a hair on his head. Not one! As he held up a candle in his outstretched hand to look me over, his skull seemed to me like a little moon in this enormous room filled with old furniture. In his puffy face there were deep furrows into which the eyes disappeared. I haggled over three of my own chairs and, giving my room number at the hotel, paid a vast sum of money for them. They were to be delivered the following morning at nine o'clock. I then left the room and with much ceremony he saw me to the door.

I made straight for the house of the central commissioner of police whom I told about the theft of my furniture and my recent rediscovery of it. He wired forthwith, requesting information from the office of the public prosecutor who originally investigated the theft, and asked me to wait till the reply came. An hour later, to my great satisfaction, he was in possession of the necessary information.

'I intend to arrest this man,' he said. 'His suspicions may have been aroused and he may try to spirit away your property. Would you like to go and have your dinner, then come back to me in two hours' time? I shall have him here by then and will question him further in your presence.'

'Most willingly, Monsieur. I'm very grateful indeed to you.'

I went and dined at my hotel, eating more heartily than I could have imagined possible, very largely I suppose because I was so glad at the prospect of the man soon being under arrest. Two hours later I returned to the police officer's house where he was waiting for me.

'Well, Monsieur,' he said, as soon as he saw me, 'we didn't manage to find your man. My officers have been unable to get hold of him.'

Oh no! I felt faint.

'But ... you found the house, didn't you?'

'Easily. It will be under surveillance and guarded till he returns. As for the man himself, he's disappeared.'

'Disappeared?'

'Disappeared. Normally he spends the evening with his neighbour, another dealer, a real old witch, the widow Bidouin. She hasn't seen him tonight and can give us no information concerning his whereabouts. We shall have to wait until morning.'

I left him. How sinister and how haunted did the streets of Rouen seem to me then. I hardly slept all night. Each time I nodded off it was into one nightmare after another. I did not wish to appear too anxious or impatient, so waited until ten o'clock the following morning before making my way to the police. The dealer had not reappeared. His shop remained closed. The commissioner said to me: 'I've gone through all the necessary procedures. The public prosecutor's office is aware of these developments. We shall make our way together to the store and have it opened up. You will show me all the items of property which are yours.'

We were whisked away in a coupe. Police officers with a locksmith in attendance were stationed at the shop entrance door which was now open. Upon entering I saw no sign of my cupboard, my armchairs, my tables, or any single one of the objects with which my house had been furnished, nothing at all—whereas the previous evening I had been unable to take a step without bumping into one or other of my former possessions.

The commissioner was surprised. At first he looked at me with suspicion.

'My God, Monsieur!' I said to him, 'isn't it a bit of a coincidence that my property should disappear at precisely the same time as the dealer?'

He smiled.

'True enough! It was a mistake to buy your own things yesterday and pay for them. It's obviously tipped him off.'

I went on: 'What I simply cannot understand is that all the space taken up by my furniture is now filled completely with other stuff.'

'Oh!' replied the commissioner, 'he's had all night ... and used accomplices, no doubt. This house is bound to lead in some way into the one next door. But don't worry, Monsieur, leave it all to me. The devil won't escape us for long, not while we're sitting on top of his lair, at least.'

Oh my heart, my poor heart! How wildly it was beating!

I stayed for about two weeks in Rouen. The man never returned. My God! My God! Who in the world would ever be able to get in *his* way? Take *him* by surprise? On the morning of my sixteenth day there I received from my gardener, whom I had left in charge of the looted and still deserted house, the following strange letter:

> Monsieur,
> May I inform Monsieur that last night something occurred here that no one, not even the police, can account for. All the furniture has come back; all, without exception and down to the smallest article. The house is now exactly as it was on the day before the robbery. We cannot get our heads around it. It happened between Friday night and the early hours of Saturday morning. The paths are all trampled over as though everything had been dragged from the gate to the front door. It was the same in reverse on the day we found them to have disappeared.
> We await instructions from Monsieur whose humble servant I remain, Raudin, Philippe.

Oh no! No! No! No! I will not go back!

I took the letter to the commissioner of Rouen.

'A clever little restitution,' he said. 'Let's play dead. We'll pick him up one of these days.'

But he's never been picked up. No, they've never managed to pick him up and now I'm as terrified of him as if I had a wild beast on my tracks. Nowhere to be found! He is nowhere to be found, that monster with the moon-skull! They'll never catch him!

He'll never go back to that place of his! What does he care about it? *I'm* the only one who can catch him and I won't do it!

I won't! I won't! I won't!

And even if he does go back, even if he does return to his shop, who could prove that my furniture was there? There's only my word to go on and I can tell that's not being seen as entirely reliable these days. Oh, no! I could no longer go on living that way. I could no longer keep secret what I had seen. I could not carry on living as normal with the fear at the back of my mind that something like that could start up again. I came to see the director of this clinic and told him everything. After a lengthy consultation, he said: 'Would you be willing, Monsieur, to come and live with us here for a while?'

'More than willing, Monsieur.'

'Do you have money?'

'Yes, Monsieur.'

'Would you like a private room?'

'Yes, Monsieur.'

'Would you like to have friends come and see you?'

'No, Monsieur, no one. The man in Rouen might want to get his own back and follow me here.'

And so I have been alone, quite alone, for three months now. I'm more or less happy. Only one thing worries me: what if the dealer went mad? What if he were brought to this clinic? You see? Even in prison you're never absolutely safe you know!

The 20th Century

Introduction to the 20th Century

By Gail Finney

Twentieth-century culture has often been divided into two principal movements or modes: modernism, spanning the first few decades of the 1900s, and postmodernism, associated with the era following the Second World War. The 20th-century works in this anthology can fruitfully be examined through the lens of this distinction. In very broad terms, modernism has been characterized as epistemologically driven, i.e., occupied with the quest for knowledge—how can I interpret the world?—whereas postmodernism has been viewed as ontologically motivated, or concerned with modes of being—which world is this?[1] Whereas modernist works typically draw on canonical literature, postmodernism is frequently playful, parodic, and/or experimental. Both movements lend themselves to the portrayal of fantasy and the supernatural.

In many modernist narratives, the reader's hesitation between reading a work as uncanny and reading it as marvelous is caused by ambiguity concerning perspective or point of view. James's *The Turn of the Screw*, for example, a quintessentially modernist work, is framed as a ghost story but is colored by perspectivism, or the belief that what we call reality is shaped by the perspective of the perceiver. First formulated systematically by Friedrich Nietzsche, this doctrine holds that there is no such thing as objective reality, since everyone perceives the world differently. This line of thought can be seen as an extension of the early German idealist view, mentioned in the "Introduction to the 19th Century" in this volume, that the human mind cannot penetrate to the essence of things but rather can only perceive appearances, meaning that reality is necessarily subjective. Whether the reader interprets the seemingly supernatural characters in *The Turn of the Screw* as actual ghosts or as figments of the governess's imagination (as the principal narrator of the tale) depends on whether one regards her as deranged or sane. The foundation of this modernist work is an epistemological quest: the reader is motivated to solve the mystery, to know the truth—but James's ingenious narrative technique, refracting the narration through several perspectives, thwarts any definitive, objective solution. The resulting hesitation in the reader places James's tale in Todorov's category of the fantastic. A similar effect is achieved by the early silent film *The Cabinet of Dr. Caligari*, in which the complicated narrative structure blurs the lines between reality and illusion, authority and subordination, and sanity and insanity.

1 Brian McHale, *Postmodernist Fiction* (New York: Methuen, 1987), esp. pp. 1–11.

Borges's work can be seen to straddle the modernist and postmodernist modes. His stories often resemble detective stories in that they present a mystery and then pursue a solution. But in "The Library of Babel" and "The Garden of Forking Paths," the narrative form prevents the reader from achieving a pat resolution: Borges rejects linearity and instead uses a narrative structure resembling a collage or web. His verbal complexity and labyrinthine style, previewed in the titles of both stories, create a kind of hesitation in the reader that is akin to the fantastic.

With Cocteau's *Beauty and the Beast* we arrive at surrealism, a movement whose cultural artifacts virtually all depict figures, events, or scenes of fantasy. Surrealist art, which flourished particularly in the 1920s and 1930s, attempts to portray the workings of the unconscious mind, so that much of it is eerie and dreamlike, yet the style employed is typically realistic. The depiction of bizarre, surprising, and incongruous subjects by means of realistic detail produces a jarring and disorienting effect on the reader or viewer. Cocteau's film is a kind of surrealist fairy tale, symbolically exploring an ancient theme in literature and art: our fear of the bestial aspects of ourselves. The figure of the benevolent beast demonstrates the fact that surface does not necessarily correspond to essence, expressed in the maxim that you can't judge a book by its cover. But this commonplace notion is conveyed by fairy-tale trappings such as magical horses and instantaneous transformations, as well as by the haunting interior of the beast's castle, fitted out with candelabra composed of human arms and statues with eyes that move. As in conventional fairy tales, the viewer accepts the magical trappings of the film as marvelous, but the surrealist quality of the setting renders the film unforgettable.

The modernist writer Kafka, who often begins his narratives by presenting an unheard-of event in a straightforward, unceremonious manner, typically relates bizarrely fantastic, dreamlike occurrences in a sober, even detached narrative voice. It is important to note Todorov's claim that his typology cannot accommodate Kafka: the dichotomy between the rational everyday world and the supernatural on which the fantastic is conventionally based is absent in Kafka's works, since the everyday world is itself incomprehensible.

Márquez's fiction exemplifies yet another subversion of realism, termed "magic realism." This mode can be seen as a subcategory of postmodernism. Magic realism is most commonly associated with Latin America, where it enjoyed a heyday from the 1940s through the 1960s, although it appears in European and North American writers as well. Márquez's stories, "A Very Old Man with Enormous Wings" and "The Handsomest Drowned Man in the World," exemplify the tendency of magic realism to blur the line between fantasy and reality, between the extraordinary and the commonplace, often by means of a narrator who is not shocked or surprised by the bizarre incidents he describes. Both the winged man and the drowned man are described so realistically and matter-of-factly that the reader, although confronted by clearly supernatural details, is uncertain about the ontological status of these characters. Hence, Márquez can be regarded as a master of the technique, so common in fantastic literature of the 1900s, of portraying unheard-of, supernatural phenomena with consummate stylistic realism, thereby achieving effects of disorientation that are appropriate for the century of unprecedented scientific and technological progress.

The Turn of the Screw

By Henry James

Introduction

The story had held us, round the fire, sufficiently breathless, but except the obvious remark that it was gruesome, as, on Christmas Eve in an old house, a strange tale should essentially be, I remember no comment uttered till somebody happened to say that it was the only case he had met in which such a visitation had fallen on a child. The case, I may mention, was that of an apparition in just such an old house as had gathered us for the occasion—an appearance, of a dreadful kind, to a little boy sleeping in the room with his mother and waking her up in the terror of it; waking her not to dissipate his dread and soothe him to sleep again, but to encounter also, herself, before she had succeeded in doing so, the same sight that had shaken him. It was this observation that drew from Douglas—not immediately, but later in the evening—a reply that had the interesting consequence to which I call attention. Someone else told a story not particularly effective, which I saw he was not following. This I took for a sign that he had himself something to produce and that we should only have to wait. We waited in fact till two nights later; but that same evening, before we scattered, he brought out what was in his mind.

"I quite agree—in regard to Griffin's ghost, or whatever it was—that its appearing first to the little boy, at so tender an age, adds a particular touch. But it's not the first occurrence of its charming kind that I know to have involved a child. If the child gives the effect another turn of the screw, what do you say to two children—?"

"We say, of course," somebody exclaimed, "that they give two turns! Also that we want to hear about them."

I can see Douglas there before the fire, to which he had got up to present his back, looking down at his interlocutor with his hands in his pockets. "Nobody but me, till now, has ever heard. It's quite too horrible." This, naturally, was declared by several voices to give the thing the utmost price, and our friend, with quiet art, prepared his triumph by turning his eyes over the rest of us and going on: "It's beyond everything. Nothing at all that I know touches it."

"For sheer terror?" I remember asking.

He seemed to say it was not so simple as that; to be really at a loss how to qualify it. He passed his hand over his eyes, made a little wincing grimace. "For dreadful—dreadfulness!"

"Oh, how delicious!" cried one of the women.

He took no notice of her; he looked at me, but as if, instead of me, he saw what he spoke of. "For general uncanny ugliness and horror and pain."

"Well then," I said, "just sit right down and begin."

He turned round to the fire, gave a kick to a log, watched it an instant. Then as he faced us again: "I can't begin. I shall have to send to town." There was a unanimous groan at this, and much reproach; after which, in his preoccupied way, he explained. "The story's written. It's in a locked drawer—it has not been out for years. I could write to my man and enclose the key; he could send down the packet as he finds it." It was to me in particular that he appeared to propound this—appeared almost to appeal for aid not to hesitate. He had broken a thickness of ice, the formation of many a winter; had had his reasons for a long silence. The others resented postponement, but it was just his scruples that charmed me. I adjured him to write by the first post and to agree with us for an early hearing; then I asked him if the experience in question had been his own. To this his answer was prompt. "Oh, thank God, no!"

"And is the record yours? You took the thing down?"

"Nothing but the impression. I took that here"—he tapped his heart. "I've never lost it."

"Then your manuscript—?"

"Is in old, faded ink, and in the most beautiful hand." He hung fire again. "A woman's. She has been dead these twenty years. She sent me the pages in question before she died." They were all listening now, and of course there was somebody to be arch, or at any rate to draw the inference. But if he put the inference by without a smile it was also without irritation. "She was a most charming person, but she was ten years older than I. She was my sister's governess," he quietly said. "She was the most agreeable woman I've ever known in her position; she would have been worthy of any whatever. It was long ago, and this episode was long before. I was at Trinity, and I found her at home on my coming down the second summer. I was much there that year—it was a beautiful one; and we had, in her off-hours, some strolls and talks in the garden—talks in which she struck me as awfully clever and nice. Oh yes; don't grin: I liked her extremely and am glad to this day to think she liked me, too. If she hadn't she wouldn't have told me. She had never told anyone. It wasn't simply that she said so, but that I knew she hadn't. I was sure; I could see. You'll easily judge why when you hear."

"Because the thing had been such a scare?"

He continued to fix me. "You'll easily judge," he repeated: "You will."

I fixed him, too. "I see. She was in love."

He laughed for the first time. "You are acute. Yes, she was in love. That is, she had been. That came out—she couldn't tell her story without its coming out. I saw it, and she saw I saw it; but neither of us spoke of it. I remember the time and the place—the corner of the lawn, the shade of the great beeches and the long, hot summer afternoon. It wasn't a scene for a shudder; but oh—!" He quitted the fire and dropped back into his chair.

"You'll receive the packet Thursday morning?" I inquired.

"Probably not till the second post."

"Well then; after dinner—"

"You'll all meet me here?" He looked us round again. "Isn't anybody going?" It was almost the tone of hope.

"Everybody will stay!"

"I will"—and "I will!" cried the ladies whose departure had been fixed. Mrs. Griffin, however, expressed the need for a little more light. "Who was it she was in love with?"

"The story will tell," I took upon myself to reply.

"Oh, I can't wait for the story!"

"The story won't tell," said Douglas; "not in any literal, vulgar way."

"More's the pity, then. That's the only way I ever understand."

"Won't you tell, Douglas?" somebody else inquired.

He sprang to his feet again. "Yes—tomorrow. Now I must go to bed. Good night." And quickly catching up a candlestick, he left us slightly bewildered. From our end of the great brown hall we heard his step on the stair; whereupon Mrs. Griffin spoke. "Well, if I don't know who she was in love with, I know who he was."

"She was ten years older," said her husband.

"Raison de plus—at that age! But it's rather nice, his long reticence."

"Forty years!" Griffin put in.

"With this outbreak at last."

"The outbreak," I returned, "will make a tremendous occasion of Thursday night;" and everyone so agreed with me that, in the light of it, we lost all attention for everything else. The last story, however incomplete and like the mere opening of a serial, had been told; we handshook and "candlestuck," as somebody said, and went to bed.

I knew the next day that a letter containing the key had, by the first post, gone off to his London apartments; but in spite of—or perhaps just on account of—the eventual diffusion of this knowledge we quite let him alone till after dinner, till such an hour of the evening, in fact, as might best accord with the kind of emotion on which our hopes were fixed. Then he became as communicative as we could desire and indeed gave us his best reason for being so. We had it from him again before the fire in the hall, as we had had our mild wonders of the previous night. It appeared that the narrative he had promised to read us really required for a proper intelligence a few words of prologue. Let me say here distinctly, to have done with it, that this narrative, from an exact transcript of my own made much later, is what I shall presently give. Poor Douglas, before his death—when it was in sight—committed to me the manuscript that reached him on the third of these days and that, on the same spot, with immense effect, he began to read to our hushed little circle on the night of the fourth. The departing ladies who had said they would stay didn't, of course, thank heaven, stay: they departed, in consequence of arrangements made, in a rage of curiosity, as they professed, produced by the touches with which he had already worked us up. But that only made his little final auditory more compact and select, kept it, round the hearth, subject to a common thrill.

The first of these touches conveyed that the written statement took up the tale at a point after it had, in a manner, begun. The fact to be in possession of was therefore that his old friend, the youngest of several daughters of a poor country parson, had, at the age of twenty, on taking service for the first time in the schoolroom, come up to London, in trepidation, to answer in person an advertisement that had already placed her in brief correspondence with the advertiser. This person proved, on her presenting herself, for judgment, at a house in Harley Street, that impressed her as vast and imposing—this prospective patron proved a gentleman, a bachelor in the prime of life, such a figure as had never risen, save in a dream or an old novel, before a fluttered, anxious girl out of a Hampshire vicarage. One could easily fix his type; it never, happily, dies out. He was handsome and bold and pleasant, offhand and gay and kind. He struck her, inevitably, as gallant and splendid, but what took her most of all and gave her the courage she afterward showed was that he put the whole thing to her as a kind of favor, an obligation he should gratefully incur. She conceived him as rich, but as fearfully extravagant—saw him all in a glow of high fashion, of good looks, of expensive habits, of charming ways with women. He had for his own town residence a big house filled with the spoils of travel and the trophies of the chase; but it was to his country home, an old family place in Essex, that he wished her immediately to proceed.

He had been left, by the death of their parents in India, guardian to a small nephew and a small niece, children of a younger, a military brother, whom he had lost two years before. These children were, by the strangest of chances for a man in his position—a lone man without the right sort of experience or a grain of patience—very heavily on his hands. It had all been a great worry and, on his own part doubtless, a series of blunders, but he immensely pitied the poor chicks and had done all he could; had in particular sent them down to his other house, the proper place for them being of course the country, and kept them there, from the first, with the best people he could find to look after them, parting even with his own servants to wait on them and going down himself, whenever he might, to see how they were doing. The awkward thing was that they had practically no other relations and that his own affairs took up all his time. He had put them in possession of Bly, which was healthy and secure, and had placed at the head of their little establishment—but below stairs only—an excellent woman, Mrs. Grose, whom he was sure his visitor would like and who had formerly been maid to his mother. She was now housekeeper and was also acting for the time as superintendent to the little girl, of whom, without children of her own, she was, by good luck, extremely fond. There were plenty of people to help, but of course the young lady who should go down as governess would be in supreme authority. She would also have, in holidays, to look after the small boy, who had been for a term at school—young as he was to be sent, but what else could be done?—and who, as the holidays were about to begin, would be back from one day to the other. There had been for the two children at first a young lady whom they had had the misfortune to lose. She had done for them quite beautifully—she was a most respectable person—till her death, the great awkwardness of which had, precisely, left no alternative but the school for little Miles. Mrs. Grose, since then, in the way of manners and things, had done as she could for Flora; and there were, further, a cook, a housemaid, a dairywoman, an old pony, an old groom, and an old gardener, all likewise thoroughly respectable.

So far had Douglas presented his picture when someone put a question. "And what did the former governess die of?—of so much respectability?"

Our friend's answer was prompt. "That will come out. I don't anticipate."

"Excuse me—I thought that was just what you are doing."

"In her successor's place," I suggested, "I should have wished to learn if the office brought with it—"

"Necessary danger to life?" Douglas completed my thought. "She did wish to learn, and she did learn. You shall hear tomorrow what she learned. Meanwhile, of course, the prospect struck her as slightly grim. She was young, untried, nervous: it was a vision of serious duties and little company, of really great loneliness. She hesitated—took a couple of days to consult and consider. But the salary offered much exceeded her modest measure, and on a second interview she faced the music, she engaged." And Douglas, with this, made a pause that, for the benefit of the company, moved me to throw in—

"The moral of which was of course the seduction exercised by the splendid young man. She succumbed to it."

He got up and, as he had done the night before, went to the fire, gave a stir to a log with his foot, then stood a moment with his back to us. "She saw him only twice."

"Yes, but that's just the beauty of her passion."

A little to my surprise, on this, Douglas turned round to me. "It was the beauty of it. There were others," he went on, "who hadn't succumbed. He told her frankly all his difficulty—that for several applicants the conditions had been prohibitive. They were, somehow, simply afraid. It sounded dull—it sounded strange; and all the more so because of his main condition."

"Which was—?"

"That she should never trouble him—but never, never: neither appeal nor complain nor write about anything; only meet all questions herself, receive all moneys from his solicitor, take the whole thing over and let him alone. She promised to do this, and she mentioned to me that when, for a moment, disburdened, delighted, he held her hand, thanking her for the sacrifice, she already felt rewarded."

"But was that all her reward?" one of the ladies asked.

"She never saw him again."

"Oh!" said the lady; which, as our friend immediately left us again, was the only other word of importance contributed to the subject till, the next night, by the corner of the hearth, in the best chair, he opened the faded red cover of a thin old-fashioned gilt-edged album. The whole thing took indeed more nights than one, but on the first occasion the same lady put another question. "What is your title?"

"I haven't one."

"Oh, I have!" I said. But Douglas, without heeding me, had begun to read with a fine clearness that was like a rendering to the ear of the beauty of his author's hand.

Chapter 1

I remember the whole beginning as a succession of flights and drops, a little seesaw of the right throbs and the wrong. After rising, in town, to meet his appeal, I had at all events a couple of very bad days—found myself doubtful again, felt indeed sure I had made a mistake. In this state of mind I spent the long hours of bumping, swinging coach that carried me to the stopping place at which I was to be met by a vehicle from the house. This convenience, I was told, had been ordered, and I found, toward the close of the June afternoon, a commodious fly in waiting for me. Driving at that hour, on a lovely day, through a country to which the summer sweetness seemed to offer me a friendly welcome, my fortitude mounted afresh and, as we turned into the avenue, encountered a reprieve that was probably but a proof of the point to which it had sunk. I suppose I had expected, or had dreaded, something so melancholy that what greeted me was a good surprise. I remember as a most pleasant impression the broad, clear front, its open windows and fresh curtains and the pair of maids looking out; I remember the lawn and the bright flowers and the crunch of my wheels on the gravel and the clustered treetops over which the rooks circled and cawed in the golden sky. The scene had a greatness that made it a different affair from my own scant home, and there immediately appeared at the door, with a little girl in her hand, a civil person who dropped me as decent a curtsy as if I had been the mistress or a distinguished visitor. I had received in Harley Street a narrower notion of the place, and that, as I recalled it, made me think the proprietor still more of a gentleman, suggested that what I was to enjoy might be something beyond his promise.

I had no drop again till the next day, for I was carried triumphantly through the following hours by my introduction to the younger of my pupils. The little girl who accompanied Mrs. Grose appeared to me on the spot a creature so charming as to make it a great fortune to have to do with her. She was the most beautiful child I had ever seen, and I afterward wondered that my employer had not told me more of her. I slept little that night—I was too much excited; and this astonished me, too, I recollect, remained with me, adding to my sense of the liberality with which I was treated. The large, impressive room, one of the best in the house, the great state bed, as I almost felt it, the full, figured draperies, the long glasses in which, for the first time, I could see myself from head to foot, all struck me—like the extraordinary charm of my small charge—as so many things thrown in. It was thrown in as well, from the first moment, that I should get on with Mrs. Grose in a relation over which, on my way, in the coach, I fear I had rather brooded. The only thing indeed that in this early outlook might have made me shrink again was the clear circumstance of her being so glad to see me. I perceived within half an hour that she was so glad—stout, simple, plain, clean, wholesome woman—as to be positively on her guard against showing it too much. I wondered even then a little why she should wish not to show it, and that, with reflection, with suspicion, might of course have made me uneasy.

But it was a comfort that there could be no uneasiness in a connection with anything so beatific as the radiant image of my little girl, the vision of whose angelic beauty had probably more than anything else to do with the restlessness that, before morning, made me several times rise and wander about my room to take in the whole picture and prospect; to watch, from my open window, the faint summer dawn, to look at such portions of the rest of the house as I could catch, and to listen, while, in the fading dusk, the first birds began to twitter, for the possible recurrence of a sound or two, less natural and not without, but within, that I had fancied I heard. There had been a moment when I believed I recognized, faint and far, the cry of a child; there had been another when I found myself just consciously starting as at the passage, before my door, of a light footstep. But these fancies were not marked enough not to be thrown off, and it is only in the light, or the gloom, I should rather say, of other and subsequent matters that they now come back to me. To watch, teach, "form" little Flora would too evidently be the making of a happy and useful life. It had been agreed between us downstairs that after this first occasion I should have her as a matter of course at night, her small white bed being already arranged, to that end, in my room. What I had undertaken was the whole care of her, and she had remained, just this last time, with Mrs. Grose only as an effect of our consideration for my inevitable strangeness and her natural timidity. In spite of this timidity—which the child herself, in the oddest way in the world, had been perfectly frank and brave about, allowing it, without a sign of uncomfortable consciousness, with the deep, sweet serenity indeed of one of Raphael's holy infants, to be discussed, to be imputed to her, and to determine us—I feel quite sure she would presently like me. It was part of what I already liked Mrs. Grose herself for, the pleasure I could see her feel in my admiration and wonder as I sat at supper with four tall candles and with my pupil, in a high chair and a bib, brightly facing me, between them, over bread and milk. There were naturally things that in Flora's presence could pass between us only as prodigious and gratified looks, obscure and roundabout allusions.

"And the little boy—does he look like her? Is he too so very remarkable?"

One wouldn't flatter a child. "Oh, miss, most remarkable. If you think well of this one!"—and she stood there with a plate in her hand, beaming at our companion, who looked from one of us to the other with placid heavenly eyes that contained nothing to check us.

"Yes; if I do—?"

"You will be carried away by the little gentleman!"

"Well, that, I think, is what I came for—to be carried away. I'm afraid, however," I remember feeling the impulse to add, "I'm rather easily carried away. I was carried away in London!"

I can still see Mrs. Grose's broad face as she took this in. "In Harley Street?"

"In Harley Street."

"Well, miss, you're not the first—and you won't be the last."

"Oh, I've no pretension," I could laugh, "to being the only one. My other pupil, at any rate, as I understand, comes back tomorrow?"

"Not tomorrow—Friday, miss. He arrives, as you did, by the coach, under care of the guard, and is to be met by the same carriage."

I forthwith expressed that the proper as well as the pleasant and friendly thing would be therefore that on the arrival of the public conveyance I should be in waiting for him with his little sister; an idea in which Mrs. Grose concurred so heartily that I somehow took her manner as a kind of comforting pledge—never falsified, thank heaven!—that we should on every question be quite at one. Oh, she was glad I was there!

What I felt the next day was, I suppose, nothing that could be fairly called a reaction from the cheer of my arrival; it was probably at the most only a slight oppression produced by a fuller measure of the scale, as I walked round them, gazed up at them, took them in, of my new circumstances. They had, as it were, an extent and mass for which I had not been prepared and in the presence of which I found myself, freshly, a little scared as well as a little proud. Lessons, in this agitation, certainly suffered some delay; I reflected that my first duty was, by the gentlest arts I could contrive, to win the child into the sense of knowing me. I spent the day with her out-of-doors; I arranged with her, to her great satisfaction, that it should be she, she only, who might show me the place. She showed it step by step and room by room and secret by secret, with droll, delightful, childish talk about it and with the result, in half an hour, of our becoming immense friends. Young as she was, I was struck, throughout our little tour, with her confidence and courage with the way, in empty chambers and dull corridors, on crooked staircases that made me pause and even on the summit of an old machicolated square tower that made me dizzy, her morning music, her disposition to tell me so many more things than she asked, rang out and led me on. I have not seen Bly since the day I left it, and I daresay that to my older and more informed eyes it would now appear sufficiently contracted. But as my little conductress, with her hair of gold and her frock of blue, danced before me round corners and pattered down passages, I had the view of a castle of romance inhabited by a rosy sprite, such a place as would somehow, for diversion of the young idea, take all color out of storybooks and fairytales. Wasn't it just a storybook over which I had fallen adoze and adream? No; it was a big, ugly, antique, but convenient house, embodying a few features of a building still older, half-replaced and half-utilized, in which I had the fancy of our being almost as lost as a handful of passengers in a great drifting ship. Well, I was, strangely, at the helm!

Chapter 2

This came home to me when, two days later, I drove over with Flora to meet, as Mrs. Grose said, the little gentleman; and all the more for an incident that, presenting itself the second evening, had deeply disconcerted me. The first day had been, on the whole, as I have expressed, reassuring; but I was to see it wind up in keen apprehension. The postbag, that evening—it came late—contained a letter for me, which, however, in the hand of my employer, I found to be composed but of a few words enclosing another, addressed to himself, with a seal still unbroken. "This, I recognize, is from the headmaster, and the headmaster's an awful bore. Read him, please; deal with him; but mind you don't report. Not a word. I'm off!" I broke the seal with a great effort—so great a one that I was a long time coming to it; took the unopened missive at last up to my room and only attacked it just before going to bed. I had better have let it wait till morning, for it gave me a second sleepless night. With no counsel to take, the next day, I was full of distress; and it finally got so the better of me that I determined to open myself at least to Mrs. Grose.

"What does it mean? The child's dismissed his school."

She gave me a look that I remarked at the moment; then, visibly, with a quick blankness, seemed to try to take it back. "But aren't they all—?"

"Sent home—yes. But only for the holidays. Miles may never go back at all."

Consciously, under my attention, she reddened. "They won't take him?"

"They absolutely decline."

At this she raised her eyes, which she had turned from me; I saw them fill with good tears. "What has he done?"

I hesitated; then I judged best simply to hand her my letter—which, however, had the effect of making her, without taking it, simply put her hands behind her. She shook her head sadly. "Such things are not for me, miss."

My counselor couldn't read! I winced at my mistake, which I attenuated as I could, and opened my letter again to repeat it to her; then, faltering in the act and folding it up once more, I put it back in my pocket. "Is he really bad?"

The tears were still in her eyes. "Do the gentlemen say so?"

"They go into no particulars. They simply express their regret that it should be impossible to keep him. That can have only one meaning." Mrs. Grose listened with dumb emotion; she forbore to ask me what this meaning might be; so that, presently, to put the thing with some coherence and with the mere aid of her presence to my own mind, I went on: "That he's an injury to the others."

At this, with one of the quick turns of simple folk, she suddenly flamed up. "Master Miles! Him an injury?"

There was such a flood of good faith in it that, though I had not yet seen the child, my very fears made me jump to the absurdity of the idea. I found myself, to meet my friend the better, offering it, on the spot, sarcastically. "To his poor little innocent mates!"

"It's too dreadful," cried Mrs. Grose, "to say such cruel things! Why, he's scarce ten years old."

"Yes, yes; it would be incredible."

She was evidently grateful for such a profession. "See him, miss, first. Then believe it!" I felt forthwith a new impatience to see him; it was the beginning of a curiosity that, for all the next hours, was to deepen almost to pain. Mrs. Grose was aware, I could judge, of what she had produced in me, and she followed it up with assurance. "You might as well believe it of the little lady. Bless her," she added the next moment— "Look at her!"

I turned and saw that Flora, whom, ten minutes before, I had established in the schoolroom with a sheet of white paper, a pencil, and a copy of nice "round o's," now presented herself to view at the open door. She expressed in her little way an extraordinary detachment from disagreeable duties, looking to me, however, with a great childish light that seemed to offer it as a mere result of the affection she had conceived for my person, which had rendered necessary that she should follow me. I needed nothing more than this to feel the full force of Mrs. Grose's comparison, and, catching my pupil in my arms, covered her with kisses in which there was a sob of atonement.

Nonetheless, the rest of the day I watched for further occasion to approach my colleague, especially as, toward evening, I began to fancy she rather sought to avoid me. I overtook her, I remember, on the staircase; we went down together, and at the bottom I detained her, holding her there with a hand on her arm. "I take what you said to me at noon as a declaration that you've never known him to be bad."

She threw back her head; she had clearly, by this time, and very honestly, adopted an attitude. "Oh, never known him—I don't pretend that!"

I was upset again. "Then you have known him—?"

"Yes indeed, miss, thank God!"

On reflection I accepted this. "You mean that a boy who never is—?"

"Is no boy for me!"

I held her tighter. "You like them with the spirit to be naughty?" Then, keeping pace with her answer, "So do I!" I eagerly brought out. "But not to the degree to contaminate—"

"To contaminate?"—my big word left her at a loss. I explained it. "To corrupt."

She stared, taking my meaning in; but it produced in her an odd laugh. "Are you afraid he'll corrupt you?" She put the question with such a fine bold humor that, with a laugh, a little silly doubtless, to match her own, I gave way for the time to the apprehension of ridicule.

But the next day, as the hour for my drive approached, I cropped up in another place. "What was the lady who was here before?"

"The last governess? She was also young and pretty—almost as young and almost as pretty, miss, even as you."

"Ah, then, I hope her youth and her beauty helped her!" I recollect throwing off. "He seems to like us young and pretty!"

"Oh, he did," Mrs. Grose assented: "it was the way he liked everyone!" She had no sooner spoken indeed than she caught herself up. "I mean that's his way—the master's."

I was struck. "But of whom did you speak first?"

She looked blank, but she colored. "Why, of him."

"Of the master?"

"Of who else?"

There was so obviously no one else that the next moment I had lost my impression of her having accidentally said more than she meant; and I merely asked what I wanted to know. "Did she see anything in the boy—?"

"That wasn't right? She never told me."

I had a scruple, but I overcame it. "Was she careful—particular?"

Mrs. Grose appeared to try to be conscientious. "About some things—yes."

"But not about all?"

Again she considered. "Well, miss—she's gone. I won't tell tales."

"I quite understand your feeling," I hastened to reply; but I thought it, after an instant, not opposed to this concession to pursue: "Did she die here?"

"No—she went off."

I don't know what there was in this brevity of Mrs. Grose's that struck me as ambiguous. "Went off to die?" Mrs. Grose looked straight out of the window, but I felt that, hypothetically, I had a right to know what young persons engaged for Bly were expected to do. "She was taken ill, you mean, and went home?"

"She was not taken ill, so far as appeared, in this house. She left it, at the end of the year, to go home, as she said, for a short holiday, to which the time she had put in had certainly given her a right. We had then a young woman—a nursemaid who had stayed on and who was a good girl and clever; and she took the children altogether for the interval. But our young lady never came back, and at the very moment I was expecting her I heard from the master that she was dead."

I turned this over. "But of what?"

"He never told me! But please, miss," said Mrs. Grose, "I must get to my work."

Chapter 3

Her thus turning her back on me was fortunately not, for my just preoccupations, a snub that could check the growth of our mutual esteem. We met, after I had brought home little Miles, more intimately than ever on the ground of my stupefaction, my general emotion: so monstrous was I then ready to pronounce it that such a child as had now been revealed to me should be under an interdict. I was a little late on the scene, and I felt, as he stood wistfully looking out for me before the door of the inn at which the coach had put him down, that I had seen him, on the instant, without and within, in the great glow of freshness, the same positive fragrance of purity, in which I had, from the first moment, seen his little sister. He was incredibly beautiful, and Mrs. Grose had put her finger on it: everything but a sort of passion of tenderness for him was swept away by his presence. What I then and there took him to my heart for was something divine that I have never found to the same degree in any child—his indescribable little air of knowing nothing in the world but love. It would have been impossible to carry a bad name with a greater sweetness of innocence, and by the time I had got back to Bly with him I remained merely bewildered—so far, that is, as I was not outraged—by the sense of the horrible letter locked up in my room, in a drawer. As soon as I could compass a private word with Mrs. Grose I declared to her that it was grotesque.

She promptly understood me. "You mean the cruel charge—?"

"It doesn't live an instant. My dear woman, look at him!"

She smiled at my pretention to have discovered his charm. "I assure you, miss, I do nothing else! What will you say, then?" she immediately added.

"In answer to the letter?" I had made up my mind. "Nothing."

"And to his uncle?"

I was incisive. "Nothing."

"And to the boy himself?"

I was wonderful. "Nothing."

She gave with her apron a great wipe to her mouth. "Then I'll stand by you. We'll see it out."

"We'll see it out!" I ardently echoed, giving her my hand to make it a vow.

She held me there a moment, then whisked up her apron again with her detached hand. "Would you mind, miss, if I used the freedom—"

"To kiss me? No!" I took the good creature in my arms and, after we had embraced like sisters, felt still more fortified and indignant.

This, at all events, was for the time: a time so full that, as I recall the way it went, it reminds me of all the art I now need to make it a little distinct. What I look back at with amazement is the situation I accepted. I had undertaken, with my companion, to see it out, and I was under a charm, apparently, that could smooth away the extent and the far and difficult connections of such an effort. I was lifted aloft on a great wave of infatuation and pity. I found it simple, in my ignorance, my confusion, and perhaps my conceit, to assume that I could deal with a boy whose education for the world was all on the point of beginning. I am unable even to remember at this day what proposal I framed for the end of his holidays and the resumption of his studies. Lessons with me, indeed, that charming summer, we all had a theory that he was to have; but I now feel that, for weeks, the lessons must have been rather my own. I learned something—at first, certainly—that had not been one of the teachings of my small, smothered life; learned to be amused, and even amusing, and not to think for the morrow. It was the first time, in a manner, that I had known space and air and freedom, all the music of summer and all the mystery of nature. And then there was consideration—and consideration was sweet. Oh, it was a trap—not designed, but deep—to my imagination, to my delicacy, perhaps to my vanity; to whatever, in me, was most excitable. The best way to picture it all is to say that I was off my guard. They gave me so little trouble—they were of a gentleness so extraordinary. I used to speculate—but even this with a dim disconnectedness—as to how the rough future (for all futures are rough!) would handle them and might bruise them. They had the bloom of health and happiness; and yet, as if I had been in charge of a pair of little grandees, of princes of the blood, for whom everything, to be right, would have to be enclosed and protected, the only form that, in my fancy, the afteryears could take for them was that of a romantic, a really royal extension of the garden and the park. It may be, of course, above all, that what suddenly broke into this gives the previous time a charm of stillness—that hush in which something gathers or crouches. The change was actually like the spring of a beast.

In the first weeks the days were long; they often, at their finest, gave me what I used to call my own hour, the hour when, for my pupils, teatime and bedtime having come and gone, I had, before my final retirement, a small interval alone. Much as I liked my companions, this hour was the thing in the day I liked most; and I liked it best of all when, as the light faded—or rather, I should say, the day lingered and the last calls of the last birds sounded, in a flushed sky, from the old trees—I could take a turn into the grounds and enjoy, almost with a sense of property that amused and flattered me, the beauty and dignity of the place. It was a pleasure at these moments to feel myself tranquil and justified; doubtless, perhaps, also to reflect that by my discretion, my quiet good sense and general high propriety, I was giving pleasure—if he ever thought of it!—to the person to whose pressure I had responded. What I was doing was what he had earnestly hoped and directly asked of me, and that I COULD, after all, do it proved even a greater joy than I had expected. I daresay I fancied myself, in short, a remarkable young woman and took comfort in the faith that this would more publicly appear. Well, I needed to be remarkable to offer a front to the remarkable things that presently gave their first sign.

It was plump, one afternoon, in the middle of my very hour: the children were tucked away, and I had come out for my stroll. One of the thoughts that, as I don't in the least shrink now from noting, used to be with me in these wanderings was that it would be as charming as a charming story suddenly to meet someone. Someone would appear there at the turn of a path and would stand before me and smile and approve. I didn't ask more than that—I only asked that he should know; and the only way to be sure he knew would be to see it, and the kind light of it, in his handsome face. That was exactly present to me—by which I mean the face was—when, on the first of these occasions, at the end of a long June day, I stopped short on emerging from one of the plantations and coming into view of the house. What arrested me on the spot—and with a shock much greater than any vision had allowed for—was the sense that my imagination had, in a flash, turned real. He did stand there!—but high up, beyond the lawn and at the very top of the tower to which, on that first morning, little Flora had conducted me. This tower was one of a pair—square, incongruous, crenelated structures—that were distinguished, for some reason, though I could see little difference, as the new and the old. They flanked opposite ends of the house and were probably architectural absurdities, redeemed in a measure indeed by not being wholly disengaged nor of a height too pretentious, dating, in their gingerbread antiquity, from a romantic revival that was already a respectable past. I admired them, had fancies about them, for we could all profit in a degree, especially when they loomed through the dusk, by the grandeur of their actual battlements; yet it was not at such an elevation that the figure I had so often invoked seemed most in place.

It produced in me, this figure, in the clear twilight, I remember, two distinct gasps of emotion, which were, sharply, the shock of my first and that of my second surprise. My second was a violent perception of the mistake of my first: the man who met my eyes was not the person I had precipitately supposed. There came to me thus a bewilderment of vision of which, after these years, there is no living view that I can hope to give. An unknown man in a lonely place is a permitted object of fear to a young woman privately bred; and the figure that faced me was—a few more seconds assured me—as little anyone else I knew as it was the image that had been in my mind. I had not seen it in Harley Street—I had not seen it anywhere. The place, moreover, in the strangest way in the world, had, on the instant, and by the very fact of its appearance, become a solitude. To me at least, making my statement here with a deliberation with which I have never made it, the whole feeling of the moment returns. It was as if, while I took in—what I did take in—all the rest of the scene had been stricken with death. I can hear again, as I write, the intense hush in which the sounds of evening dropped. The rooks stopped cawing in the golden sky, and the friendly hour lost, for the minute, all its voice. But there was no other change in nature, unless indeed it were a change that I saw with a stranger sharpness. The gold was still in the sky, the clearness in the air, and the man who looked at me over the battlements was as definite as a picture in a frame. That's how I thought, with extraordinary quickness, of each person that he might have been and that he was not. We were confronted across our distance quite long enough for me to ask myself with intensity who then he was and to feel, as an effect of my inability to say, a wonder that in a few instants more became intense.

The great question, or one of these, is, afterward, I know, with regard to certain matters, the question of how long they have lasted. Well, this matter of mine, think what you will of it, lasted while I caught at a dozen possibilities, none of which made a difference for the better, that I could see, in there having been in the house—and for how long, above all?—a person of whom I was in ignorance. It lasted while I just bridled a little with the sense that my office demanded that there should be no such ignorance and no such person. It lasted while this visitant, at all events—and there was a touch of the strange freedom, as I remember, in the sign of familiarity of his wearing no hat—seemed to fix me, from his position, with just the question, just the scrutiny through the fading light, that his own presence provoked. We were too far apart to call to each other, but there was a moment at which, at shorter range, some challenge between us, breaking the hush, would have been the right result of our straight mutual stare. He was in one of the angles, the one away from the house, very erect, as it struck me, and with both hands on the ledge. So I saw him as I see the letters I form on this page; then, exactly, after a minute, as if to add to the spectacle, he slowly changed his place—passed, looking at me hard all the while, to the opposite corner of the platform. Yes, I had the sharpest sense that during this transit he never took his eyes from me, and I can see at this moment the way his hand, as he went, passed from one of the crenelations to the next. He stopped at the other corner, but less long, and even as he turned away still markedly fixed me. He turned away; that was all I knew.

Chapter 4

It was not that I didn't wait, on this occasion, for more, for I was rooted as deeply as I was shaken. Was there a "secret" at Bly—a mystery of Udolpho or an insane, an unmentionable relative kept in unsuspected confinement? I can't say how long I turned it over, or how long, in a confusion of curiosity and dread, I remained where I had had my collision; I only recall that when I re-entered the house darkness had quite closed in. Agitation, in the interval, certainly had held me and driven me, for I must, in circling about the place, have walked three miles; but I was to be, later on, so much more overwhelmed that this mere dawn of alarm was a comparatively human chill. The most singular part of it, in fact—singular as the rest had been—was the part I became, in the hall, aware of in meeting Mrs. Grose. This picture comes back to me in the general train—the impression, as I received it on my return, of the wide white panelled space, bright in the lamplight and with its portraits and red carpet, and of the good surprised look of my friend, which immediately told me she had missed me. It came to me straightway, under her contact, that, with plain heartiness, mere relieved anxiety at my appearance, she knew nothing whatever that could bear upon the incident I had there ready for her. I had not suspected in advance that her comfortable face would pull me up, and I somehow measured the importance of what I had seen by my thus finding myself hesitate to mention it. Scarce anything in the whole history seems to me so odd as this fact that my real beginning of fear was one, as I may say, with the instinct of sparing my companion. On the spot, accordingly, in the pleasant hall and with her eyes on me, I, for a reason that I couldn't then have phrased, achieved an inward resolution—offered a vague pretext for my lateness and, with the plea of the beauty of the night and of the heavy dew and wet feet, went as soon as possible to my room.

Here it was another affair; here, for many days after, it was a queer affair enough. There were hours, from day to day—or at least there were moments, snatched even from clear duties—when I had to shut myself up to think. It was not so much yet that I was more nervous than I could bear to be as that I was remarkably afraid of becoming so; for the truth I had now to turn over was, simply and clearly, the truth that I could arrive at no account whatever of the visitor with whom I had been so inexplicably and yet, as it seemed to me, so intimately concerned. It took little time to see that I could sound without forms of inquiry and without exciting remark any domestic complications. The shock I had suffered must have sharpened all my senses; I felt sure, at the end of three days and as the result of mere closer attention, that I had not been practiced upon by the servants nor made the object of any "game." Of whatever it was that I knew, nothing was known around me. There was but one sane inference: someone had taken a liberty rather gross. That was what, repeatedly, I dipped into my room and locked the door to say to myself. We had been, collectively, subject to an intrusion; some unscrupulous traveler, curious in old houses, had made his way in unobserved, enjoyed the prospect from the best point of view, and then stolen out as he came. If he had given me such a bold hard stare, that was but a part of his indiscretion. The good thing, after all, was that we should surely see no more of him.

This was not so good a thing, I admit, as not to leave me to judge that what, essentially, made nothing else much signify was simply my charming work. My charming work was just my life with Miles and Flora, and through nothing could I so like it as through feeling that I could throw myself into it in trouble. The attraction of my small charges was a constant joy, leading me to wonder afresh at the vanity of my original fears, the distaste I had begun by entertaining for the probable gray prose of my office. There was to be no gray prose, it appeared, and no long grind; so how could work not be charming that presented itself as daily beauty? It was all the romance of the nursery and the poetry of the schoolroom. I don't mean by this, of course, that we studied only fiction and verse; I mean I can express no otherwise the sort of interest my companions inspired. How can I describe that except by saying that instead of growing used to them—and it's a marvel for a governess: I call the sisterhood to witness!—I made constant fresh discoveries. There was one direction, assuredly, in which these discoveries stopped: deep obscurity continued to cover the region of the boy's conduct at school. It had been promptly given me, I have noted, to face that mystery without a pang. Perhaps even it would be nearer the truth to say that—without a word—he himself had cleared it up. He had made the whole charge absurd. My conclusion bloomed there with the real rose flush of his innocence: he was only too fine and fair for the little horrid, unclean school world, and he had paid a price for it. I reflected acutely that the sense of such differences, such superiorities of quality, always, on the part of the majority—which could include even stupid, sordid headmasters—turn infallibly to the vindictive.

Both the children had a gentleness (it was their only fault, and it never made Miles a muff) that kept them—how shall I express it?—almost impersonal and certainly quite unpunishable. They were like the cherubs of the anecdote, who had—morally, at any rate—nothing to whack! I remember feeling with Miles in especial as if he had had, as it were, no history. We expect of a small child a scant one, but there was in this beautiful little boy something extraordinarily sensitive, yet extraordinarily happy, that, more than in any creature of his age I have seen, struck me as beginning anew each day. He had never for a second suffered. I took this as a direct disproof of his having really been chastised. If he had been wicked he would have "caught" it, and I should have caught it by the rebound—I should have found the trace. I found nothing at all, and he was therefore an angel. He never spoke of his school, never mentioned a comrade or a master; and I, for my part, was quite too much disgusted to allude to them. Of course I was under the spell, and the wonderful part is that, even at the time, I perfectly knew I was. But I gave myself up to it; it was an antidote to any pain, and I had more pains than one. I was in receipt in these days of disturbing letters from home, where things were not going well. But with my children, what things in the world mattered? That was the question I used to put to my scrappy retirements. I was dazzled by their loveliness.

There was a Sunday—to get on—when it rained with such force and for so many hours that there could be no procession to church; in consequence of which, as the day declined, I had arranged with Mrs. Grose that, should the evening show improvement, we would attend together the late service. The rain happily stopped, and I prepared for our walk, which, through the park and by the good road to the village, would be a matter of twenty minutes. Coming downstairs to meet my colleague in the hall, I remembered a pair of gloves that had required three stitches and that had received them—with a publicity perhaps not edifying—while I sat with the children at their tea, served on Sundays, by exception, in that cold, clean temple of mahogany and brass, the "grown-up" dining room. The gloves had been dropped there, and I turned in to recover them. The day was gray enough, but the afternoon light still lingered, and it enabled me, on crossing the threshold, not only to recognize, on a chair near the wide window, then closed, the articles I wanted, but to become aware of a person on the other side of the window and looking straight in. One step into the room had sufficed; my vision was instantaneous; it was all there. The person looking straight in was the person who had already appeared to me. He appeared thus again with I won't say greater distinctness, for that was impossible, but with a nearness that represented a forward stride in our intercourse and made me, as I met him, catch my breath and turn cold. He was the same—he was the same, and seen, this time, as he had been seen before, from the waist up, the window, though the dining room was on the ground floor, not going down to the terrace on which he stood. His face was close to the glass, yet the effect of this better view was, strangely, only to show me how intense the former had been. He remained but a few seconds—long enough to convince me he also saw and recognized; but it was as if I had been looking at him for years and had known him always. Something, however, happened this time that had not happened before; his stare into my face, through the glass and across the room, was as deep and hard as then, but it quitted me for a moment during which I could still watch it, see it fix successively several other things. On the spot there came to me the added shock of a certitude that it was not for me he had come there. He had come for someone else.

The flash of this knowledge—for it was knowledge in the midst of dread—produced in me the most extraordinary effect, started as I stood there, a sudden vibration of duty and courage. I say courage because I was beyond all doubt already far gone. I bounded straight out of the door again, reached that of the house, got, in an instant, upon the drive, and, passing along the terrace as fast as I could rush, turned a corner and came full in sight. But it was in sight of nothing now—my visitor had vanished. I stopped, I almost dropped, with the real relief of this; but I took in the whole scene—I gave him time to reappear. I call it time, but how long was it? I can't speak to the purpose today of the duration of these things. That kind of measure must have left me: they couldn't have lasted as they actually appeared to me to last. The terrace and the whole place, the lawn and the garden beyond it, all I could see of the park, were empty with a great emptiness. There were shrubberies and big trees, but I remember the clear assurance I felt that none of them concealed him. He was there or was not there: not there if I didn't see him. I got hold of this; then, instinctively, instead of returning as I had come, went to the window. It was confusedly present to me that I ought to place myself where he had stood. I did so; I applied my face to the pane and looked, as he had looked, into the room. As if, at this moment, to show me exactly what his range had been, Mrs. Grose, as I had done for himself just before, came in from the hall. With this I had the full image of a repetition of what had already occurred. She saw me as I had seen my own visitant; she pulled up short as I had done; I gave her something of the shock that I had received. She turned white, and this made me ask myself if I had blanched as much. She stared, in short, and retreated on just my lines, and I knew she had then passed out and come round to me and that I should presently meet her. I remained where I was, and while I waited I thought of more things than one. But there's only one I take space to mention. I wondered why she should be scared.

Chapter 5

Oh, she let me know as soon as, round the corner of the house, she loomed again into view. "What in the name of goodness is the matter—?" She was now flushed and out of breath.

I said nothing till she came quite near. "With me?" I must have made a wonderful face. "Do I show it?"

"You're as white as a sheet. You look awful."

I considered; I could meet on this, without scruple, any innocence. My need to respect the bloom of Mrs. Grose's had dropped, without a rustle, from my shoulders, and if I wavered for the instant it was not with what I kept back. I put out my hand to her and she took it; I held her hard a little, liking to feel her close to me. There was a kind of support in the shy heave of her surprise. "You came for me for church, of course, but I can't go."

"Has anything happened?"

"Yes. You must know now. Did I look very queer?"

"Through this window? Dreadful!"

"Well," I said, "I've been frightened." Mrs. Grose's eyes expressed plainly that she had no wish to be, yet also that she knew too well her place not to be ready to share with me any marked inconvenience. Oh, it was quite settled that she must share! "Just what you saw from the dining room a minute ago was the effect of that. What I saw—just before—was much worse."

Her hand tightened. "What was it?"

"An extraordinary man. Looking in."

"What extraordinary man?"

"I haven't the least idea."

Mrs. Grose gazed round us in vain. "Then where is he gone?"

"I know still less."

"Have you seen him before?"

"Yes—once. On the old tower."

She could only look at me harder. "Do you mean he's a stranger?"

"Oh, very much!"

"Yet you didn't tell me?"

"No—for reasons. But now that you've guessed—"

Mrs. Grose's round eyes encountered this charge. "Ah, I haven't guessed!" she said very simply. "How can I if you don't imagine?"

"I don't in the very least."

"You've seen him nowhere but on the tower?"

"And on this spot just now."

Mrs. Grose looked round again. "What was he doing on the tower?"

"Only standing there and looking down at me."

She thought a minute. "Was he a gentleman?"

I found I had no need to think. "No." She gazed in deeper wonder. "No."

"Then nobody about the place? Nobody from the village?"

"Nobody—nobody. I didn't tell you, but I made sure."

She breathed a vague relief: this was, oddly, so much to the good. It only went indeed a little way. "But if he isn't a gentleman—"

"What is he? He's a horror."

"A horror?"

"He's—God help me if I know what he is!"

Mrs. Grose looked round once more; she fixed her eyes on the duskier distance, then, pulling herself together, turned to me with abrupt inconsequence. "It's time we should be at church."

"Oh, I'm not fit for church!"

"Won't it do you good?"

"It won't do them—! I nodded at the house.

"The children?"

"I can't leave them now."

"You're afraid—?"

I spoke boldly. "I'm afraid of him."

Mrs. Grose's large face showed me, at this, for the first time, the faraway faint glimmer of a consciousness more acute: I somehow made out in it the delayed dawn of an idea I myself had not given her and that was as yet quite obscure to me. It comes back to me that I thought instantly of this as something I could get from her; and I felt it to be connected with the desire she presently showed to know more. "When was it—on the tower?"

"About the middle of the month. At this same hour."

"Almost at dark," said Mrs. Grose.

"Oh, no, not nearly. I saw him as I see you."

"Then how did he get in?"

"And how did he get out?" I laughed. "I had no opportunity to ask him! This evening, you see," I pursued, "he has not been able to get in."

"He only peeps?"

"I hope it will be confined to that!" She had now let go my hand; she turned away a little. I waited an instant; then I brought out: "Go to church. Goodbye. I must watch."

Slowly she faced me again. "Do you fear for them?"

We met in another long look. "Don't you?" Instead of answering she came nearer to the window and, for a minute, applied her face to the glass. "You see how he could see," I meanwhile went on.

She didn't move. "How long was he here?"

"Till I came out. I came to meet him."

Mrs. Grose at last turned round, and there was still more in her face. "I couldn't have come out."

"Neither could I!" I laughed again. "But I did come. I have my duty."

"So have I mine," she replied; after which she added: "What is he like?"

"I've been dying to tell you. But he's like nobody."

"Nobody?" she echoed.

"He has no hat." Then seeing in her face that she already, in this, with a deeper dismay, found a touch of picture, I quickly added stroke to stroke. "He has red hair, very red, close-curling, and a pale face, long in shape, with straight, good features and little, rather queer whiskers that are as red as his hair. His eyebrows are, somehow, darker; they look particularly arched and as if they might move a good deal. His eyes are sharp, strange—awfully; but I only know clearly that they're rather small and very fixed. His mouth's wide, and his lips are thin, and except for his little whiskers he's quite clean-shaven. He gives me a sort of sense of looking like an actor."

"An actor!" It was impossible to resemble one less, at least, than Mrs. Grose at that moment.

"I've never seen one, but so I suppose them. He's tall, active, erect," I continued, "but never—no, never!—a gentleman."

My companion's face had blanched as I went on; her round eyes started and her mild mouth gaped. "A gentleman?" she gasped, confounded, stupefied: "a gentleman he?"

"You know him then?"

She visibly tried to hold herself. "But he is handsome?"

I saw the way to help her. "Remarkably!"

"And dressed—?"

"In somebody's clothes. "They're smart, but they're not his own."

She broke into a breathless affirmative groan: "They're the master's!"

I caught it up. "You do know him?"

She faltered but a second. "Quint!" she cried.

"Quint?"

"Peter Quint—his own man, his valet, when he was here!"

"When the master was?"

Gaping still, but meeting me, she pieced it all together. "He never wore his hat, but he did wear—well, there were waistcoats missed. They were both here—last year. Then the master went, and Quint was alone."

I followed, but halting a little. "Alone?"

"Alone with us." Then, as from a deeper depth, "In charge," she added.

"And what became of him?"

She hung fire so long that I was still more mystified. "He went, too," she brought out at last.

"Went where?"

Her expression, at this, became extraordinary. "God knows where! He died."

"Died?" I almost shrieked.

She seemed fairly to square herself, plant herself more firmly to utter the wonder of it. "Yes. Mr. Quint is dead."

Chapter 6

It took of course more than that particular passage to place us together in presence of what we had now to live with as we could—my dreadful liability to impressions of the order so vividly exemplified, and my companion's knowledge, henceforth—a knowledge half consternation and half compassion—of that liability. There had been, this evening, after the revelation left me, for an hour, so prostrate—there had been, for either of us, no attendance on any service but a little service of tears and vows, of prayers and promises, a climax to the series of mutual challenges and pledges that had straightway ensued on our retreating together to the schoolroom and shutting ourselves up there to have everything out. The result of our having everything out was simply to reduce our situation to the last rigor of its elements. She herself had seen nothing, not the shadow of a shadow, and nobody in the house but the governess was in the governess's plight; yet she accepted without directly impugning my sanity the truth as I gave it to her, and ended by showing me, on this ground, an awestricken tenderness, an expression of the sense of my more than questionable privilege, of which the very breath has remained with me as that of the sweetest of human charities.

What was settled between us, accordingly, that night, was that we thought we might bear things together; and I was not even sure that, in spite of her exemption, it was she who had the best of the burden. I knew at this hour, I think, as well as I knew later, what I was capable of meeting to shelter my pupils; but it took me some time to be wholly sure of what my honest ally was prepared for to keep terms with so compromising a contract. I was queer company enough—quite as queer as the company I received; but as I trace over what we went through I see how much common ground we must have found in the one idea that, by good fortune, could steady us. It was the idea, the second movement, that led me straight out, as I may say, of the inner chamber of my dread. I could take the air in the court, at least, and there Mrs. Grose could join me. Perfectly can I recall now the particular way strength came to me before we separated for the night. We had gone over and over every feature of what I had seen.

"He was looking for someone else, you say—someone who was not you?"

"He was looking for little Miles." A portentous clearness now possessed me. "That's whom he was looking for."

"But how do you know?"

"I know, I know, I know!" My exaltation grew. "And you know, my dear!"

She didn't deny this, but I required, I felt, not even so much telling as that. She resumed in a moment, at any rate: "What if he should see him?"

"Little Miles? That's what he wants!"

She looked immensely scared again. "The child?"

"Heaven forbid! The man. He wants to appear to them." That he might was an awful conception, and yet, somehow, I could keep it at bay; which, moreover, as we lingered there, was what I succeeded in practically proving. I had an absolute certainty that I should see again what I had already seen, but something within me said that by offering myself bravely as the sole subject of such experience, by accepting, by inviting, by surmounting it all, I should serve as an expiatory victim and guard the tranquility of my companions. The children, in especial, I should thus fence about and absolutely save. I recall one of the last things I said that night to Mrs. Grose.

"It does strike me that my pupils have never mentioned—"

She looked at me hard as I musingly pulled up. "His having been here and the time they were with him?"

"The time they were with him, and his name, his presence, his history, in any way."

"Oh, the little lady doesn't remember. She never heard or knew."

"The circumstances of his death?" I thought with some intensity. "Perhaps not. But Miles would remember—Miles would know."

"Ah, don't try him!" broke from Mrs. Grose.

I returned her the look she had given me. "Don't be afraid." I continued to think. "It IS rather odd."

"That he has never spoken of him?"

"Never by the least allusion. And you tell me they were 'great friends'?"

"Oh, it wasn't him!" Mrs. Grose with emphasis declared. "It was Quint's own fancy. To play with him, I mean—to spoil him." She paused a moment; then she added: "Quint was much too free."

This gave me, straight from my vision of his face—such a face!—a sudden sickness of disgust. "Too free with my boy?"

"Too free with everyone!"

I forbore, for the moment, to analyze this description further than by the reflection that a part of it applied to several of the members of the household, of the half-dozen maids and men who were still of our small colony. But there was everything, for our apprehension, in the lucky fact that no discomfortable legend, no perturbation of scullions, had ever, within anyone's memory attached to the kind old place. It had neither bad name nor ill fame, and Mrs. Grose, most apparently, only desired to cling to me and to quake in silence. I even put her, the very last thing of all, to the test. It was when, at midnight, she had her hand on the schoolroom door to take leave. "I have it from you then—for it's of great importance—that he was definitely and admittedly bad?"

"Oh, not admittedly. I knew it—but the master didn't."

"And you never told him?"

"Well, he didn't like tale-bearing—he hated complaints. He was terribly short with anything of that kind, and if people were all right to him—"

"He wouldn't be bothered with more?" This squared well enough with my impressions of him: he was not a trouble-loving gentleman, nor so very particular perhaps about some of the company he kept. All the same, I pressed my interlocutress. "I promise you I would have told!"

She felt my discrimination. "I daresay I was wrong. But, really, I was afraid."

"Afraid of what?"

"Of things that man could do. Quint was so clever—he was so deep."

I took this in still more than, probably, I showed. "You weren't afraid of anything else? Not of his effect—?"

"His effect?" she repeated with a face of anguish and waiting while I faltered.

"On innocent little precious lives. They were in your charge."

"No, they were not in mine!" she roundly and distressfully returned. "The master believed in him and placed him here because he was supposed not to be well and the country air so good for him. So he had everything to say. Yes"—she let me have it—"even about them."

"Them—that creature?" I had to smother a kind of howl. "And you could bear it!"

"No. I couldn't—and I can't now!" And the poor woman burst into tears.

A rigid control, from the next day, was, as I have said, to follow them; yet how often and how passionately, for a week, we came back together to the subject! Much as we had discussed it that Sunday night, I was, in the immediate later hours in especial—for it may be imagined whether I slept—still haunted with the shadow of something she had not told me. I myself had kept back nothing, but there was a word Mrs. Grose had kept back. I was sure, moreover, by morning, that this was not from a failure of frankness, but because on every side there were fears. It seems to me indeed, in retrospect, that by the time the morrow's sun was high I had restlessly read into the fact before us almost all the meaning they were to receive from subsequent and more cruel occurrences. What they gave me above all was just the sinister figure of the living man—the dead one would keep awhile!—and of the months he had continuously passed at Bly, which, added up, made a formidable stretch. The limit of this evil time had arrived only when, on the dawn of a winter's morning, Peter Quint was found, by a laborer going to early work, stone dead on the road from the village: a catastrophe explained—superficially at least—by a visible wound to his head; such a wound as might have been produced—and as, on the final evidence, had been—by a fatal slip, in the dark and after leaving the public house, on the steepish icy slope, a wrong path altogether, at the bottom of which he lay. The icy slope, the turn mistaken at night and in liquor, accounted for much—practically, in the end and after the inquest and boundless chatter, for everything; but there had been matters in his life—strange passages and perils, secret disorders, vices more than suspected—that would have accounted for a good deal more.

I scarce know how to put my story into words that shall be a credible picture of my state of mind; but I was in these days literally able to find a joy in the extraordinary flight of heroism the occasion demanded of me. I now saw that I had been asked for a service admirable and difficult; and there would be a greatness in letting it be seen—oh, in the right quarter!—that I could succeed where many another girl might have failed. It was an immense help to me—I confess I rather applaud myself as I look back!—that I saw my service so strongly and so simply. I was there to protect and defend the little creatures in the world the most bereaved and the most lovable, the appeal of whose helplessness had suddenly become only too explicit, a deep, constant ache of one's own committed heart. We were cut off, really, together; we were united in our danger. They had nothing but me, and I—well, I had them. It was in short a magnificent chance. This chance presented itself to me in an image richly material. I was a screen—I was to stand before them. The more I saw, the less they would. I began to watch them in a stifled suspense, a disguised excitement that might well, had it continued too long, have turned to something like madness. What saved me, as I now see, was that it turned to something else altogether. It didn't last as suspense—it was superseded by horrible proofs. Proofs, I say, yes—from the moment I really took hold.

This moment dated from an afternoon hour that I happened to spend in the grounds with the younger of my pupils alone. We had left Miles indoors, on the red cushion of a deep window seat; he had wished to finish a book, and I had been glad to encourage a purpose so laudable in a young man whose only defect was an occasional excess of the restless. His sister, on the contrary, had been alert to come out, and I strolled with her half an hour, seeking the shade, for the sun was still high and the day exceptionally warm. I was aware afresh, with her, as we went, of how, like her brother, she contrived—it was the charming thing in both children—to let me alone without appearing to drop me and to accompany me without appearing to surround. They were never importunate and yet never listless. My attention to them all really went to seeing them amuse themselves immensely without me: this was a spectacle they seemed actively to prepare and that engaged me as an active admirer. I walked in a world of their invention—they had no occasion whatever to draw upon mine; so that my time was taken only with being, for them, some remarkable person or thing that the game of the moment required and that was merely, thanks to my superior, my exalted stamp, a happy and highly distinguished sinecure. I forget what I was on the present occasion; I only remember that I was something very important and very quiet and that Flora was playing very hard. We were on the edge of the lake, and, as we had lately begun geography, the lake was the Sea of Azof.

Suddenly, in these circumstances, I became aware that, on the other side of the Sea of Azof, we had an interested spectator. The way this knowledge gathered in me was the strangest thing in the world—the strangest, that is, except the very much stranger in which it quickly merged itself. I had sat down with a piece of work—for I was something or other that could sit—on the old stone bench which overlooked the pond; and in this position I began to take in with certitude, and yet without direct vision, the presence, at a distance, of a third person. The old trees, the thick shrubbery, made a great and pleasant shade, but it was all suffused with the brightness of the hot, still hour. There was no ambiguity in anything; none whatever, at least, in the conviction I from one moment to another found myself forming as to what I should see straight before me and across the lake as a consequence of raising my eyes. They were attached at this juncture to the stitching in which I was engaged, and I can feel once more the spasm of my effort not to move them till I should so have steadied myself as to be able to make up my mind what to do. There was an alien object in view—a figure whose right of presence I instantly, passionately questioned. I recollect counting over perfectly the possibilities, reminding myself that nothing was more natural, for instance, then the appearance of one of the men about the place, or even of a messenger, a postman, or a tradesman's boy, from the village. That reminder had as little effect on my practical certitude as I was conscious—still even without looking—of its having upon the character and attitude of our visitor. Nothing was more natural than that these things should be the other things that they absolutely were not.

Of the positive identity of the apparition I would assure myself as soon as the small clock of my courage should have ticked out the right second; meanwhile, with an effort that was already sharp enough, I transferred my eyes straight to little Flora, who, at the moment, was about ten yards away. My heart had stood still for an instant with the wonder and terror of the question whether she too would see; and I held my breath while I waited for what a cry from her, what some sudden innocent sign either of interest or of alarm, would tell me. I waited, but nothing came; then, in the first place—and there is something more dire in this, I feel, than in anything I have to relate—I was determined by a sense that, within a minute, all sounds from her had previously dropped; and, in the second, by the circumstance that, also within the minute, she had, in her play, turned her back to the water. This was her attitude when I at last looked at her—looked with the confirmed conviction that we were still, together, under direct personal notice. She had picked up a small flat piece of wood, which happened to have in it a little hole that had evidently suggested to her the idea of sticking in another fragment that might figure as a mast and make the thing a boat. This second morsel, as I watched her, she was very markedly and intently attempting to tighten in its place. My apprehension of what she was doing sustained me so that after some seconds I felt I was ready for more. Then I again shifted my eyes—I faced what I had to face.

Chapter 7

I got hold of Mrs. Grose as soon after this as I could; and I can give no intelligible account of how I fought out the interval. Yet I still hear myself cry as I fairly threw myself into her arms: "They know—it's too monstrous: they know, they know!"

"And what on earth—?" I felt her incredulity as she held me.

"Why, all that we know—and heaven knows what else besides!" Then, as she released me, I made it out to her, made it out perhaps only now with full coherency even to myself. "Two hours ago, in the garden"—I could scarce articulate—"Flora saw!"

Mrs. Grose took it as she might have taken a blow in the stomach. "She has told you?" she panted.

"Not a word—that's the horror. She kept it to herself! The child of eight, that child!" Unutterable still, for me, was the stupefaction of it.

Mrs. Grose, of course, could only gape the wider. "Then how do you know?"

"I was there—I saw with my eyes: saw that she was perfectly aware."

"Do you mean aware of him?"

"No—of her." I was conscious as I spoke that I looked prodigious things, for I got the slow reflection of them in my companion's face. "Another person—this time; but a figure of quite as unmistakable horror and evil: a woman in black, pale and dreadful—with such an air also, and such a face!—on the other side of the lake. I was there with the child—quiet for the hour; and in the midst of it she came."

"Came how—from where?"

"From where they come from! She just appeared and stood there—but not so near."

"And without coming nearer?"

"Oh, for the effect and the feeling, she might have been as close as you!"

My friend, with an odd impulse, fell back a step. "Was she someone you've never seen?" "Yes. But someone the child has. Someone you have." Then, to show how I had thought it all out: "My predecessor—the one who died."

"Miss Jessel?"

"Miss Jessel. You don't believe me?" I pressed.

She turned right and left in her distress. "How can you be sure?"

This drew from me, in the state of my nerves, a flash of impatience. "Then ask Flora—she's sure!" But I had no sooner spoken than I caught myself up. "No, for God's sake, don't!" She'll say she isn't—she'll lie!"

Mrs. Grose was not too bewildered instinctively to protest. "Ah, how can you?"

"Because I'm clear. Flora doesn't want me to know."

"It's only then to spare you."

"No, no—there are depths, depths! The more I go over it, the more I see in it, and the more I see in it, the more I fear. I don't know what I don't see—what I don't fear!"

Mrs. Grose tried to keep up with me. "You mean you're afraid of seeing her again?"

"Oh, no; that's nothing—now!" Then I explained. "It's of not seeing her."

But my companion only looked wan. "I don't understand you."

"Why, it's that the child may keep it up—and that the child assuredly will—without my knowing it."

At the image of this possibility Mrs. Grose for a moment collapsed, yet presently to pull herself together again, as if from the positive force of the sense of what, should we yield an inch, there would really be to give way to. "Dear, dear—we must keep our heads! And after all, if she doesn't mind it—!" She even tried a grim joke. "Perhaps she likes it!"

"Likes such things—a scrap of an infant!"

"Isn't it just a proof of her blessed innocence?" my friend bravely inquired.

She brought me, for the instant, almost round. "Oh, we must clutch at that—we must cling to it! If it isn't a proof of what you say, it's a proof of—God knows what! For the woman's a horror of horrors."

Mrs. Grose, at this, fixed her eyes a minute on the ground; then at last raising them, "Tell me how you know," she said.

"Then you admit it's what she was?" I cried.

"Tell me how you know," my friend simply repeated.

"Know? By seeing her! By the way she looked."

"At you, do you mean—so wickedly?"

"Dear me, no—I could have borne that. She gave me never a glance. She only fixed the child."

Mrs. Grose tried to see it. "Fixed her?"

"Ah, with such awful eyes!"

She stared at mine as if they might really have resembled them. "Do you mean of dislike?"

"God help us, no. Of something much worse."

"Worse than dislike?—this left her indeed at a loss.

"With a determination—indescribable. With a kind of fury of intention."

I made her turn pale. "Intention?"

"To get hold of her." Mrs. Grose—her eyes just lingering on mine—gave a shudder and walked to the window; and while she stood there looking out I completed my statement. "that's what Flora knows."

After a little she turned round. "The person was in black, you say?"

"In mourning—rather poor, almost shabby. But—yes—with extraordinary beauty." I now recognized to what I had at last, stroke by stroke, brought the victim of my confidence, for she quite visibly weighed this. "Oh, handsome—very, very," I insisted; "wonderfully handsome. But infamous."

She slowly came back to me. "Miss Jessel—was infamous." She once more took my hand in both her own, holding it as tight as if to fortify me against the increase of alarm I might draw from this disclosure. "They were both infamous," she finally said.

So, for a little, we faced it once more together; and I found absolutely a degree of help in seeing it now so straight. "I appreciate," I said, "the great decency of your not having hitherto spoken; but the time has certainly come to give me the whole thing." She appeared to assent to this, but still only in silence; seeing which I went on: "I must have it now. Of what did she die? Come, there was something between them."

"There was everything."

"In spite of the difference—?"

"Oh, of their rank, their condition"—she brought it woefully out. "She was a lady."

I turned it over; I again saw. "Yes—she was a lady."

"And he so dreadfully below," said Mrs. Grose.

I felt that I doubtless needn't press too hard, in such company, on the place of a servant in the scale; but there was nothing to prevent an acceptance of my companion's own measure of my predecessor's abasement. There was a way to deal with that, and I dealt; the more readily for my full vision—on the evidence—of our employer's late clever, good-looking "own" man; impudent, assured, spoiled, depraved. "The fellow was a hound."

Mrs. Grose considered as if it were perhaps a little a case for a sense of shades. "I've never seen one like him. He did what he wished."

"With her?"

"With them all."

It was as if now in my friend's own eyes Miss Jessel had again appeared. I seemed at any rate, for an instant, to see their evocation of her as distinctly as I had seen her by the pond; and I brought out with decision: "It must have been also what she wished!"

Mrs. Grose's face signified that it had been indeed, but she said at the same time: "Poor woman—she paid for it!"

"Then you do know what she died of?" I asked.

"No—I know nothing. I wanted not to know; I was glad enough I didn't; and I thanked heaven she was well out of this!"

"Yet you had, then, your idea—"

"Of her real reason for leaving? Oh, yes—as to that. She couldn't have stayed. Fancy it here—for a governess! And afterward I imagined—and I still imagine. And what I imagine is dreadful."

"Not so dreadful as what I do," I replied; on which I must have shown her—as I was indeed but too conscious—a front of miserable defeat. It brought out again all her compassion for me, and at the renewed touch of her kindness my power to resist broke down. I burst, as I had, the other time, made her burst, into tears; she took me to her motherly breast, and my lamentation overflowed. "I don't do it!" I sobbed in despair; "I don't save or shield them! It's far worse than I dreamed—they're lost!"

Chapter 8

What I had said to Mrs. Grose was true enough: there were in the matter I had put before her depths and possibilities that I lacked resolution to sound; so that when we met once more in the wonder of it we were of a common mind about the duty of resistance to extravagant fancies. We were to keep our heads if we should keep nothing else—difficult indeed as that might be in the face of what, in our prodigious experience, was least to be questioned. Late that night, while the house slept, we had another talk in my room, when she went all the way with me as to its being beyond doubt that I had seen exactly what I had seen. To hold her perfectly in the pinch of that, I found I had only to ask her how, if I had "made it up," I came to be able to give, of each of the persons appearing to me, a picture disclosing, to the last detail, their special marks—a portrait on the exhibition of which she had instantly recognized and named them. She wished of course—small blame to her!—to sink the whole subject; and I was quick to assure her that my own interest in it had now violently taken the form of a search for the way to escape from it. I encountered her on the ground of a probability that with recurrence—for recurrence we took for granted—I should get used to my danger, distinctly professing that my personal exposure had suddenly become the least of my discomforts. It was my new suspicion that was intolerable; and yet even to this complication the later hours of the day had brought a little ease.

On leaving her, after my first outbreak, I had of course returned to my pupils, associating the right remedy for my dismay with that sense of their charm which I had already found to be a thing I could positively cultivate and which had never failed me yet. I had simply, in other words, plunged afresh into Flora's special society and there become aware—it was almost a luxury!—that she could put her little conscious hand straight upon the spot that ached. She had looked at me in sweet speculation and then had accused me to my face of having "cried." I had supposed I had brushed away the ugly signs: but I could literally—for the time, at all events—rejoice, under this fathomless charity, that they had not entirely disappeared. To gaze into the depths of blue of the child's eyes and pronounce their loveliness a trick of premature cunning was to be guilty of a cynicism in preference to which I naturally preferred to abjure my judgment and, so far as might be, my agitation. I couldn't abjure for merely wanting to, but I could repeat to Mrs. Grose—as I did there, over and over, in the small hours—that with their voices in the air, their pressure on one's heart, and their fragrant faces against one's cheek, everything fell to the ground but their incapacity and their beauty. It was a pity that, somehow, to settle this once for all, I had equally to re-enumerate the signs of subtlety that, in the afternoon, by the lake had made a miracle of my show of self-possession. It was a pity to be obliged to reinvestigate the certitude of the moment itself and repeat how it had come to me as a revelation that the inconceivable communion I then surprised was a matter, for either party, of habit. It was a pity that I should have had to quaver out again the reasons for my not having, in my delusion, so much as questioned that the little girl saw our visitant even as I actually saw Mrs. Grose herself, and that she wanted, by just so much as she did thus see, to make me suppose she didn't, and at the same time, without showing anything, arrive at a guess as to whether I myself did! It was a pity that I needed once more to describe the portentous little activity by which she sought to divert my attention—the perceptible increase of movement, the greater intensity of play, the singing, the gabbling of nonsense, and the invitation to romp.

Yet if I had not indulged, to prove there was nothing in it, in this review, I should have missed the two or three dim elements of comfort that still remained to me. I should not for instance have been able to asseverate to my friend that I was certain—which was so much to the good—that I at least had not betrayed myself. I should not have been prompted, by stress of need, by desperation of mind—I scarce know what to call it—to invoke such further aid to intelligence as might spring from pushing my colleague fairly to the wall. She had told me, bit by bit, under pressure, a great deal; but a small shifty spot on the wrong side of it all still sometimes brushed my brow like the wing of a bat; and I remember how on this occasion—for the sleeping house and the concentration alike of our danger and our watch seemed to help—I felt the importance of giving the last jerk to the curtain. "I don't believe anything so horrible," I recollect saying; "no, let us put it definitely, my dear, that I don't. But if I did, you know, there's a thing I should require now, just without sparing you the least bit more—oh, not a scrap, come!—to get out of you. What was it you had in mind when, in our distress, before Miles came back, over the letter from his school, you said, under my insistence, that you didn't pretend for him that he had not literally ever been 'bad'? He has not literally 'ever,' in these weeks that I myself have lived with him and so closely watched him; he has been an imperturbable little prodigy of delightful, lovable goodness. Therefore you might perfectly have made the claim for him if you had not, as it happened, seen an exception to take. What was your exception, and to what passage in your personal observation of him did you refer?"

It was a dreadfully austere inquiry, but levity was not our note, and, at any rate, before the gray dawn admonished us to separate I had got my answer. What my friend had had in mind proved to be immensely to the purpose. It was neither more nor less than the circumstance that for a period of several months Quint and the boy had been perpetually together. It was in fact the very appropriate truth that she had ventured to criticize the propriety, to hint at the incongruity, of so close an alliance, and even to go so far on the subject as a frank overture to Miss Jessel. Miss Jessel had, with a most strange manner, requested her to mind her business, and the good woman had, on this, directly approached little Miles. What she had said to him, since I pressed, was that she liked to see young gentlemen not forget their station.

I pressed again, of course, at this. "You reminded him that Quint was only a base menial?"

"As you might say! And it was his answer, for one thing, that was bad."

"And for another thing?" I waited. "He repeated your words to Quint?"

"No, not that. It's just what he wouldn't!" she could still impress upon me. "I was sure, at any rate," she added, "that he didn't. But he denied certain occasions."

"What occasions?"

"When they had been about together quite as if Quint were his tutor—and a very grand one—and Miss Jessel only for the little lady. When he had gone off with the fellow, I mean, and spent hours with him."

"He then prevaricated about it—he said he hadn't?" Her assent was clear enough to cause me to add in a moment: "I see. He lied."

"Oh!" Mrs. Grose mumbled. This was a suggestion that it didn't matter; which indeed she backed up by a further remark. "You see, after all, Miss Jessel didn't mind. She didn't forbid him."

I considered. "Did he put that to you as a justification?"

At this she dropped again. "No, he never spoke of it."

"Never mentioned her in connection with Quint?"

She saw, visibly flushing, where I was coming out. "Well, he didn't show anything. He denied," she repeated; "he denied."

Lord, how I pressed her now! "So that you could see he knew what was between the two wretches?"

"I don't know—I don't know!" the poor woman groaned.

"You do know, you dear thing," I replied; "only you haven't my dreadful boldness of mind, and you keep back, out of timidity and modesty and delicacy, even the impression that, in the past, when you had, without my aid, to flounder about in silence, most of all made you miserable. But I shall get it out of you yet! There was something in the boy that suggested to you," I continued, "that he covered and concealed their relation."

"Oh, he couldn't prevent—"

"Your learning the truth? I daresay! But, heavens," I fell, with vehemence, athinking, "what it shows that they must, to that extent, have succeeded in making of him!"

"Ah, nothing that's not nice now!" Mrs. Grose lugubriously pleaded.

"I don't wonder you looked queer," I persisted, "when I mentioned to you the letter from his school!"

"I doubt if I looked as queer as you!" she retorted with homely force. "And if he was so bad then as that comes to, how is he such an angel now?"

"Yes, indeed—and if he was a fiend at school! How, how, how? Well," I said in my torment, "you must put it to me again, but I shall not be able to tell you for some days. Only, put it to me again!" I cried in a way that made my friend stare. "There are directions in which I must not for the present let myself go." Meanwhile I returned to her first example—the one to which she had just previously referred—of the boy's happy capacity for an occasional slip. "If Quint—on your remonstrance at the time you speak of—was a base menial, one of the things Miles said to you, I find myself guessing, was that you were another." Again her admission was so adequate that I continued: "And you forgave him that?"

"Wouldn't you?"

"Oh, yes!" And we exchanged there, in the stillness, a sound of the oddest amusement. Then I went on: "At all events, while he was with the man—"

"Miss Flora was with the woman. It suited them all!"

It suited me, too, I felt, only too well; by which I mean that it suited exactly the particularly deadly view I was in the very act of forbidding myself to entertain. But I so far succeeded in checking the expression of this view that I will throw, just here, no further light on it than may be offered by the mention of my final observation to Mrs. Grose. "His having lied and been impudent are, I confess, less engaging specimens than I had hoped to have from you of the outbreak in him of the little natural man. Still," I mused, "They must do, for they make me feel more than ever that I must watch."

It made me blush, the next minute, to see in my friend's face how much more unreservedly she had forgiven him than her anecdote struck me as presenting to my own tenderness an occasion for doing. This came out when, at the schoolroom door, she quitted me. "Surely you don't accuse him—"

"Of carrying on an intercourse that he conceals from me? Ah, remember that, until further evidence, I now accuse nobody." Then, before shutting her out to go, by another passage, to her own place, "I must just wait," I wound up.

Chapter 9

I waited and waited, and the days, as they elapsed, took something from my consternation. A very few of them, in fact, passing, in constant sight of my pupils, without a fresh incident, sufficed to give to grievous fancies and even to odious memories a kind of brush of the sponge. I have spoken of the surrender to their extraordinary childish grace as a thing I could actively cultivate, and it may be imagined if I neglected now to address myself to this source for whatever it would yield. Stranger than I can express, certainly, was the effort to struggle against my new lights; it would doubtless have been, however, a greater tension still had it not been so frequently successful. I used to wonder how my little charges could help guessing that I thought strange things about them; and the circumstances that these things only made them more interesting was not by itself a direct aid to keeping them in the dark. I trembled lest they should see that they were so immensely more interesting. Putting things at the worst, at all events, as in meditation I so often did, any clouding of their innocence could only be—blameless and foredoomed as they were—a reason the more for taking risks. There were moments when, by an irresistible impulse, I found myself catching them up and pressing them to my heart. As soon as I had done so I used to say to myself: "What will they think of that? Doesn't it betray too much?" It would have been easy to get into a sad, wild tangle about how much I might betray; but the real account, I feel, of the hours of peace that I could still enjoy was that the immediate charm of my companions was a beguilement still effective even under the shadow of the possibility that it was studied. For if it occurred to me that I might occasionally excite suspicion by the little outbreaks of my sharper passion for them, so too I remember wondering if I mightn't see a queerness in the traceable increase of their own demonstrations.

They were at this period extravagantly and preternaturally fond of me; which, after all, I could reflect, was no more than a graceful response in children perpetually bowed over and hugged. The homage of which they were so lavish succeeded, in truth, for my nerves, quite as well as if I never appeared to myself, as I may say, literally to catch them at a purpose in it. They had never, I think, wanted to do so many things for their poor protectress; I mean—though they got their lessons better and better, which was naturally what would please her most—in the way of diverting, entertaining, surprising her; reading her passages, telling her stories, acting her charades, pouncing out at her, in disguises, as animals and historical characters, and above all astonishing her by the "pieces" they had secretly got by heart and could interminably recite. I should never get to the bottom—were I to let myself go even now—of the prodigious private commentary, all under still more private correction, with which, in these days, I overscored their full hours. They had shown me from the first a facility for everything, a general faculty which, taking a fresh start, achieved remarkable flights. They got their little tasks as if they loved them, and indulged, from the mere exuberance of the gift, in the most unimposed little miracles of memory. They not only popped out at me as tigers and as Romans, but as Shakespeareans, astronomers, and navigators. This was so singularly the case that it had presumably much to do with the fact as to which, at the present day, I am at a loss for a different explanation: I allude to my unnatural composure on the subject of another school for Miles. What I remember is that I was content not, for the time, to open the question, and that contentment must have sprung from the sense of his perpetually striking show of cleverness. He was too clever for a bad governess, for a parson's daughter, to spoil; and the strangest if not the brightest thread in the pensive embroidery I just spoke of was the impression I might have got, if I had dared to work it out, that he was under some influence operating in his small intellectual life as a tremendous incitement.

If it was easy to reflect, however, that such a boy could postpone school, it was at least as marked that for such a boy to have been "kicked out" by a schoolmaster was a mystification without end. Let me add that in their company now—and I was careful almost never to be out of it—I could follow no scent very far. We lived in a cloud of music and love and success and private theatricals. The musical sense in each of the children was of the quickest, but the elder in especial had a marvelous knack of catching and repeating. The schoolroom piano broke into all gruesome fancies; and when that failed there were confabulations in corners, with a sequel of one of them going out in the highest spirits in order to "come in" as something new. I had had brothers myself, and it was no revelation to me that little girls could be slavish idolaters of little boys. What surpassed everything was that there was a little boy in the world who could have for the inferior age, sex, and intelligence so fine a consideration. They were extraordinarily at one, and to say that they never either quarreled or complained is to make the note of praise coarse for their quality of sweetness. Sometimes, indeed, when I dropped into coarseness, I perhaps came across traces of little understandings between them by which one of them should keep me occupied while the other slipped away. There is a naive side, I suppose, in all diplomacy; but if my pupils practiced upon me, it was surely with the minimum of grossness. It was all in the other quarter that, after a lull, the grossness broke out.

I find that I really hang back; but I must take my plunge. In going on with the record of what was hideous at Bly, I not only challenge the most liberal faith—for which I little care; but—and this is another matter—I renew what I myself suffered, I again push my way through it to the end. There came suddenly an hour after which, as I look back, the affair seems to me to have been all pure suffering; but I have at least reached the heart of it, and the straightest road out is doubtless to advance. One evening—with nothing to lead up or to prepare it—I felt the cold touch of the impression that had breathed on me the night of my arrival and which, much lighter then, as I have mentioned, I should probably have made little of in memory had my subsequent sojourn been less agitated. I had not gone to bed; I sat reading by a couple of candles. There was a roomful of old books at Bly—last-century fiction, some of it, which, to the extent of a distinctly deprecated renown, but never to so much as that of a stray specimen, had reached the sequestered home and appealed to the unavowed curiosity of my youth. I remember that the book I had in my hand was Fielding's Amelia; also that I was wholly awake. I recall further both a general conviction that it was horribly late and a particular objection to looking at my watch. I figure, finally, that the white curtain draping, in the fashion of those days, the head of Flora's little bed, shrouded, as I had assured myself long before, the perfection of childish rest. I recollect in short that, though I was deeply interested in my author, I found myself, at the turn of a page and with his spell all scattered, looking straight up from him and hard at the door of my room. There was a moment during which I listened, reminded of the faint sense I had had, the first night, of there being something undefinably astir in the house, and noted the soft breath of the open casement just move the half-drawn blind. Then, with all the marks of a deliberation that must have seemed magnificent had there been anyone to admire it, I laid down my book, rose to my feet, and, taking a candle, went straight out of the room and, from the passage, on which my light made little impression, noiselessly closed and locked the door.

I can say now neither what determined nor what guided me, but I went straight along the lobby, holding my candle high, till I came within sight of the tall window that presided over the great turn of the staircase. At this point I precipitately found myself aware of three things. They were practically simultaneous, yet they had flashes of succession. My candle, under a bold flourish, went out, and I perceived, by the uncovered window, that the yielding dusk of earliest morning rendered it unnecessary. Without it, the next instant, I saw that there was someone on the stair. I speak of sequences, but I required no lapse of seconds to stiffen myself for a third encounter with Quint. The apparition had reached the landing halfway up and was therefore on the spot nearest the window, where at sight of me, it stopped short and fixed me exactly as it had fixed me from the tower and from the garden. He knew me as well as I knew him; and so, in the cold, faint twilight, with a glimmer in the high glass and another on the polish of the oak stair below, we faced each other in our common intensity. He was absolutely, on this occasion, a living, detestable, dangerous presence. But that was not the wonder of wonders; I reserve this distinction for quite another circumstance: the circumstance that dread had unmistakably quitted me and that there was nothing in me there that didn't meet and measure him.

I had plenty of anguish after that extraordinary moment, but I had, thank God, no terror. And he knew I had not—I found myself at the end of an instant magnificently aware of this. I felt, in a fierce rigor of confidence, that if I stood my ground a minute I should cease—for the time, at least—to have him to reckon with; and during the minute, accordingly, the thing was as human and hideous as a real interview: hideous just because it was human, as human as to have met alone, in the small hours, in a sleeping house, some enemy, some adventurer, some criminal. It was the dead silence of our long gaze at such close quarters that gave the whole horror, huge as it was, its only note of the unnatural. If I had met a murderer in such a place and at such an hour, we still at least would have spoken. Something would have passed, in life, between us; if nothing had passed, one of us would have moved. The moment was so prolonged that it would have taken but little more to make me doubt if even I were in life. I can't express what followed it save by saying that the silence itself—which was indeed in a manner an attestation of my strength—became the element into which I saw the figure disappear; in which I definitely saw it turn as I might have seen the low wretch to which it had once belonged turn on receipt of an order, and pass, with my eyes on the villainous back that no hunch could have more disfigured, straight down the staircase and into the darkness in which the next bend was lost.

Chapter 10

I remained awhile at the top of the stair, but with the effect presently of understanding that when my visitor had gone, he had gone: then I returned to my room. The foremost thing I saw there by the light of the candle I had left burning was that Flora's little bed was empty; and on this I caught my breath with all the terror that, five minutes before, I had been able to resist. I dashed at the place in which I had left her lying and over which (for the small silk counterpane and the sheets were disarranged) the white curtains had been deceivingly pulled forward; then my step, to my unutterable relief, produced an answering sound: I perceived an agitation of the window blind, and the child, ducking down, emerged rosily from the other side of it. She stood there in so much of her candor and so little of her nightgown, with her pink bare feet and the golden glow of her curls. She looked intensely grave, and I had never had such a sense of losing an advantage acquired (the thrill of which had just been so prodigious) as on my consciousness that she addressed me with a reproach. "You naughty: where have you been?"—instead of challenging her own irregularity I found myself arraigned and explaining. She herself explained, for that matter, with the loveliest, eagerest simplicity. She had known suddenly, as she lay there, that I was out of the room, and had jumped up to see what had become of me. I had dropped, with the joy of her reappearance, back into my chair—feeling then, and then only, a little faint; and she had pattered straight over to me, thrown herself upon my knee, given herself to be held with the flame of the candle full in the wonderful little face that was still flushed with sleep. I remember closing my eyes an instant, yieldingly, consciously, as before the excess of something beautiful that shone out of the blue of her own. "You were looking for me out of the window?" I said. "You thought I might be walking in the grounds?"

"Well, you know, I thought someone was"—she never blanched as she smiled out that at me.

Oh, how I looked at her now! "And did you see anyone?"

"Ah, no!" she returned, almost with the full privilege of childish inconsequence, resentfully, though with a long sweetness in her little drawl of the negative.

At that moment, in the state of my nerves, I absolutely believed she lied; and if I once more closed my eyes it was before the dazzle of the three or four possible ways in which I might take this up. One of these, for a moment, tempted me with such singular intensity that, to withstand it, I must have gripped my little girl with a spasm that, wonderfully, she submitted to without a cry or a sign of fright. Why not break out at her on the spot and have it all over?—give it to her straight in her lovely little lighted face? "You see, you see, you KNOW that you do and that you already quite suspect I believe it; therefore, why not frankly confess it to me, so that we may at least live with it together and learn perhaps, in the strangeness of our fate, where we are and what it means?" This solicitation dropped, alas, as it came: if

I could immediately have succumbed to it I might have spared myself—well, you'll see what. Instead of succumbing I sprang again to my feet, looked at her bed, and took a helpless middle way. "Why did you pull the curtain over the place to make me think you were still there?"

Flora luminously considered; after which, with her little divine smile: "Because I don't like to frighten you!"

"But if I had, by your idea, gone out—?"

She absolutely declined to be puzzled; she turned her eyes to the flame of the candle as if the question were as irrelevant, or at any rate as impersonal, as Mrs. Marcet or nine-times-nine. "Oh, but you know," she quite adequately answered, "that you might come back, you dear, and that you have!" And after a little, when she had got into bed, I had, for a long time, by almost sitting on her to hold her hand, to prove that I recognized the pertinence of my return.

You may imagine the general complexion, from that moment, of my nights. I repeatedly sat up till I didn't know when; I selected moments when my roommate unmistakably slept, and, stealing out, took noiseless turns in the passage and even pushed as far as to where I had last met Quint. But I never met him there again; and I may as well say at once that I on no other occasion saw him in the house. I just missed, on the staircase, on the other hand, a different adventure. Looking down it from the top I once recognized the presence of a woman seated on one of the lower steps with her back presented to me, her body half-bowed and her head, in an attitude of woe, in her hands. I had been there but an instant, however, when she vanished without looking round at me. I knew, nonetheless, exactly what dreadful face she had to show; and I wondered whether, if instead of being above I had been below, I should have had, for going up, the same nerve I had lately shown Quint. Well, there continued to be plenty of chance for nerve. On the eleventh night after my latest encounter with that gentleman—they were all numbered now—I had an alarm that perilously skirted it and that indeed, from the particular quality of its unexpectedness, proved quite my sharpest shock. It was precisely the first night during this series that, weary with watching, I had felt that I might again without laxity lay myself down at my old hour. I slept immediately and, as I afterward knew, till about one o'clock; but when I woke it was to sit straight up, as completely roused as if a hand had shook me. I had left a light burning, but it was now out, and I felt an instant certainty that Flora had extinguished it. This brought me to my feet and straight, in the darkness, to her bed, which I found she had left. A glance at the window enlightened me further, and the striking of a match completed the picture.

The child had again got up—this time blowing out the taper, and had again, for some purpose of observation or response, squeezed in behind the blind and was peering out into the night. That she now saw—as she had not, I had satisfied myself, the previous time—was proved to me by the fact that she was disturbed neither by my reillumination nor by the haste I made to get into slippers and into a wrap. Hidden, protected, absorbed, she evidently rested on the sill—the casement opened forward—and gave herself up. There was a great still moon to help her, and this fact had counted in my quick decision. She was face to face with the apparition we had met at the lake, and could now communicate with it as she had not then been able to do. What I, on my side, had to care for was, without disturbing her, to reach, from the corridor, some other window in the same quarter. I got to the door without her hearing me; I got out of it, closed it, and listened, from the other side, for some sound from her. While I stood in the passage I had my eyes on her brother's door, which was but ten steps off and which, indescribably, produced in me a renewal of the strange impulse that I lately spoke of as my temptation. What if I should go straight in and march to his window?—what if, by risking to his boyish bewilderment a revelation of my motive, I should throw across the rest of the mystery the long halter of my boldness?

This thought held me sufficiently to make me cross to his threshold and pause again. I preternaturally listened; I figured to myself what might portentously be; I wondered if his bed were also empty and he too were secretly at watch. It was a deep, soundless minute, at the end of which my impulse failed. He was quiet; he might be innocent; the risk was hideous; I turned away. There was a figure in the grounds—a figure prowling for a sight, the visitor with whom Flora was engaged; but it was not the visitor most concerned with my boy. I hesitated afresh, but on other grounds and only for a few seconds; then I had made my choice. There were empty rooms at Bly, and it was only a question of choosing the right one. The right one suddenly presented itself to me as the lower one—though high above the gardens—in the solid corner of the house that I have spoken of as the old tower. This was a large, square chamber, arranged with some state as a bedroom, the extravagant size of which made it so inconvenient that it had not for years, though kept by Mrs. Grose in exemplary order, been occupied. I had often admired it and I knew my way about in it; I had only, after just faltering at the first chill gloom of its disuse, to pass across it and unbolt as quietly as I could one of the shutters. Achieving this transit, I uncovered the glass without a sound and, applying my face to the pane, was able, the darkness without being much less than within, to see that I commanded the right direction. Then I saw something more. The moon made the night extraordinarily penetrable and showed me on the lawn a person, diminished by distance, who stood there motionless and as if fascinated, looking up to where I had appeared—looking, that is, not so much straight at me as at something that was apparently above me. There was clearly another person above me—there was a person on the tower; but the presence on the lawn was not in the least what I had conceived and had confidently hurried to meet. The presence on the lawn—I felt sick as I made it out—was poor little Miles himself.

Chapter 11

It was not till late next day that I spoke to Mrs. Grose; the rigor with which I kept my pupils in sight making it often difficult to meet her privately, and the more as we each felt the importance of not provoking—on the part of the servants quite as much as on that of the children—any suspicion of a secret flurry or that of a discussion of mysteries. I drew a great security in this particular from her mere smooth aspect. There was nothing in her fresh face to pass on to others my horrible confidences. She believed me, I was sure, absolutely: if she hadn't I don't know what would have become of me, for I couldn't have borne the business alone. But she was a magnificent monument to the blessing of a want of imagination, and if she could see in our little charges nothing but their beauty and amiability, their happiness and cleverness, she had no direct communication with the sources of my trouble. If they had been at all visibly blighted or battered, she would doubtless have grown, on tracing it back, haggard enough to match them; as matters stood, however, I could feel her, when she surveyed them, with her large white arms folded and the habit of serenity in all her look, thank the Lord's mercy that if they were ruined the pieces would still serve. Flights of fancy gave place, in her mind, to a steady fireside glow, and I had already begun to perceive how, with the development of the conviction that—as time went on without a public accident—our young things could, after all, look out for themselves, she addressed her greatest solicitude to the sad case presented by their instructress. That, for myself, was a sound simplification: I could engage that, to the world, my face should tell no tales, but it would have been, in the conditions, an immense added strain to find myself anxious about hers.

At the hour I now speak of she had joined me, under pressure, on the terrace, where, with the lapse of the season, the afternoon sun was now agreeable; and we sat there together while, before us, at a distance, but within call if we wished, the children strolled to and fro in one of their most manageable moods. They moved slowly, in unison, below us, over the lawn, the boy, as they went, reading aloud from a storybook and passing his arm round his sister to keep her quite in touch. Mrs. Grose watched them with positive placidity; then I caught the suppressed intellectual creak with which she conscientiously turned to take from me a view of the back of the tapestry. I had made her a receptacle of lurid things, but there was an odd recognition of my superiority—my accomplishments and my function—in her patience under my pain. She offered her mind to my disclosures as, had I wished to mix a witch's broth and proposed it with assurance, she would have held out a large clean saucepan. This had become thoroughly her attitude by the time that, in my recital of the events of the night, I reached the point of what Miles had said to me when, after seeing him, at such a monstrous hour, almost on the very spot where he happened now to be, I had gone down to bring him in; choosing then, at the window, with a concentrated need of not alarming the house, rather that method than a signal more resonant. I had left her meanwhile in little doubt of my small hope of representing with success even to her actual sympathy my sense of the real splendor of the little inspiration with which, after I had got him into the house, the boy met my final articulate challenge. As soon as I appeared in the moonlight on the terrace, he had come to me as straight as possible; on which I had taken his hand without a word and led him, through the dark spaces, up the staircase where Quint had so hungrily hovered for him, along the lobby where I had listened and trembled, and so to his forsaken room.

Not a sound, on the way, had passed between us, and I had wondered—oh, how I had wondered!—if he were groping about in his little mind for something plausible and not too grotesque. It would tax his invention, certainly, and I felt, this time, over his real embarrassment, a curious thrill of triumph. It was a sharp trap for the inscrutable! He couldn't play any longer at innocence; so how the deuce would he get out of it? There beat in me indeed, with the passionate throb of this question an equal dumb appeal as to how the deuce I should. I was confronted at last, as never yet, with all the risk attached even now to sounding my own horrid note. I remember in fact that as we pushed into his little chamber, where the bed had not been slept in at all and the window, uncovered to the moonlight, made the place so clear that there was no need of striking a match—I remember how I suddenly dropped, sank upon the edge of the bed from the force of the idea that he must know how he really, as they say, "had" me. He could do what he liked, with all his cleverness to help him, so long as I should continue to defer to the old tradition of the criminality of those caretakers of the young who minister to superstitions and fears. He "had" me indeed, and in a cleft stick; for who would ever absolve me, who would consent that I should go unhung, if, by the faintest tremor of an overture, I were the first to introduce into our perfect intercourse an element so dire? No, no: it was useless to attempt to convey to Mrs. Grose, just as it is scarcely less so to attempt to suggest here, how, in our short, stiff brush in the dark, he fairly shook me with admiration. I was of course thoroughly kind and merciful; never, never yet had I placed on his little shoulders hands of such tenderness as those with which, while I rested against the bed, I held him there well under fire. I had no alternative but, in form at least, to put it to him.

"You must tell me now—and all the truth. What did you go out for? What were you doing there?"

I can still see his wonderful smile, the whites of his beautiful eyes, and the uncovering of his little teeth shine to me in the dusk. "If I tell you why, will you understand?" My heart, at this, leaped into my mouth. Would he tell me why? I found no sound on my lips to press it, and I was aware of replying only with a vague, repeated, grimacing nod. He was gentleness itself, and while I wagged my head at him he stood there more than ever a little fairy prince. It was his brightness indeed that gave me a respite. Would it be so great if he were really going to tell me? "Well," he said at last, "just exactly in order that you should do this."

"Do what?"

"Think me—for a change—bad!" I shall never forget the sweetness and gaiety with which he brought out the word, nor how, on top of it, he bent forward and kissed me. It was practically the end of everything. I met his kiss and I had to make, while I folded him for a minute in my arms, the most stupendous effort not to cry. He had given exactly the account of himself that permitted least of my going behind it, and it was only with the effect of confirming my acceptance of it that, as I presently glanced about the room, I could say—

"Then you didn't undress at all?"

He fairly glittered in the gloom. "Not at all. I sat up and read."

"And when did you go down?"

"At midnight. When I'm bad I am bad!"

"I see, I see—it's charming. But how could you be sure I would know it?"

"Oh, I arranged that with Flora." His answers rang out with a readiness! "She was to get up and look out."

"Which is what she did do." It was I who fell into the trap!

"So she disturbed you, and, to see what she was looking at, you also looked—you saw."

"While you," I concurred, "caught your death in the night air!"

He literally bloomed so from this exploit that he could afford radiantly to assent. "How otherwise should I have been bad enough?" he asked. Then, after another embrace, the incident and our interview closed on my recognition of all the reserves of goodness that, for his joke, he had been able to draw upon.

Chapter 12

The particular impression I had received proved in the morning light, I repeat, not quite successfully presentable to Mrs. Grose, though I reinforced it with the mention of still another remark that he had made before we separated. "It all lies in half a dozen words," I said to her, "words that really settle the matter. 'Think, you know, what I might do!' He threw that off to show me how good he is. He knows down to the ground what he 'might' do. That's what he gave them a taste of at school."

"Lord, you do change!" cried my friend.

"I don't change—I simply make it out. The four, depend upon it, perpetually meet. If on either of these last nights you had been with either child, you would clearly have understood. The more I've watched and waited the more I've felt that if there were nothing else to make it sure it would be made so by the systematic silence of each. Never, by a slip of the tongue, have they so much as alluded to either of their old friends, any more than Miles has alluded to his expulsion. Oh, yes, we may sit here and look at them, and they may show off to us there to their fill; but even while they pretend to be lost in their fairytale they're steeped in their vision of the dead restored. He's not reading to her," I declared; "they're talking of them—they're talking horrors! I go on, I know, as if I were crazy; and it's a wonder I'm not. What I've seen would have made you so; but it has only made me more lucid, made me get hold of still other things."

My lucidity must have seemed awful, but the charming creatures who were victims of it, passing and repassing in their interlocked sweetness, gave my colleague something to hold on by; and I felt how tight she held as, without stirring in the breath of my passion, she covered them still with her eyes. "Of what other things have you got hold?"

"Why, of the very things that have delighted, fascinated, and yet, at bottom, as I now so strangely see, mystified and troubled me. Their more than earthly beauty, their absolutely unnatural goodness. It's a game," I went on; "it's a policy and a fraud!"

"On the part of little darlings—?"

"As yet mere lovely babies? Yes, mad as that seems!" The very act of bringing it out really helped me to trace it—follow it all up and piece it all together. "They haven't been good—they've only been absent. It has been easy to live with them, because they're simply leading a life of their own. They're not mine—they're not ours. They're his and they're hers!"

"Quint's and that woman's?"

"Quint's and that woman's. They want to get to them."

Oh, how, at this, poor Mrs. Grose appeared to study them! "But for what?"

"For the love of all the evil that, in those dreadful days, the pair put into them. And to ply them with that evil still, to keep up the work of demons, is what brings the others back."

"Laws!" said my friend under her breath. The exclamation was homely, but it revealed a real acceptance of my further proof of what, in the bad time—for there had been a worse even than this!—must have occurred. There could have been no such justification for me as the plain assent of her experience to whatever depth of depravity I found credible in our brace of scoundrels. It was in obvious submission of memory that she brought out after a moment: "They were rascals! But what can they now do?" she pursued.

"Do?" I echoed so loud that Miles and Flora, as they passed at their distance, paused an instant in their walk and looked at us. "Don't they do enough?" I demanded in a lower tone, while the children, having smiled and nodded and kissed hands to us, resumed their exhibition. We were held by it a minute; then I answered: "They can destroy them!" At this my companion did turn, but the inquiry she launched was a silent one, the effect of which was to make me more explicit. "They don't know, as yet, quite how—but they're trying hard. They're seen only across, as it were, and beyond—in strange places and on high places, the top of towers, the roof of houses, the outside of windows, the further edge of pools; but there's a deep design, on either side, to shorten the distance and overcome the obstacle; and the success of the tempters is only a question of time. They've only to keep to their suggestions of danger."

"For the children to come?"

"And perish in the attempt!" Mrs. Grose slowly got up, and I scrupulously added: "Unless, of course, we can prevent!"

Standing there before me while I kept my seat, she visibly turned things over. "Their uncle must do the preventing.

He must take them away."

"And who's to make him?"

She had been scanning the distance, but she now dropped on me a foolish face. "You, miss."

"By writing to him that his house is poisoned and his little nephew and niece mad?"

"But if they are, miss?"

"And if I am myself, you mean? That's charming news to be sent him by a governess whose prime undertaking was to give him no worry."

Mrs. Grose considered, following the children again. "Yes, he do hate worry. That was the great reason—"

"Why those fiends took him in so long? No doubt, though his indifference must have been awful. As I'm not a fiend, at any rate, I shouldn't take him in."

My companion, after an instant and for all answer, sat down again and grasped my arm. "Make him at any rate come to you."

I stared. "To me?" I had a sudden fear of what she might do. "'Him'?"

"He ought to be here—he ought to help."

I quickly rose, and I think I must have shown her a queerer face than ever yet. "You see me asking him for a visit?" No, with her eyes on my face she evidently couldn't. Instead of it even—as a woman reads another—she could see what I myself saw: his derision, his amusement, his contempt for the breakdown of my resignation at being left alone and for the fine machinery I had set in motion to attract his attention to my slighted charms. She didn't know—no one knew—how proud I had been to serve him and to stick to our terms; yet she nonetheless took the measure, I think, of the warning I now gave her. "If you should so lose your head as to appeal to him for me—"

She was really frightened. "Yes, miss?"

"I would leave, on the spot, both him and you."

Chapter 13

It was all very well to join them, but speaking to them proved quite as much as ever an effort beyond my strength—offered, in close quarters, difficulties as insurmountable as before. This situation continued a month, and with new aggravations and particular notes, the note above all, sharper and sharper, of the small ironic consciousness on the part of my pupils. It was not, I am as sure today as I was sure then, my mere infernal imagination: it was absolutely traceable that they were aware of my predicament and that this strange relation made, in a manner, for a long time, the air in which we moved. I don't mean that they had their tongues in their cheeks or did anything vulgar, for that was not one of their dangers: I do mean, on the other hand, that the element of the unnamed and untouched became, between us, greater than any other, and that so much avoidance could not have been so successfully effected without a great deal of tacit arrangement. It was as if, at moments, we were perpetually coming into sight of subjects before which we must stop short, turning suddenly out of alleys that we perceived to be blind, closing with a little bang that made us look at each other—for, like all bangs, it was something louder than we had intended—the doors we had indiscreetly opened. All roads lead to Rome, and there were times when it might have struck us that almost every branch of study or subject of conversation skirted forbidden ground. Forbidden ground was the question of the return of the dead in general and of whatever, in especial, might survive, in memory, of the friends little children had lost. There were days when I could have sworn that one of them had, with a small invisible nudge, said to the other: "She thinks she'll do it this time—but she won't!" To "do it" would have been to indulge for instance—and for once in a way—in some direct reference to the lady who had prepared them for my discipline. They had a delightful endless appetite for passages in my own history, to which I had again and again treated them; they were in possession of everything that had ever happened to me, had had, with every circumstance the story of my smallest adventures and of those of my brothers and sisters and of the cat and the dog at home, as well as many particulars of the eccentric nature of my father, of the furniture and arrangement of our house, and of the conversation of the old women of our village. There were things enough, taking one with another, to chatter about, if one went very fast and knew by instinct when to go round. They pulled with an art of their own the strings of my invention and my memory; and nothing else perhaps, when I thought of such occasions afterward, gave me so the suspicion of being watched from under cover. It was in any case over my life, my past, and my friends alone that we could take anything like our ease—a state of affairs that led them sometimes without the least pertinence to break out into sociable reminders. I was invited—with no visible connection—to repeat afresh Goody Gosling's celebrated mot or to confirm the details already supplied as to the cleverness of the vicarage pony.

It was partly at such junctures as these and partly at quite different ones that, with the turn my matters had now taken, my predicament, as I have called it, grew most sensible. The fact that the days passed for me without another encounter ought, it would have appeared, to have done something toward soothing my nerves. Since the light brush, that second night on the upper landing, of the presence of a woman at the foot of the stair, I had seen nothing, whether in or out of the house, that one had better not have seen. There was many a corner round which I expected to come upon Quint, and many a situation that, in a merely sinister way, would have favored the appearance of Miss Jessel. The summer had turned, the summer had gone; the autumn had dropped upon Bly and had blown out half our lights. The place, with its gray sky and withered garlands, its bared spaces and scattered dead leaves, was like a theater after the performance—all strewn with crumpled playbills. There were exactly states of the air, conditions of sound and of stillness, unspeakable impressions of the kind of ministering moment, that brought back to me, long enough to catch it, the feeling of the medium in which, that June evening out of doors, I had had my first sight of Quint, and in which, too, at those other instants, I had, after seeing him through the window, looked for him in vain in the circle of shrubbery. I recognized the signs, the portents—I recognized the moment, the spot. But they remained unaccompanied and empty, and I continued unmolested; if unmolested one could call a young woman whose sensibility had, in the most extraordinary fashion, not declined but deepened. I had said in my talk with Mrs. Grose on that horrid scene of Flora's by the lake—and had perplexed her by so saying—that it would from that moment distress me much more to lose my power than to keep it. I had then expressed what was vividly in my mind: the truth that, whether the children really saw or not—since, that is, it was not yet definitely proved—I greatly preferred, as a safeguard, the fullness of my own exposure. I was ready to know the very worst that was to be known. What I had then had an ugly glimpse of was that my eyes might be sealed just while theirs were most opened. Well, my eyes were sealed, it appeared, at present—a consummation for which it seemed blasphemous not to thank God. There was, alas, a difficulty about that: I would have thanked him with all my soul had I not had in a proportionate measure this conviction of the secret of my pupils.

How can I retrace today the strange steps of my obsession? There were times of our being together when I would have been ready to swear that, literally, in my presence, but with my direct sense of it closed, they had visitors who were known and were welcome. Then it was that, had I not been deterred by the very chance that such an injury might prove greater than the injury to be averted, my exultation would have broken out. "They're here, they're here, you little wretches," I would have cried, "and you can't deny it now!" The little wretches denied it with all the added volume of their sociability and their tenderness, in just the crystal depths of which—like the flash of a fish in a stream—the mockery of their advantage peeped up. The shock, in truth, had sunk into me still deeper than I knew on the night when, looking out to see either Quint or Miss Jessel under the stars, I had beheld the boy over whose rest I watched and who had immediately brought in with him—had straightway, there, turned it on me—the lovely upward look with which, from the battlements above me, the hideous apparition of Quint had played. If it was a question of a scare, my discovery on this occasion had scared me more than any other, and it was in the condition of nerves produced by it that I made my actual inductions. They harassed me so that sometimes, at odd moments, I shut myself up audibly to rehearse—it was at once a fantastic relief and a renewed despair—the manner in which I might come to the point. I approached it from one side and the other while, in my room, I flung myself about, but I always broke down in the monstrous utterance of names. As they died away on my lips, I said to myself that I should indeed help them to represent something infamous, if, by pronouncing them, I should violate as rare a little case of instinctive delicacy as any schoolroom, probably, had ever known. When I said to myself: "They have the manners to be silent, and you, trusted as you are, the baseness to speak!" I felt myself crimson and I covered my face with my hands. After these secret scenes I chattered more than ever, going on volubly enough till one of our prodigious, palpable hushes occurred—I can call them nothing else—the strange, dizzy lift or swim (I try for terms!) into a stillness, a pause of all life, that had nothing to do with the more or less noise that at the moment we might be engaged in making and that I could hear through any deepened exhilaration or quickened recitation or louder strum of the piano. Then it was that the others, the outsiders, were there. Though they were not angels, they "passed," as the French say, causing me, while they stayed, to tremble with the fear of their addressing to their younger victims some yet more infernal message or more vivid image than they had thought good enough for myself.

What it was most impossible to get rid of was the cruel idea that, whatever I had seen, Miles and Flora saw more—things terrible and unguessable and that sprang from dreadful passages of intercourse in the past. Such things naturally left on the surface, for the time, a chill which we vociferously denied that we felt; and we had, all three, with repetition, got into such splendid training that we went, each time, almost automatically, to mark the close of the incident, through the very same movements. It was striking of the children, at all events, to kiss me inveterately with a kind of wild irrelevance and never to fail—one or the other—of the precious question that had helped us through many a peril. "When do you think he will come? Don't you think we ought to write?"—there was nothing like that inquiry, we found by experience, for carrying off an awkwardness. "He" of course was their uncle in Harley Street; and we lived in much profusion of theory that he might at any moment arrive to mingle in our circle. It was impossible to have given less encouragement than he had done to such a doctrine, but if we had not had the doctrine to fall back upon we should have deprived each other of some of our finest exhibitions. He never wrote to them—that may have been selfish, but it was a part of the flattery of his trust of me; for the way in which a man pays his highest tribute to a woman is apt to be but by the more festal celebration of one of the sacred laws of his comfort; and I held that I carried out the spirit of the pledge given not to appeal to him when I let my charges understand that their own letters were but charming literary exercises. They were too beautiful to be posted; I kept them myself; I have them all to this hour. This was a rule indeed which only added to the satiric effect of my being plied with the supposition that he might at any moment be among us. It was exactly as if my charges knew how almost more awkward than anything else that might be for me. There appears to me, moreover, as I look back, no note in all this more extraordinary than the mere fact that, in spite of my tension and of their triumph, I never lost patience with them. Adorable they must in truth have been, I now reflect, that I didn't in these days hate them! Would exasperation, however, if relief had longer been postponed, finally have betrayed me? It little matters, for relief arrived. I call it relief, though it was only the relief that a snap brings to a strain or the burst of a thunderstorm to a day of suffocation. It was at least change, and it came with a rush.

Chapter 14

Walking to church a certain Sunday morning, I had little Miles at my side and his sister, in advance of us and at Mrs. Grose's, well in sight. It was a crisp, clear day, the first of its order for some time; the night had brought a touch of frost, and the autumn air, bright and sharp, made the church bells almost gay. It was an odd accident of thought that I should have happened at such a moment to be particularly and very gratefully struck with the obedience of my little charges. Why did they never resent my inexorable, my perpetual society? Something or other had brought nearer home to me that I had all but pinned the boy to my shawl and that, in the way our companions were marshaled before me, I might have appeared to provide against some danger of rebellion. I was like a gaoler with an eye to possible surprises and escapes. But all this belonged—I mean their magnificent little surrender—just to the special array of the facts that were most abysmal. Turned out for Sunday by his uncle's tailor, who had had a free hand and a notion of pretty waistcoats and of his grand little air, Miles's whole title to independence, the rights of his sex and situation, were so stamped upon him that if he had suddenly struck for freedom I should have had nothing to say. I was by the strangest of chances wondering how I should meet him when the revolution unmistakably occurred. I call it a revolution because I now see how, with the word he spoke, the curtain rose on the last act of my dreadful drama, and the catastrophe was precipitated. "Look here, my dear, you know," he charmingly said, "when in the world, please, am I going back to school?"

Transcribed here the speech sounds harmless enough, particularly as uttered in the sweet, high, casual pipe with which, at all interlocutors, but above all at his eternal governess, he threw off intonations as if he were tossing roses. There was something in them that always made one "catch," and I caught, at any rate, now so effectually that I stopped as short as if one of the trees of the park had fallen across the road. There was something new, on the spot, between us, and he was perfectly aware that I recognized it, though, to enable me to do so, he had no need to look a whit less candid and charming than usual. I could feel in him how he already, from my at first finding nothing to reply, perceived the advantage he had gained. I was so slow to find anything that he had plenty of time, after a minute, to continue with his suggestive but inconclusive smile: "You know, my dear, that for a fellow to be with a lady always—!" His "my dear" was constantly on his lips for me, and nothing could have expressed more the exact shade of the sentiment with which I desired to inspire my pupils than its fond familiarity. It was so respectfully easy.

But, oh, how I felt that at present I must pick my own phrases! I remember that, to gain time, I tried to laugh, and I seemed to see in the beautiful face with which he watched me how ugly and queer I looked. "And always with the same lady?" I returned.

He neither blanched nor winked. The whole thing was virtually out between us. "Ah, of course, she's a jolly, 'perfect' lady; but, after all, I'm a fellow, don't you see? that's—well, getting on."

I lingered there with him an instant ever so kindly. "Yes, you're getting on." Oh, but I felt helpless!

I have kept to this day the heartbreaking little idea of how he seemed to know that and to play with it. "And you can't say I've not been awfully good, can you?"

I laid my hand on his shoulder, for, though I felt how much better it would have been to walk on, I was not yet quite able. "No, I can't say that, Miles."

"Except just that one night, you know—!"

"That one night?" I couldn't look as straight as he.

"Why, when I went down—went out of the house."

"Oh, yes. But I forget what you did it for."

"You forget?"—he spoke with the sweet extravagance of childish reproach. "Why, it was to show you I could!"

"Oh, yes, you could."

"And I can again."

I felt that I might, perhaps, after all, succeed in keeping my wits about me. "Certainly. But you won't."

"No, not that again. It was nothing."

"It was nothing," I said. "But we must go on."

He resumed our walk with me, passing his hand into my arm. "Then when am I going back?"

I wore, in turning it over, my most responsible air. "Were you very happy at school?"

He just considered. "Oh, I'm happy enough anywhere!"

"Well, then," I quavered, "if you're just as happy here—!"

"Ah, but that isn't everything! Of course you know a lot—"

"But you hint that you know almost as much?" I risked as he paused.

"Not half I want to!" Miles honestly professed. "But it isn't so much that."

"What is it, then?"

"Well—I want to see more life."

"I see; I see." We had arrived within sight of the church and of various persons, including several of the household of Bly, on their way to it and clustered about the door to see us go in. I quickened our step; I wanted to get there before the question between us opened up much further; I reflected hungrily that, for more than an hour, he would have to be silent; and I thought with envy of the comparative dusk of the pew and of the almost spiritual help of the hassock on which I might bend my knees. I seemed literally to be running a race with some confusion to which he was about to reduce me, but I felt that he had got in first when, before we had even entered the churchyard, he threw out—

"I want my own sort!"

It literally made me bound forward. "There are not many of your own sort, Miles!" I laughed. "Unless perhaps dear little Flora!"

"You really compare me to a baby girl?"

This found me singularly weak. "Don't you, then, love our sweet Flora?"

"If I didn't—and you, too; if I didn't—!" he repeated as if retreating for a jump, yet leaving his thought so unfinished that, after we had come into the gate, another stop, which he imposed on me by the pressure of his arm, had become inevitable. Mrs. Grose and Flora had passed into the church, the other worshippers had followed, and we were, for the minute, alone among the old, thick graves. We had paused, on the path from the gate, by a low, oblong, tablelike tomb.

"Yes, if you didn't—?"

He looked, while I waited, at the graves. "Well, you know what!" But he didn't move, and he presently produced something that made me drop straight down on the stone slab, as if suddenly to rest. "Does my uncle think what you think?"

I markedly rested. "How do you know what I think?"

"Ah, well, of course I don't; for it strikes me you never tell me. But I mean does he know?"

"Know what, Miles?"

"Why, the way I'm going on."

I perceived quickly enough that I could make, to this inquiry, no answer that would not involve something of a sacrifice of my employer. Yet it appeared to me that we were all, at Bly, sufficiently sacrificed to make that venial. "I don't think your uncle much cares."

Miles, on this, stood looking at me. "Then don't you think he can be made to?"

"In what way?"

"Why, by his coming down."

"But who'll get him to come down?"

"I will!" the boy said with extraordinary brightness and emphasis. He gave me another look charged with that expression and then marched off alone into church.

Chapter 15

The business was practically settled from the moment I never followed him. It was a pitiful surrender to agitation, but my being aware of this had somehow no power to restore me. I only sat there on my tomb and read into what my little friend had said to me the fullness of its meaning; by the time I had grasped the whole of which I had also embraced, for absence, the pretext that I was ashamed to offer my pupils and the rest of the congregation such an example of delay. What I said to myself above all was that Miles had got something out of me and that the proof of it, for him, would be just this awkward collapse. He had got out of me that there was something I was much afraid of and that he should probably be able to make use of my fear to gain, for his own purpose, more freedom. My fear was of having to deal with the intolerable question of the grounds of his dismissal from school, for that was really but the question of the horrors gathered behind. That his uncle should arrive to treat with me of these things was a solution that, strictly speaking, I ought now to have desired to bring on; but I could so little face the ugliness and the pain of it that I simply procrastinated and lived from hand to mouth. The boy, to my deep discomposure, was immensely in the right, was in a position to say to me: "Either you clear up with my guardian the mystery of this interruption of my studies, or you cease to expect me to lead with you a life that's so unnatural for a boy." What was so unnatural for the particular boy I was concerned with was this sudden revelation of a consciousness and a plan.

That was what really overcame me, what prevented my going in. I walked round the church, hesitating, hovering; I reflected that I had already, with him, hurt myself beyond repair. Therefore I could patch up nothing, and it was too extreme an effort to squeeze beside him into the pew: he would be so much more sure than ever to pass his arm into mine and make me sit there for an hour in close, silent contact with his commentary on our talk. For the first minute since his arrival I wanted to get away from him. As I paused beneath the high east window and listened to the sounds of worship, I was taken with an impulse that might master me, I felt, completely should I give it the least encouragement. I might easily put an end to my predicament by getting away altogether. Here was my chance; there was no one to stop me; I could give the whole thing up—turn my back and retreat. It was only a question of hurrying again, for a few preparations, to the house which the attendance at church of so many of the servants would practically have left unoccupied. No one, in short, could blame me if I should just drive desperately off. What was it to get away if I got away only till dinner? That would be in a couple of hours, at the end of which—I had the acute prevision—my little pupils would play at innocent wonder about my nonappearance in their train.

"What did you do, you naughty, bad thing? Why in the world, to worry us so—and take our thoughts off, too, don't you know?—did you desert us at the very door?" I couldn't meet such questions nor, as they asked them, their false little lovely eyes; yet it was all so exactly what I should have to meet that, as the prospect grew sharp to me, I at last let myself go.

I got, so far as the immediate moment was concerned, away; I came straight out of the churchyard and, thinking hard, retraced my steps through the park. It seemed to me that by the time I reached the house I had made up my mind I would fly. The Sunday stillness both of the approaches and of the interior, in which I met no one, fairly excited me with a sense of opportunity. Were I to get off quickly, this way, I should get off without a scene, without a word. My quickness would have to be remarkable, however, and the question of a conveyance was the great one to settle. Tormented, in the hall, with difficulties and obstacles, I remember sinking down at the foot of the staircase—suddenly collapsing there on the lowest step and then, with a revulsion, recalling that it was exactly where more than a month before, in the darkness of night and just so bowed with evil things, I had seen the specter of the most horrible of women. At this I was able to straighten myself; I went the rest of the way up; I made, in my bewilderment, for the schoolroom, where there were objects belonging to me that I should have to take. But I opened the door to find again, in a flash, my eyes unsealed. In the presence of what I saw I reeled straight back upon my resistance.

Seated at my own table in clear noonday light I saw a person whom, without my previous experience, I should have taken at the first blush for some housemaid who might have stayed at home to look after the place and who, availing herself of rare relief from observation and of the schoolroom table and my pens, ink, and paper, had applied herself to the considerable effort of a letter to her sweetheart. There was an effort in the way that, while her arms rested on the table, her hands with evident weariness supported her head; but at the moment I took this in I had already become aware that, in spite of my entrance, her attitude strangely persisted. Then it was—with the very act of its announcing itself—that her identity flared up in a change of posture. She rose, not as if she had heard me, but with an indescribable grand melancholy of indifference and detachment, and, within a dozen feet of me, stood there as my vile predecessor. Dishonored and tragic, she was all before me; but even as I fixed and, for memory, secured it, the awful image passed away. Dark as midnight in her black dress, her haggard beauty and her unutterable woe, she had looked at me long enough to appear to say that her right to sit at my table was as good as mine to sit at hers. While these instants lasted, indeed, I had the extraordinary chill of feeling that it was I who was the intruder. It was as a wild protest against it that, actually addressing her—"You terrible, miserable woman!"—I heard myself break into a sound that, by the open door, rang through the long passage and the empty house. She looked at me as if she heard me, but I had recovered myself and cleared the air. There was nothing in the room the next minute but the sunshine and a sense that I must stay.

Chapter 16

I had so perfectly expected that the return of my pupils would be marked by a demonstration that I was freshly upset at having to take into account that they were dumb about my absence. Instead of gaily denouncing and caressing me, they made no allusion to my having failed them, and I was left, for the time, on perceiving that she too said nothing, to study Mrs. Grose's odd face. I did this to such purpose that I made sure they had in some way bribed her to silence; a silence that, however, I would engage to break down on the first private opportunity. This opportunity came before tea: I secured five minutes with her in the housekeeper's room, where, in the twilight, amid a smell of lately baked bread, but with the place all swept and garnished, I found her sitting in pained placidity before the fire. So I see her still, so I see her best: facing the flame from her straight chair in the dusky, shining room, a large clean image of the "put away"—of drawers closed and locked and rest without a remedy.

"Oh, yes, they asked me to say nothing; and to please them—so long as they were there—of course I promised. But what had happened to you?"

"I only went with you for the walk," I said. "I had then to come back to meet a friend."

She showed her surprise. "A friend—you?"

"Oh, yes, I have a couple!" I laughed. "But did the children give you a reason?"

"For not alluding to your leaving us? Yes; they said you would like it better. Do you like it better?"

My face had made her rueful. "No, I like it worse!" But after an instant I added: "Did they say why I should like it better?"

"No; Master Miles only said, "We must do nothing but what she likes!"

"I wish indeed he would. And what did Flora say?"

"Miss Flora was too sweet. She said, 'Oh, of course, of course!'—and I said the same."

I thought a moment. "You were too sweet, too—I can hear you all. But nonetheless, between Miles and me, it's now all out."

"All out?" My companion stared. "But what, miss?"

"Everything. It doesn't matter. I've made up my mind. I came home, my dear," I went on, "for a talk with Miss Jessel."

I had by this time formed the habit of having Mrs. Grose literally well in hand in advance of my sounding that note; so that even now, as she bravely blinked under the signal of my word, I could keep her comparatively firm. "A talk! Do you mean she spoke?"

"It came to that. I found her, on my return, in the schoolroom."

"And what did she say?" I can hear the good woman still, and the candor of her stupefaction.

"That she suffers the torments—!"

It was this, of a truth, that made her, as she filled out my picture, gape. "Do you mean," she faltered,"—of the lost?"

"Of the lost. Of the damned. And that's why, to share them-" I faltered myself with the horror of it.

But my companion, with less imagination, kept me up. "To share them—?"

"She wants Flora." Mrs. Grose might, as I gave it to her, fairly have fallen away from me had I not been prepared. I still held her there, to show I was. "As I've told you, however, it doesn't matter."

"Because you've made up your mind? But to what?"

"To everything."

"And what do you call 'everything'?"

"Why, sending for their uncle."

"Oh, miss, in pity do," my friend broke out.

"Ah, but I will, I will! I see it's the only way. What's 'out,' as I told you, with Miles is that if he thinks I'm afraid to—and has ideas of what he gains by that—he shall see he's mistaken. Yes, yes; his uncle shall have it here from me on the spot (and before the boy himself, if necessary) that if I'm to be reproached with having done nothing again about more school—"

"Yes, miss—" my companion pressed me.

"Well, there's that awful reason."

There were now clearly so many of these for my poor colleague that she was excusable for being vague. "But—a—which?"

"Why, the letter from his old place."

"You'll show it to the master?"

"I ought to have done so on the instant."

"Oh, no!" said Mrs. Grose with decision.

"I'll put it before him," I went on inexorably, "that I can't undertake to work the question on behalf of a child who has been expelled—"

"For we've never in the least known what!" Mrs. Grose declared.

"For wickedness. For what else—when he's so clever and beautiful and perfect? Is he stupid? Is he untidy? Is he infirm? Is he ill-natured? He's exquisite—so it can be only that; and that would open up the whole thing. After all," I said, "it's their uncle's fault. If he left here such people—!"

"He didn't really in the least know them. The fault's mine." She had turned quite pale.

"Well, you shan't suffer," I answered.

"The children shan't!" she emphatically returned.

I was silent awhile; we looked at each other. "Then what am I to tell him?"

"You needn't tell him anything. I'll tell him."

I measured this. "Do you mean you'll write—?" Remembering she couldn't, I caught myself up. "How do you communicate?"

"I tell the bailiff. He writes."

"And should you like him to write our story?"

My question had a sarcastic force that I had not fully intended, and it made her, after a moment, inconsequently break down. The tears were again in her eyes. "Ah, miss, you write!"

"Well—tonight," I at last answered; and on this we separated.

Chapter 17

I went so far, in the evening, as to make a beginning. The weather had changed back, a great wind was abroad, and beneath the lamp, in my room, with Flora at peace beside me, I sat for a long time before a blank sheet of paper and listened to the lash of the rain and the batter of the gusts. Finally I went out, taking a candle; I crossed the passage and listened a minute at Miles's door. What, under my endless obsession, I had been impelled to listen for was some betrayal of his not being at rest, and I presently caught one, but not in the form I had expected. His voice tinkled out. "I say, you there—come in." It was a gaiety in the gloom!

I went in with my light and found him, in bed, very wide awake, but very much at his ease. "Well, what are you up to?" he asked with a grace of sociability in which it occurred to me that Mrs. Grose, had she been present, might have looked in vain for proof that anything was "out."

I stood over him with my candle. "How did you know I was there?"

"Why, of course I heard you. Did you fancy you made no noise? You're like a troop of cavalry!" he beautifully laughed.

"Then you weren't asleep?"

"Not much! I lie awake and think."

I had put my candle, designedly, a short way off, and then, as he held out his friendly old hand to me, had sat down on the edge of his bed. "What is it," I asked, "that you think of?"

"What in the world, my dear, but you?"

"Ah, the pride I take in your appreciation doesn't insist on that! I had so far rather you slept."

"Well, I think also, you know, of this queer business of ours."

I marked the coolness of his firm little hand. "Of what queer business, Miles?"

"Why, the way you bring me up. And all the rest!"

I fairly held my breath a minute, and even from my glimmering taper there was light enough to show how he smiled up at me from his pillow. "What do you mean by all the rest?"

"Oh, you know, you know!"

I could say nothing for a minute, though I felt, as I held his hand and our eyes continued to meet, that my silence had all the air of admitting his charge and that nothing in the whole world of reality was perhaps at that moment so fabulous as our actual relation. "Certainly you shall go back to school," I said, "if it be that that troubles you. But not to the old place—we must find another, a better. How could I know it did trouble you, this question, when you never told me so, never spoke of it at all?" His clear, listening face, framed in its smooth whiteness, made him for the minute as appealing as some wistful patient in a children's hospital; and I would have given, as the resemblance came to me, all I possessed on earth really to be the nurse or the sister of charity who might have helped to cure him. Well, even as it was, I perhaps might help! "Do you know you've never said a word to me about your school—I mean the old one; never mentioned it in any way?"

He seemed to wonder; he smiled with the same loveliness. But he clearly gained time; he waited, he called for guidance. "Haven't I?" It wasn't for me to help him—it was for the thing I had met!

Something in his tone and the expression of his face, as I got this from him, set my heart aching with such a pang as it had never yet known; so unutterably touching was it to see his little brain puzzled and his little resources taxed to play, under the spell laid on him, a part of innocence and consistency. "No, never—from the hour you came back. You've never mentioned to me one of your masters, one of your comrades, nor the least little thing that ever happened to you at school. Never, little Miles—no, never—have you given me an inkling of anything that may have happened there. Therefore you can fancy how much I'm in the dark. Until you came out, that way, this morning, you had, since the first hour I saw you, scarce even made a reference to anything in your previous life. You seemed so perfectly to accept the present." It was extraordinary how my absolute conviction of his secret precocity (or whatever I might call the poison of an influence that I dared but half to phrase) made him, in spite of the faint breath of his inward trouble, appear as accessible as an older person—imposed him almost as an intellectual equal. "I thought you wanted to go on as you are."

It struck me that at this he just faintly colored. He gave, at any rate, like a convalescent slightly fatigued, a languid shake of his head. "I don't—I don't. I want to get away."

"You're tired of Bly?"

"Oh, no, I like Bly."

"Well, then—?"

"Oh, you know what a boy wants!"

I felt that I didn't know so well as Miles, and I took temporary refuge. "You want to go to your uncle?"

Again, at this, with his sweet ironic face, he made a movement on the pillow. "Ah, you can't get off with that!"

I was silent a little, and it was I, now, I think, who changed color. "My dear, I don't want to get off!"

"You can't, even if you do. You can't, you can't!"—he lay beautifully staring. "My uncle must come down, and you must completely settle things."

"If we do," I returned with some spirit, "you may be sure it will be to take you quite away."

"Well, don't you understand that that's exactly what I'm working for? You'll have to tell him—about the way you've let it all drop: you'll have to tell him a tremendous lot!"

The exultation with which he uttered this helped me somehow, for the instant, to meet him rather more. "And how much will you, Miles, have to tell him? There are things he'll ask you!"

He turned it over. "Very likely. But what things?"

"The things you've never told me. To make up his mind what to do with you. He can't send you back—"

"Oh, I don't want to go back!" he broke in. "I want a new field."

He said it with admirable serenity, with positive unimpeachable gaiety; and doubtless it was that very note that most evoked for me the poignancy, the unnatural childish tragedy, of his probable reappearance at the end of three months with all this bravado and still more dishonor. It overwhelmed me now that I should never be able to bear that, and it made me let myself go. I threw myself upon him and in the tenderness of my pity I embraced him. "Dear little Miles, dear little Miles—!"

My face was close to his, and he let me kiss him, simply taking it with indulgent good humor. "Well, old lady?"

"Is there nothing—nothing at all that you want to tell me?"

He turned off a little, facing round toward the wall and holding up his hand to look at as one had seen sick children look. "I've told you—I told you this morning."

Oh, I was sorry for him! "That you just want me not to worry you?"

He looked round at me now, as if in recognition of my understanding him; then ever so gently, "To let me alone," he replied.

There was even a singular little dignity in it, something that made me release him, yet, when I had slowly risen, linger beside him. God knows I never wished to harass him, but I felt that merely, at this, to turn my back on him was to abandon or, to put it more truly, to lose him. "I've just begun a letter to your uncle," I said.

"Well, then, finish it!"

I waited a minute. "What happened before?"

He gazed up at me again. "Before what?"

"Before you came back. And before you went away."

For some time he was silent, but he continued to meet my eyes. "What happened?"

It made me, the sound of the words, in which it seemed to me that I caught for the very first time a small faint quaver of consenting consciousness—it made me drop on my knees beside the bed and seize once more the chance of possessing him. "Dear little Miles, dear little Miles, if you knew how I want to help you! It's only that, it's nothing but that, and I'd rather die than give you a pain or do you a wrong—I'd rather die than hurt a hair of you. Dear little Miles"—oh, I brought it out now even if I should go too far—"I just want you to help me to save you!" But I knew in a moment after this that I had gone too far. The answer to my appeal was instantaneous, but it came in the form of an extraordinary blast and chill, a gust of frozen air, and a shake of the room as great as if, in the wild wind, the casement had crashed in. The boy gave a loud, high shriek, which, lost in the rest of the shock of sound, might have seemed, indistinctly, though I was so close to him, a note either of jubilation or of terror. I jumped to my feet again and was conscious of darkness. So for a moment we remained, while I stared about me and saw that the drawn curtains were unstirred and the window tight. "Why, the candle's out!" I then cried.

"It was I who blew it, dear!" said Miles.

Chapter 18

The next day, after lessons, Mrs. Grose found a moment to say to me quietly: "Have you written, miss?"

"Yes—I've written." But I didn't add—for the hour—that my letter, sealed and directed, was still in my pocket. There would be time enough to send it before the messenger should go to the village. Meanwhile there had been, on the part of my pupils, no more brilliant, more exemplary morning. It was exactly as if they had both had at heart to gloss over any recent little friction. They performed the dizziest feats of arithmetic, soaring quite out of my feeble range, and perpetrated, in higher spirits than ever, geographical and historical jokes. It was conspicuous of course in Miles in particular that he appeared to wish to show how easily he could let me down. This child, to my memory, really lives in a setting of beauty and misery that no words can translate; there was a distinction all his own in every impulse he revealed; never was a small natural creature, to the uninitiated eye all frankness and freedom, a more ingenious, a more extraordinary little gentleman. I had perpetually to guard against the wonder of contemplation into which my initiated view betrayed me; to check the irrelevant gaze and discouraged sigh in which I constantly both attacked and renounced the enigma of what such a little gentleman could have done that deserved a penalty. Say that, by the dark prodigy I knew, the imagination of all evil had been opened up to him: all the justice within me ached for the proof that it could ever have flowered into an act.

He had never, at any rate, been such a little gentleman as when, after our early dinner on this dreadful day, he came round to me and asked if I shouldn't like him, for half an hour, to play to me. David playing to Saul could never have shown a finer sense of the occasion. It was literally a charming exhibition of tact, of magnanimity, and quite tantamount to his saying outright: "The true knights we love to read about never push an advantage too far. I know what you mean now: you mean that—to be let alone yourself and not followed up—you'll cease to worry and spy upon me, won't keep me so close to you, will let me go and come. Well, I 'come,' you see—but I don't go! There'll be plenty of time for that. I do really delight in your society, and I only want to show you that I contended for a principle." It may be imagined whether I resisted this appeal or failed to accompany him again, hand in hand, to the schoolroom. He sat down at the old piano and played as he had never played; and if there are those who think he had better have been kicking a football I can only say that I wholly agree with them. For at the end of a time that under his influence I had quite ceased to measure, I started up with a strange sense of having literally slept at my post. It was after luncheon, and by the schoolroom fire, and yet I hadn't really, in the least, slept: I had only done something much worse—I had forgotten. Where, all this time, was Flora? When I put the question to Miles, he played on a minute before answering and then could only say: "Why, my dear, how do I know?"—breaking moreover into a happy laugh which, immediately after, as if it were a vocal accompaniment, he prolonged into incoherent, extravagant song.

I went straight to my room, but his sister was not there; then, before going downstairs, I looked into several others. As she was nowhere about she would surely be with Mrs. Grose, whom, in the comfort of that theory, I accordingly proceeded in quest of. I found her where I had found her the evening before, but she met my quick challenge with blank, scared ignorance. She had only supposed that, after the repast, I had carried off both the children; as to which she was quite in her right, for it was the very first time I had allowed the little girl out of my sight without some special provision. Of course now indeed she might be with the maids, so that the immediate thing was to look for her without an air of alarm. This we promptly arranged between us; but when, ten minutes later and in pursuance of our arrangement, we met in the hall, it was only to report on either side that after guarded inquiries we had altogether failed to trace her. For a minute there, apart from observation, we exchanged mute alarms, and I could feel with what high interest my friend returned me all those I had from the first given her.

"She'll be above," she presently said—"in one of the rooms you haven't searched."

"No; she's at a distance." I had made up my mind. "She has gone out."

Mrs. Grose stared. "Without a hat?"

I naturally also looked volumes. "Isn't that woman always without one?"

"She's with her?"

"She's with her!" I declared. "We must find them."

My hand was on my friend's arm, but she failed for the moment, confronted with such an account of the matter, to respond to my pressure. She communed, on the contrary, on the spot, with her uneasiness. "And where's Master Miles?"

"Oh, he's with Quint. They're in the schoolroom."

"Lord, miss!" My view, I was myself aware—and therefore I suppose my tone—had never yet reached so calm an assurance.

"The trick's played," I went on; "they've successfully worked their plan. He found the most divine little way to keep me quiet while she went off."

"'Divine'?" Mrs. Grose bewilderedly echoed.

"Infernal, then!" I almost cheerfully rejoined. "He has provided for himself as well. But come!"

She had helplessly gloomed at the upper regions. "You leave him—?"

"So long with Quint? Yes—I don't mind that now."

She always ended, at these moments, by getting possession of my hand, and in this manner she could at present still stay me. But after gasping an instant at my sudden resignation, "Because of your letter?" she eagerly brought out.

I quickly, by way of answer, felt for my letter, drew it forth, held it up, and then, freeing myself, went and laid it on the great hall table. "Luke will take it," I said as I came back. I reached the house door and opened it; I was already on the steps.

My companion still demurred: the storm of the night and the early morning had dropped, but the afternoon was damp and gray. I came down to the drive while she stood in the doorway. "You go with nothing on?"

"What do I care when the child has nothing? I can't wait to dress," I cried, "and if you must do so, I leave you. Try meanwhile, yourself, upstairs."

"With them?" Oh, on this, the poor woman promptly joined me!

Chapter 19

We went straight to the lake, as it was called at Bly, and I daresay rightly called, though I reflect that it may in fact have been a sheet of water less remarkable than it appeared to my untraveled eyes. My acquaintance with sheets of water was small, and the pool of Bly, at all events on the few occasions of my consenting, under the protection of my pupils, to affront its surface in the old flat-bottomed boat moored there for our use, had impressed me both with its extent and its agitation. The usual place of embarkation was half a mile from the house, but I had an intimate conviction that, wherever Flora might be, she was not near home. She had not given me the slip for any small adventure, and, since the day of the very great one that I had shared with her by the pond, I had been aware, in our walks, of the quarter to which she most inclined. This was why I had now given to Mrs. Grose's steps so marked a direction—a direction that made her, when she perceived it, oppose a resistance that showed me she was freshly mystified. "You're going to the water, Miss?—you think she's in—?"

"She may be, though the depth is, I believe, nowhere very great. But what I judge most likely is that she's on the spot from which, the other day, we saw together what I told you."

"When she pretended not to see—?"

"With that astounding self-possession? I've always been sure she wanted to go back alone. And now her brother has managed it for her."

Mrs. Grose still stood where she had stopped. "You suppose they really talk of them?"

"I could meet this with a confidence! "They say things that, if we heard them, would simply appall us."

"And if she is there—"

"Yes?"

"Then Miss Jessel is?"

"Beyond a doubt. You shall see."

"Oh, thank you!" my friend cried, planted so firm that, taking it in, I went straight on without her. By the time I reached the pool, however, she was close behind me, and I knew that, whatever, to her apprehension, might befall me, the exposure of my society struck her as her least danger. She exhaled a moan of relief as we at last came in sight of the greater part of the water without a sight of the child. There was no trace of Flora on that nearer side of the bank where my observation of her had been most startling, and none on the opposite edge, where, save for a margin of some twenty yards, a thick copse came down to the water. The pond, oblong in shape, had a width so scant compared to its length that, with its ends out of view, it might have been taken for a scant river. We looked at the empty expanse, and then I felt the suggestion of my friend's eyes. I knew what she meant and I replied with a negative headshake.

"No, no; wait! She has taken the boat."

My companion stared at the vacant mooring place and then again across the lake. "Then where is it?"

"Our not seeing it is the strongest of proofs. She has used it to go over, and then has managed to hide it."

"All alone—that child?"

"She's not alone, and at such times she's not a child: she's an old, old woman." I scanned all the visible shore while Mrs. Grose took again, into the queer element I offered her, one of her plunges of submission; then I pointed out that the boat might perfectly be in a small refuge formed by one of the recesses of the pool, an indentation masked, for the hither side, by a projection of the bank and by a clump of trees growing close to the water.

"But if the boat's there, where on earth's she?" my colleague anxiously asked.

"That's exactly what we must learn." And I started to walk further.

"By going all the way round?"

"Certainly, far as it is. It will take us but ten minutes, but it's far enough to have made the child prefer not to walk. She went straight over."

"Laws!" cried my friend again; the chain of my logic was ever too much for her. It dragged her at my heels even now, and when we had got halfway round—a devious, tiresome process, on ground much broken and by a path choked with overgrowth—I paused to give her breath. I sustained her with a grateful arm, assuring her that she might hugely help me; and this started us afresh, so that in the course of but few minutes more we reached a point from which we found the boat to be where I had supposed it. It had been intentionally left as much as possible out of sight and was tied to one of the stakes of a fence that came, just there, down to the brink and that had been an assistance to disembarking. I recognized, as I looked at the pair of short, thick oars, quite safely drawn up, the prodigious character of the feat for a little girl; but I had lived, by this time, too long among wonders and had panted to too many livelier measures. There was a gate in the fence, through which we passed, and that brought us, after a trifling interval, more into the open. Then, "There she is!" we both exclaimed at once.

Flora, a short way off, stood before us on the grass and smiled as if her performance was now complete. The next thing she did, however, was to stoop straight down and pluck—quite as if it were all she was there for—a big, ugly spray of withered fern. I instantly became sure she had just come out of the copse. She waited for us, not herself taking a step, and I was conscious of the rare solemnity with which we presently approached her. She smiled and smiled, and we met; but it was all done in a silence by this time flagrantly ominous. Mrs. Grose was the first to break the spell: she threw herself on her knees and, drawing the child to her breast, clasped in a long embrace the little tender, yielding body. While this dumb convulsion lasted I could only watch it—which I did the more intently when I saw Flora's face peep at me over our companion's shoulder. It was serious now—the flicker had left it; but it strengthened the pang with which I at that moment envied Mrs. Grose the simplicity of her relation. Still, all this while, nothing more passed between us save that Flora had let her foolish fern again drop to the ground. What she and I had virtually said to each other was that pretexts were useless now. When Mrs. Grose finally got up she kept the child's hand, so that the two were still before me; and the singular reticence of our communion was even more marked in the frank look she launched me. "I'll be hanged," it said, "if I'll speak!"

It was Flora who, gazing all over me in candid wonder, was the first. She was struck with our bare-headed aspect. "Why, where are your things?"

"Where yours are, my dear!" I promptly returned.

She had already got back her gaiety, and appeared to take this as an answer quite sufficient. "And where's Miles?" she went on.

There was something in the small valor of it that quite finished me: these three words from her were, in a flash like the glitter of a drawn blade, the jostle of the cup that my hand, for weeks and weeks, had held high and full to the brim that now, even before speaking, I felt overflow in a deluge. "I'll tell you if you'll tell me—" I heard myself say, then heard the tremor in which it broke.

"Well, what?"

Mrs. Grose's suspense blazed at me, but it was too late now, and I brought the thing out handsomely. "Where, my pet, is Miss Jessel?"

Chapter 20

Just as in the churchyard with Miles, the whole thing was upon us. Much as I had made of the fact that this name had never once, between us, been sounded, the quick, smitten glare with which the child's face now received it fairly likened my breach of the silence to the smash of a pane of glass. It added to the interposing cry, as if to stay the blow, that Mrs. Grose, at the same instant, uttered over my violence—the shriek of a creature scared, or rather wounded, which, in turn, within a few seconds, was completed by a gasp of my own. I seized my colleague's arm. "She's there, she's there!"

Miss Jessel stood before us on the opposite bank exactly as she had stood the other time, and I remember, strangely, as the first feeling now produced in me, my thrill of joy at having brought on a proof. She was there, and I was justified; she was there, and I was neither cruel nor mad. She was there for poor scared Mrs. Grose, but she was there most for Flora; and no moment of my monstrous time was perhaps so extraordinary as that in which I consciously threw out to her—with the sense that, pale and ravenous demon as she was, she would catch and understand it—an inarticulate message of gratitude. She rose erect on the spot my friend and I had lately quitted, and there was not, in all the long reach of her desire, an inch of her evil that fell short. This first vividness of vision and emotion were things of a few seconds, during which Mrs. Grose's dazed blink across to where I pointed struck me as a sovereign sign that she too at last saw, just as it carried my own eyes precipitately to the child. The revelation then of the manner in which Flora was affected startled me, in truth, far more than it would have done to find her also merely agitated, for direct dismay was of course not what I had expected. Prepared and on her guard as our pursuit had actually made her, she would repress every betrayal; and I was therefore shaken, on the spot, by my first glimpse of the particular one for which I had not allowed. To see her, without a convulsion of her small pink face, not even feign to glance in the direction of the prodigy I announced, but only, instead of that, turn at me an expression of hard, still gravity, an expression absolutely new and unprecedented and that appeared to read and accuse and judge me—this was a stroke that somehow converted the little girl herself into the very presence that could make me quail. I quailed even though my certitude that she thoroughly saw was never greater than at that instant, and in the immediate need to defend myself I called it passionately to witness. "She's there, you little unhappy thing—there, there, there, and you see her as well as you see me!" I had said shortly before to Mrs. Grose that she was not at these times a child, but an old, old woman, and that description of her could not have been more strikingly confirmed than in the way in which, for all answer to this, she simply showed me, without a concession, an admission, of her eyes, a countenance of deeper and deeper, of indeed suddenly quite fixed, reprobation. I was by this time—if I can put the whole thing at all together—more appalled at what I may properly call her manner than at anything else, though it was simultaneously with this that I became aware of having Mrs. Grose also, and very formidably, to reckon with. My elder companion, the next moment, at any rate, blotted out everything but her own flushed face and her loud, shocked protest, a burst of high disapproval. "What a dreadful turn, to be sure, miss! Where on earth do you see anything?"

I could only grasp her more quickly yet, for even while she spoke the hideous plain presence stood undimmed and undaunted. It had already lasted a minute, and it lasted while I continued, seizing my colleague, quite thrusting her at it and presenting her to it, to insist with my pointing hand. "You don't see her exactly as we see?—you mean to say you don't now—now? She's as big as a blazing fire! Only look, dearest woman, look—!" She looked, even as I did, and gave me, with her deep groan of negation, repulsion, compassion—the mixture with her pity of her relief at her exemption—a sense, touching to me even then, that she would have backed me up if she could. I might well have needed that, for with this hard blow of the proof that her eyes were hopelessly sealed I felt my own situation horribly crumble, I felt—I saw—my livid predecessor press, from her position, on my defeat, and I was conscious, more than all, of what I should have from this instant to deal with in the astounding little attitude of Flora. Into this attitude Mrs. Grose immediately and violently entered, breaking, even while there pierced through my sense of ruin a prodigious private triumph, into breathless reassurance.

"She isn't there, little lady, and nobody's there—and you never see nothing, my sweet! How can poor Miss Jessel—when poor Miss Jessel's dead and buried? We know, don't we, love?—and she appealed, blundering in, to the child. "It's all a mere mistake and a worry and a joke—and we'll go home as fast as we can!"

Our companion, on this, had responded with a strange, quick primness of propriety, and they were again, with Mrs. Grose on her feet, united, as it were, in pained opposition to me. Flora continued to fix me with her small mask of reprobation, and even at that minute I prayed God to forgive me for seeming to see that, as she stood there holding tight to our friend's dress, her incomparable childish beauty had suddenly failed, had quite vanished. I've said it already—she was literally, she was hideously, hard; she had turned common and almost ugly. "I don't know what you mean. I see nobody. I see nothing. I never have. I think you're cruel. I don't like you!" Then, after this deliverance, which might have been that of a vulgarly pert little girl in the street, she hugged Mrs. Grose more closely and buried in her skirts the dreadful little face. In this position she produced an almost furious wail. "Take me away, take me away—oh, take me away from her!"

"From me?" I panted.

"From you—from you!" she cried.

Even Mrs. Grose looked across at me dismayed, while I had nothing to do but communicate again with the figure that, on the opposite bank, without a movement, as rigidly still as if catching, beyond the interval, our voices, was as vividly there for my disaster as it was not there for my service. The wretched child had spoken exactly as if she had got from some outside source each of her stabbing little words, and I could therefore, in the full despair of all I had to accept, but sadly shake my head at her. "If I had ever doubted, all my doubt would at present have gone. I've been living with the miserable truth, and now it has only too much closed round me. Of course I've lost you: I've interfered, and you've seen—under her dictation"—with which I faced, over the pool again, our infernal witness—"the easy and perfect way to meet it. I've done my best, but I've lost you. Goodbye." For Mrs. Grose I had an imperative, an almost frantic "Go, go!" before which, in infinite distress, but mutely possessed of the little girl and clearly convinced, in spite of her blindness, that something awful had occurred and some collapse engulfed us, she retreated, by the way we had come, as fast as she could move.

Of what first happened when I was left alone I had no subsequent memory. I only knew that at the end of, I suppose, a quarter of an hour, an odorous dampness and roughness, chilling and piercing my trouble, had made me understand that I must have thrown myself, on my face, on the ground and given way to a wildness of grief. I must have lain there long and cried and sobbed, for when I raised my head the day was almost done. I got up and looked a moment, through the twilight, at the gray pool and its blank, haunted edge, and then I took, back to the house, my dreary and difficult course. When I reached the gate in the fence the boat, to my surprise, was gone, so that I had a fresh reflection to make on Flora's extraordinary command of the situation. She passed that night, by the most tacit, and I should add, were not the word so grotesque a false note, the happiest of arrangements, with Mrs. Grose. I saw neither of them on my return, but, on the other hand, as by an ambiguous compensation, I saw a great deal of Miles. I saw—I can use no other phrase—so much of him that it was as if it were more than it had ever been. No evening I had passed at Bly had the portentous quality of this one; in spite of which—and in spite also of the deeper depths of consternation that had opened beneath my feet—there was literally, in the ebbing actual, an extraordinarily sweet sadness. On reaching the house I had never so much as looked for the boy; I had simply gone straight to my room to change what I was wearing and to take in, at a glance, much material testimony to Flora's rupture. Her little belongings had all been removed. When later, by the schoolroom fire, I was served with tea by the usual maid, I indulged, on the article of my other pupil, in no inquiry whatever. He had his freedom now—he might have it to the end! Well, he did have it; and it consisted—in part at least—of his coming in at about eight o'clock and sitting down with me in silence. On the removal of the tea things I had blown out the candles and drawn my chair closer: I was conscious of a mortal coldness and felt as if I should never again be warm. So, when he appeared, I was sitting in the glow with my thoughts. He paused a moment by the door as if to look at me; then—as if to share them—came to the other side of the hearth and sank into a chair. We sat there in absolute stillness; yet he wanted, I felt, to be with me.

Chapter 21

Before a new day, in my room, had fully broken, my eyes opened to Mrs. Grose, who had come to my bedside with worse news. Flora was so markedly feverish that an illness was perhaps at hand; she had passed a night of extreme unrest, a night agitated above all by fears that had for their subject not in the least her former, but wholly her present, governess. It was not against the possible re-entrance of Miss Jessel on the scene that she protested—it was conspicuously and passionately against mine. I was promptly on my feet of course, and with an immense deal to ask; the more that my friend had discernibly now girded her loins to meet me once more. This I felt as soon as I had put to her the question of her sense of the child's sincerity as against my own. "She persists in denying to you that she saw, or has ever seen, anything?"

My visitor's trouble, truly, was great. "Ah, miss, it isn't a matter on which I can push her! Yet it isn't either, I must say, as if I much needed to. It has made her, every inch of her, quite old."

"Oh, I see her perfectly from here. She resents, for all the world like some high little personage, the imputation on her truthfulness and, as it were, her respectability. 'Miss Jessel indeed—she!' Ah, she's 'respectable,' the chit! The impression she gave me there yesterday was, I assure you, the very strangest of all; it was quite beyond any of the others. I did put my foot in it! She'll never speak to me again."

Hideous and obscure as it all was, it held Mrs. Grose briefly silent; then she granted my point with a frankness which, I made sure, had more behind it. "I think indeed, miss, she never will. She do have a grand manner about it!"

"And that manner"—I summed it up—"is practically what's the matter with her now!"

Oh, that manner, I could see in my visitor's face, and not a little else besides! "She asks me every three minutes if I think you're coming in."

"I see—I see." I, too, on my side, had so much more than worked it out. "Has she said to you since yesterday—except to repudiate her familiarity with anything so dreadful—a single other word about Miss Jessel?"

"Not one, miss. And of course you know," my friend added, "I took it from her, by the lake, that, just then and there at least, there was nobody."

"Rather! and, naturally, you take it from her still."

"I don't contradict her. What else can I do?"

"Nothing in the world! You've the cleverest little person to deal with. They've made them—their two friends, I mean—still cleverer even than nature did; for it was wondrous material to play on! Flora has now her grievance, and she'll work it to the end."

"Yes, miss; but to what end?"

"Why, that of dealing with me to her uncle. She'll make me out to him the lowest creature—!"

I winced at the fair show of the scene in Mrs. Grose's face; she looked for a minute as if she sharply saw them together. "And him who thinks so well of you!"

"He has an odd way—it comes over me now," I laughed, "—of proving it! But that doesn't matter. What Flora wants, of course, is to get rid of me."

My companion bravely concurred. "Never again to so much as look at you."

"So that what you've come to me now for," I asked, "is to speed me on my way?" Before she had time to reply, however, I had her in check. "I've a better idea—the result of my reflections. My going would seem the right thing, and on Sunday I was terribly near it. Yet that won't do. It's you who must go. You must take Flora."

My visitor, at this, did speculate. "But where in the world—?"

"Away from here. Away from them. Away, even most of all, now, from me. Straight to her uncle."

"Only to tell on you—?"

"No, not 'only'! To leave me, in addition, with my remedy."

She was still vague. "And what is your remedy?"

"Your loyalty, to begin with. And then Miles's."

She looked at me hard. "Do you think he—?"

"Won't, if he has the chance, turn on me? Yes, I venture still to think it. At all events, I want to try. Get off with his sister as soon as possible and leave me with him alone." I was amazed, myself, at the spirit I had still in reserve, and therefore perhaps a trifle the more disconcerted at the way in which, in spite of this fine example of it, she hesitated. "There's one thing, of course," I went on: "they mustn't, before she goes, see each other for three seconds." Then it came over me that, in spite of Flora's presumable sequestration from the instant of her return from the pool, it might already be too late. "Do you mean," I anxiously asked, "that they have met?"

At this she quite flushed. "Ah, miss, I'm not such a fool as that! If I've been obliged to leave her three or four times, it has been each time with one of the maids, and at present, though she's alone, she's locked in safe. And yet—and yet!" There were too many things.

"And yet what?"

"Well, are you so sure of the little gentleman?"

"I'm not sure of anything but you. But I have, since last evening, a new hope. I think he wants to give me an opening. I do believe that—poor little exquisite wretch!—he wants to speak. Last evening, in the firelight and the silence, he sat with me for two hours as if it were just coming."

Mrs. Grose looked hard, through the window, at the gray, gathering day. "And did it come?"

"No, though I waited and waited, I confess it didn't, and it was without a breach of the silence or so much as a faint allusion to his sister's condition and absence that we at last kissed for good night. All the same," I continued, "I can't, if her uncle sees her, consent to his seeing her brother without my having given the boy—and most of all because things have got so bad—a little more time."

My friend appeared on this ground more reluctant than I could quite understand. "What do you mean by more time?"

"Well, a day or two—really to bring it out. He'll then be on my side—of which you see the importance. If nothing comes, I shall only fail, and you will, at the worst, have helped me by doing, on your arrival in town, whatever you may have found possible." So I put it before her, but she continued for a little so inscrutably embarrassed that I came again to her aid. "Unless, indeed," I wound up, "you really want not to go."

I could see it, in her face, at last clear itself; she put out her hand to me as a pledge. "I'll go—I'll go. I'll go this morning."

I wanted to be very just. "If you should wish still to wait, I would engage she shouldn't see me."

"No, no: it's the place itself. She must leave it." She held me a moment with heavy eyes, then brought out the rest. "Your idea's the right one. I myself, miss—"

"Well?"

"I can't stay."

The look she gave me with it made me jump at possibilities. "You mean that, since yesterday, you have seen—?"

She shook her head with dignity. "I've heard—!"

"Heard?"

"From that child—horrors! There!" she sighed with tragic relief. "On my honor, miss, she says things—!" But at this evocation she broke down; she dropped, with a sudden sob, upon my sofa and, as I had seen her do before, gave way to all the grief of it.

It was quite in another manner that I, for my part, let myself go. "Oh, thank God!"

She sprang up again at this, drying her eyes with a groan. "'Thank God'?"

"It so justifies me!"

"It does that, miss!"

I couldn't have desired more emphasis, but I just hesitated. "She's so horrible?"

I saw my colleague scarce knew how to put it. "Really shocking."

"And about me?"

"About you, miss—since you must have it. It's beyond everything, for a young lady; and I can't think wherever she must have picked up—"

"The appalling language she applied to me? I can, then!" I broke in with a laugh that was doubtless significant enough.

It only, in truth, left my friend still more grave. "Well, perhaps I ought to also—since I've heard some of it before! Yet I can't bear it," the poor woman went on while, with the same movement, she glanced, on my dressing table, at the face of my watch. "But I must go back."

I kept her, however. "Ah, if you can't bear it—!"

"How can I stop with her, you mean? Why, just for that: to get her away. Far from this," she pursued, "far from them—"

"She may be different? She may be free?" I seized her almost with joy. "Then, in spite of yesterday, you believe—"

"In such doings?" Her simple description of them required, in the light of her expression, to be carried no further, and she gave me the whole thing as she had never done. "I believe."

Yes, it was a joy, and we were still shoulder to shoulder: if I might continue sure of that I should care but little what else happened. My support in the presence of disaster would be the same as it had been in my early need of confidence, and if my friend would answer for my honesty, I would answer for all the rest. On the point of taking leave of her, nonetheless, I was to some extent embarrassed. "There's one thing, of course—it occurs to me—to remember. My letter, giving the alarm, will have reached town before you."

I now perceived still more how she had been beating about the bush and how weary at last it had made her. "Your letter won't have got there. Your letter never went."

"What then became of it?"

"Goodness knows! Master Miles—"

"Do you mean he took it?" I gasped.

She hung fire, but she overcame her reluctance. "I mean that I saw yesterday, when I came back with Miss Flora, that it wasn't where you had put it. Later in the evening I had the chance to question Luke, and he declared that he had neither noticed nor touched it." We could only exchange, on this, one of our deeper mutual soundings, and it was Mrs. Grose who first brought up the plumb with an almost elated "You see!"

"Yes, I see that if Miles took it instead he probably will have read it and destroyed it."

"And don't you see anything else?"

I faced her a moment with a sad smile. "It strikes me that by this time your eyes are open even wider than mine."

They proved to be so indeed, but she could still blush, almost, to show it. "I make out now what he must have done at school." And she gave, in her simple sharpness, an almost droll disillusioned nod. "He stole!"

I turned it over—I tried to be more judicial. "Well—perhaps."

She looked as if she found me unexpectedly calm. "He stole letters!"

She couldn't know my reasons for a calmness after all pretty shallow; so I showed them off as I might. "I hope then it was to more purpose than in this case! The note, at any rate, that I put on the table yesterday," I pursued, "will have given him so scant an advantage—for it contained only the bare demand for an interview—that he is already much ashamed of having gone so far for so little, and that what he had on his mind last evening was precisely the need of confession." I seemed to myself, for the instant, to have mastered it, to see it all. "Leave us, leave us"—I was already, at the door, hurrying her off. "I'll get it out of him. He'll meet me—he'll confess. If he confesses, he's saved. And if he's saved—"

"Then you are?" The dear woman kissed me on this, and I took her farewell. "I'll save you without him!" she cried as she went.

Chapter 22

Yet it was when she had got off—and I missed her on the spot—that the great pinch really came. If I had counted on what it would give me to find myself alone with Miles, I speedily perceived, at least, that it would give me a measure. No hour of my stay in fact was so assailed with apprehensions as that of my coming down to learn that the carriage containing Mrs. Grose and my younger pupil had already rolled out of the gates. Now I was, I said to myself, face to face with the elements, and for much of the rest of the day, while I fought my weakness, I could consider that I had been supremely rash. It was a tighter place still than I had yet turned round in; all the more that, for the first time, I could see in the aspect of others a confused reflection of the crisis. What had happened naturally caused them all to stare; there was too little of the explained, throw out whatever we might, in the suddenness of my colleague's act. The maids and the men looked blank; the effect of which on my nerves was an aggravation until I saw the necessity of making it a positive aid. It was precisely, in short, by just clutching the helm that I avoided total wreck; and I dare say that, to bear up at all, I became, that morning, very grand and very dry. I welcomed the consciousness that I was charged with much to do, and I caused it to be known as well that, left thus to myself, I was quite remarkably firm. I wandered with that manner, for the next hour or two, all over the place and looked, I have no doubt, as if I were ready for any onset. So, for the benefit of whom it might concern, I paraded with a sick heart.

The person it appeared least to concern proved to be, till dinner, little Miles himself. My perambulations had given me, meanwhile, no glimpse of him, but they had tended to make more public the change taking place in our relation as a consequence of his having at the piano, the day before, kept me, in Flora's interest, so beguiled and befooled. The stamp of publicity had of course been fully given by her confinement and departure, and the change itself was now ushered in by our nonobservance of the regular custom of the schoolroom. He had already disappeared when, on my way down, I pushed open his door, and I learned below that he had breakfasted—in the presence of a couple of the maids—with Mrs. Grose and his sister. He had then gone out, as he said, for a stroll; than which nothing, I reflected, could better have expressed his frank view of the abrupt transformation of my office. What he would not permit this office to consist of was yet to be settled: there was a queer relief, at all events—I mean for myself in especial—in the renouncement of one pretension. If so much had sprung to the surface, I scarce put it too strongly in saying that what had perhaps sprung highest was the absurdity of our prolonging the fiction that I had anything more to teach him. It sufficiently stuck out that, by tacit little tricks in which even more than myself he carried out the care for my dignity, I had had to appeal to him to let me off straining to meet him on the ground of his true capacity. He had at any rate his freedom now; I was never to touch it again; as I had amply shown, moreover, when, on his joining me in the schoolroom the previous night, I had uttered, on the subject of the interval just concluded, neither challenge nor hint. I had too much, from this moment, my other ideas. Yet when he at last arrived, the difficulty of applying them, the accumulations of my problem, were brought straight home to me by the beautiful little presence on which what had occurred had as yet, for the eye, dropped neither stain nor shadow.

To mark, for the house, the high state I cultivated I decreed that my meals with the boy should be served, as we called it, downstairs; so that I had been awaiting him in the ponderous pomp of the room outside of the window of which I had had from Mrs. Grose, that first scared Sunday, my flash of something it would scarce have done to call light. Here at present I felt afresh—for I had felt it again and again—how my equilibrium depended on the success of my rigid will, the will to shut my eyes as tight as possible to the truth that what I had to deal with was, revoltingly, against nature. I could only get on at all by taking "nature" into my confidence and my account, by treating my monstrous ordeal as a push in a direction unusual, of course, and unpleasant, but demanding, after all, for a fair front, only another turn of the screw of ordinary human virtue. No attempt, nonetheless, could well require more tact than just this attempt to supply, one's self, all the nature. How could I put even a little of that article into a suppression of reference to what had occurred? How, on the other hand, could I make reference without a new plunge into the hideous obscure? Well, a sort of answer, after a time, had come to me, and it was so far confirmed as that I was met, incontestably, by the quickened vision of what was rare in my little companion. It was indeed as if he had found even now—as he had so often found at lessons—still some other delicate way to ease me off. Wasn't there light in the fact which, as we shared our solitude, broke out with a specious glitter it had never yet quite worn?—the fact that (opportunity aiding, precious opportunity which had now come) it would be preposterous, with a child so endowed, to forego the help one might wrest from absolute intelligence? What had his intelligence been given him for but to save him? Mightn't one, to reach his mind, risk the stretch of an angular arm over his character? It was as if, when we were face to face in the dining room, he had literally shown me the way. The roast mutton was on the table, and I had dispensed with attendance. Miles, before he sat down, stood a moment with his hands in his pockets and looked at the joint, on which he seemed on the point of passing some humorous judgment. But what he presently produced was: "I say, my dear, is she really very awfully ill?"

"Little Flora? Not so bad but that she'll presently be better. London will set her up. Bly had ceased to agree with her. Come here and take your mutton."

He alertly obeyed me, carried the plate carefully to his seat, and, when he was established, went on. "Did Bly disagree with her so terribly suddenly?"

"Not so suddenly as you might think. One had seen it coming on."

"Then why didn't you get her off before?"

"Before what?"

"Before she became too ill to travel."

I found myself prompt. "She's not too ill to travel: she only might have become so if she had stayed. This was just the moment to seize. The journey will dissipate the influence"—oh, I was grand!—"and carry it off."

"I see, I see"—Miles, for that matter, was grand, too. He settled to his repast with the charming little "table manner" that, from the day of his arrival, had relieved me of all grossness of admonition. Whatever he had been driven from school for, it was not for ugly feeding. He was irreproachable, as always, today; but he was unmistakably more conscious. He was discernibly trying to take for granted more things than he found, without assistance, quite easy; and he dropped into peaceful silence while he felt his situation. Our meal was of the briefest—mine a vain pretense, and I had the things immediately removed. While this was done Miles stood again with his hands in his little pockets and his back to me—stood and looked out of the wide window through which, that other day, I had seen what pulled me up. We continued silent while the maid was with us—as silent, it whimsically occurred to me, as some young couple who, on their wedding journey, at the inn, feel shy in the presence of the waiter. He turned round only when the waiter had left us. "Well—so we're alone!"

Chapter 23

"Oh, more or less." I fancy my smile was pale. "Not absolutely. We shouldn't like that!" I went on.

"No—I suppose we shouldn't. Of course we have the others."

"We have the others—we have indeed the others," I concurred.

"Yet even though we have them," he returned, still with his hands in his pockets and planted there in front of me, "they don't much count, do they?"

I made the best of it, but I felt wan. "It depends on what you call 'much'!"

"Yes"—with all accommodation—"everything depends!" On this, however, he faced to the window again and presently reached it with his vague, restless, cogitating step. He remained there awhile, with his forehead against the glass, in contemplation of the stupid shrubs I knew and the dull things of November. I had always my hypocrisy of "work," behind which, now, I gained the sofa. Steadying myself with it there as I had repeatedly done at those moments of torment that I have described as the moments of my knowing the children to be given to something from which I was barred, I sufficiently obeyed my habit of being prepared for the worst. But an extraordinary impression dropped on me as

I extracted a meaning from the boy's embarrassed back—none other than the impression that I was not barred now. This inference grew in a few minutes to sharp intensity and seemed bound up with the direct perception that it was positively he who was. The frames and squares of the great window were a kind of image, for him, of a kind of failure. I felt that I saw him, at any rate, shut in or shut out. He was admirable, but not comfortable: I took it in with a throb of hope. Wasn't he looking, through the haunted pane, for something he couldn't see?—and wasn't it the first time in the whole business that he had known such a lapse? The first, the very first: I found it a splendid portent. It made him anxious, though he watched himself; he had been anxious all day and, even while in his usual sweet little manner he sat at table, had needed all his small strange genius to give it a gloss. When he at last turned round to meet me, it was almost as if this genius had succumbed. "Well, I think I'm glad Bly agrees with me!"

"You would certainly seem to have seen, these twenty-four hours, a good deal more of it than for some time before. I hope," I went on bravely, "that you've been enjoying yourself."

"Oh, yes, I've been ever so far; all round about—miles and miles away. I've never been so free."

He had really a manner of his own, and I could only try to keep up with him. "Well, do you like it?"

He stood there smiling; then at last he put into two words—"Do you?"—more discrimination than I had ever heard two words contain. Before I had time to deal with that, however, he continued as if with the sense that this was an impertinence to be softened. "Nothing could be more charming than the way you take it, for of course if we're alone together now it's you that are alone most. But I hope," he threw in, "you don't particularly mind!"

"Having to do with you?" I asked. "My dear child, how can I help minding? Though I've renounced all claim to your company—you're so beyond me—I at least greatly enjoy it. What else should I stay on for?"

He looked at me more directly, and the expression of his face, graver now, struck me as the most beautiful I had ever found in it. "You stay on just for that?"

"Certainly. I stay on as your friend and from the tremendous interest I take in you till something can be done for you that may be more worth your while. That needn't surprise you." My voice trembled so that I felt it impossible to suppress the shake. "Don't you remember how I told you, when I came and sat on your bed the night of the storm, that there was nothing in the world I wouldn't do for you?"

"Yes, yes!" He, on his side, more and more visibly nervous, had a tone to master; but he was so much more successful than I that, laughing out through his gravity, he could pretend we were pleasantly jesting. "Only that, I think, was to get me to do something for you!"

"It was partly to get you to do something," I conceded. "But, you know, you didn't do it."

"Oh, yes," he said with the brightest superficial eagerness, "you wanted me to tell you something."

"That's it. Out, straight out. What you have on your mind, you know."

"Ah, then, is that what you've stayed over for?"

He spoke with a gaiety through which I could still catch the finest little quiver of resentful passion; but I can't begin to express the effect upon me of an implication of surrender even so faint. It was as if what I had yearned for had come at last only to astonish me. "Well, yes—I may as well make a clean breast of it. it was precisely for that."

He waited so long that I supposed it for the purpose of repudiating the assumption on which my action had been founded; but what he finally said was: "Do you mean now—here?"

"There couldn't be a better place or time." He looked round him uneasily, and I had the rare—oh, the queer!—impression of the very first symptom I had seen in him of the approach of immediate fear. It was as if he were suddenly afraid of me—which struck me indeed as perhaps the best thing to make him. Yet in the very pang of the effort I felt it vain to try sternness, and I heard myself the next instant so gentle as to be almost grotesque. "You want so to go out again?"

"Awfully!" He smiled at me heroically, and the touching little bravery of it was enhanced by his actually flushing with pain. He had picked up his hat, which he had brought in, and stood twirling it in a way that gave me, even as I was just nearly reaching port, a perverse horror of what I was doing. To do it in any way was an act of violence, for what did it consist of but the obtrusion of the idea of grossness and guilt on a small helpless creature who had been for me a revelation of the possibilities of beautiful intercourse? Wasn't it base to create for a being so exquisite a mere alien awkwardness? I suppose I now read into our situation a clearness it couldn't have had at the time, for I seem to see our poor eyes already lighted with some spark of a prevision of the anguish that was to come. So we circled about, with terrors and scruples, like fighters not daring to close. But it was for each other we feared! That kept us a little longer suspended and unbruised. "I'll tell you everything," Miles said—"I mean I'll tell you anything you like. You'll stay on with me, and we shall both be all right, and I will tell you—I will. But not now."

"Why not now?"

My insistence turned him from me and kept him once more at his window in a silence during which, between us, you might have heard a pin drop. Then he was before me again with the air of a person for whom, outside, someone who had frankly to be reckoned with was waiting. "I have to see Luke."

I had not yet reduced him to quite so vulgar a lie, and I felt proportionately ashamed. But, horrible as it was, his lies made up my truth. I achieved thoughtfully a few loops of my knitting. "Well, then, go to Luke, and I'll wait for what you promise. Only, in return for that, satisfy, before you leave me, one very much smaller request."

He looked as if he felt he had succeeded enough to be able still a little to bargain. "Very much smaller—?"

"Yes, a mere fraction of the whole. Tell me"—oh, my work preoccupied me, and I was offhand!—"if, yesterday afternoon, from the table in the hall, you took, you know, my letter."

Chapter 24

My sense of how he received this suffered for a minute from something that I can describe only as a fierce split of my attention—a stroke that at first, as I sprang straight up, reduced me to the mere blind movement of getting hold of him, drawing him close, and, while I just fell for support against the nearest piece of furniture, instinctively keeping him with his back to the window. The appearance was full upon us that I had already had to deal with here: Peter Quint had come into view like a sentinel before a prison. The next thing I saw was that, from outside, he had reached the window, and then I knew that, close to the glass and glaring in through it, he offered once more to the room his white face of damnation. It represents but grossly what took place within me at the sight to say that on the second my decision was made; yet I believe that no woman so overwhelmed ever in so short a time recovered her grasp of the act. It came to me in the very horror of the immediate presence that the act would be, seeing and facing what I saw and faced, to keep the boy himself unaware. The inspiration—I can call it by no other name—was that I felt how voluntarily, how transcendently, I might. It was like fighting with a demon for a human soul, and when I had fairly so appraised it I saw how the human soul—held out, in the tremor of my hands, at arm's length—had a perfect dew of sweat on a lovely childish forehead. The face that was close to mine was as white as the face against the glass, and out of it presently came a sound, not low nor weak, but as if from much further away, that I drank like a waft of fragrance.

"Yes—I took it."

At this, with a moan of joy, I enfolded, I drew him close; and while I held him to my breast, where I could feel in the sudden fever of his little body the tremendous pulse of his little heart, I kept my eyes on the thing at the window and saw it move and shift its posture. I have likened it to a sentinel, but its slow wheel, for a moment, was rather the prowl of a baffled beast. My present quickened courage, however, was such that, not too much to let it through, I had to shade, as it were, my flame. Meanwhile the glare of the face was again at the window, the scoundrel fixed as if to watch and wait. It was the very confidence that I might now defy him, as well as the positive certitude, by this time, of the child's unconsciousness, that made me go on. "What did you take it for?"

"To see what you said about me."

"You opened the letter?"

"I opened it."

My eyes were now, as I held him off a little again, on Miles's own face, in which the collapse of mockery showed me how complete was the ravage of uneasiness. What was prodigious was that at last, by my success, his sense was sealed and his communication stopped: he knew that he was in presence, but knew not of what, and knew still less that I also was and that I did know. And what did this strain of trouble matter when my eyes went back to the window only to see that the air was clear again and—by my personal triumph—the influence quenched? There was nothing there. I felt that the cause was mine and that I should surely get all. "And you found nothing!"—I let my elation out.

He gave the most mournful, thoughtful little headshake. "Nothing."

"Nothing, nothing!" I almost shouted in my joy.

"Nothing, nothing," he sadly repeated.

I kissed his forehead; it was drenched. "So what have you done with it?"

"I've burned it."

"Burned it?" It was now or never. "Is that what you did at school?"

Oh, what this brought up! "At school?"

"Did you take letters?—or other things?"

"Other things?" He appeared now to be thinking of something far off and that reached him only through the pressure of his anxiety. Yet it did reach him. "Did I steal?"

I felt myself redden to the roots of my hair as well as wonder if it were more strange to put to a gentleman such a question or to see him take it with allowances that gave the very distance of his fall in the world. "Was it for that you mightn't go back?"

The only thing he felt was rather a dreary little surprise. "Did you know I mightn't go back?"

"I know everything."

He gave me at this the longest and strangest look. "Everything?"

"Everything. Therefore did you—?" But I couldn't say it again.

Miles could, very simply. "No. I didn't steal."

My face must have shown him I believed him utterly; yet my hands—but it was for pure tenderness—shook him as if to ask him why, if it was all for nothing, he had condemned me to months of torment. "What then did you do?"

He looked in vague pain all round the top of the room and drew his breath, two or three times over, as if with difficulty. He might have been standing at the bottom of the sea and raising his eyes to some faint green twilight. "Well—I said things."

"Only that?"

"They thought it was enough!"

"To turn you out for?"

Never, truly, had a person "turned out" shown so little to explain it as this little person! He appeared to weigh my question, but in a manner quite detached and almost helpless. "Well, I suppose I oughtn't."

"But to whom did you say them?"

He evidently tried to remember, but it dropped—he had lost it. "I don't know!"

He almost smiled at me in the desolation of his surrender, which was indeed practically, by this time, so complete that I ought to have left it there. But I was infatuated—I was blind with victory, though even then the very effect that was to have brought him so much nearer was already that of added separation. "Was it to everyone?" I asked.

"No; it was only to—" But he gave a sick little headshake. "I don't remember their names."

"Were they then so many?"

"No—only a few. Those I liked."

Those he liked? I seemed to float not into clearness, but into a darker obscure, and within a minute there had come to me out of my very pity the appalling alarm of his being perhaps innocent. It was for the instant confounding and bottomless, for if he were innocent, what then on earth was I? Paralyzed, while it lasted, by the mere brush of the question, I let him go a little, so that, with a deep-drawn sigh, he turned away from me again; which, as he faced toward the clear window, I suffered, feeling that I had nothing now there to keep him from. "And did they repeat what you said?" I went on after a moment.

He was soon at some distance from me, still breathing hard and again with the air, though now without anger for it, of being confined against his will. Once more, as he had done before, he looked up at the dim day as if, of what had hitherto sustained him, nothing was left but an unspeakable anxiety. "Oh, yes," he nevertheless replied—"they must have repeated them. To those they liked," he added.

There was, somehow, less of it than I had expected; but I turned it over. "And these things came round—?"

"To the masters? Oh, yes!" he answered very simply. "But I didn't know they'd tell."

"The masters? They didn't—they've never told. That's why I ask you."

He turned to me again his little beautiful fevered face. "Yes, it was too bad."

"Too bad?"

"What I suppose I sometimes said. To write home."

I can't name the exquisite pathos of the contradiction given to such a speech by such a speaker; I only know that the next instant I heard myself throw off with homely force: "Stuff and nonsense!" But the next after that I must have sounded stern enough. "What were these things?"

My sternness was all for his judge, his executioner; yet it made him avert himself again, and that movement made me, with a single bound and an irrepressible cry, spring straight upon him. For there again, against the glass, as if to blight his confession and stay his answer, was the hideous author of our woe—the white face of damnation. I felt a sick swim at the drop of my victory and all the return of my battle, so that the wildness of my veritable leap only served as a great betrayal. I saw him, from the midst of my act, meet it with a divination, and on the perception that even now he only guessed, and that the window was still to his own eyes free, I let the impulse flame up to convert the climax of his dismay into the very proof of his liberation. "No more, no more, no more!" I shrieked, as I tried to press him against me, to my visitant.

"Is she here?" Miles panted as he caught with his sealed eyes the direction of my words. Then as his strange "she" staggered me and, with a gasp, I echoed it, "Miss Jessel, Miss Jessel!" he with a sudden fury gave me back.

I seized, stupefied, his supposition—some sequel to what we had done to Flora, but this made me only want to show him that it was better still than that. "It's not Miss Jessel! But it's at the window—straight before us. It's there—the coward horror, there for the last time!"

At this, after a second in which his head made the movement of a baffled dog's on a scent and then gave a frantic little shake for air and light, he was at me in a white rage, bewildered, glaring vainly over the place and missing wholly, though it now, to my sense, filled the room like the taste of poison, the wide, overwhelming presence. "It's he?"

I was so determined to have all my proof that I flashed into ice to challenge him. "Whom do you mean by 'he'?"

"Peter Quint—you devil!" His face gave again, round the room, its convulsed supplication. "Where?"

They are in my ears still, his supreme surrender of the name and his tribute to my devotion. "What does he matter now, my own?—what will he ever matter? I have you," I launched at the beast, "but he has lost you forever!" Then, for the demonstration of my work, "There, there!" I said to Miles.

But he had already jerked straight round, stared, glared again, and seen but the quiet day. With the stroke of the loss I was so proud of he uttered the cry of a creature hurled over an abyss, and the grasp with which I recovered him might have been that of catching him in his fall. I caught him, yes, I held him—it may be imagined with what a passion; but at the end of a minute I began to feel what it truly was that I held. We were alone with the quiet day, and his little heart, dispossessed, had stopped.

The Metamorphosis

By Franz Kafka

The Metamorphosis

One morning, as Gregor Samsa was waking up from anxious dreams, he discovered that in his bed he had been changed into a monstrous verminous bug. He lay on his armour-hard back and saw, as he lifted his head up a little, his brown, arched abdomen divided up into rigid bow-like sections. From this height the blanket, just about ready to slide off completely, could hardly stay in place. His numerous legs, pitifully thin in comparison to the rest of his circumference, flickered helplessly before his eyes.

"What's happened to me," he thought. It was no dream. His room, a proper room for a human being, only somewhat too small, lay quietly between the four well-known walls. Above the table, on which an unpacked collection of sample cloth goods was spread out—Samsa was a travelling salesman—hung the picture which he had cut out of an illustrated magazine a little while ago and set in a pretty gilt frame. It was a picture of a woman with a fur hat and a fur boa. She sat erect there, lifting up in the direction of the viewer a solid fur muff into which her entire forearm had disappeared.

Gregor's glance then turned to the window. The dreary weather—the rain drops were falling audibly down on the metal window ledge—made him quite melancholy. "Why don't I keep sleeping for a little while longer and forget all this foolishness," he thought. But this was entirely impractical, for he was used to sleeping on his right side, but in his present state he could not get himself into this position. No matter how hard he threw himself onto his right side, he always rolled onto his back again. He must have tried it a hundred times, closing his eyes so that he would not have to see the wriggling legs, and gave up only when he began to feel a light, dull pain in his side which he had never felt before.

"O God," he thought, "what a demanding job I've chosen! Day in, day out, on the road. The stresses of selling are much greater than the actual work going on at head office, and, in addition to that, I still have to cope with the problems of travelling, the worries about train connections, irregular bad food, temporary and constantly changing human relationships, which never come from the heart. To hell with it all!" He felt a slight itching on the top of his abdomen. He slowly pushed himself on his back closer to the bed post so that he could lift his head more easily, found the itchy part, which was entirely covered with small white spots—he did not know what to make of them and wanted to feel the place with a leg. But he retracted it immediately, for the contact felt like a cold shower all over him.

He slid back again into his earlier position. "This getting up early," he thought, "makes a man quite idiotic. A man must have his sleep. Other travelling salesmen live like harem women. For instance, when I come back to the inn during the course of the morning to write up the necessary orders, these gentlemen are just sitting down to breakfast. If I were to try that with my boss, I'd be thrown out on the spot. Still, who knows whether that mightn't be really good for me. If I didn't hold back for my parents' sake, I'd have quit ages ago. I would've gone to the boss and told him just what I think from the bottom of my heart. He would've fallen right off his desk! How weird it is to sit up at that desk and talk down to the employee from way up there. What's more, the boss has trouble hearing, so the employee has to step up quite close to him. Anyway, I haven't completely given up that hope yet. Once I've got together the money to pay off my parents' debt to him—that should take another five or six years—I'll do it for sure. Then I'll make the big break. In any case, right now I have to get up. My train leaves at five o'clock."

He looked over at the alarm clock ticking away by the chest of drawers. "Good God!" he thought. It was half past six, and the hands were going quietly on. It was even past the half hour, already nearly quarter to. Could the alarm have failed to ring? One saw from the bed that it was properly set for four o'clock. Certainly it had rung. Yes, but was it possible to sleep peacefully through that noise which made the furniture shake? Now, it is true he had not slept peacefully, but evidently he had slept all the more deeply. Still, what should he do now? The next train left at seven o'clock. To catch that one, he would have to go in a mad rush. The sample collection was not packed up yet, and he really did not feel particularly fresh and active. And even if he caught the train, there was no avoiding a blow-up with the boss, because the firm's errand boy would have waited for the five o'clock train and reported the news of his absence long ago. He was the boss's minion, without backbone and intelligence. Well then, what if he reported in sick? But that would be extremely embarrassing and suspicious, because during his five years' service Gregor had not been sick even once. The boss would certainly come with the doctor from the health insurance company and would reproach his parents for their lazy son and cut short all objections with the insurance doctor's comments; for him everyone was completely healthy but really lazy about work. And besides, would the doctor in this case be totally wrong? Apart from a really excessive drowsiness after the long sleep, Gregor, in fact, felt quite well and even had a really strong appetite.

As he was thinking all this over in the greatest haste, without being able to make the decision to get out of bed—the alarm clock was indicating exactly quarter to seven—there was a cautious knock on the door by the head of the bed. "Gregor," a voice called—it was his mother—"it's quarter to seven. Don't you want to be on your way?" The soft voice! Gregor was startled when he heard his voice answering. It was clearly and unmistakably his earlier voice, but in it was intermingled, as if from below, an irrepressible, painful squeaking, which left the words positively distinct only in the first moment and distorted them in the reverberation, so that one did not know if one had heard correctly. Gregor wanted to answer in detail and explain everything, but in these circumstances he confined himself to saying, "Yes, yes, thank you mother. I'm getting up right away." Because of the wooden door the change in Gregor's voice was not really noticeable outside, so his mother calmed down with this explanation and shuffled off. However, as a result of the short conversation, the other family members became aware that Gregor was unexpectedly still at home, and already his father was knocking on one side door, weakly but with his fist. "Gregor, Gregor," he called out, "what's going on?" And, after a short while, he urged him on again in a deeper voice: "Gregor! Gregor!" At the other side door, however, his sister knocked lightly. "Gregor? Are you all right? Do you need anything?" Gregor directed answers in both directions, "I'll be ready right away." He made an effort with the most careful articulation and inserted long pauses between the individual words to remove everything remarkable from his voice. His father turned back to his breakfast. However, the sister whispered, "Gregor, open the door—I beg you." Gregor had no intention of opening the door, but congratulated himself on his precaution, acquired from travelling, of locking all doors during the night, even at home.

First he wanted to stand up quietly and undisturbed, get dressed, above all have breakfast, and only then consider further action, for—he noticed this clearly—by thinking things over in bed he would not reach a reasonable conclusion. He remembered that he had already often felt some light pain or other in bed, perhaps the result of an awkward lying position, which later, once he stood up, turned out to be purely imaginary, and he was eager to see how his present fantasies would gradually dissipate. That the change in his voice was nothing other than the onset of a real chill, an occupational illness of commercial travellers, of that he had not the slightest doubt.

It was very easy to throw aside the blanket. He needed only to push himself up a little, and it fell by itself. But to continue was difficult, particularly because he was so unusually wide. He needed arms and hands to push himself upright. Instead of these, however, he had only many small limbs, which were incessantly moving with very different motions and which, in addition, he was unable to control. If he wanted to bend one of them, then it was the first to extend itself, and if he finally succeeded doing what he wanted with this limb, in the meantime all the others, as if left free, moved around in an excessively painful agitation. "But I must not stay in bed uselessly," said Gregor to himself.

At first he wanted to get out of bed with the lower part of his body, but this lower part—which, by the way, he had not yet looked at and which he also could not picture clearly—proved itself too difficult to move. The attempt went so slowly. When, having become almost frantic, he finally hurled himself forward with all his force and without thinking, he chose his direction incorrectly, and he hit the lower bedpost hard. The violent pain he felt revealed to him that the lower part of his body was at the moment probably the most sensitive.

Thus, he tried to get his upper body out of the bed first and turned his head carefully toward the edge of the bed. He managed to do this easily, and in spite of its width and weight his body mass at last slowly followed the turning of his head. But as he finally raised his head outside the bed in the open air, he became anxious about moving forward any further in this manner, for if he allowed himself eventually to fall by this process, it would really take a miracle to prevent his head from getting injured. And at all costs he must not lose consciousness right now. He preferred to remain in bed.

However, after a similar effort, while he lay there again, sighing as before, and once again saw his small limbs fighting one another, if anything even worse than earlier, and did not see any chance of imposing quiet and order on this arbitrary movement, he told himself again that he could not possibly remain in bed and that it might be the most reasonable thing to sacrifice everything if there was even the slightest hope of getting himself out of bed in the process. At the same moment, however, he did not forget to remind himself from time to time of the fact that calm—indeed the calmest—reflection might be much better than confused decisions. At such moments, he directed his gaze as precisely as he could toward the window, but unfortunately there was little confident cheer to be had from a glance at the morning mist, which concealed even the other side of the narrow street. "It's already seven o'clock," he told himself at the latest sounds from the alarm clock, "already seven o'clock and still such a fog." And for a little while longer he lay quietly with weak breathing, as if perhaps waiting for normal and natural conditions to re-emerge out of the complete stillness.

But then he said to himself, "Before it strikes a quarter past seven, whatever happens I must be completely out of bed. Besides, by then someone from the office will arrive to inquire about me, because the office will open before seven o'clock." And he made an effort then to rock his entire body length out of the bed with a uniform motion. If he let himself fall out of the bed in this way, his head, which in the course of the fall he intended to lift up sharply, would probably remain uninjured. His back seemed to be hard; nothing would really happen to that as a result of the fall onto the carpet. His greatest reservation was a worry about the loud noise which the fall must create and which presumably would arouse, if not fright, then at least concern on the other side of all the doors. However, he had to take that chance.

As Gregor was already in the process of lifting himself half out of bed—the new method was more of a game than an effort; he needed only to rock with a series of jerks—it struck him how easy all this would be if someone were to come to his aid. Two strong people—he thought of his father and the servant girl—would have been quite sufficient. They would only have had to push their arms under his arched back to get him out of the bed, to bend down with their load, and then merely to exercise patience so that he could complete the flip onto the floor, where his diminutive legs would then, he hoped, acquire a purpose. Now, quite apart from the fact that the doors were locked, should he really call out for help? In spite of all his distress, he was unable to suppress a smile at this idea.

He had already got to the point where, by rocking more strongly, he maintained his equilibrium with difficulty, and very soon he would finally have to make a final decision, for in five minutes it would be a quarter past seven. Then there was a ring at the door of the apartment. "That's someone from the office," he told himself, and he almost froze, while his small limbs only danced around all the faster. For one moment everything remained still. "They aren't opening," Gregor said to himself, caught up in some absurd hope. But of course then, as usual, the servant girl with her firm tread went to the door and opened it. Gregor needed to hear only the first word of the visitor's greeting to recognize immediately who it was, the manager himself. Why was Gregor the only one condemned to work in a firm where, at the slightest lapse, someone at once attracted the greatest suspicion? Were all the employees then collectively, one and all, scoundrels? Among them was there then no truly devoted person who, if he failed to use just a couple of hours in the morning for office work, would become abnormal from pangs of conscience and really be in no state to get out of bed? Was it really not enough to let an apprentice make inquiries, if such questioning was even generally necessary? Must the manager himself come, and in the process must it be demonstrated to the entire innocent family that the investigation of this suspicious circumstance could be entrusted only to the intelligence of the manager? And more as a consequence of the excited state in which this idea put Gregor than as a result of an actual decision, he swung himself with all his might out of the bed. There was a loud thud, but not a real crash. The fall was absorbed somewhat by the carpet and, in addition, his back was more elastic than Gregor had thought. For that reason the dull noise was not quite so conspicuous. But he had not held his head up with sufficient care and had hit it. He turned his head, irritated and in pain, and rubbed it on the carpet.

"Something has fallen in there," said the manager in the next room on the left. Gregor tried to imagine to himself whether anything similar to what was happening to him today could have also happened at some point to the manager. At least one had to concede the possibility of such a thing. However, as if to give a rough answer to this question, the manager now, with a squeak of his polished boots, took a few determined steps in the next room. From the neighbouring room on the right the sister was whispering to inform Gregor: "Gregor, the manager is here." "I know," said Gregor to himself. But he did not dare make his voice loud enough so that his sister could hear.

"Gregor," his father now said from the neighbouring room on the left, "Mr. Manager has come and is asking why you have not left on the early train. We don't know what we should tell him. Besides, he also wants to speak to you personally. So please open the door. He will be good enough to forgive the mess in your room." In the middle of all this, the manager called out in a friendly way, "Good morning, Mr. Samsa." "He is not well," said his mother to the manager, while his father was still talking at the door, "He is not well, believe me, Mr. Manager. Otherwise how would Gregor miss a train? The young man has nothing in his head except business. I'm almost angry that he never goes out in the evening. Right now he's been in the city eight days, but he's been at home every evening. He sits here with us at the table and reads the newspaper quietly or studies his travel schedules. It's a quite a diversion for him to busy himself with fretwork. For instance, he cut out a small frame over the course of two or three evenings. You'd be amazed how pretty it is. It's hanging right inside the room. You'll see it immediately, as soon as Gregor opens the door. Anyway, I'm happy that you're here, Mr. Manager. By ourselves, we would never have made Gregor open the door. He's so stubborn, and he's certainly not well, although he denied that this morning." "I'm coming right away," said Gregor slowly and deliberately and didn't move, so as not to lose one word of the conversation. "My dear lady, I cannot explain it to myself in any other way," said the manager; "I hope it is nothing serious. On the other hand, I must also say that we business people, luckily or unluckily, however one looks at it, very often simply have to overcome a slight indisposition for business reasons." "So can Mr. Manager come in to see you now?" asked his father impatiently and knocked once again on the door. "No," said Gregor. In the neighbouring room on the left an awkward stillness descended. In the neighbouring room on the right the sister began to sob.

Why did his sister not go to the others? She had probably just got up out of bed now and had not even started to get dressed yet. Then why was she crying? Because he was not getting up and letting the manager in, because he was in danger of losing his position, and because then his boss would badger his parents once again with the old demands? Those were probably unnecessary worries right now. Gregor was still here and was not thinking at all about abandoning his family. At the moment he was lying right there on the carpet, and no one who knew about his condition would have seriously demanded that he let the manager in. But Gregor would not be casually dismissed right way because of this small discourtesy, for which he would find an easy and suitable excuse later on. It seemed to Gregor that it might be far more reasonable to leave him in peace at the moment, instead of disturbing him with crying and conversation. But it was the very uncertainty which distressed the others and excused their behaviour.

"Mr. Samsa," the manager was now shouting, his voice raised, "what's the matter? You are barricading yourself there in your room, answering with only a yes and a no, are making serious and unnecessary trouble for your parents, and neglecting—I mention this only incidentally—your commercial duties in a truly unheard of manner. I am speaking here in the name of your parents and your employer, and I am requesting you in all seriousness for an immediate and clear explanation. I am amazed. I am amazed. I thought I knew you as a calm, reasonable person, and now you appear suddenly to want to start parading around in weird moods. The Chief indicated to me earlier this very day a possible explanation for your neglect—it concerned the collection of cash entrusted to you a short while ago—but in truth I almost gave him my word of honour that this explanation could not be correct. However, now I see here your unimaginable pig headedness, and I am totally losing any desire to speak up for you in the slightest. And your position is not at all the most secure. Originally I intended to mention all this to you privately, but since you are letting me waste my time here uselessly, I don't know why the matter shouldn't come to the attention of your parents as well. Your productivity has also been very unsatisfactory recently. Of course, it's not the time of year to conduct exceptional business, we recognize that, but a time of year for conducting no business, there is no such thing at all, Mr. Samsa, and such a thing must not be permitted."

"But Mr. Manager," called Gregor, beside himself and, in his agitation, forgetting everything else, "I'm opening the door immediately, this very moment. A slight indisposition, a dizzy spell, has prevented me from getting up. I'm still lying in bed right now. But I'm quite refreshed once again. I'm in the midst of getting out of bed. Just have patience for a short moment! Things are not yet going as well as I thought. But things are all right with me. How suddenly this can overcome someone! Only yesterday evening everything was fine with me. My parents certainly know that. Actually just yesterday evening I had a small premonition. People must have seen that in me. Why have I not reported that to the office? But people always think that they'll get over sickness without having to stay at home. Mr. Manager! Take it easy on my parents! There is really no basis for the criticisms which you're now making against me. Nobody has said a word to me about that. Perhaps you have not read the latest orders which I sent in. Besides, now I'm setting out on my trip on the eight o'clock train; the few hours' rest have made me stronger. Mr. Manager, do not stay. I will be at the office in person right away. Please have the goodness to say that and to convey my respects to the Chief."

While Gregor was quickly blurting all this out, hardly aware of what he was saying, he had moved close to the chest of drawers without effort, probably as a result of the practice he had already had in bed, and now he was trying to raise himself up on it. Actually, he wanted to open the door. He really wanted to let himself be seen and to speak with the manager. He was keen to witness what the others now asking about him would say when they saw him. If they were startled, then Gregor had no more responsibility and could be calm. But if they accepted everything quietly, then he would have no reason to get excited and, if he got a move on, could really be at the station around eight o'clock. At first he slid down a few times on the smooth chest of drawers. But at last he gave himself a final swing and stood upright there. He was no longer at all aware of the pains in his lower body, no matter how they might still sting. Now he let himself fall against the back of a nearby chair, on the edge of which he braced himself with his small limbs. By doing this he gained control over himself and kept quiet, for he could now hear the manager.

"Did you understand even a single word?" the manager asked the parents, "Is he playing the fool with us?" "For God's sake," cried the mother, already in tears, "perhaps he's very ill, and we're upsetting him. Grete! Grete!" she yelled at that point. "Mother?" called the sister from the other side. They were making themselves understood through Gregor's room. "You must go to the doctor right away. Gregor is sick. Hurry to the doctor. Did you hear Gregor speak just now?" "That was an animal's voice," said the manager, remarkably quiet in comparison to the mother's cries. "Anna! Anna!" yelled the father through the hall into the kitchen, clapping his hands, "Fetch a locksmith right away!" The two young women were already running through the hall with swishing skirts—how had his sister dressed herself so quickly?—and pulled open the doors of the apartment. One could not hear the doors closing at all. They probably had left them open, as is customary in an apartment where a huge misfortune has taken place.

However, Gregor had become much calmer. All right, people did not understand his words any more, although they seemed clear enough to him, clearer than previously, perhaps because his ears had got used to them. But at least people now thought that things were not completely all right with him and were prepared to help him. The confidence and assurance with which the first arrangements had been carried out made him feel good. He felt himself included once again in the circle of humanity and was expecting from both the doctor and the locksmith, without differentiating between them with any real precision, splendid and surprising results. In order to get as clear a voice as possible for the critical conversation which was imminent, he coughed a little, and certainly took the trouble to do this in a really subdued way, since it was possible that even this noise sounded like something different from a human cough. He no longer trusted himself to decide any more. Meanwhile in the next room it had become really quiet. Perhaps his parents were sitting with the manager at the table whispering; perhaps they were all leaning against the door and listening.

Gregor pushed himself slowly towards the door, with the help of the easy chair, let go of it there, threw himself against the door, held himself upright against it—the balls of his tiny limbs had a little sticky stuff on them—and rested there momentarily from his exertion. Then he made an effort to turn the key in the lock with his mouth. Unfortunately it seemed that he had no real teeth. How then was he to grab hold of the key? But to make up for that his jaws were naturally very strong; with their help he managed to get the key really moving. He did not notice that he was obviously inflicting some damage on himself, for a brown fluid came out of his mouth, flowed over the key, and dripped onto the floor. "Just listen," said the manager in the next room. "He's turning the key." For Gregor that was a great encouragement. But they should all have called out to him, including his father and mother, "Come on, Gregor," they should have shouted. "Keep going, keep working on the lock!" Imagining that all his efforts were being followed with suspense, he bit down frantically on the key with all the force he could muster. As the key turned more, he danced around the lock. Now he was holding himself upright only with his mouth, and he had to hang onto the key or then press it down again with the whole weight of his body, as necessary. The quite distinct click of the lock as it finally snapped really woke Gregor up. Breathing heavily he said to himself, "So I didn't need the locksmith," and he set his head against the door handle to open the door completely.

Because he had to open the door in this way, it was already open really wide without him yet being visible. He first had to turn himself slowly around the edge of the door, very carefully, of course, if he did not want to fall awkwardly on his back right at the entrance into the room. He was still preoccupied with this difficult movement and had no time to pay attention to anything else, when he heard the manager exclaim a loud "Oh!"—it sounded like the wind whistling—and now he saw him, nearest to the door, pressing his hand against his open mouth and moving slowly back, as if an invisible constant force was pushing him away. His mother—in spite of the presence of the manager she was standing here with her hair sticking up on end, still a mess from the night—first looked at his father with her hands clasped, then went two steps towards Gregor and collapsed right in the middle of her skirts, which were spread out all around her, her face sunk on her breast, completely concealed. His father clenched his fist with a hostile expression, as if he wished to push Gregor back into his room, then looked uncertainly around the living room, covered his eyes with his hands, and cried so that his mighty breast shook.

At this point Gregor did not take one step into the room, but leaned his body from the inside against the firmly bolted wing of the door, so that only half his body was visible, as well as his head, tilted sideways, with which he peeped over at the others. Meanwhile it had become much brighter. Standing out clearly from the other side of the street was a section of the endless gray-black house situated opposite—it was a hospital—with its severe regular windows breaking up the facade. The rain was still coming down, but only in large individual drops visibly and firmly thrown down one by one onto the ground. Countless breakfast dishes were standing piled around on the table, because for his father breakfast was the most important meal time in the day, which he prolonged for hours by reading various newspapers. Directly across on the opposite wall hung a photograph of Gregor from the time of his military service; it was a picture of him as a lieutenant, as he, smiling and worry free, with his hand on his sword, demanded respect for his bearing and uniform. The door to the hall was ajar, and since the door to the apartment was also open, one could see out into the landing of the apartment and the start of the staircase going down.

"Now," said Gregor, well aware that he was the only one who had kept his composure. "I'll get dressed right away, pack up the collection of samples, and set off. You'll allow me to set out on my way, will you not? You see, Mr. Manager, I am not pig-headed, and I am happy to work. Travelling is exhausting, but I couldn't live without it. Where are you going, Mr. Manager? To the office? Really? Will you report everything truthfully? A person can be incapable of work momentarily, but that's precisely the best time to remember the earlier achievements and to consider that later, after the obstacles have been shoved aside, the person will certainly work all the more diligently and intensely. I am really so indebted to Mr. Chief—you know that perfectly well. On the other hand, I am concerned about my parents and my sister. I'm in a fix, but I'll work myself out of it again. Don't make things more difficult for me than they already are. Speak up on my behalf in the office! People don't like travelling salesmen. I know that. People think they earn pots of money and thus lead a fine life. People don't even have any special reason to think through this judgment more clearly. But you, Mr. Manager, you have a better perspective on what's involved than other people, even, I tell you in total confidence, a better perspective than Mr. Chief himself, who in his capacity as the employer may easily let his judgment make mistakes at the expense of an employee. You also know well enough that the travelling salesman who is outside the office almost the entire year can become so easily a victim of gossip, coincidences, and groundless complaints, against which it's totally impossible for him to defend himself, since for the most part he doesn't hear about them at all and only then when he's exhausted after finishing a trip and at home gets to feel in his own body the nasty consequences, which can't be thoroughly explored back to their origins. Mr. Manager, don't leave without speaking a word indicating to me that you'll at least concede that I'm a little in the right!"

But at Gregor's first words the manager had already turned away, and now he looked back with pursed lips at Gregor over his twitching shoulders. During Gregor's speech he was not still for a moment but kept moving away towards the door, without taking his eyes off Gregor, but really gradually, as if there was a secret ban on leaving the room. He was already in the hall, and given the sudden movement with which he finally pulled his foot out of the living room, one could have believed that he had just burned the sole of his foot. In the hall, however, he stretched his right hand out away from his body towards the staircase, as if some truly supernatural relief was waiting for him there.

Gregor realized that he must not under any circumstances allow the manager to go away in this frame of mind, especially if his position in the firm was not to be placed in the greatest danger. His parents did not understand all this very well. Over the long years, they had developed the conviction that Gregor was set up for life in this firm and, in addition, they had so much to do nowadays with their present troubles that all foresight was foreign to them. But Gregor had this foresight. The manager must be held back, calmed down, convinced, and finally won over. The future of Gregor and his family really depended on it! If only the sister had been there! She was clever. She had already cried while Gregor was still lying quietly on his back. And the manager, this friend of the ladies, would certainly let himself be guided by her. She would have closed the door to the apartment and talked him out of his fright in the hall. But the sister was not even there. Gregor must deal with it himself. And without thinking that as yet he did not know anything about his present ability to move and without thinking that his speech possibly—indeed probably—had once again not been understood, he left the wing of the door, pushed himself through the opening, and wanted to go over to the manager, who was already holding tight with both hands gripping the handrail on the landing in a ridiculous way. But as Gregor looked for something to steady himself, with a small scream he immediately fell down onto his numerous little legs. Scarcely had this happened, when he felt for the first time that morning a general physical well being. The small limbs had firm floor under them; they obeyed perfectly, as he noticed to his joy, and even strove to carry him forward in the direction he wanted. Right away he believed that the final amelioration of all his suffering was immediately at hand. But at the very moment when he lay on the floor rocking in a restrained manner quite close and directly across from his mother, who had apparently totally sunk into herself, she suddenly sprang right up with her arms spread far apart and her fingers extended and cried out, "Help, for God's sake, help!" She held her head bowed down, as if she wanted to view Gregor better, but ran senselessly back, contradicting that gesture, forgetting that behind her stood the table with all the dishes on it. When she reached the table, she sat down heavily on it, as if absent-mindedly, and did not appear to notice at all that next to her coffee was pouring out onto the carpet in a full stream from the large, overturned container.

"Mother, mother," said Gregor quietly and looked over towards her. The manager had momentarily vanished completely from his mind. On the other hand, when he saw the flowing coffee Gregor could not stop himself snapping his jaws in the air a few times. At that his mother screamed all over again, hurried from the table, and collapsed into the arms of his father, who was rushing towards her. But Gregor had no time right now for his parents—the manager was already on the staircase. With his chin on the bannister, the manager looked back for the last time. Gregor took an initial movement to catch up to him if possible. But the manager must have suspected something, because he made a leap down over a few stairs and disappeared, still shouting "Huh!" The sound echoed throughout the entire stairwell.

But now unfortunately this flight of the manager seemed to bewilder his father completely. Earlier he had been relatively calm. For instead of running after the manager himself or at least not hindering Gregor from his pursuit, with his right hand he grabbed hold of the manager's cane, which he had left behind on a chair with his hat and overcoat. With his left hand, his father grabbed a large newspaper from the table and, stamping his feet on the floor, he set out to drive Gregor back into his room by waving the cane and the newspaper. No request of Gregor's was of any use; no request would even be understood. No matter how willing he was to turn his head respectfully, his father just stomped all the harder with his feet. Across the room from him his mother had pulled open a window, in spite of the cool weather, and leaning out with her hands on her cheeks, she pushed her face far outside the window. Between the lane and the stairwell a strong draught came up, the curtains on the window flew around, the newspapers on the table rustled, and individual sheets fluttered down over the floor. The father relentlessly pushed his way forward, hissing like a wild man. Now, Gregor still had no practice at all in going backwards—it was really very slow going. If Gregor only had been allowed to turn himself around, he would have been in his room right away, but he was afraid to make his father impatient by the time-consuming process of turning around, and each moment he faced the threat of a mortal blow on his back or his head from the cane in his father's hand. Finally Gregor had no other option, for he noticed with horror that he did not understand yet how to maintain his direction going backwards. And so he began, amid constantly anxious sideways glances in his father's direction, to turn himself around as quickly as possible, although in truth this was only done very slowly. Perhaps his father noticed his good intentions, for he did not disrupt Gregor in this motion, but with the tip of the cane from a distance he even directed Gregor's rotating movement now and then. If only his father had not hissed so unbearably! Because of that Gregor totally lost his head. He was already almost totally turned around, when, always with this hissing in his ear, he just made a mistake and turned himself back a little. But when he finally was successful in getting his head in front of the door opening, it became clear that his body was too wide to go through any further. Naturally his father, in his present mental state, had no idea of, say, opening the other wing of the door a bit to create a suitable passage for Gregor to get through. His single fixed thought was that Gregor must get into his room as quickly as possible. He would never have allowed the elaborate preparations that Gregor required to orient himself and thus perhaps in this way to get through the door. Perhaps with his excessive noise he was now driving Gregor forwards as if there were no obstacle. Behind Gregor the sound at this point was no longer like the voice of only a single father. Now it was really no longer a joke, and Gregor forced himself, come what might, into the door. One side of his body was lifted up. He lay at an angle in the door opening. His one flank was really sore from the scraping. On the white door ugly blotches were left. Soon he was stuck fast and would not have been able to move any more on his own. The tiny legs on one side hung twitching in the air above, and the ones on the other side were pushed painfully into the floor. Then his father gave him one really strong liberating push from behind, and he scurried, bleeding severely, far into the interior of his room. The door was slammed shut with the cane, and then finally it was quiet.

Gregor first woke up from his heavy swoon-like sleep in the evening twilight. He would certainly have woken up soon afterwards even without any disturbance, for he felt himself sufficiently rested and wide awake, although it appeared to him as if a hurried step and a cautious closing of the door to the hall had roused him. Light from the electric streetlamps lay pale here and there on the ceiling of his room and on the higher parts of the furniture, but underneath around Gregor it was dark. He pushed himself slowly toward the door, still groping awkwardly with his feelers, which he now learned to value for the first time, to check what was happening there. His left side seemed one single long unpleasantly stretched scar, and he really had to hobble on his two rows of legs. In addition, one small leg had been seriously wounded in the course of the morning incident—it was almost a miracle that only one had been hurt—and dragged lifelessly behind.

By the door he first noticed what had really lured him there: it was the smell of something to eat. For a bowl stood there, filled with sweetened milk, in which swam tiny pieces of white bread. He almost laughed with joy, for he had an even greater hunger than in the morning, and he immediately dipped his head almost up to and over his eyes down into the milk. But he soon drew it back again in disappointment, not just because it was difficult for him to eat on account of his delicate left side—he could eat only if his entire panting body worked in a coordinated way—but also because the milk, which otherwise was his favourite drink and which his sister had certainly placed there for that reason, did not appeal to him at all. He turned away from the bowl almost with aversion and crept back into the middle of the room.

In the living room, as Gregor saw through the crack in the door, the gas was lit, but where, on other occasions at this time of day, his father was accustomed to read the afternoon newspaper in a loud voice to his mother and sometimes also to his sister, at the moment no sound was audible. Now, perhaps this reading aloud, about which his sister had always spoken and written to him, had recently fallen out of their general routine. But it was so still all around, in spite of the fact that the apartment was certainly not empty. "What a quiet life the family leads," said Gregor to himself, and, as he stared fixedly out in front of him into the darkness, he felt a great pride that he had been able to provide such a life for his parents and his sister in such a beautiful apartment. But how would things go if now all tranquillity, all prosperity, all contentment should come to a horrible end? In order not to lose himself in such thoughts, Gregor preferred to set himself moving, so he crawled up and down in his room.

Once during the long evening one side door and then the other door were opened just a tiny crack and quickly closed again. Someone presumably needed to come in but had then thought better of it. Gregor immediately took up a position by the living room door, determined to bring in the hesitant visitor somehow or other or at least to find out who it might be. But now the door was not opened any more, and Gregor waited in vain. Earlier, when the door had been barred, they had all wanted to come in to him; now, when he had opened one door and when the others had obviously been opened during the day, no one came any more, and now the keys were stuck in the locks on the outside.

The light in the living room was turned off only late at night, and it was now easy to establish that his parents and his sister had stayed awake all this time, for one could hear them clearly as all three moved away on tiptoe. Now it was certain that no one would come in to Gregor any more until the morning. Thus, he had a long time to think undisturbed about how he should reorganize his life from scratch. But the high, open room, in which he was compelled to lie flat on the floor, made him anxious, without his being able to figure out the reason, for he had lived in the room for five years. With a half-unconscious turn and not without a little shame he scurried under the couch, where, in spite of the fact that his back was a little cramped and he could no longer lift up his head, he felt very comfortable right away and was sorry only that his body was too wide to fit completely under the couch.

There he remained the entire night, which he spent partly in a state of semi-sleep, out of which his hunger constantly woke him with a start, but partly in a state of worry and murky hopes, which all led to the conclusion that for the time being he would have to keep calm and with patience and the greatest consideration for his family tolerate the troubles which in his present condition he was now forced to cause them.

Already early in the morning—it was still almost night—Gregor had an opportunity to test the power of the decisions he had just made, for his sister, almost fully dressed, opened the door from the hall into his room and looked eagerly inside. She did not find him immediately, but when she noticed him under the couch—God, he had to be somewhere or other, for he could hardly fly away—she got such a shock that, without being able to control herself, she slammed the door shut once again from the outside. However, as if she was sorry for her behaviour, she immediately opened the door again and walked in on her tiptoes, as if she was in the presence of a serious invalid or a total stranger. Gregor had pushed his head forward just to the edge of the couch and was observing her. Would she really notice that he had left the milk standing, not indeed from any lack of hunger, and would she bring in something else to eat more suitable for him? If she did not do it on her own, he would sooner starve to death than call her attention to the fact, although he had a really powerful urge to move beyond the couch, throw himself at his sister's feet, and beg her for something or other good to eat. But his sister noticed right away with astonishment that the bowl was still full, with only a little milk spilled around it. She picked it up immediately, although not with her bare hands but with a rag, and took it out of the room. Gregor was extremely curious what she would bring as a substitute, and he pictured to himself very different ideas about it. But he never could have guessed what his sister, out of the goodness of her heart, in fact, did. To test his taste, she brought him an entire selection, all spread out on an old newspaper. There were old half-rotten vegetables, bones from the evening meal, covered with a white sauce which had almost solidified, some raisins and almonds, cheese which Gregor had declared inedible two days earlier, a slice of dry bread, a slice with butter, and a slice of salted bread smeared with butter. In addition to all this, she put down the bowl—probably designated once and for all as Gregor's—into which she had poured some water. And out of her delicacy of feeling, since she knew that Gregor would not eat in front of her, she went away very quickly and even turned the key in the lock, so that Gregor could now know that he might make himself as comfortable as he wished. Gregor's small limbs buzzed now that the time for eating had come. His wounds must, in any case, have already healed completely. He felt no handicap on that score. He was astonished at that and thought about how more than a month ago he had cut his finger very slightly with a knife and how this wound had hurt enough even the day before yesterday. "Am I now going to be less sensitive?" he thought, already sucking greedily on the cheese, which had strongly attracted him right away, more than all the other foods. Quickly and with his eyes watering with satisfaction, he ate one after the other the cheese, the vegetables, and the sauce. The fresh food, by contrast, did not taste good to him. He could not even bear the smell and carried the things he wanted to eat a little distance away. By the time his sister slowly turned the key as a sign that he should withdraw, he was long finished with everything and now lay lazily in the same spot. The noise immediately startled him, in spite of the fact that he was already almost asleep, and he scurried back again under the couch. But it cost him great self-control to remain under the couch, even for the short time his sister was in the room, because his body had filled out somewhat on account of the rich meal and in the narrow space there he could scarcely breathe. In the midst of minor attacks of asphyxiation, he looked at her with somewhat protruding eyes, as his unsuspecting sister swept up with a broom, not just the remnants, but even the foods which Gregor had not touched at all, as if these were also now useless, and as she dumped everything quickly into a bucket, which she closed with a wooden lid, and then carried all of it out of the room. She had hardly turned around before Gregor had already dragged himself out from under the couch, stretched out, and let his body expand.

In this way Gregor now got his food every day, once in the morning, when his parents and the servant girl were still asleep, and a second time after the common noon meal, for his parents were asleep then for a little while, and the servant girl was sent off by his sister on some errand or other. They certainly would not have wanted Gregor to starve to death, but perhaps they could not have endured finding out what he ate other than by hearsay. Perhaps his sister also wanted to spare them what was possibly only a small grief, for they were really suffering quite enough already.

What sorts of excuses people had used on that first morning to get the doctor and the locksmith out of the house again Gregor was completely unable to ascertain. Since they could not understand him, no one, not even his sister, thought that he might be able to understand others, and thus, when his sister was in his room, he had to be content with listening now and then to her sighs and invocations to the saints. Only later, when she had grown somewhat accustomed to everything—naturally there could never be any talk of her growing completely accustomed to it—Gregor sometimes caught a comment which was intended to be friendly or could be interpreted as such. "Well, today it tasted good to him," she said, if Gregor had really cleaned up what he had to eat; whereas, in the reverse situation, which gradually repeated itself more and more frequently, she used to say almost sadly, "Now everything has been left again."

But while Gregor could get no new information directly, he did hear a good deal from the room next door, and as soon as he heard voices, he scurried right away to the appropriate door and pressed his entire body against it. In the early days especially, there was no conversation which was not concerned with him in some way or other, even if only in secret. For two days at all meal times discussions of that subject could be heard on how people should now behave; but they also talked about the same subject in the times between meals, for there were always at least two family members at home, since no one really wanted to remain in the house alone and people could not under any circumstances leave the apartment completely empty. In addition, on the very first day the servant girl—it was not completely clear what and how much she knew about what had happened—on her knees had begged his mother to let her go immediately, and when she said good bye about fifteen minutes later, she thanked them for the dismissal with tears in her eyes, as if she was receiving the greatest favour which people had shown her there, and, without anyone demanding it from her, she swore a fearful oath not to reveal anything to anyone, not even the slightest detail.

Now his sister had to team up with his mother to do the cooking, although that did not create much trouble because people were eating almost nothing. Again and again Gregor listened as one of them vainly invited another one to eat and received no answer other than "Thank you. I've had enough" or something like that. And perhaps they had stopped having anything to drink, too. His sister often asked his father whether he wanted to have a beer and gladly offered to fetch it herself, and when his father was silent, she said, in order to remove any reservations he might have, that she could send the caretaker's wife to get it. But then his father finally said a resounding "No," and nothing more would be spoken about it.

Already during the first day his father laid out all the financial circumstances and prospects to his mother and to his sister as well. From time to time he stood up from the table and pulled out of the small lockbox salvaged from his business, which had collapsed five years previously, some document or other or some notebook. The sound was audible as he opened up the complicated lock and, after removing what he was looking for, locked it up again. These explanations by his father were, in part, the first enjoyable thing that Gregor had the chance to listen to since his imprisonment. He had thought that nothing at all was left over for his father from that business; at least his father had told him nothing to contradict that view, and Gregor in any case had not asked him about it. At the time Gregor's only concern had been to use everything he had in order to allow his family to forget as quickly as possible the business misfortune which had brought them all into a state of complete hopelessness. And so at that point he had started to work with a special intensity and from a minor assistant had become, almost overnight, a travelling salesman, who naturally had entirely different possibilities for earning money and whose successes at work were converted immediately into the form of cash commissions, which could be set out on the table at home for his astonished and delighted family. Those had been beautiful days, and they had never come back afterwards, at least not with the same splendour, in spite of the fact that Gregor later earned so much money that he was in a position to bear the expenses of the entire family, costs which he, in fact, did bear. They had become quite accustomed to it, both the family and Gregor as well. They took the money with thanks, and he happily surrendered it, but a special warmth was no longer present. Only the sister had remained still close to Gregor, and it was his secret plan to send her next year to the Conservatory, regardless of the great expense which that necessarily involved and which would be made up in other ways. In contrast to Gregor, she loved music very much and knew how to play the violin charmingly. Now and then during Gregor's short stays in the city the Conservatory was mentioned in conversations with his sister, but always merely as a beautiful dream, whose realization was unimaginable, and their parents never listened to these innocent expectations with pleasure. But Gregor thought about them with scrupulous consideration and intended to explain the matter in all seriousness on Christmas Eve.

In his present situation, such completely futile ideas went through his head, while he pushed himself right up against the door and listened. Sometimes in his general exhaustion he could not listen any more and let his head bang listlessly against the door, but he immediately pulled himself together once more, for even the small sound which he made by this motion was heard near by and silenced everyone. "There he goes on again," said his father after a while, clearly turning towards the door, and only then would the interrupted conversation gradually be resumed again.

Now, Gregor found out clearly enough—for his father tended to repeat himself from time to time in his explanations, partly because he had not personally concerned himself with these matters for a long time now, and partly because his mother did not understand everything right away the first time—that, in spite all bad luck, an amount of money, although a very small one, was still available from the old times and that the interest, which had not been touched, had in the intervening time allowed it to increase a little. Furthermore, in addition to this, the money which Gregor had brought home every month—he had kept only a few crowns for himself—had not been completely spent and had grown into a small capital amount. Gregor, behind his door, nodded eagerly, rejoicing over this unanticipated foresight and frugality. True, with this excess money, he could really have paid off more of his father's debt to his employer and the day on which he could be rid of this position would have been a lot closer, but now things were doubtless better the way his father had arranged them.

At the moment, however, this money was not nearly sufficient to permit the family to live on the interest payments. Perhaps it would be enough to maintain the family for one or at most two years, that was all. Thus, it only added up to an amount which one should not really draw upon and which must be set aside for an emergency. But they had to earn money to live on. Now, it's true his father was indeed a healthy man, but he was old and had not worked for five years and thus could not be counted on for very much. He had in these five years, the first holidays of his laborious but unsuccessful life, put on a good deal of fat and thus had become really heavy. And should his old mother now perhaps work for money, a woman who suffered from asthma, for whom wandering through the apartment even now was a great strain and who spent every second day on the sofa by the open window having trouble with her breathing? Should his sister earn money, a girl who was still a seventeen-year-old child and whose earlier life style had been so very delightful that it had consisted of dressing herself nicely, sleeping in late, helping around the house, taking part in a few modest enjoyments and, above all, playing the violin? When it came to talking about this need to earn money, at first Gregor went away from the door and threw himself on the cool leather sofa beside the door, for he was quite hot from shame and sorrow.

Often he lay there all night long, not sleeping at all, just scratching on the leather for hours at a time. Or he undertook the very difficult task of pushing a chair over to the window. Then he crept up on the window sill and, braced on the chair, leaned against the window to look out, obviously with some memory or other of the liberating sense which looking out the window used to bring him in earlier times. For, in fact, from day to day he perceived things with less and less clarity, even those only a short distance away: the hospital across the street, the all-too-frequent sight of which he had previously cursed, was not visible at all any more, and if he had not been very well aware that he lived in the quiet but completely urban Charlotte Street, he could have believed that from his window he was peering out at a featureless wasteland, in which the gray heaven and the gray earth had merged and were indistinguishable. His observant sister only had to notice a couple of times that the chair stood by the window; then, after cleaning up the room, each time, she pushed the chair back right against the window again and from now on she even left the inner casements open.

If Gregor had only been able to speak to his sister and thank her for everything that she had to do for him, he would have tolerated her service more easily. As it was, he suffered under it. The sister admittedly sought to cover up the awkwardness of everything as much as possible, and, as time went by, she naturally became more successful at it. But with the passing of time Gregor also came to understand everything much more clearly. Even her entrance was terrible for him. As soon as she came in, she ran straight to the window, without taking the time to shut the door, in spite of the fact that she was otherwise very considerate in sparing anyone the sight of Gregor's room, and yanked the window open with eager hands, as if she was almost suffocating, and remained for a while by the window breathing deeply, even when it was still so cold. With this running and noise she frightened Gregor twice every day. The entire time he trembled under the couch, and yet he knew very well that she would certainly have spared him gladly if it had only been possible to remain with the window closed in a room where Gregor lived.

On one occasion—about one month had already gone by since Gregor's transformation, and there was now no particular reason any more for his sister to be startled at Gregor's appearance—she arrived a little earlier than usual and came upon Gregor as he was still looking out the window, immobile and well positioned to frighten someone. It would not have come as a surprise to Gregor if she had not come in, since his position was preventing her from opening the window immediately. But not only did she not step inside; she even retreated and shut the door. A stranger really could have concluded from this that Gregor had been lying in wait for her and wanted to bite her. Of course, Gregor immediately concealed himself under the couch, but he had to wait until noon before his sister returned, and she seemed much less calm than usual. From this he realized that his appearance was still intolerable to her and must remain intolerable to her in future, and that she really had to exert a lot of self-control not to run away from a glimpse of only the small part of his body which stuck out from under the couch. In order to spare her even this sight, one day he dragged the sheet on his back and onto the couch—this task took him four hours—and arranged it in such a way that he was now completely concealed and his sister, even if she bent down, could not see him. If this sheet was not necessary as far as she was concerned, then she could remove it, for it was clear enough that Gregor could not derive any pleasure from isolating himself away so completely. But she left the sheet just as it was, and Gregor believed he even caught a look of gratitude when, on one occasion, he carefully lifted up the sheet a little with his head to check, as his sister took stock of the new arrangement.

In the first two weeks his parents could not bring themselves to visit him, and he often heard how they fully acknowledged his sister's present work; whereas, earlier they had often got annoyed at his sister because she had seemed to them a somewhat useless young woman. However, now both his father and his mother frequently waited in front of Gregor's door while his sister cleaned up inside, and as soon as she came out, she had to explain in great detail how things looked in the room, what Gregor had eaten, how he had behaved this time, and whether perhaps a slight improvement was perceptible. In any event, his mother comparatively soon wanted to visit Gregor, but his father and his sister restrained her, at first with reasons which Gregor listened to very attentively and which he completely endorsed. Later, however, they had to hold her back forcefully, and when she then cried "Let me go to Gregor. He's my unfortunate son! Don't you understand that I have to go to him?" Gregor then thought that perhaps it would be a good thing if his mother came in, not every day, of course, but maybe once a week. She understood everything much better than his sister, who, in spite of all her courage, was still merely a child and, in the last analysis, had perhaps undertaken such a difficult task only out of childish recklessness.

Gregor's wish to see his mother was soon realized. While during the day Gregor, out of consideration for his parents, did not want to show himself by the window, he could not crawl around very much on the few square metres of the floor. He found it difficult to bear lying quietly during the night, and soon eating no longer gave him the slightest pleasure. So for diversion he acquired the habit of crawling back and forth across the walls and ceiling. He was especially fond of hanging from the ceiling. The experience was quite different from lying on the floor. It was easier to breathe, a slight vibration went through his body, and in the midst of the almost happy amusement which Gregor found up there, it could happen that, to his own surprise, he let go and hit the floor. However, now he naturally controlled his body quite differently than before, and he did not injure himself in such a great fall. Now, his sister noticed immediately the new amusement which Gregor had found for himself—for as he crept around he left behind here and there traces of his sticky stuff—and so she got the idea of making the area where Gregor could creep around as large as possible and thus of removing the furniture which got in the way, especially the chest of drawers and the writing desk. But she was in no position to do this by herself. She did not dare to ask her father to help, and the servant girl would certainly not have assisted her, for although this girl, about sixteen years old, had courageously remained since the dismissal of the previous cook, she had begged for the privilege of being allowed to stay permanently confined to the kitchen and of having to open the door only in answer to a special summons. Thus, his sister had no other choice but to involve his mother at a time when his father was absent. His mother approached Gregor's room with cries of excited joy, but she fell silent at the door. Of course, his sister first checked whether everything in the room was in order. Only then did she let his mother enter. Gregor had drawn the sheet down with the greatest haste even further and wrinkled it more. The whole thing really looked just like a coverlet thrown carelessly over the couch. On this occasion, Gregor also held back from spying out from under the sheet. He refrained from looking at his mother this time and was merely happy that she had now come. "Come on; you can't see him," said his sister and evidently led his mother by the hand. Now Gregor listened as these two weak women shifted the still heavy old chest of drawers from its position and as his sister constantly took on herself the greatest part of the work, without listening to the warnings of his mother, who was afraid that she would strain herself. The work lasted a very long time. After about a quarter of an hour had already gone by, his mother said it would be better if they left the chest of drawers where it was, because, in the first place, it was too heavy: they would not be finished before his father's arrival, and leaving the chest of drawers in the middle of the room would block all Gregor's pathways, but, in the second place, they could not be at all certain that Gregor would be pleased with the removal of the furniture. To her the reverse seemed to be true; the sight of the empty walls pierced her right to the heart, and why should Gregor not feel the same, since he had been accustomed to the room furnishings for a long time and would therefore feel himself abandoned in an empty room. "And is it not the case," his mother concluded very quietly, almost whispering, as if she wished to prevent Gregor, whose exact location she really did not know, from hearing even the sound of her voice—for she was convinced that he did not understand her words—"and isn't it a fact that by removing the furniture we're showing that we're giving up all hope of an improvement and are leaving him to his own resources without any consideration? I think it would be best if we tried to keep the room exactly in the condition it was in before, so that, when Gregor returns to us, he finds everything unchanged and can forget the intervening time all the more easily."

As he heard his mother's words Gregor realized that the lack of all immediate human contact, together with the monotonous life surrounded by the family over the course of these two months, must have confused his understanding, because otherwise he could not explain to himself how he, in all seriousness, could have been so keen to have his room emptied. Was he really eager to let the warm room, comfortably furnished with pieces he had inherited, be turned into a cavern in which he would, of course, then be able to crawl about in all directions without disturbance, but at the same time with a quick and complete forgetting of his human past as well? Was he then at this point already on the verge of forgetting and was it only the voice of his mother, which he had not heard for a long time, that had aroused him? Nothing was to be removed—everything must remain. In his condition he could not function without the beneficial influences of his furniture. And if the furniture prevented him from carrying out his senseless crawling about all over the place, then there was no harm in that, but rather a great benefit.

But his sister unfortunately thought otherwise. She had grown accustomed, certainly not without justification, so far as the discussion of matters concerning Gregor was concerned, to act as an special expert with respect to their parents, and so now the mother's advice was for his sister sufficient reason to insist on the removal, not only of the chest of drawers and the writing desk, which were the only items she had thought about at first, but also of all the furniture, with the exception of the indispensable couch. Of course, it was not only childish defiance and her recent very unexpected and hard won self-confidence which led her to this demand. She had also actually observed that Gregor needed a great deal of room to creep about; the furniture, on the other hand, as far as one could see, was not the slightest use. But perhaps the enthusiastic sensibility of young women of her age also played a role. This feeling sought release at every opportunity, and with it Grete now felt tempted to want to make Gregor's situation even more terrifying, so that then she would be able to do even more for him than she had up to now. For surely no one except Grete would ever trust themselves to enter a room in which Gregor ruled the empty walls all by himself.

And so she did not let herself be dissuaded from her decision by her mother, who in this room seemed uncertain of herself in her sheer agitation and soon kept quiet, helping his sister with all her energy to get the chest of drawers out of the room. Now, Gregor could still do without the chest of drawers if need be, but the writing desk really had to stay. And scarcely had the women left the room with the chest of drawers, groaning as they pushed it, when Gregor stuck his head out from under the sofa to see how he could intervene, cautiously and with as much consideration as possible. But unfortunately it was his mother who came back into the room first, while Grete had her arms wrapped around the chest of drawers in the next room and was rocking it back and forth by herself, of course without moving it from its position. But his mother was not used to the sight of Gregor; he could have made her ill, and so, frightened, Gregor scurried backwards right to the other end of the sofa. However, he could no longer prevent the sheet from moving forward a little. That was enough to catch his mother's attention. She came to a halt, stood still for a moment, and then went back to Grete.

Although Gregor kept repeating to himself over and over that really nothing unusual was going on, that only a few pieces of furniture were being rearranged, he soon had to admit to himself that the movements of the women to and fro, their quiet conversations, and the scraping of the furniture on the floor affected him like a great commotion stirred up on all sides, and, so firmly was he pulling in his head and legs and pressing his body into the floor, he had to tell himself unequivocally that he would not be able to endure all this much longer. They were cleaning out his room, taking away from him everything he cherished; they had already dragged out the chest of drawers in which the fret saw and other tools were kept, and they were now loosening the writing desk which was fixed tight to the floor, the desk on which he, as a business student, a school student, indeed even as an elementary school student, had written out his assignments. At that moment he really did not have any more time to check the good intentions of the two women, whose existence he had in any case almost forgotten, because in their exhaustion they were working really silently, and the heavy stumbling of their feet was the only sound to be heard.

And so he scuttled out—the women were just propping themselves up on the writing desk in the next room in order to take a short breather. He changed the direction of his path four times. He really did not know what he should rescue first. Then he saw hanging conspicuously on the wall, which was otherwise already empty, the picture of the woman dressed in nothing but fur. He quickly scurried up over it and pressed himself against the glass which held it in place and which made his hot abdomen feel good. At least this picture, which Gregor at the moment completely concealed, surely no one would now take away. He twisted his head towards the door of the living room to observe the women as they came back in.

They had not allowed themselves very much rest and were coming back right away. Grete had placed her arm around her mother and held her tightly. "So what shall we take now?" said Grete and looked around her. Then her glance met Gregor's from the wall. She kept her composure only because her mother was there. She bent her face towards her mother in order to prevent her from looking around, and said, although in a trembling voice and too quickly, "Come, wouldn't it be better to go back to the living room for just another moment?" Grete's purpose was clear to Gregor: she wanted to bring his mother to a safe place and then chase him down from the wall. Well, let her just try! He squatted on his picture and did not hand it over. He would sooner spring into Grete's face.

But Grete's words had immediately made the mother very uneasy. She walked to the side, caught sight of the enormous brown splotch on the flowered wallpaper, and, before she became truly aware that what she was looking at was Gregor, screamed out in a high-pitched raw voice "Oh God, oh God" and fell with outstretched arms, as if she was surrendering everything, down onto the couch and lay there motionless. "Gregor, you …" cried out his sister with a raised fist and an urgent glare. Since his transformation these were the first words which she had directed right at him. She ran into the room next door to bring some spirits or other with which she could revive her mother from her fainting spell. Gregor wanted to help as well—there was time enough to save the picture—but he was stuck fast on the glass and had to tear himself loose forcibly. Then he also scurried into the next room, as if he could give his sister some advice, as in earlier times, but then he had to stand there idly behind her, while she rummaged about among various small bottles. Still, she was frightened when she turned around. A bottle fell onto the floor and shattered. A splinter of glass wounded Gregor in the face, and some corrosive medicine or other dripped over him. Now, without lingering any longer, Grete took as many small bottles as she could hold and ran with them in to her mother. She slammed the door shut with her foot. Gregor was now shut off from his mother, who was perhaps near death, thanks to him. He could not open the door; he did not want to chase away his sister, who had to remain with her mother. At this point he had nothing to do but wait, and, overwhelmed with self-reproach and worry, he began to creep and crawl over everything: walls, furniture, and ceiling. Finally, in his despair, as the entire room started to spin around him, he fell onto the middle of the large table.

A short time elapsed. Gregor lay there limply. All around was still. Perhaps that was a good sign. Then there was ring at the door. The servant girl was naturally shut up in her kitchen, and therefore Grete had to go to open the door. The father had arrived. "What's happened?" were his first words. Grete's appearance had told him everything. Grete replied with a dull voice; evidently she was pressing her face against her father's chest: "Mother fainted, but she's getting better now. Gregor has broken loose." "Yes, I have expected that," said his father, "I always warned you of that, but you women don't want to listen." It was clear to Gregor that his father had badly misunderstood Grete's all-too-brief message and was assuming that Gregor had committed some violent crime or other. Thus, Gregor now had to find his father to calm him down, for he had neither the time nor the ability to explain things to him. And so he rushed away to the door of his room and pushed himself against it, so that his father could see right away as he entered from the hall that Gregor fully intended to return at once to his room, that it was not necessary to drive him back, but that one only needed to open the door, and he would disappear immediately.

But his father was not in the mood to observe such niceties. "Ah!" he yelled as soon as he entered, with a tone as if he were at once angry and pleased. Gregor pulled his head back from the door and raised it in the direction of his father. He had not really pictured his father as he now stood there. Of course, what with his new style of creeping all around, he had in the past while neglected to pay attention to what was going on in the rest of the apartment, as he had done before, and really should have grasped the fact that he would encounter different conditions. And yet, and yet, was that still his father? Was that the same man who had lain exhausted and buried in bed in earlier days when Gregor was setting out on a business trip, who had received him on the evenings of his return in a sleeping gown and arm chair, totally incapable of standing up, who had only lifted his arm as a sign of happiness, and who in their rare strolls together a few Sundays a year and on the most important holidays made his way slowly forwards between Gregor and his mother—who themselves moved slowly—always a bit more slowly than them, bundled up in his old coat, working hard to move forwards and always setting down his walking stick carefully, and who, when he had wanted to say something, almost always stood still and gathered his entourage around him? But now he was standing up really straight, dressed in a tight-fitting blue uniform with gold buttons, like the ones servants wear in a banking company. Above the high stiff collar of his jacket his firm double chin stuck out prominently, beneath his bushy eyebrows the glance of his black eyes was fresh and alert, and his usually dishevelled white hair was combed down into a shining and carefully exact parting. He threw his cap, on which a gold monogram, probably the symbol of a bank, was affixed, in an arc across the entire room onto the sofa and, thrusting back the edges of the long coat of his uniform, with his hands in his trouser pockets and a grim face, moved right up to Gregor. He really did not know what he had in mind, but he raised his foot uncommonly high anyway, and Gregor was astonished at the gigantic size of the sole of his boot. However, he did not linger on that point, for he had known even from the first day of his new life that, as far as he was concerned, his father considered the only appropriate response to be the greatest force. And so he scurried away from his father, stopped when his father remained standing, and scampered forward again when his father merely stirred. In this way they made their way around the room repeatedly, without anything decisive taking place. In fact, because of the slow pace, it did not look like a chase. So Gregor remained on the floor for the time being, especially since he was afraid that his father could interpret a flight up onto the wall or the ceiling as an act of real malice. At any event, Gregor had to tell himself that he could not keep up this running around for a long time, because whenever his father took a single step, he had to go through a large number of movements. Already he was starting to feel a shortage of breath, just as in his earlier days when his lungs had been quite unreliable. As he now staggered around in this way in order to gather all his energies for running, hardly keeping his eyes open and feeling so listless that he had no notion at all of any escape other than by running and had almost already forgotten that the walls were available to him, although here they were obstructed by carefully carved furniture full of sharp points and spikes, at that moment something or other thrown casually flew close by and rolled in front of him. It was an apple. Immediately a second one flew after it. Gregor stood still in fright. Further running away was useless, for his father had decided to bombard him. From the fruit bowl on the sideboard his father had filled his pockets, and now, without for the moment taking accurate aim, he was throwing apple after apple. These small red apples rolled around on the floor, as if electrified, and collided with each other. A weakly thrown apple grazed Gregor's back but skidded off harmlessly. However, another thrown immediately after that one drove into Gregor's back really hard. Gregor wanted to drag himself off, as if he could make the unexpected and incredible pain go away if he changed his position. But he felt as if he was nailed in place and lay stretched out completely confused in all his senses. Only with his final glance did he notice how the door of his room was pulled open and how, right in front of his screaming sister, his mother ran out in her underbodice, for his sister had loosened her clothing in order to give her some freedom to breathe in her fainting spell, and how his mother then ran up to his father—on the way her loosened petticoats slipped toward the floor one after the other—and how, tripping over them, she hurled herself onto his father and, throwing her arms around him, in complete union with him—but at this moment Gregor's powers of sight gave way—as her hands reached around his father's neck, and she begged him to spare Gregor's life.

III

Gregor's serious wound, from which he suffered for over a month—since no one ventured to remove the apple, it remained in his flesh as a visible reminder—seemed by itself to have reminded the father that, in spite of Gregor's present unhappy and hateful appearance, he was a member of the family and should not be treated as an enemy, but that it was, on the contrary, a requirement of family duty to suppress one's aversion and to endure—nothing else, just endure.

And if through his wound Gregor had now also apparently lost for good his ability to move and for the time being needed many, many minutes to crawl across his room, like an aged invalid—so far as creeping up high was concerned, that was unimaginable—nevertheless, for this worsening of his condition, in his view he did get completely satisfactory compensation, because every day towards evening the door to the living room, which he was in the habit of keeping a sharp eye on even one or two hours beforehand, was opened, so that he, lying down in the darkness of his room, invisible from the living room, could see the entire family at the illuminated table and listen to their conversation, to a certain extent with their common permission, a situation quite different from what had happened before.

Of course, it was no longer the animated social interaction of former times, which in small hotel rooms Gregor had always thought about with a certain longing, when, tired out, he had had to throw himself into the damp bedclothes. For the most part what went on now was only very quiet. After the evening meal, the father soon fell asleep in his arm chair. The mother and sister warned each other to be quiet. Bent far over the light, the mother sewed fine undergarments for a fashion shop. The sister, who had taken on a job as a salesgirl, in the evening studied stenography and French, so as perhaps to obtain a better position later on. Sometimes the father woke up and, as if he was quite ignorant that he had been asleep, said to the mother "How long you have been sewing again today!" and went right back to sleep, while the mother and the sister smiled tiredly to each other.

With a sort of stubbornness the father refused to take off his servant's uniform even at home, and while his sleeping gown hung unused on the coat hook, the father dozed completely dressed in his place, as if he was always ready for his responsibility and even here was waiting for the voice of his superior. As a result, in spite of all the care from the mother and sister, his uniform, which even at the start was not new, grew dirty, and Gregor looked, often for the entire evening, at this clothing, with stains all over it and with its gold buttons always polished, in which the old man, although very uncomfortable, nonetheless was sleeping peacefully.

As soon as the clock struck ten, the mother tried gently encouraging the father to wake up and then persuading him to go to bed, on the ground that he could not get a proper sleep here and that the father, who had to report for service at six o'clock, really needed a good sleep. But in his stubbornness, which had gripped him since he had become a servant, he always insisted on staying even longer by the table, although he regularly fell asleep and then could be prevailed upon only with the greatest difficulty to trade his chair for the bed. No matter how much the mother and sister might at that point work on him with small admonitions, for a quarter of an hour he would remain shaking his head slowly, his eyes closed, without standing up. The mother would pull him by the sleeve and speak flattering words into his ear; the sister would leave her work to help her mother, but that would not have the desired effect on the father. He would merely settle himself even more deeply into his arm chair. Only when the two women grabbed him under the armpits would he throw his eyes open, look back and forth at the mother and sister, and habitually say "This is a life. This is the peace and quiet of my old age." And propped up by both women, he would heave himself up elaborately, as if for him it was the greatest trouble, allow himself to be led to the door by the women, wave them away there, and proceed on his own from that point, while the mother quickly threw down her sewing implements and the sister her pen in order to run after the father and help him some more.

In this overworked and exhausted family who had time to worry any longer about Gregor more than was absolutely necessary? The household was constantly getting smaller. The servant girl was now let go. A huge bony cleaning woman with white hair flying all over her head came in the morning and evening to do the heaviest work. The mother took care of everything else, in addition to her considerable sewing work. It even happened that various pieces of family jewellery, which previously the mother and sister had been overjoyed to wear on social and festive occasions, were sold, as Gregor found out in the evening from the general discussion of the prices they had fetched. But the greatest complaint was always that they could not leave this apartment, which was much too big for their present means, since it was impossible to imagine how Gregor might be moved. But Gregor fully recognized that it was not just consideration for him which was preventing a move, for he could have been transported easily in a suitable box with a few air holes. The main thing holding the family back from a change in living quarters was far more their complete hopelessness and the idea that they had been struck by a misfortune like no one else in their entire circle of relatives and acquaintances. What the world demands of poor people they now carried out to an extreme degree. The father bought breakfast to the petty officials at the bank, the mother sacrificed herself for the undergarments of strangers, the sister behind her desk was at the beck and call of customers, but the family's energies did not extend any further. And the wound in his back began to pain Gregor all over again, when his mother and sister, after they had escorted the father to bed, now came back, let their work lie, moved close together, and sat cheek to cheek and when his mother would now say, pointing to Gregor's room, "Close the door, Grete," and when Gregor was again in the darkness, while close by the women mingled their tears or, quite dry eyed, stared at the table.

Gregor spent his nights and days with hardly any sleep. Sometimes he thought that the next time the door opened he would take over the family arrangements just as he had earlier. In his imagination appeared again, after a long time, his boss and the manager, the chief clerk and the apprentices, the excessively spineless custodian, two or three friends from other businesses, a chambermaid from a hotel in the provinces, a loving, fleeting memory, a female cashier from a hat shop, whom he had seriously but too slowly courted—they all appeared mixed in with strangers or people he had already forgotten, but instead of helping him and his family, they were all unapproachable, and he was happy to see them disappear. But then again he was in no mood to worry about his family. He was filled with sheer anger over the wretched care he was getting, even though he could not imagine anything which he might have an appetite for. Still, he made plans about how he could get into the larder to take there what he at all accounts deserved, even if he was not hungry. Without thinking any more about how they might be able to give Gregor special pleasure, the sister very quickly kicked some food or other, whatever she felt like, into his room in the morning and at noon, before she ran off to her shop. And in the evening, quite indifferent to whether the food had perhaps only been tasted or, what happened most frequently, remained entirely undisturbed, she whisked it out with one sweep of her broom. The task of cleaning his room, which she now always carried out in the evening, could not have been done any more quickly. Streaks of dirt ran along the walls; here and there lay tangles of dust and garbage. At first, when his sister arrived, Gregor positioned himself in a particularly filthy corner in order with this posture to make something of a protest. But he could well have stayed there for weeks without his sister's doing the job any better. In fact, she perceived the dirt as much as he did, but she had decided just to let it stay. In this business, with a touchiness which was quite new to her and which had generally taken over the entire family, she kept watch to see that the cleaning of Gregor's room remained reserved for her. His mother had once undertaken a major clean up of his room, which she had only completed successfully after using a few buckets of water. But the extensive dampness made Gregor sick, and he lay spread out, embittered and immobile, on the couch. However, the mother's punishment did not fail to materialize. For in the evening the sister had hardly observed the change in Gregor's room before she ran into the living room mightily offended and, in spite of her mother's hand lifted high in entreaty, broke out in a fit of crying. Her parents—the father had, of course, woken up with a start in his arm chair—at first looked at her astonished and helpless, until they started to get agitated. Turning to his right, the father heaped reproaches on the mother that she had not left the cleaning of Gregor's room to the sister and, turning to his left, he shouted at the sister that she would no longer be allowed to clean Gregor's room ever again, while the mother tried to pull the father, beside himself in his excitement, into the bed room. The sister, shaken by her crying fit, pounded on the table with her tiny fists, and Gregor hissed at all this, angry that no one thought about shutting the door and sparing him the sight of this commotion.

But even when the sister, exhausted from her daily work, had grown tired of caring for Gregor as she had before, even then the mother did not have to come at all in her place. And Gregor did not have to be neglected. For now the cleaning woman was there. This old widow, whose bony frame had enabled her to survive the worst a long life can offer, had no real horror of Gregor. Without being in the least curious, she had once accidentally opened Gregor's door. At the sight of Gregor, who, totally surprised, began to scamper here and there, although no one was chasing him, she remained standing with her hands folded across her stomach staring at him. Since then she did not fail to open the door furtively a little every morning and evening and look in on Gregor. At first, she also called him to her with words which she probably thought were friendly, like "Come here for a bit, old dung beetle!" or "Hey, look at the old dung beetle!" Addressed in such a manner, Gregor made no answer, but remained motionless in his place, as if the door had not been opened at all. If only, instead of allowing this cleaning woman to disturb him uselessly whenever she felt like it, they had given her orders to clean up his room every day! Once in the early morning—a hard downpour, perhaps already a sign of the coming spring, struck the window panes—when the cleaning woman started up once again with her usual conversation, Gregor was so bitter that he turned towards her, as if for an attack, although slowly and weakly. But instead of being afraid of him, the cleaning woman merely lifted up a chair standing close by the door and, as she stood there with her mouth wide open, her intention was clear: she would close her mouth only when the chair in her hand had been thrown down on Gregor's back. "This goes no further, all right?" she asked, as Gregor turned himself around again, and she placed the chair calmly back in the corner.

Gregor ate hardly anything any more. Only when he chanced to move past the food which had been prepared did he, as a game, take a bit into his mouth, hold it there for hours, and generally spit it out again. At first he thought it might be his sadness over the condition of his room which kept him from eating, but he very soon became reconciled to the alterations in his room. People had grown accustomed to discard in there things which they could not put anywhere else, and at this point there were many such items, now that they had rented one room of the apartment to three lodgers. These solemn gentlemen—all three had full beards, as Gregor once found out through a crack in the door—were meticulously intent on tidiness, not only in their own room but, since they had now rented a room here, in the entire household, particularly in the kitchen. They simply did not tolerate any useless or shoddy stuff. Moreover, for the most part they had brought with them their own pieces of furniture. Thus, many items had become superfluous, and these were not really things one could sell or things people wanted to throw out. All these pieces ended up in Gregor's room, even the box of ashes and the garbage pail from the kitchen. The cleaning woman, always in a great hurry, simply flung anything that was for the moment useless into Gregor's room. Fortunately Gregor generally saw only the relevant object and the hand which held it. The cleaning woman perhaps was intending, when time and opportunity allowed, to take the stuff out again or to throw everything out all at once, but in fact the things remained lying there, wherever they had ended up at the first throw, unless Gregor squirmed his way through the accumulation of junk and moved it. At first he was forced to do this because otherwise there was no room for him to creep around, but later he did it with a growing pleasure, although after such movements, tired to death and feeling wretched, he did not budge again for hours.

Because the lodgers sometimes also took their evening meal at home in the common living room, the door to it stayed shut on many evenings. But Gregor had no trouble at all going without the open door. Already on many evenings when it was open he had not availed himself of it, but, without the family noticing, was stretched out in the darkest corner of his room. However, on one occasion the cleaning woman had left the door to the living room slightly ajar, and it remained open even when the lodgers came in as evening fell and the lights were put on. They sat down at the head of the table, where in earlier days the mother, the father, and Gregor had eaten, unfolded their serviettes, and picked up their knives and forks. The mother immediately appeared in the door with a dish of meat and right behind her the sister with a dish piled high with potatoes. The food gave off a lot of steam. The gentlemen lodgers bent over the plates set before them, as if they wanted to check them before eating, and in fact the one who sat in the middle—for the other two he seemed to serve as the authority—cut off a piece of meat still on the dish, obviously to establish whether it was sufficiently tender and whether or not it should be sent back to the kitchen. He was satisfied, and mother and sister, who had looked on in suspense, began to breathe easily and to smile.

The family itself ate in the kitchen. In spite of that, before the father went into the kitchen, he came into the living room and with a single bow, cap in hand, made a tour of the table. The lodgers rose up collectively and murmured something into their beards. Then, when they were alone, they ate almost in complete silence. It seemed odd to Gregor that, out of all the many different sorts of sounds of eating, what was always audible was their chewing teeth, as if by that Gregor should be shown that people needed their teeth to eat and that nothing could be done even with the most handsome toothless jawbone. "I really do have an appetite," Gregor said to himself sorrowfully, "but not for these things. How these lodgers stuff themselves, and I am dying of hunger!"

On this very evening the violin sounded from the kitchen. Gregor did not remember hearing it all through this period. The lodgers had already ended their night meal, the middle one had pulled out a newspaper and had given each of the other two a page, and they were now leaning back, reading and smoking. When the violin started playing, they became attentive, got up, and went on tiptoe to the hall door, at which they remained standing pressed up against one another. They must have been audible from the kitchen, because the father called out, "Perhaps the gentlemen don't like the playing? It can be stopped at once." "On the contrary," stated the lodger in the middle, "might the young woman not come into us and play in the room here, where it is really much more comfortable and cheerful?" "Oh, certainly," cried the father, as if he were the one playing the violin. The men stepped back into the room and waited. Soon the father came with the music stand, the mother with the sheet music, and the sister with the violin. The sister calmly prepared everything for the recital. The parents, who had never previously rented a room and therefore exaggerated their politeness to the lodgers, dared not sit on their own chairs. The father leaned against the door, his right hand stuck between two buttons of his buttoned-up uniform. The mother, however, accepted a chair offered by one of the lodgers. Since she let the chair stay where the gentleman had chanced to put it, she sat to one side in a corner.

The sister began to play. The father and mother, one on each side, followed attentively the movements of her hands. Attracted by the playing, Gregor had ventured to advance a little further forward, and his head was already in the living room. He scarcely wondered about the fact that recently he had had so little consideration for the others. Earlier this consideration had been something he was proud of. And for that very reason he would have had at this moment more reason to hide away, because as a result of the dust which lay all over his room and flew around with the slightest movement, he was totally covered in dirt. On his back and his sides he carted around with him threads, hair, and remnants of food. His indifference to everything was much too great for him to lie on his back and scour himself on the carpet, as he had done earlier several times a day. In spite of this condition he had no timidity about inching forward a bit on the spotless floor of the living room.

In any case, no one paid him any attention. The family was all caught up in the violin playing. The lodgers, by contrast, who for the moment had placed themselves, hands in their trouser pockets, behind the music stand much too close to the sister, so that they could all see the sheet music, something that must certainly have bothered the sister, soon drew back to the window conversing in low voices with bowed heads, where they then remained, anxiously observed by the father. It now seemed really clear that, having assumed they were to hear a beautiful or entertaining violin recital, they were disappointed; they had had enough of the entire performance and were allowing their peace and quiet to be disturbed only out of politeness. In particular, the way in which they all blew the smoke from their cigars out of their noses and mouths up into the air led one to conclude that they were very irritated. And yet his sister was playing so beautifully. Her face was turned to the side, her eyes following the score intently and sadly. Gregor crept forward still a little further, keeping his head close against the floor in order to be able to catch her gaze if possible. Was he an animal that music so captivated him? For him it was as if the way to the unknown nourishment he craved was revealing itself. He was determined to press forward right up to his sister, to tug at her dress, and to indicate to her in this way that she might still come with her violin into his room, because here no one valued the recital as he wanted to value it. He did not wish to let her go from his room any more, at least not so long as he lived. His frightening appearance would for the first time become useful for him. He wanted to be at all the doors of his room simultaneously and snarl back at the attackers. However, his sister should not be compelled but would remain with him voluntarily. She would sit next to him on the sofa, bend down her ear to him, and he would then confide in her that he firmly intended to send her to the Conservatory and that, if his misfortune had not arrived in the interim, he would have declared all this last Christmas—had Christmas really already come and gone?—and would have brooked no argument. After this explanation his sister would break out in tears of emotion, and Gregor would lift himself up to her armpit and kiss her throat, which she, from the time she had been going to work, had left exposed without a band or a collar.

"Mr. Samsa!" called out the middle lodger to the father and, without uttering a further word, pointed his index finger at Gregor as he was moving slowly forward. The violin fell silent. The middle lodger smiled, first shaking his head at his friends, and then looked down at Gregor once more. Rather than driving Gregor back, the father seemed to consider it more important for the time being to calm down the lodgers, although they were not at all upset and Gregor seemed to entertain them more than the violin recital. The father hurried over to them and with outstretched arms tried to push them into their own room and at the same time to block their view of Gregor with his own body. At this point they became really somewhat irritated, although one no longer knew whether that was because of the father's behaviour or because of the knowledge they had just acquired that they had, without being aware of it, a neighbour like Gregor. They demanded explanations from his father, raised their arms to make their points, tugged agitatedly at their beards, and moved back towards their room quite slowly. In the meantime, the isolation which had suddenly fallen upon his sister after the unexpected breaking off of the recital had overwhelmed her. She had held onto the violin and bow in her limp hands for a little while and had continued to look at the sheet music as if she was still playing. All at once she pulled herself together, placed the instrument in her mother's lap—the mother was still sitting in her chair having trouble breathing, for her lungs were labouring hard—and had run into the next room, which the lodgers, pressured by the father, were already approaching more rapidly. One could observe how under the sister's practised hands the covers and pillows on the beds were thrown high and then rearranged. Even before the lodgers had reached the room, she had finished fixing the beds and was slipping out. The father seemed once again so gripped by his stubbornness that he forgot about the respect which, after all, he must show his lodgers. He pressed on and on, until right in the door of the room the middle gentleman stamped loudly with his foot and thus brought the father to a standstill. "I hereby declare," the middle lodger said, raising his hand and casting his glance both on the mother and the sister, "that considering the disgraceful conditions prevailing in this apartment and family"—with this he spat decisively on the floor—"I immediately cancel my room. I will, of course, pay nothing at all for the days which I have lived here; on the contrary, I shall think about whether or not I will initiate some sort of action against you, something which—believe me—will be very easy to establish." He fell silent and looked directly in front of him, as if he was waiting for something. In fact, his two friends immediately joined in with their opinions, "We also give immediate notice." At that he seized the door handle and with a bang slammed the door shut.

The father groped his way tottering to his chair and let himself fall in it. It looked as if he was stretching out for his usual evening snooze, but the heavy nodding of his head, which appeared as if it had no support, showed that he was not sleeping at all. Gregor had lain motionless the entire time in the spot where the lodgers had caught him. Disappointment with the collapse of his plan and perhaps also weakness brought on by his severe hunger made it impossible for him to move. He was afraid and reasonably certain that they might launch a combined attack against him at any moment, and he waited. He was not even startled when the violin fell from the mother's lap, out from under her trembling fingers, and gave off a reverberating tone.

"My dear parents," said the sister banging her hand on the table by way of an introduction, "things cannot go on any longer in this way. Maybe if you don't understand that, well, I do. I will not utter my brother's name in front of this monster, and thus I say only that we must try to get rid of it. We have tried what is humanly possible to take care of it and to be patient. I believe that no one can criticize us in the slightest."

"She is right in a thousand ways," said the father to himself. The mother, who was still incapable of breathing properly, began to cough numbly with her hand held up over her mouth and a manic expression in her eyes.

The sister hurried over to her mother and held her forehead. The sister's words seemed to have led the father to certain reflections. He sat upright, played with his service hat among the plates, which still lay on the table from the lodgers' evening meal, and looked now and then at the motionless Gregor.

"We must try to get rid of it," the sister now said decisively to the father, for the mother, in her coughing fit, was not listening to anything. "It is killing you both. I see it coming. When people have to work as hard as we all do, they cannot also tolerate this endless torment at home. I just can't go on any more." And she broke out into such a crying fit that her tears flowed out down onto her mother's face. She wiped them off her mother with mechanical motions of her hands.

"Child," said the father sympathetically and with obvious appreciation, "then what should we do?"

The sister only shrugged her shoulders as a sign of the perplexity which, in contrast to her previous confidence, had now come over her while she was crying.

"If he understood us," said the father in a semi-questioning tone. The sister, in the midst of her sobbing, shook her hand energetically as a sign that there was no point thinking of that.

"If he understood us," repeated the father and by shutting his eyes he absorbed the sister's conviction of the impossibility of this point, "then perhaps some compromise would be possible with him. But as it is ..."

"It has to go," cried the sister. "That is the only way, father. You must try to get rid of the idea that this is Gregor. The fact that we have believed this for so long, that is truly our real misfortune. But how can it be Gregor? If it were Gregor, he would have long ago realized that a communal life among human beings is not possible with such a creature and would have gone away voluntarily. Then we would not have a brother, but we could go on living and honour his memory. But this animal plagues us. It drives away the lodgers, will obviously take over the entire apartment, and leave us to spend the night in the lane. Just look, father," she suddenly cried out, "he's already starting up again." With a fright which was totally incomprehensible to Gregor, the sister even left the mother, literally pushed herself away from her chair, as if she would sooner sacrifice her mother than remain in Gregor's vicinity, and rushed behind her father who, excited merely by her behaviour, also stood up and half raised his arms in front of the sister as though to protect her.

But Gregor did not have any notion of wishing to create problems for anyone and certainly not for his sister. He had just started to turn himself around in order to creep back into his room, quite a startling sight, since, as a result of his suffering condition, he had to guide himself through the difficulty of turning around with his head, in this process lifting and striking it against the floor several times. He paused and looked around. His good intentions seemed to have been recognized. The fright had lasted only for a moment. Now they looked at him in silence and sorrow. His mother lay in her chair, with her legs stretched out and pressed together, her eyes almost shut from weariness. The father and sister sat next to one another. The sister had put her hands around the father's neck.

"Now perhaps I can actually turn myself around," thought Gregor and began the task again. He couldn't stop puffing at the effort and had to rest now and then. Besides, no one was urging him on. It was all left to him on his own. When he had completed turning around, he immediately began to wander straight back. He was astonished at the great distance which separated him from his room and did not understand in the least how in his weakness he had covered the same distance a short time before, almost without noticing it. Always intent only on creeping along quickly, he hardly paid any attention to the fact that no word or cry from his family interrupted him. Only when he was already in the doorway did he turn his head, not completely, because he felt his neck growing stiff. At any rate, he still saw that behind him nothing had changed. Only the sister was standing up. His last glimpse brushed over the mother, who was now completely asleep.

He was only just inside his room when the door was pushed shut very quickly, bolted fast, and barred. Gregor was startled by the sudden commotion behind him, so much so that his little limbs bent double under him. It was his sister who had been in such a hurry. She was already standing up, had waited, and then sprung forward nimbly. Gregor had not heard anything of her approach. She cried out "Finally!" to her parents, as she turned the key in the lock.

"What now?" Gregor asked himself and looked around him in the darkness. He soon made the discovery that he could no longer move at all. He was not surprised at that. On the contrary, it struck him as unnatural that up to this point he had really been able up to move around with these thin little legs. Besides he felt relatively content. True, he had pains throughout his entire body, but it seemed to him that they were gradually becoming weaker and weaker and would finally go away completely. The rotten apple in his back and the inflamed surrounding area, entirely covered with white dust, he hardly noticed. He remembered his family with deep feelings of love. In this business, his own thought that he had to disappear was, if possible, even more decisive than his sister's. He remained in this state of empty and peaceful reflection until the tower clock struck three in the morning. In front of the window he witnessed the beginning of the outside growing generally lighter. Then without willing it, his head sank all the way down, and from his nostrils his last breath flowed weakly out.

Early in the morning the cleaning woman came. In her sheer energy and haste she banged all the doors—in precisely the way people had already frequently asked her to avoid—so much so that once she arrived a quiet sleep was no longer possible anywhere in the entire apartment. In her customarily brief visit to Gregor she at first found nothing special. She thought he lay so immobile there on purpose and was playing the offended party. She gave him credit for as complete an understanding as possible. Since she happened to be holding the long broom in her hand, she tried to tickle Gregor with it from the door. When that was quite unsuccessful, she became irritated and poked Gregor a little, and only when she had shoved him from his place without any resistance did she become attentive. When she quickly realized the true state of affairs, her eyes grew large and she whistled to herself. However, she didn't restrain herself for long. She pulled open the door of the bedroom and yelled in a loud voice into the darkness, "Come and look. It's kicked the bucket. It's lying there. It's completely snuffed it!"

The Samsas sat upright in their marriage bed and had to get over their fright at the cleaning woman before they managed to grasp her message. But then Mr. and Mrs. Samsa climbed very quickly out of bed, one on either side. Mr. Samsa threw the bedspread over his shoulders, Mrs. Samsa came out only in her nightshirt, and like this they stepped into Gregor's room. Meanwhile, the door of the living room, in which Grete had slept since the lodgers had arrived on the scene, had also opened. She was fully clothed, as if she had not slept at all; her white face also seemed to indicate that. "Dead?" said Mrs. Samsa and looked questioningly at the cleaning woman, although she could have checked everything on her own and it was clear even without a check. "I should say so," said the cleaning woman and, by way of proof, poked Gregor's body with the broom a considerable distance more to the side. Mrs. Samsa made a movement, as if she wished to restrain the broom, but did not do it. "Well," said Mr. Samsa, "now we can give thanks to God." He crossed himself, and the three women followed his example. Grete, who did not take her eyes off the corpse, said, "Just look how thin he was. He has eaten nothing for such a long time. The meals which came in here came out again exactly the same." In fact, Gregor's body was completely flat and dry. That was apparent really for the first time, now that he was no longer raised on his small limbs and nothing else distracted one from looking.

"Grete, come into us for a moment," said Mrs. Samsa with a melancholy smile, and Grete went, not without looking back at the corpse, behind her parents into the bed room. The cleaning woman shut the door and opened the window wide. In spite of the early morning, the fresh air was partly tinged with warmth. It was already almost the end of March.

The three lodgers stepped out of their room and looked around for their breakfast, astonished that they had been forgotten. The middle one of the gentlemen asked the cleaning woman grumpily "Where is the breakfast?" However, she laid her finger to her lips and then quickly and silently indicated to the lodgers that they could come into Gregor's room. So they came and stood in the room, which was already quite bright, around Gregor's corpse, their hands in the pockets of their somewhat worn jackets.

Then the door of the bed room opened, and Mr. Samsa appeared in his uniform, with his wife on one arm and his daughter on the other. All were a little tear stained. Now and then Grete pressed her face into her father's arm.

"Get out of my apartment immediately," said Mr. Samsa and pointed to the door, without letting go of the women. "What do you mean?" said the middle lodger, somewhat dismayed and with a sugary smile. The two others kept their hands behind them and constantly rubbed them against each other, as if in joyful anticipation of a great squabble which must end up in their favour. "I mean exactly what I say," replied Mr. Samsa and went directly up to the lodger with his two female companions. The latter at first stood there motionless and looked at the floor, as if matters were arranging themselves in a new way in his head. "All right, then we'll go," he said and looked up at Mr. Samsa as if, suddenly overcome by humility, he was even asking fresh permission for this decision. Mr. Samsa merely nodded briefly and repeatedly to him with his eyes open wide. Following that, with long strides the lodger actually went out immediately into the hall. His two friends had already been listening for a while with their hands quite still, and now they hopped smartly after him, as if afraid that Mr. Samsa could step into the hall ahead of them and disturb their reunion with their leader. In the hall all three of them took their hats from the coat rack, pulled their canes from the umbrella stand, bowed silently, and left the apartment. In what turned out to be an entirely groundless mistrust, Mr. Samsa stepped with the two women out onto the landing, leaned against the railing, and looked over as the three lodgers slowly but steadily made their way down the long staircase, disappeared on each floor in a certain turn of the stairwell, and in a few seconds reappeared again. The further down they went, the more the Samsa family lost interest in them, and when a butcher with a tray on his head came up to meet them and then with a proud bearing ascended the stairs high above them, Mr. Samsa, together with the women, soon left the bannister, and they all returned, as if relieved, back into their apartment.

They decided to pass that day resting and going for a stroll. Not only had they earned this break from work, but there was no question that they really needed it. And so they sat down at the table and wrote three letters of apology: Mr. Samsa to his supervisor, Mrs. Samsa to her client, and Grete to her proprietor. During the writing the cleaning woman came in to say that she was going off, for her morning work was finished. The three people writing at first merely nodded, without glancing up. Only when the cleaning woman was still unwilling to depart, did they look up annoyed. "Well?" asked Mr. Samsa. The cleaning woman stood smiling in the doorway, as if she had a great stroke of luck to report to the family but would only do it if she was questioned thoroughly. The almost upright small ostrich feather in her hat, which had irritated Mr. Samsa during her entire service with them, swayed lightly in all directions. "All right then, what do you really want?" asked Mrs. Samsa, whom the cleaning lady respected more than the others. "Well," answered the cleaning woman, smiling so happily she couldn't go on speaking right away, "you mustn't worry about throwing out that rubbish from the next room. It's all taken care of." Mrs. Samsa and Grete bent down to their letters, as though they wanted to go on writing. Mr. Samsa, who noticed that the cleaning woman now wanted to start describing everything in detail, decisively prevented her with an outstretched hand. But since she was not allowed to explain, she remembered the great hurry she was in, and called out, clearly insulted, "Bye bye, everyone," then turned around furiously and left the apartment with a fearful slamming of the door.

"This evening she'll be given notice," said Mr. Samsa, but he got no answer from either his wife or from his daughter, because the cleaning woman seemed to have once again upset the tranquillity they had just attained. The women got up, went to the window, and remained there, with their arms about each other. Mr. Samsa turned around in his chair in their direction and observed them quietly for a while. Then he called out, "All right, come here then. Let's finally get rid of old things. And have a little consideration for me." The women attended to him at once. They rushed to him, caressed him, and quickly ended their letters.

Then all three left the apartment together, something they had not done for months now, and took the electric tram into the open air outside the city. The car in which they were sitting by themselves was totally engulfed by the warm sun. Leaning back comfortably in their seats, they talked to each other about future prospects, and they discovered that on closer observation these were not at all bad, for the three of them had employment, about which they had not really questioned each other at all, which was extremely favourable and with especially promising future prospects. The greatest improvement in their situation at this point, of course, had to come from a change of dwelling. Now they wanted to rent a smaller and cheaper apartment but better situated and generally more practical than the present one, which Gregor had chosen. While they amused themselves in this way, it struck Mr. and Mrs. Samsa, almost at the same moment, as they looked at their daughter, who was getting more animated all the time, how she had blossomed recently, in spite of all the troubles which had made her cheeks pale, into a beautiful and voluptuous young woman. Growing more silent and almost unconsciously understanding each other in their glances, they thought that the time was now at hand to seek out a good honest man for her. And it was something of a confirmation of their new dreams and good intentions when at the end of their journey their daughter stood up first and stretched her young body.

A Country Doctor

By Franz Kafka

A Country Doctor

I was in great difficulty. An urgent journey was facing me. A seriously ill man was waiting for me in a village ten miles distant. A severe snowstorm filled the space between him and me. I had a carriage—a light one, with large wheels, entirely suitable for our country roads. Wrapped up in furs with the bag of instruments in my hand, I was already standing in the courtyard ready for the journey; but the horse was missing—the horse. My own horse had died the previous night, as a result of overexertion in this icy winter. My servant girl was at that very moment running around the village to see if she could borrow a horse, but it was hopeless—I knew that—and I stood there useless, increasingly covered with snow, becoming all the time more immobile. The girl appeared at the gate, alone. She was swinging the lantern. Of course, who is now going to lend his horse for such a journey? I walked once again across the courtyard. I couldn't see what to do. Distracted and tormented, I kicked my foot against the cracked door of the pig sty which had not been used for years. The door opened and banged to and fro on its hinges. A warmth and smell as if from horses came out. A dim stall lantern on a rope swayed inside. A man huddled down in the stall below showed his open blue-eyed face. "Shall I hitch up?" he asked, crawling out on all fours. I didn't know what to say and merely bent down to see what was still in the stall. The servant girl stood beside me. "One doesn't know the sorts of things one has stored in one's own house," she said, and we both laughed. "Hey, Brother, hey Sister," the groom cried out, and two horses, powerful animals with strong flanks, shoved their way one behind the other, legs close to the bodies, lowering their well-formed heads like camels, and getting through the door space, which they completely filled, only through the powerful movements of their rumps. But right away they stood up straight, long legged, with thick steaming bodies. "Help him," I said, and the girl obediently hurried to hand the wagon harness to the groom. But as soon as she was beside him, the groom puts his arms around her and pushes his face against hers. She screams out and runs over to me. On the girl's cheek are red marks from two rows of teeth. "You brute," I cry out in fury, "do you want the whip?" But I immediately remember that he is a stranger, that I don't know where he comes from, and that he's helping me out of his own free will, when everyone else is refusing to. As if he knows what I am thinking, he takes no offence at my threat, but turns around to me once more, still busy with the horses. Then he says, "Climb in," and, in fact, everything is ready. I notice that I have never before traveled with such a beautiful team of horses, and I climb in happily. "But I'll take the reins. You don't know the way," I say. "Of course," he says; "I'm not going with you. I'm staying with Rosa." "No," screams Rosa and runs into the house, with an accurate premonition of the inevitability of her fate. I hear the door chain rattling as she sets it in place. I hear the lock click. I see how in addition she chases down the corridor and through the rooms putting out all the lights in order to make herself impossible to find. "You're coming with me," I say to the groom, "or I'll give up the journey, no matter how urgent it is. It's not my intention to give you the girl as the price of the trip." "Giddy up," he says and claps his hands. The carriage is torn away, like a piece of wood in a current. I still hear how the door of my house is breaking down and splitting apart under the groom's onslaught, and then my eyes and ears are filled with a roaring sound which overwhelms all my senses at once. But only for a moment. Then I am already there, as if the farm yard of my invalid opens up immediately in front of my courtyard gate. The horses stand quietly. The snowfall has stopped, moonlight all around. The sick man's parents rush out of the house, his sister behind them. They almost lift me out of the carriage. I get nothing from their confused talking. In the sick room one can hardly breathe the air. The neglected cooking stove is smoking. I want to push open the window, but first I'll look at the sick man. Thin, without fever, not cold, not warm, with empty eyes, without a shirt, the young man under the stuffed quilt heaves himself up, hangs around my throat, and whispers in my ear, "Doctor, let me die." I look around. No one has heard. The parents stand silently, leaning forward, and wait for my judgment. The sister has brought a stool for my handbag. I open the bag and look among my instruments. The young man constantly gropes at me from the bed to remind me of his request. I take some tweezers, test them in the candle light, and put them back. "Yes," I think blasphemously, "in such cases the gods do help. They send the missing horse, even add a second one because it's urgent, and even throw in a groom as a bonus." Now for the first time I think once more of Rosa. What am I doing? How am I saving her? How do I pull her out from under this groom, ten miles away from her, with uncontrollable horses in the front of my carriage? These horses, who have now somehow loosened their straps, are pushing open the window from outside, I don't know how. Each one is sticking its head through a window and, unmoved by the crying of the family, is observing the invalid. "I'll go back right away," I think, as if the horses were ordering me to journey back, but I allow the sister, who thinks I am in a daze because of the heat, to take off my fur coat. A glass of rum is prepared for me. The old man claps me on the shoulder; the sacrifice of his treasure justifies this familiarity. I shake my head. In the narrow circle of the old man's thinking I was not well; that's the only reason I refuse to drink. The mother stands by the bed and entices me over. I follow and, as a horse neighs loudly at the ceiling, lay my head on the young man's chest, which trembles under my wet beard. That confirms what I know: the young man is healthy. His circulation is a little off, saturated with coffee by his caring mother, but he's healthy and best pushed out of bed with a shove. I'm no improver of the world and let him lie there. I am employed by the district and do my duty to the full, right to the point where it's almost too much. Badly paid, but I'm generous and ready to help the poor. I still have to look after Rosa, and then the young man may have his way, and I want to die, too. What am I doing here in this endless winter! My horse is dead, and there is no one in the village who'll lend me his. I have to drag my team out of the pig sty. If they hadn't happened to be horses, I'd have had to travel with pigs. That's the way it is. And I nod to the family. They know nothing about it, and if they did know, they wouldn't believe it. Incidentally, it's easy to write prescriptions, but difficult to come to an understanding with people. Now, at this point my visit might have come to an end—they have once more called for my help unnecessarily. I'm used to that. With the help of my night bell the entire region torments me, but that this time I had to sacrifice Rosa as well, this beautiful girl, who lives in my house all year long and whom I scarcely notice—this sacrifice is too great, and I must somehow in my own head subtly rationalize it away for the moment, in order not to leave this family who cannot, even with their best will, give me Rosa back again. But as I am closing up by hand bag and calling for my fur coat, the family is standing together, the father sniffing the glass of rum in his hand, the mother, probably disappointed in me—what more do these people really expect?—tearfully biting her lips, and the sister flapping a very bloody hand towel, I am somehow ready, in the circumstances, to concede that the young man is perhaps nonetheless sick. I go to him. He smiles up at me, as if I was bringing him the most nourishing kind of soup—ah, now both horses are whinnying, the noise is probably supposed to come from higher regions in order to illuminate my examination—and now I find out that, yes indeed, the young man is ill. On his right side, in the region of the hip, a wound the size of the palm of one's hand has opened up. Rose coloured, in many different shadings, dark in the depths, brighter on the edges, delicately grained, with uneven patches of blood, open to the light like a mining pit. That's what it looks like from a distance. Close up a complication is apparent. Who can look at that without whistling softly? Worms, as thick and long as my little finger, themselves rose coloured and also spattered with blood, are wriggling their white bodies with many limbs from their stronghold in the inner of the wound towards the light. Poor young man, there's no helping you. I have found out your great wound. You are dying from this flower on your side. The family is happy; they see me doing something. The sister says that to the mother, the mother tells the father, the father tells a few guests who are coming in on tip toe through the moonlight of the open door, balancing themselves with outstretched arms. "Will you save me?" whispers the young man, sobbing, quite blinded by the life inside his wound. That's how people are in my region. Always demanding the impossible from the doctor. They have lost the old faith. The priest sits at home and tears his religious robes to pieces, one after the other. But the doctor is supposed to achieve everything with his delicate surgeon's hand. Well, it's what they like to think. I have not offered myself. If they use me for sacred purposes, I let that happen to me as well. What more do I want, an old country doctor, robbed of my servant girl! And they come, the family and the village elders, and are taking my clothes off. A choir of school children with the teacher at the head stands in front of the house and sings an extremely simple melody with the words

> Take his clothes off, then he'll heal,
> and if he doesn't cure, then kill him.
> It's only a doctor; it's only a doctor.

Then I am stripped of my clothes and, with my fingers in my beard and my head tilted to one side, I look at the people quietly. I am completely calm and clear about everything and stay that way, too, although it is not helping me at all, for they are now taking me by the head and feet and dragging me into the bed. They lay me against the wall on the side of wound. Then they all go out of the room. The door is shut. The singing stops. Clouds move in front of the moon. The bedclothes lie warmly around me. In the open space of the windows the horses' heads sway like shadows. "Do you know," I hear someone saying in my ear, "my confidence in you is very small. You were only shaken out from somewhere. You don't come on your own feet. Instead of helping, you give me less room on my deathbed. The best thing would be if I scratch your eyes out." "Right," I say, "it's a disgrace. But now I'm a doctor. What am I supposed to do? Believe me, things are not easy for me either." "Should I be satisfied with this excuse? Alas, I'll probably have to be. I always have to make do. I came into the world with a beautiful wound; that was all I was furnished with." "Young friend," I say, "your mistake is that you have no perspective. I've already been in all the sick rooms, far and wide, and I tell you your wound is not so bad. Made in a tight corner with two blows from an axe. Many people offer their side and hardly hear the axe in the forest, to say nothing of the fact that it's coming closer to them." "Is that really so, or are you deceiving me in my fever?" "It is truly so. Take the word of honour of a medical doctor." He took my word and grew still. But now it was time to think about my escape. The horses were still standing loyally in their place. Clothes, fur coat, and bag were quickly gathered up. I didn't want to delay by getting dressed; if the horses rushed as they had on the journey out, I should, in fact, be springing out of that bed into my own, as it were. One horse obediently pulled back from the window. I threw the bundle into the carriage. The fur coat flew too far and was caught on a hook by only one arm. Good enough. I swung myself up onto the horse. The reins dragging loosely, one horse barely harnessed to the other, the carriage swaying behind, last of all the fur coat in the snow. "Giddy up," I said, but there was no giddying up about it. We dragged slowly through the snowy desert like old men; for a long time the fresh but inaccurate singing of the children resounded behind us:

"Enjoy yourselves, you patients.
The doctor's laid[1] [*sic*] in bed with you."

I'll never come home at this rate. My flourishing practice is lost. A successor is robbing me, but to no avail, for he cannot replace me. In my house the disgusting groom is wreaking havoc. Rosa is his victim. I will not think it through. Naked, abandoned to the frost of this unhappy age, with an earthly carriage and unearthly horses, I drive around by myself, an old man. My fur coat hangs behind the wagon, but I cannot reach it, and no one from the nimble rabble of patients lifts a finger. Betrayed! Betrayed! Once one responds to a false alarm on the night bell, there's no making it good again—not ever.

1 Ed. note: lain

The Library of Babel*

By Jorge Luis Borges

By this art you may contemplate the variation of the 23 letters …
—*The Anatomy of Melancholy,* Part 2, Sect. II, Mem. IV.

The universe (which others call the Library) is composed of an indefinite, perhaps an infinite, number of hexagonal galleries, with enormous ventilation shafts in the middle, encircled by very low railings. From any hexagon the upper or lower stories are visible, interminably. The distribution of the galleries is invariable. Twenty shelves—five long shelves per side—cover all sides except two; their height, which is that of each floor, scarcely exceeds that of an average librarian. One of the free sides gives upon a narrow entrance way, which leads to another gallery, identical to the first and to all the others. To the left and to the right of the entrance way are two miniature rooms. One allows standing room for sleeping; the other, the satisfaction of fecal necessities. Through this section passes the spiral staircase, which plunges down into the abyss and rises up to the heights. In the entrance way hangs a mirror, which faithfully duplicates appearances. People are in the habit of inferring from this mirror that the Library is not infinite (if it really were, why this illusory duplication?); I prefer to dream that the polished surfaces feign and promise infinity. …

Light comes from some spherical fruits called by the name of lamps. There are two, running transversally, in each hexagon. The light they emit is insufficient, incessant

Like all men of the Library, I have traveled in my youth, I have journeyed in search of a book, perhaps of the catalogue of catalogues; now that my eyes can scarcely decipher what I write, I am preparing to die a few leagues from the hexagon in which I was born. Once dead, there will not lack pious hands to hurl me over the banister; my sepulchre shall be the unfathomable air: my body will sink lengthily and will corrupt and dissolve in the wind engendered by the fall, which is infinite. I affirm that the Library is interminable. The idealists argue that the hexagonal halls are a necessary form of absolute space or, at least, of our intuition of space. They contend that a triangular or pentagonal hall is inconceivable. (The

* It should, perhaps, be recalled that for years Jorge Luis Borges has been director of the National Library of Argentina.
—*Editor's note.*

mystics claim that to them ecstasy reveals a round chamber containing a great book with a continuous back circling the walls of the room; but their testimony is suspect; their words, obscure. That cyclical book is God.) Let it suffice me, for the time being, to repeat the classic dictum: *The Library is a sphere whose consummate center is any hexagon, and whose circumference is inaccessible.*

Five shelves correspond to each one of the walls of each hexagon; each shelf contains thirty-two books of a uniform format; each book is made up of four hundred and ten pages; each page, of forty lines; each line, of some eighty black letters. There are also letters on the spine of each book; these letters do not indicate or prefigure what the pages will say. I know that such a lack of relevance, at one time, seemed mysterious. Before summarizing the solution (whose disclosure, despite its tragic implications, is perhaps the capital fact of this history), I want to recall certain axioms.

The first: The Library exists *ab aeterno.* No reasonable mind can doubt this truth, whose immediate corollary is the future eternity of the world. Man, the imperfect librarian may be the work of chance or of malevolent demiurges; the universe, with its elegant endowment of shelves, of enigmatic volumes, of indefatigable ladders for the voyager, and of privies for the seated librarian, can only be the work of a god. In order to perceive the distance which exists between the divine and the human, it is enough to compare the rude tremulous symbols which my fallible hand scribbles on the end pages of a book with the organic letters inside: exact, delicate, intensely black, inimitably symmetric.

The second: *The number of orthographic symbols is twenty-five.*[1] This bit of evidence permitted the formulation, three hundred years ago, of a general theory of the Library and the satisfactory resolution of the problem which no conjecture had yet made clear: the formless and chaotic nature of almost all books. One of these books, which my father saw in a hexagon of the circuit number fifteen ninety-four, was composed of the letters MCV perversely repeated from the first line to the last. Another, very much consulted in this zone, is a mere labyrinth of letters, but on the next-to-the-last page, one may read *O Time your pyramids.* As is well known: for one reasonable line or one straightforward note there are leagues of insensate cacaphony, of verbal farragoes and incoherencies. (I know of a wild region whose librarians repudiate the vain superstitious custom of seeking any sense in books and compare it to looking for meaning in dreams or in the chaotic lines of one's hands. ... They admit that the inventors of writing imitated the twenty-five natural symbols, but they maintain that this application is accidental and that books in themselves mean nothing. This opinion—we shall see—is not altogether false.) For a long time it was believed that these impenetrable books belonged to past or remote languages. It is true that the most ancient men, the first librarians, made use of a language quite different from the one we speak today; it is true that some miles to the right the language is dialectical and that ninety stories up it is incomprehensible. All this, 1 repeat, is true; but four hundred and ten pages of unvarying MCVs do not correspond to any language, however dialectical or rudimentary it might be. Some librarians insinuated that each letter could influence the next, and that the value of MCV on the third line of page 71 was not the same as that of the same series in another position on another page; but this vague thesis did not prosper. Still other men thought in terms of cryptographs; this conjecture has come to be universally accepted, though not in the sense in which it was formulated by its inventors.

[1] The original manuscript of the present note does not contain digits or capital letters. The punctuation is limited to the comma and the period. These two signs, plus the space sign and the twenty-two letters of the alphabet, make up the twenty-five sufficient symbols enumerated by the unknown author.

Five hundred years ago, the chief of an upper hexagon[2] came upon a book as confusing as all the rest but which contained nearly two pages of homogenous lines. He showed his find to an ambulant decipherer, who told him the lines were written in Portuguese. Others told him they were in Yiddish. In less than a century the nature of the language was finally established: it was a Samoyed-Lithuanian dialect of Guarany with classical Arabic inflections. The contents were also deciphered: notions of combinational analysis, illustrated by examples of variations with unlimited repetition. These examples made it possible for a librarian of genius to discover the fundamental law of the Library. This thinker observed that all the books, however diverse, are made up of uniform elements: the period, the comma, the space, the twenty-two letters of the alphabet. He also adduced a circumstance confirmed by all travelers: *There are not, in the whole vast Library, two identical books.* From all these incontrovertible premises he deduced that the Library is total and that its shelves contain all the possible combinations of the twenty-odd orthographic symbols (whose number, though vast, is not infinite); that is, everything which can be expressed, in all languages. Everything is there: the minute history of the future, the autobiographies of the archangels, the faithful catalogue of the Library, thousands and thousands of false catalogues, a demonstration of the fallacy of these catalogues, a demonstration of the fallacy of the true catalogue, the Gnostic gospel of Basilides, the commentary on this gospel, the commentary on the commentary of this gospel, the veridical account of your death, a version of each book in all languages, the interpolations of every book in all books.

When it was proclaimed that the Library comprised all books, the first impression was one of extravagant joy. All men felt themselves lords of a secret, intact treasure. There was no personal or universal problem whose eloquent solution did not exist—in some hexagon. The universe was justified, the universe suddenly expanded to the limitless dimensions of hope. At that time there was much talk of the Vindications: books of apology and prophecy, which vindicated for all time the actions of every man in the world and established a store of prodigious arcana for the future. Thousands of covetous persons abandoned their dear natal hexagons and crowded up the stairs, urged on by the vain aim of finding their Vindication. These pilgrims disputed in the narrow corridors, hurled dark maledictions, strangled each other on the divine stairways, flung the deceitful books to the bottom of the tunnels, and died as they were thrown into space by men from remote regions. Some went mad.... The Vindications do exist. I have myself seen two of these books, which were concerned with future people, people who were perhaps not imaginary. But the searchers did not remember that the calculable possibility of a man's finding his own book, or some perfidious variation of his own book, is close to zero.

The clarification of the basic mysteries of humanity—the origin of the Library and of time—was also expected. It is credible that those grave mysteries can be explained in words: if the language of the philosophers does not suffice, the multiform Library will have produced the unexpected language required and the necessary vocabularies and grammars for this language.

It is now four centuries since men have been wearying the hexagons....

There are official searchers, *inquisitors.* I have observed them carrying out their functions: they are always exhausted. They speak of a staircase without steps where they were almost killed. They speak of

[2] Formerly, for each three hexagons there was one man. Suicide and pulmonary diseases have destroyed this proportion. My memory recalls scenes of unspeakable melancholy: there have been many nights when I have ventured down corridors and polished staircases without encountering a single librarian.

galleries and stairs with the local librarian. From time to time they will pick up the nearest book and leaf through its pages, in search of infamous words. Obviously, no one expects to discover anything.

The uncommon hope was followed, naturally enough, by deep depression. The certainty that some shelf in some hexagon contained precious books and that these books were inaccessible seemed almost intolerable. A blasphemous sect suggested that all searches be given up and that men everywhere shuffle letters and symbols until they succeeded in composing, by means of an improbable stroke of luck, the canonical books. The authorities found themselves obliged to issue severe orders. The sect disappeared, but in my childhood I still saw old men who would hide out in the privies for long periods of time, and, with metal disks in a forbidden dicebox, feebly mimic the divine disorder.

Other men, inversely, thought that the primary task was to eliminate useless works. They would invade the hexagons, exhibiting credentials which were not always false, skim through a volume with annoyance, and then condemn entire bookshelves to destruction: their ascetic, hygenic fury is responsible for the senseless loss of millions of books. Their name is execrated; but those who mourn the "treasures" destroyed by this frenzy, overlook two notorious facts. One: the Library is so enormous that any reduction undertaken by humans is infinitesimal. Two: each book is unique, irreplaceable, but (inasmuch as the Library is total) there are always several hundreds of thousands of imperfect facsimiles—of works which differ only by one letter or one comma. Contrary to public opinion, I dare suppose that the consequences of the depredations committed by the Purifiers have been exaggerated by the horror which these fanatics provoked. They were spurred by the delirium of storming the books in the Crimson Hexagon: books of a smaller than ordinary format, omnipotent, illustrated, magical.

We know, too, of another superstition of that time: the Man of the Book. In some shelf of some hexagon, men reasoned, there must exist a book which is the cipher and perfect compendium of *all the rest:* some librarian has perused it, and it is analogous to a god. Vestiges of the worship of that remote functionary still persist in the language of this zone. Many pilgrimages have sought Him out. For a century they trod the most diverse routes in vain, How to locate the secret hexagon which harbored it? Someone proposed a regressive approach: in order to locate book A, first consult book B which will indicate the location of A; in order to locate book B, first consult book C, and so on ad infinitum. …

I have squandered and consumed my years in adventures of this type. To me, it does not seem unlikely that on some shelf of the universe there lies a total book.[3] I pray the unknown gods that some man—even if only one man, and though it have been thousands of years ago!—may have examined and read it. If honor and wisdom and happiness are not for me, let them be for others. May heaven exist, though my place be in hell. Let me be outraged and annihilated, but may Thy enormous Library be justified, for one instant, in one being.

The impious assert that absurdities are the norm in the Library and that anything reasonable (even humble and pure coherence) is an almost miraculous exception. They speak (I know) of "the febrile Library, whose hazardous volumes run the constant risk of being changed into others and in which everything is affirmed, denied, and confused as by a divinity in delirium." These words, which not only denounce disorder but exemplify it as well, manifestly demonstrate the bad taste of the speakers and

[3] I repeat: it is enough that a book be possible for it to exist. Only the impossible is excluded. For example: no book is also a stairway, though doubtless there are books that discuss and deny and demonstrate this possibility and others whose structure corresponds to that of a stairway.

their desperate ignorance. Actually, the Library includes all verbal structures, all the variations allowed by the twenty-five orthographic symbols, but it does not permit of one absolute absurdity. It is pointless to observe that the best book in the numerous hexagons under my administration is entitled *Combed Clap of Thunder;* or that another is called *The Plaster Cramp;* and still another *Axaxaxas Mlö.* Such propositions as are contained in these titles, at first sight incoherent, doubtless yield a cryptographic or allegorical justification. Since they are verbal, these justifications already figure, *ex hypothesi* in the Library. I can not combine certain letters, as *dhcmrlchtdj,* which the divine Library has not already foreseen in combination, and which in one of its secret languages does not encompass some terrible meaning. No one can articulate a syllable which is not full of tenderness and fear, and which is not, in one of those languages, the powerful name of some god. To speak is to fall into tautologies. This useless and wordy epistle itself already exists in one of the thirty volumes of the five shelves in one of the uncountable hexagons—and so does its refutation. (An *n* number of possible languages makes use of the same vocabulary; in some of them, the symbol *library* admits of the correct definition *ubiquitous and everlasting system of hexagonal galleries* but *library* is *bread* or *pyramid* or anything else, and the seven words which define it possess another value. You who read me, are you sure you understand my language?)

Methodical writing distracts me from the present condition of men. But the certainty that everything has been already written nullifies or makes phantoms of us all. I know of districts where the youth prostrate themselves before books and barbarously kiss the pages, though they do not know how to make out a single letter. Epidemics, heretical disagreements, the pilgrimages which inevitably degenerate into banditry, have decimated the population. I believe I have mentioned the suicides, more frequent each year. Perhaps I am deceived by old age and fear, but I suspect that the human species—the unique human species—is on the road to extinction, while the Library will last on forever: illuminated, solitary, infinite, perfectly immovable, filled with precious volumes, useless, incorruptible, secret.

Infinite I have just written. I have not interpolated this adjective merely from rhetorical habit. It is not illogical, I say, to think that the world is infinite. Those who judge it to be limited, postulate that in remote places the corridors and stairs and hexagons could inconceivably cease—a manifest absurdity. Those who imagined it to be limitless forget that the possible number of books is limited. I dare insinuate the following solution to this ancient problem: *The Library is limitless and periodic.* If an eternal voyager were to traverse it in any direction, he would find, after many centuries, that the same volumes are repeated in the same disorder (which, thus repeated, would be an order: the Order). My solitude is gladdened by this elegant hope.[4]

[4] Letizia Álvarez de Toledo has observed that this vast Library is useless: rigorously speaking, a single volume would be sufficient, a volume of ordinary format, printed in nine or ten point type, containing an infinite number if infinitely thin leaves. (In the early seventeenth century, Cavalieri said that all solid bodies are the superimposition of an infinite number of planes.) The handling of this silky *vade mecum* would not be convenient: each apparent page would unfold into other analogous ones; the inconceivable middle page would have no reverse.

The Garden of Forking Paths

By Jorge Luis Borges

To Victoria Ocampo

In his *A History of the World War* (page 212), Captain Liddell Hart reports that a planned offensive by thirteen British divisions, supported by fourteen hundred artillery pieces, against the German line at Serre-Montauban, scheduled for July 24, 1916, had to be postponed* until the morning of the 29th, He comments that torrential rain caused this delay—which lacked any special significance. The following deposition, dictated by, read over, and then signed by Dr. Yu Tsun, former teacher of English at the Tsingtao *Hochschule,* casts unsuspected light upon this event. The first two pages are missing.

* * *

... and I hung up the phone. Immediately I recollected the voice that had spoken in German. It was that of Captain Richard Madden. Madden, in Viktor Runeberg's office, meant the end of all our work and—though this seemed a secondary matter, *or should have seemed so to me*—of our lives also. His being there meant that Runeberg had been arrested or murdered.[1] Before the sun set on this same day, I ran the same risk. Madden was implacable. Rather, to be more accurate, he was obliged to be implacable. An Irishman in the service of England, a man suspected of equivocal feelings if not of actual treachery, how could he fail to welcome and seize upon this extraordinary piece of luck: the discovery, capture and perhaps the deaths of two agents of Imperial Germany?

I went up to my bedroom. Absurd though the gesture was, I closed and locked the door. I threw myself down on my narrow iron bed, and waited on my back. The never changing rooftops filled the

[1] A malicious and outlandish statement. In point of fact, Captain Richard Madden had been attacked by the Prussian spy Hans Rabener, alias Viktor Runeberg, who drew an automatic pistol when Madden appeared with orders for the spy's arrest. Madden, in self defense, had inflicted wounds of which the spy later died.—*Note by the manuscript editor.*

window, and the hazy six o'clock sun hung in the sky. It seemed incredible that this day, a day without warnings or omens, might be that of my implacable death. In despite of my dead father, in despite of having been a child in one of the symmetrical gardens of Hai Feng, was I to die now?

Then I reflected that all things happen, happen to one, precisely *now*. Century follows century, and things happen only in the present. There are countless men in the air, on land and at sea, and all that really happens happens to me. … The almost unbearable memory of Madden's long horseface put an end to these wandering thoughts.

In the midst of my hatred and terror (now that it no longer matters to me to speak of terror, now that I have outwitted Richard Madden, now that my neck hankers for the hangman's noose), I knew that the fast-moving and doubtless happy soldier did not suspect that I possessed the Secret—the name of the exact site of the new British artillery park on the Ancre. A bird streaked across the misty sky and, absently, I turned it into an airplane and then that airplane into many in the skies of France, shattering the artillery park under a rain of bombs. If only my mouth, before it should be silenced by a bullet, could shout this name in such a way that it could be heard in Germany. … My voice, my human voice, was weak. How could it reach the ear of the Chief? The ear of that sick and hateful man who knew nothing of Runeberg or of me except that we were in Staffordshire. A man who, sitting in his arid Berlin office, leafed infinitely through newspapers, looking in vain for news from us, I said aloud, "I must flee."

I sat up on the bed, in senseless and perfect silence, as if Madden was already peering at me. Something—perhaps merely a desire to prove my total penury to myself—made me empty out my pockets. I found just what I knew I was going to find. The American watch, the nickel-plated chain and the square coin, the key ring with the useless but compromising keys to Runeberg's office, the notebook, a letter which I decided to destroy at once (and which I did not destroy), a five shilling piece, two single shillings and some pennies, a red and blue pencil, a handkerchief—and a revolver with a single bullet. Absurdly I held it and weighed it in my hand, to give myself courage. Vaguely I thought that a pistol shot can be heard for a great distance.

In ten minutes I had developed my plan. The telephone directory gave me the name of the one person capable of passing on the information. He lived in a suburb of Fenton, less than half an hour away by train.

I am a timorous man. I can say it now, now that I have brought my incredibly risky plan to an end. It was not easy to bring about, and I know that its execution was terrible. I did not do it for Germany—no! Such a barbarous country is of no importance to me, particularly since it had degraded me by making me become a spy. Furthermore, I knew an Englishman—a modest man—who, for me, is as great as Goethe. I did not speak with him for more than an hour, but during that time, he *was* Goethe.

I carried out my plan because I felt the Chief had some fear of those of my race, of those uncountable forebears whose culmination lies in me. I wished to prove to him that a yellow man could save his armies. Besides, I had to escape the Captain. His hands and voice could, at any moment, knock and beckon at my door.

racial element

Silently, I dressed, took leave of myself in the mirror, went down the stairs, sneaked a look at the quiet street, and went out. The station was not far from my house, but I thought it more prudent to take a cab. I told myself that I thus ran less chance of being recognized. The truth is that, in the deserted street, I felt infinitely visible and vulnerable. I recall that I told the driver to stop short of the main entrance. I got out with a painful and deliberate slowness.

I was going to the village of Ashgrove, but took a ticket for a station further on. The train would leave in a few minutes, at eight-fifty. I hurried, for the next would not go until half past nine. There was almost no one on the platform. I walked through the carriages. I remember some farmers, a woman dressed in mourning, a youth deep in Tacitus' *Annals* and a wounded, happy soldier.

At last the train pulled out. A man I recognized ran furiously, but vainly, the length of the platform. It was Captain Richard Madden. Shattered, trembling, I huddled in the distant corner of the seat, as far as possible from the fearful window.

From utter terror I passed into a state of almost abject happiness. I told myself that the duel had already started and that I had won the first encounter by besting my adversary in his first attack—even if it was only for forty minutes—by an accident of fate. I argued that so small a victory prefigured a total victory. I argued that it was not so trivial, that were it not for the precious accident of the train schedule, I would be in prison or dead. I argued, with no less sophism, that my timorous happiness was proof that I was man enough to bring this adventure to a successful conclusion. From my weakness I drew strength that never left me.

I foresee that man will resign himself each day to new abominations, that soon only soldiers and bandits will be left. To them I offer this advice: *Whosoever would undertake some atrocious enterprise should act as if it were already accomplished, should impose upon himself a future as irrevocable as the past.*

Thus I proceeded, while the eyes of a man already dead, I contemplated the fluctuations of the day that would probably be my last, and watched the diffuse coming of night.

The train crept along gently, amid as trees. It slowed down and stopped, almost in the middle of a field. No one called the name of a station. "Ashgrove?" I asked some children on the platform. "Ashgrove," they replied. I got out.

A lamp lit the platform, but the children's faces remained in a shadow. One of them asked me: "Are you going to Dr. Stephen Albert's house?" Without waiting for my answer, another said: "The house is a good distance away but you won't get lost if you take the road to the left and bear to the left at every crossroad." I threw them a coin (my last), went down some stone steps and started along a deserted road. At a slight incline, the road ran downhill. It was a plain dirt way, and overhead the branches of trees intermingled, while a round moon hung low in the sky as if to keep me company.

For a moment I thought that Richard Madden might in some way have divined my desperate intent. At once I realized that this would be impossible. The advice about turning always to the left reminded me that such was the common formula for finding the central courtyard of certain labyrinths. I know something about labyrinths. Not for nothing am I the great-grandson of Ts'ui Pên. He was Governor of Yunnan and gave up temporal power to write a novel with more characters than there are in *Hung Lou Mêng*, and to create a maze in which all men would lose themselves. He spent thirteen years on these oddly assorted tasks before he was assassinated by a stranger. His novel had no sense to it and nobody ever found his labyrinth.

Under the trees of England I meditated on this lost and perhaps mythical labyrinth. I imagined it untouched and perfect on the secret summit of some mountain; I imagined it drowned under rice paddies or beneath the sea; I imagined it infinite, made not only of eight-sided pavilions and of twisting paths but also of rivers, provinces and kingdoms. … I thought of a maze of mazes, of a sinuous, ever growing maze which would take in both past and future and would somehow involve the stars.

Lost in these imaginary illusions I forgot my destiny—that of the hunted. For an undetermined period of time I felt myself cut off from the world, an abstract spectator. The hazy and murmuring countryside, the moon, the decline of the evening, stirred within me. Going down the gently sloping road I could not feel fatigue. The evening was at once intimate and infinite.

The road kept descending and branching off, through meadows misty in the twilight. A high-pitched and almost syllabic music kept coming and going, moving with the breeze, blurred by the leaves and by distance.

I thought that a man might be an enemy of other men, of the differing moments of other men, but never an enemy of a country: not of fireflies, words, gardens, streams, or the West wind.

Meditating thus I arrived at a high, rusty iron gate. Through the railings I could see an avenue bordered with poplar trees and also a kind of summer house or pavilion. Two things dawned on me at once, the first trivial and the second almost incredible: the music came from the pavilion and that music was Chinese. That was why I had accepted it fully, without paying it any attention. I do not remember whether there was a bell, a push-button, or whether 1 attracted attention by clapping my hands. The stuttering sparks of the music kept on.

But from the end of the avenue, from the main house, a lantern approached; a lantern which alternately, from moment to moment, was crisscrossed or put out by the trunks of the trees; a paper lantern shaped like a drum and colored like the moon. A tall man carried it. I could not see his face for the light blinded me.

He opened the gate and spoke slowly in my language.

"I see that the worthy Hsi P'eng has troubled himself to see to relieving my solitude. No doubt you want to see the garden?"

Recognizing the name of one of our consuls, I replied, somewhat taken aback.

"The garden?"

"The garden of forking paths."

Something stirred in my memory and I said, with incomprehensible assurance:

"The garden of my ancestor, Ts'ui Pên."

"Your ancestor? Your illustrious ancestor? Come in."

The damp path zigzagged like those of my childhood. When we reached the house we went into a library filled with books from both East and West. I recognized some large volumes bound in yellow silk—manuscripts of the Lost Encyclopedia which was edited by the Third Emperor of the Luminous Dynasty. They had never been printed. A phonograph record was spinning near a bronze phoenix. I remember also a rose-glazed jar and yet another, older by many centuries, of that blue color which our potters copied from the Persians. ...

Stephen Albert was watching me with a smile on his face. He was, as I have said, remarkably tall. His face was deeply lined and he had gray eyes and a gray beard. There was about him something of the priest, and something of the sailor. Later, he told me he had been a missionary in Tientsin before he "had aspired to become a Sinologist."

We sat down, I upon a large, low divan, he with his back to the window and to a large circular clock. I calculated that my pursuer, Richard Madden, could not arrive in less than an hour. My irrevocable decision could wait.

"A strange destiny," said Stephen Albert, "that of Ts'ui Pên—Governor of his native province, learned in astronomy, in astrology and tireless in the interpretation of the canonical books, a chess player, a famous poet and a calligrapher. Yet he abandoned all to make a book and a labyrinth. He gave up all the pleasures of oppression, justice, of a well-stocked bed, of banquets, and even of erudition, and shut himself up in the Pavilion of the Limpid Sun for thirteen years. At his death, his heirs found only a mess of manuscripts. The family, as you doubtless know, wished to consign them to the fire, but the executor of the estate—a Taoist or a Buddhist monk—insisted on their publication."

"Those of the blood of Ts'ui Pên," I replied, "still curse the memory of that monk. Such a publication was madness. The book is a shapeless mass of contradictory rough drafts. I examined it once upon a time: the hero dies in the third chapter, while in the fourth he is alive. As for that other enterprise of Ts'ui Pên … his Labyrinth. …"

"Here is the Labyrinth," Albert said, pointing to a tall, lacquered writing cabinet.

"An ivory labyrinth?" I exclaimed. "A tiny labyrinth indeed … !"

"A symbolic labyrinth," he corrected me. "An invisible labyrinth of time. I, a barbarous Englishman, have been given the key to this transparent mystery. After more than a hundred years most of the details are irrecoverable, lost beyond all recall, but it isn't hard to image what must have happened. At one time, Ts'ui Pên must have said; 'I am going into seclusion to write a book,' and at another, 'I am retiring to construct a maze.' Everyone assumed these were separate activities. No one realized that the book and the labyrinth were one and the same. The Pavillion of the Limpid Sun was set in the middle of an intricate garden. This may have suggested the idea of a physical maze.

"Ts'ui Pên died. In all the vast lands which once belonged to your family, no one could find the labyrinth. The novel's confusion suggested that *it* was the labyrinth. Two circumstances showed me the direct solution to the problem. First, the curious legend that Ts'ui Pên had proposed to create an infinite maze, second, a fragment of a letter which I discovered."

Albert rose. For a few moments he turned his back to me. He opened the top drawer in the high black and gilded writing cabinet. He returned holding in his hand a piece of paper which had once been crimson but which had faded with the passage of time: it was rose colored, tenuous, quadrangular. Ts'ui Pên's calligraphy was justly famous. Eagerly, but without understanding, I read the words which a man of my own blood had written with a small brush: "I leave to various future times, but not to all, my garden of forking paths."

I handed back the sheet of paper in silence. Albert went on:

"Before I discovered this letter, I kept asking myself how a book could be infinite. I could not imagine any other than a cyclic volume, circular. A volume whose last page would be the same as the first and so have the possibility of continuing indefinitely. I recalled, too, the night in the middle of *The Thousand and One Nights* when Queen Scheherezade, through a magical mistake on the part of her copyist, started to tell the story of *The Thousand and One Nights,* with the risk of again arriving at the night upon which she will relate it, and thus on to infinity. I also imagined a Platonic hereditary work, passed on from father to son, to which each individual would add a new chapter or correct, with pious care, the work of his elders.

"These conjectures gave me amusement, but none seemed to have the remotest application to the contradictory chapters of Ts'ui Pên. At this point, I was sent from Oxford the manuscript you have just seen.

"Naturally, my attention was caught by the sentence, 'I leave to various future times, but not to all, my garden of forking paths.' I had no sooner read this, than I understood. *The Garden of Forking Paths* was the chaotic novel itself. The phrase 'to various future times, but not to all' suggested the image of bifurcating in time, not in space. Rereading the whole work confirmed this theory. In all fiction, when a man is faced with alternatives he chooses one at the expense of the others. In the almost unfathomable Ts'ui Pên, he chooses—simultaneously—all of them. He thus *creates* various futures, various times which start others that will in their turn branch out and bifurcate in other times. This is the cause of the contradictions in the novel.

"Fang, let us say, has a secret. A stranger knocks at his door. Fang makes up his mind to kill him. Naturally there are various possible outcomes. Fang can kill the intruder, the intruder can kill Fang, both can be saved, both can die and so on and so on. In Ts'ui Pên's work, all the possible solutions occur, each one being the point of departure for other bifurcations. Sometimes the pathways of this labyrinth converge. For example, you come to this house; but in other possible pasts you are my enemy; in others my friend.

"If you will put up with my atrocious pronunciation, I would like to read you a few pages of your ancestor's work."

His countenance, in the bright circle of lamplight, was certainly that of an ancient, but it shone with something unyielding, even immortal.

With slow precision, he read two versions of the same epic chapter. In the first, an army marches into battle over a desolate mountain pass. The bleak and somber aspect of the rocky landscape made the soldiers feel that life itself was of little value, and so they won the battle easily. In the second, the same army passes through a palace where a banquet is in progress. The splendor of the feast remained a memory throughout the glorious battle, and so victory followed.

With proper veneration I listened to these old tales, although perhaps with less admiration for them in themselves than for the fact that they had been thought out by one of my own blood, and that a man of a distant empire had given them back to me, in the last stage of a desperate adventure, on a Western island. I remember the final words, repeated at the end of each version like a secret command: "Thus the heroes fought, with tranquil heart and bloody sword. They were resigned to killing and to dying."

At that moment I felt within me and around me something invisible and intangible pullulating. It was not the pullulation of two divergent, parallel, and finally converging armies, but an agitation more inaccessible, more intimate, prefigured by them in some way. Stephen Albert continued:

"I do not think that your illustrious ancestor toyed idly with variations. I do not find it believable that he would waste thirteen years laboring over a never, ending experiment in, rhetoric. In your country the novel is an inferior genre; in Ts'ui Pên's period, it was a despised one. Ts'ui Pên was a fine novelist but he was also a man of letters who, doubtless, considered himself more than a mere novelist. The testimony of his contemporaries attests to this, and certainly the known facts of his life confirm his leanings toward the metaphysical and the mystical. Philosophical conjectures take up the greater part of his novel. I know that of all problems, none disquieted him more, and none concerned him more than the profound one of time. Now then, this is the *only* problem that does not figure in the pages of *The Garden.* He does not even use the word which means *time.* How can these voluntary omissions be explained?"

I proposed various solutions, all of them inadequate. We discussed them. Finally Stephen Albert said: "In a guessing game to which the answer is chess, which word is the only one prohibited?" I thought for a moment and then replied:

"The word is *chess.*"

"Precisely," said Albert. "*The Garden of Forking Paths* is an enormous guessing game, or parable,in which the subject is time. The rules of the game forbid the use of the word itself. To eliminate a word completely, to refer to it by means of inept phrases and obvious paraphrases, is perhaps the best way of drawing attention to it. This, then, is the tortuous method of approach preferred by the oblique Ts'ui Pên in every meandering of his interminable novel. I have gone over hundreds of manuscripts, I have corrected errors introduced by careless copyists, I have worked out the plan from this chaos, I have restored, or believe I have restored, the original. I have translated the whole work. I can state categorically that not once has the word *time* been used in the whole book.

"The explanation is obvious. *The Garden of Forking Paths* is a picture, incomplete yet not false, of the universe such as Ts'ui Pên conceived it to be. Differing from Newton and Schopenhauer, your ancestor did not think of time as absolute and uniform. He believed in an infinite series of times, in a dizzily growing, ever spreading network of diverging, converging and parallel times. This web of time—the strands of which approach one another, bifurcate, intersect or ignore each other through the centuries—embraces *every* possibility. We do not exist in most of them. In some you exist and not I, while in others I do, and you do not, and in yet others both of us exist. In this one, in which chance has favored me, you have come to my gate. In another, you, crossing the garden, have found me dead. In yet another, I say these very same words, but am an error, a phantom."

"In all of them," I enunciated, with a tremor in my voice. "I deeply appreciate and am grateful to you for the restoration of Ts'ui Pên's garden."

"Not in *all*" he murmured with a smile. "Time is forever dividing itself toward innumerable futures and in one of them I am your enemy."

Once again I sensed the pullulation of which I have already spoken. It seemed to me that the dew-damp garden surrounding the house was infinitely saturated with invisible people. All were Albert and myself, secretive, busy and multiform in other dimensions of time. I lifted my eyes and the short nightmare disappeared. In the black and yellow garden there was only a single man, but this man was as strong as a statue and this man was walking up the path and he was Captain Richard Madden.

"The future exists now," "I replied. "But I am your friend. Can I take another look at the letter?"

Albert rose from his seat. He stood up tall as he opened the top drawer of the high writing cabinet. For a moment his back was again turned to me. I had the revolver ready. I fired with the utmost care: Albert fell without a murmur, at once. I swear that his death was instantaneous, as if he had been struck by lightning.

What remains is unreal and unimportant. Madden broke in and arrested me. I have been condemned to hang. Abominably, I have yet triumphed! The secret name of the city to be attacked got through to Berlin. Yesterday it was bombed. I read the news in the same English newspapers which were trying to solve the riddle of the murder of the learned Sinologist Stephen Albert by the unknown Yu Tsun. The Chief, however, had already solved this mystery. He knew that my problem was to shout, with my feeble voice, above the tumult of war, the name of the city called Albert, and that I had no other course open to me than to kill someone of that name. He does not know, for no one can, of my infinite penitence and sickness of the heart.

—*Translated by* Helen Temple *and* Ruthven Todd

A Very Old Man with Enormous Wings

By Gabriel García Márquez

On the third day of rain they had killed so many crabs inside the house that Pelayo had to cross his drenched courtyard and throw them into the sea, because the newborn child had a temperature all night and they thought it was due to the stench. The world had been sad since Tuesday. Sea and sky were a single ash-gray thing and the sands of the beach, which on March nights glimmered like powdered light, had become a stew of mud and rotten shellfish. The light was so weak at noon that when Pelayo was coming back to the house after throwing away the crabs, it was hard for him to see what it was that was moving and groaning in the rear of the courtyard. He had to go very close to see that it was an old man, a very old man, lying face down in the mud, who, in spite of his tremendous efforts, couldn't get up, impeded by his enormous wings.

Frightened by that nightmare, Pelayo ran to get Elisenda, his wife, who was putting compresses on the sick child, and he took her to the rear of the courtyard. They both looked at the fallen body with mute stupor. He was dressed like a ragpicker. There were only a few faded hairs left on his bald skull and very few teeth in his mouth, and his pitiful condition of a drenched great-grandfather had taken away any sense of grandeur he might have had. His huge buzzard wings, dirty and half-plucked, were forever entangled in the mud. They looked at him so long and so closely that Pelayo and Elisenda very soon overcame their surprise and in the end found him familiar. Then they dared speak to him, and he answered in an incomprehensible dialect with a strong sailor's voice. That was how they skipped over the inconvenience of the wings and quite intelligently concluded that he was a lonely castaway from some foreign ship wrecked by the storm. And yet, they called in a neighbor woman who knew everything about life and death to see him, and all she needed was one look to show them their mistake.

"He's an angel," she told them. "He must have been coming for the child, but the poor fellow is so old that the rain knocked him down."

On the following day everyone knew that a flesh-and-blood angel was held captive in Pelayo's house. Against the judgment of the wise neighbor woman, for whom angels in those times were the fugitive survivors of a celestial conspiracy, they did not have the heart to club him to death. Pelayo watched over him all afternoon from the kitchen, armed with his bailiffs club, and before going to bed he dragged him out of the mud and locked him up with the hens in the wire chicken coop. In the middle of the night, when the rain stopped, Pelayo and Elisenda were still killing crabs. A short time afterward the child woke up without a fever and with a desire to eat. Then they felt magnanimous and decided to put the angel on a raft with fresh water and provisions for three days and leave him to his fate on the high seas. But when they went out into the courtyard with the first light of dawn, they found the whole neighborhood in front of the chicken coop having fun with the angel, without the slightest reverence, tossing him things to eat through the openings in the wire as if he weren't a supernatural creature but a circus animal.

Father Gonzaga arrived before seven o'clock, alarmed at the strange news. By that time onlookers less frivolous than those at dawn had already arrived and they were making all kinds of conjectures concerning the captive's future. The simplest among them thought that he should be named mayor of the world. Others of sterner mind felt that he should be promoted to the rank of five-star general in order to win all wars. Some visionaries hoped that he could be put to stud in order to implant on earth a race of winged wise men who could take charge of the universe. But Father Gonzaga, before becoming a priest, had been a robust woodcutter. Standing by the wife, he reviewed his catechism in an instant and asked them to open the door so that he could take a close look at that pitiful man who looked more like a huge decrepit hen among the fascinated chickens. He was lying in a corner drying his open wings in the sunlight among the fruit peels and breakfast left overs that the early risers had thrown him. Alien to the impertinences of the world, he only lifted his antiquarian eyes and murmured something in his dialect when Father Gonzaga went into the chicken coop and said good morning to him in Latin. The parish priest had his first suspicion of an when he saw that he did not understand the language of God or know how to greet His ministers. Then he noticed that seen close up he was much too human: he had an unbearable smell of the outdoors, the back side of his wings was strewn with parasites and his main feathers had been mistreated by terrestrial winds, and nothing about him measured up to the proud dignity of angels. Then he came out of the chicken coop and in a brief sermon warned the curious against the risks of being ingenuous. He reminded them that the devil had the bad habit of making use of carnival tricks in order to confuse the unwary. He argued that if wings were not the essential element in determining the difference between a hawk and an airplane, they were even less so in the recognition of angels. Nevertheless, he promised to write a letter to his bishop so that the latter would write to his primate so that the latter would write to the Supreme Pontiff in order to get the final verdict from the highest courts.

His prudence fell on sterile hearts. The news of the captive angel spread with such rapidity that after a few hours the courtyard had the bustle of a marketplace and they had to call in troops with fixed bayonets to disperse the mob that was about to knock the house down. Elisenda, her spine all twisted from sweeping up so much marketplace trash, then got the idea of fencing in the yard and charging five cents admission to see the angel.

The curious came from far away. A traveling carnival arrived with a flying acrobat who buzzed over the crowd several times, but no one paid any attention to him because his wings were not those of an angel but, rather, those of a sidereal bat. The most unfortunate invalids on earth came in search of health: a poor woman who since childhood had been counting her heartbeats and had run out of numbers; a

Portuguese man who couldn't sleep because the noise of the stars disturbed him; a sleepwalker who got up at night to undo the things he had done while awake; and many others with less serious ailments. In the midst of that shipwreck disorder that made the earth tremble, Pelayo and Elisenda were happy with fatigue, for in less than a week they had crammed their rooms with money and the line of pilgrims waiting their turn to enter still reached beyond the horizon.

The angel was the only one who took no part in his own act. He spent his time trying to get comfortable in his borrowed nest, befuddled by the hellish heat of the oil lamps and sacramental candles that had been placed along the wire. At first they tried to make him eat some mothballs, which, according to the wisdom of the wise neighbor woman, were the food prescribed for angels. But he turned them down, just as he turned down the papal lunches that the penitents brought him, and they never found out whether it was because he was an angel or because he was an old man that in the end he ate nothing but eggplant mush. His only supernatural virtue seemed to be patience. Especially during the first days, when the hens pecked at him, searching for the stellar parasites that proliferated in his wings, and the cripples pulled out feathers to touch their defective parts with, and even the most merciful threw stones at him, trying to get him to rise so they could see him standing. The only time they succeeded in arousing him was when they burned his side with an iron for branding steers, for he had been motionless for so many hours that they thought he was dead. He awoke with a start, ranting in his hermetic language and with tears in his eyes, and he flapped his wings a couple of times, which brought on a whirlwind of chicken dung and lunar dust and a gale of panic that did not seem to be of this world. Although many thought that his reaction had been one not of rage but of pain, from then on they were careful not to annoy him, because the majority understood that his passivity was not that of a hero taking his ease but that of a cataclysm in repose.

Father Gonzaga held back the crowd's frivolity with formulas of maidservant inspiration while awaiting the arrival of a final judgment on the nature of the captive But the mail from Rome showed no sense of urgency. They spent their time finding out if the prisoner had a navel, if his dialect had any connection with Aramaic, how many times he could fit on the head of a pin, or whether he wasn't just a Norwegian with wings. Those meager letters might have come and gone until the end of time if a providential event had not put an end to the priest's tribulations.

It so happened that during those days, among so many other carnival attractions, there arrived in town the traveling show of the woman who had been changed into a spider for having disobeyed her parents. The admission to see her was not only less than the admission to see the angel, but people were permitted to ask her all manner of questions about her absurd state and to examine her up and down so that no one would ever doubt the truth of her horror. She was a frightful tarantula the size of a ram and with the head of a sad maiden. What was most heartrending, however, was not her outlandish shape but the sincere affliction with which she recounted the details of her misfortune. While still practically a child she had sneaked out of her parents' house to go to a dance, and while she was coming back through the woods after having danced all night without permission, a fearful thunderclap rent the sky in two and through the crack came the lightning bolt of brimstone that changed her into a spider. Her only nourishment came from the meatballs that charitable souls chose to toss into her mouth. A spectacle like that, full of so much human truth and with such a fearful lesson, was bound to defeat without even trying that of a haughty angel who scarcely deigned to look at mortals. Besides, the few miracles attributed to the angel showed a certain mental disorder, like the blind man who didn't recover his sight but grew three new teeth, or the paralytic who didn't get to walk but almost won the lottery, and the leper whose sores sprouted sunflowers. Those consolation miracles, which were more like mocking fun, had already ruined the angel's reputation when the woman who had been changed into a spider finally crushed him completely. That was how Father Gonzaga was cured forever of his insomnia and Pelayo's courtyard went back to being as empty as during the time it had rained for three days and crabs walked through the bedrooms.

The owners of the house had no reason to lament. With the money they saved they built a two-story mansion with balconies and gardens and high netting so that crabs wouldn't get in during the winter, and with iron bars on the windows so that angels wouldn't get in. Pelayo also set up a rabbit warren close to town and gave up his job as bailiff for good, and Elisenda bought some satin pumps with high heels and many dresses of iridescent silk, the kind worn on Sunday by the most desirable women in those times. The chicken coop was the only thing that didn't receive any attention. If they washed it down with creolin and burned tears of myrrh inside it every so often, it was not in homage to the angel but to drive away the dungheap stench that still hung everywhere like a ghost and was turning the new house into an old one. At first, when the child learned to walk, they were careful that he not get too close to the chicken coop. But then they began to lose their fears and got used to the smell, and before the child got his second teeth he'd gone inside the chicken coop to play, where the wires were falling apart. The angel was no less standoffish with him than with other mortals, but he tolerated the most ingenious infamies with the patience of a dog who had no illusions. They both came down with chicken pox at the same time. The doctor who took care of the child couldn't resist the temptation to listen to the angel's heart, and he found so much whistling in the heart and so many sounds in his kidneys that it seemed impossible for him to be alive. What surprised him most, however, was the logic of his wings. They seemed so natural on that completely human organism that he couldn't understand why other men didn't have them too.

When the child began school it had been some time since the sun and rain had caused the collapse of the chicken coop. The angel went dragging himself about here and there like a stray dying man. They would drive him out of the bedroom with a broom and a moment later find him in the kitchen. He seemed to be in so many places at the same time that they grew to think that he'd been duplicated, that he was reproducing himself all through the house, and the exasperated and unhinged Elisenda shouted that it was awful living in that hell full of angels. He could scarcely eat and his antiquarian eyes had also become so foggy that he went about bumping into posts. All he had left were the bare cannulae of his last feathers. Pelayo threw a blanket over him and extended him the charity of letting him sleep in the shed, and only then did they notice that he had a temperature at night, and was delirious with the tongue twisters of an old Norwegian. That was one of the few times they became alarmed, for they thought he was going to die and not even the wise neighbor woman had been able to tell them what to do with dead angels.

And yet he not only survived his worst winter, but seemed improved with the first sunny days. He remained motionless for several days in the farthest corner of the courtyard, where no one would see him, and at the beginning of December some large, stiff feathers began to grow on his wings, the feathers of a scarecrow, which looked more like another misfortune of decrepitude. But he must have known the reason for those changes, for he was quite careful that no one should notice them, that no one should hear the sea chanteys that he sometimes sang under the stars. One morning Elisenda was cutting some bunches of onions for lunch when a wind that seemed to come from the high seas blew into the kitchen.

Then she went to the window and caught the angel in his first attempts at flight. They were so clumsy that his fingernails opened a furrow in the vegetable patch and he was on the point of knocking the shed down with the ungainly flapping that slipped on the light and couldn't get a grip on the air. But he did manage to gain altitude. Elisenda let out a sigh of relief, for herself and for him, when she saw him pass over the last houses, holding himself up in some way with the risky flapping of a senile vulture. She kept watching him even when she was through cutting the onions and she kept on watching until it was no longer possible for her to see him, because then he was no longer an annoyance in her life but an imaginary dot on the horizon of the sea.

(1968)

divinity as elusive

2-sided nature of divide (Kafka)

- question power & existence of divine

↳ healing power but dirty & falling apart

"A God who abandons his people" ↳ In Latin ↳

Man assign ≠ diff IDs

→ don't apply rational to irrational phenomena

The Handsomest Drowned Man in the World

By Gabriel García Márquez

The first children who saw the dark and slinky bulge approaching through the sea let themselves think it was an enemy ship. Then they saw it had no flags or masts and they thought it was a whale. But when it was washed up on the beach, they removed the clumps of seaweed, the jellyfish tentacles, and the remains of fish and flotsam, and only then did they see that it was a drowned man.

They had been playing with him all afternoon, burying him in the sand and digging him up again, when someone chanced to see them and spread the alarm in the village. The men who carried him to the nearest house noticed that he weighed more than any dead man they had ever known, almost as much as a horse, and they said to each other that maybe he'd been floating too long and the water had got into his bones. When they laid him on the floor they said he'd been taller than all other men because there was barely enough room for him in the house, but they thought that maybe the ability to keep on growing after death was part of the nature of certain drowned men. He had the smell of the sea about him and only his shape gave one to suppose that it was the corpse of a human being, because the skin was covered with a crust of mud and scales.

They did not even have to clean off his face to know that the dead man was a stranger. The village was made up of only twenty-odd wooden houses that had stone courtyards with no flowers and which were spread about on the end of a desertlike cape. There was so little land that mothers always went about with the fear that the wind would carry off their children and the few dead that the years had caused among them had to be thrown off the cliffs. But the sea was calm and bountiful and all the men fit into seven boats. So when they found the drowned man they simply had to look at one another to see that they were all there.

That night they did not go out to work at sea. While the men went to find out if anyone was missing in neighboring villages, the women stayed behind to care for the drowned man. They took the mud off with grass swabs, they removed the underwater stones entangled in his hair, and they scraped the crust off with tools used for scaling fish. As they were doing that they noticed that the vegetation on him came

Gabriel García Márquez, "The Handsomest Drowned Man in the World," *Collected Stories*, trans. Gregory Rabassa, pp. 230-236.

from faraway oceans and deep water and that his clothes were in tatters, as if he had sailed through labyrinths of coral. They noticed too that he bore his death with pride, for he did not have the lonely look of other drowned men who came out of the sea or that haggard, needy look of men who drowned in rivers. But only when they finished cleaning him off did they become aware of the kind of man he was and it left them breathless. Not only was he the tallest, strongest, most virile, and best built man they had ever seen, but even though they were looking at him there was no room for him in their imagination.

They could not find a bed in the village large enough to lay him on nor was there a table solid enough to use for his wake. The tallest mens' holiday pants would not fit him, not the fattest ones' Sunday shirts, nor the shoes of the one with the biggest feet. Fascinated by his huge size and his beauty, the women then decided to make him some pants from a large piece of sail and a shirt from some bridal brabant linen so that he could continue through his death with dignity. As they sewed, sitting in a circle and gazing at the corpse between stitches, it seemed to them that the wind had never been so steady nor the sea so restless as on that night and they supposed that the change had something to do with the dead man. They thought that if that magnificent man had lived in the village, his house would have had the widest doors, the highest ceiling, and the strongest floor, his bedstead would have been made from a midship frame held together by iron bolts, and his wife would have been the happiest woman. They thought that he would have had so much authority that he could have drawn fish out of the sea simply by calling their names and that he would have put so much work into his land that springs would have burst forth from among the rocks so that he would have been able to plant flowers on the cliffs. They secretly compared him to their own men, thinking that for all their lives theirs were incapable of doing what he could do in one night, and they ended up dismissing them deep in their hearts as the weakest, meanest, and most useless creatures on earth. They were wandering through that maze of fantasy when the oldest woman, who as the oldest had looked upon the drowned man with more compassion than passion, sighed:

"He has the face of someone called Esteban."

It was true. Most of them had only to take another look at him to see that he could not have any other name. The more stubborn among them, who were the youngest, still lived for a few hours with the illusion that when they put his clothes on and he lay among the flowers in patent leather shoes his name might be Lautaro. But it was a vain illusion. There had not been enough canvas, the poorly cut and worse sewn pants were too tight, and the hidden strength of his heart popped the buttons on his shirt. After midnight the whistling of the wind died down and the sea fell into its Wednesday drowsiness. The silence put an end to any last doubts: he was Esteban. The women who had dressed him, who had combed his hair, had cut his nails and shaved him were unable to hold back a shudder of pity when they had to resign themselves to his being dragged along the ground. It was then that they understood how unhappy he must have been with that huge body since it bothered him even after death. They could see him in life, condemned to going through doors sideways, cracking his head on crossbeams, remaining on his feet during visits, not knowing what to do with his soft, pink, sea lion hands while the lady of the house looked for her most resistant chair and begged him, frightened to death, sit here, Esteban, please, and he, leaning against the wall, smiling, don't bother, ma'am, I'm fine where I am, his heels raw and his back roasted from having done the same thing so many times whenever he paid a visit, don't bother, ma'am, I'm fine where I am, just to avoid the embarrassment of breaking up the chair, and never knowing perhaps that the ones who said don't go, Esteban, at least wait till the coffee's ready, were the ones who later on would whisper the big boob finally left, how nice, the handsome fool has gone. That was what the women were thinking beside the body a little before dawn. Later, when they covered his face with a handkerchief so that the light would not bother him, he looked so forever dead, so defenseless, so much like their men that the first furrows of tears opened in their hearts. It was one of the younger ones who began the weeping. The others, coming to, went from sighs to wails, and the more they sobbed the more they felt like weeping, because the drowned man was becoming all the more Esteban for them, and so they wept so much, for he was the most destitute, most peaceful, and most obliging man on earth, poor Esteban. So when the men returned with the news that the drowned man was not from the neighboring villages either, the women felt an opening of jubilation in the midst of their tears.

"Praise the Lord," they sighed, "he's ours!"

The men thought the fuss was only womanish frivolity. Fatigued because of the difficult nighttime inquiries, all they wanted was to get rid of the bother of the newcomer once and for all before the sun grew strong on that arid, windless day. They improvised a litter with the remains of foremasts and gaffs, tying it together with rigging so that it would bear the weight of the body until they reached the cliffs. They wanted to tie the anchor from a cargo ship to him so that he would sink easily into the deepest waves, where fish are blind and divers die of nostalgia, and bad currents would not bring him back to shore, as had happened with other bodies. But the more they hurried, the more the women thought of ways to waste time. They walked about like startled hens, pecking with the sea charms on their breasts, some interfering on one side to put a scapular of the good wind on the drowned man, some on the other side to put a wrist compass on him, and after a great deal of *get away from there, woman, stay out of the way, look, you almost made me fall on top of the dead man,* the men began to feel mistrust in their livers and started grumbling about why so many main-altar decorations for a stranger, because no matter how many nails and holy-water jars he had on him, the sharks would chew him all the same, but the women kept piling on their junk relics, running back and forth, stumbling, while they released in sighs what they did not in tears, so that the men finally exploded with *since when has there ever been such a fuss over a drifting corpse, a drowned nobody, a piece of cold Wednesday meat.* One of the women, mortified by so much lack of care, then removed the handkerchief from the dead man's face and the men were left breathless too.

He was Esteban. It was not necessary to repeat it for them to recognize him. If they had been told Sir Walter Raleigh, even they might have been impressed with his gringo accent, the macaw on his shoulder, his cannibal-killing blunderbuss, but there could be only one Esteban in the world and there he was, stretched out like a sperm whale, shoeless, wearing the pants of an undersized child, and with those stony nails that had to be cut with a knife. They only had to take the hand kerchief off his face to see that he was ashamed, that it was not his fault that he was so big or so heavy or so handsome, and if he had known that this was going to happen, he would have looked for a more discreet place to drown in, seriously, I even would have tied the anchor off a galleon around my neck and staggered off a cliff like someone who doesn't like things in order not to be upsetting people now with this Wednesday dead body, as you people say, in order not to be bothering anyone with this filthy piece of cold meat that doesn't have anything to do with me. There was so much truth in his manner that even the most mistrustful men, the ones who felt the bitterness of endless nights at sea fearing that their women would tire of dreaming about them and begin to dream of drowned men, even they and others who were harder still shuddered in the marrow of their bones at Esteban's sincerity.

That was how they came to hold the most splendid funeral they could conceive of for an abandoned drowned man. Some women who had gone to get flowers in the neighboring villages returned with other women who could not believe what they had been told, and those women went back for more flowers when they saw the dead man, and they brought more and more until there were so many flowers and so many people that it was hard to walk about. At the final moment it pained them to return him to the waters as an orphan and they chose a father and mother from among the best people, and aunts and uncles and cousins, so that through him all the inhabitants of the village became kinsmen. Some sailors who heard the weeping from a distance went off course and people heard of one who had himself tied to the mainmast, remembering ancient fables about sirens. While they fought for the privilege of carrying him on their shoulders along the steep escarpment by the cliffs, men and women became aware for the first time of the desolation of their streets, the dryness of their courtyards, the narrowness of their dreams as they faced the splendor and beauty of their drowned man. They let him go without an anchor so that he could come back if he wished and whenever he wished, and they all held their breath for the fraction of centuries the body took to fall into the abyss. They did not need to look at one another to realize that they were no longer all present, that they would never be. But they also knew that everything would be different from then on, that their houses would have wider doors, higher ceilings, and stronger floors so that Esteban's memory could go everywhere without bumping into beams and so that no one in the future would dare whisper the big boob finally died, too bad, the handsome fool has finally died, because they were going to paint their house fronts gay colors to make Esteban's memory eternal and they were going to break their backs digging for springs among the stones and planting flowers on the cliffs so that in future years at dawn the passengers on great liners would awaken, suffocated by the smell of gardens on the high seas, and the captain would have to come down from the bridge in his dress uniform, with his astrolabe, his pole star, and his row of war medals and, pointing to the promontory of roses on the horizon, he would say in fourteen languages, look there, where the wind is so peaceful now that it's gone to sleep beneath the beds, over there, where the sun's so bright that the sunflowers don't know which way to turn, yes, over there, that's Esteban's village.

(1968)

infinite room of imagination (?)

Figure represent : Heroic (cultural-village)
ie political, hollywood, sports, etc. Heros in U.S. culture

Subconscious supernatural
(compared to conscious supernatural in Poe)
→ Part of everyday life

CPSIA information can be obtained
at www.ICGtesting.com
Printed in the USA
FSOW01n1613010415
6140FS

9 781621 314219